The Music Within Your Heart

Isaac Samuel Miller

BookLocker

Trenton, Georgia

The Music Within Your Heart
Copyright © 2023 by Isaac Samuel Miller

Print ISBN: 978-1-958890-04-2
Ebook ISBN: 979-8-88531-521-0

Published by BookLocker.com, Inc., Trenton, Georgia.

Printed on acid-free paper.

The characters and events in this book are fictitious. Any similarity to real persons, living or dead, is coincidental and not intended by the author.

BookLocker.com, Inc.
2023

First Edition

Library of Congress Cataloguing in Publication Data
Miller, Isaac Samuel
The Music Within Your Heart by Isaac Samuel Miller
Library of Congress Control Number: 2023909569

Table of Contents

Prologue

Los Angeles, California
July 23rd, 2003
10a.m.

I roll out of my king-sized bed and sit at the edge, rubbing my morning eyes before a massive yawn echoes throughout my bedroom. I rise and stretch my slightly toned arms into the air as I stand, five-feet-and-seven-inches-tall. My toasty brown skin is clear with only a few wrinkles.

I walk toward my balcony and slide open a double door with a clear view. I walk outside to embrace nature's cool breeze. With a big smile, I look over the mountain view from my balcony. I grip the rails, then my knees pop as I rub my lips together.

"The music within my heart…" Staring into the mountains, my dark brown eyes beam under my thick eyebrows as I continue to sing. "The music within my heart..."

That's my favorite song. It still holds the key to my heart, even until this day. If only I'd known that things would've turned out the way they have, I would've done a lot of things differently.

I turn around and lean into the balcony with my arms behind me, my hands maintaining an overhand grip on the rails. I step forward to walk back into my bedroom, hesitating before proceeding to the studio downstairs. My bedroom's heavenly aroma lifts my nostrils wide open. I exhale. *I love that strawberry smell!* Glancing at my messy bed, I shift slightly to the right, bending over to stretch the tension in my lower back. *I guess it's time to record my final album.*

My bedroom door squeaks as I exit my room. Strolling toward the studio, I grab and hold a medium-sized roll of fat encapsulated around my belly. *I need to get back into eating properly again.*

A few seconds later, I enter the studio, looking in the mirror in front of me and wrapping my long black hair into a ponytail. Twisting my body from side-to-side, I gently slide my hands down my waistline and sigh," I really wish my frame was still slim like it was back in the day." I take a few steps to my right near the sound system controllers before sitting down in one of the studio's chairs.

Leaning forward, I toss my hands into the air before planting my face into my hands as tears flow into the crevices of my small fingers. I lament before shaking my head. "Oh Sammie, life gave us so many obstacles!" Sitting back with my legs crossed, I place my right hand underneath my chin as my tears form specks atop the gray tile on the floor. Grief-stricken, I reminisce on my past life.

After discovering my life's true purpose, my life was filled with good things that were often overshadowed by unwanted surprises. A description of my life as a rollercoaster ride is a gross understatement. For two decades, I was forced to endure challenging trials. The worst part during my life's drought was giving birth after the ordeal with Kyle amid still being madly in love with Sammie. During that time, I didn't have the comfort that would have come from knowing it was possible for me to reunite with the things that truly make me happy.

I stand after adjusting the controllers on the studio mixer. Looking downward, I rub my chin with my right hand while taking a deep breath. I pause and place my hands atop the studio desk, leaning heavily on it. Memories rush through my heart and mind like the pain of an open wound.

I expel an extended sigh. *My life took my heart on a twenty-four year long journey that compelled me to question the value of my* existence. *It's been forty years and I'm still bewildered as I ponder how I ended up where I am in my life right now.* I push my hands away from the studio mixer and grab a paper towel to my left, drying the tears on my cheeks.

Putting aside a now soaked paper towel, I grab a notepad to my right to attempt to write a song. "Shoot, I forgot about my engagement today!" I gaze at my wristwatch. *I can still make it on time.* I take a few steps toward the studio door, grabbing a thin gray jacket I left on the floor a couple of days ago. I exit the studio and hop into my silver convertible Porsche. While taking in the beauty of the morning sky, I let the top down, and my ponytail brushes against the gentle wind of the day. With the engine roaring, I drive away while continuing to cerebrate.

Grabbing the steering wheel with force, I increase my car's speed to sixty miles an hour. I stare at the speedometer as the wind lifts my loosely fitted sunglasses off my face. Placing my right hand across my forehead, I squeeze my wrinkle-free skin. *Mom and Timmy would be very proud if they knew how my life had unfolded.*

I am fifty years old, and I can't help but relive my nostalgic feelings as I drive over the bridge that created distance between me and the only guy my heart ever lived for. *I used to think that if things were meant to be between us, my life would one day produce the circumstances I fought for.*

I slant my head toward my left as several cars pass me by. *I can still hear my dad's raspy voice saying to my mom, "Debra, I know you love the Novato neighborhood, but sweetheart, we have to leave. We aren't safe here anymore!"* My mom's reply still sends chills down my spine. She always lifted her right eyebrow when she was disturbed. With a bitter tone, she replied, *"Anthony, what are we going to do about Timothy? We have to seek justice for our only son!"*

I scoff as I feel my speed decrease to fifty miles an hour. Suddenly, I realize that I am unconsciously pressing down on the brake pedal. I perk up my mouth and squeeze my lips together while looking at the time on the dashboard. *Every summer, I volunteer at The University of Marin County. And every time I visit, I am reminded of the significance of helping people to pursue their passions. I don't want another soul to experience the pain of regret that I feel at times. I still have a hard time forgiving myself from withholding my special gift from the world for so many years.*

My biggest regret is not saying what I should have said to him during our encounter forty years ago in the midnight forest. I wonder how my life would have evolved if I didn't wait twenty-five years to follow what I know now as the music within my heart.

While driving across the beautiful bridge that started my life's history, I begin to drift into thoughts of emptiness, reliving the pain of not knowing if I would marry my intended soulmate.

I glance in the rearview mirror and dry my teary eyes. *I'm so happy my sweet husband is away right now on his business trip. I like to be alone whenever my mind starts to travel back into my past.*" I just can't today." *There's no way I can do the engagement today, I'm just not in the right headspace.*

I exit off the bridge and take the Marin County exit to head to a nearby park. At a traffic light, I look around, prying my cellphone from the crevice of the passenger seat. I call the event coordinator for my engagement and inform her that I'm suddenly not feeling well. I ask to reschedule the event and the coordinator obliges my request. After hanging up with her, I look up at the sunny sky as the massive clouds slowly split apart, exposing the openness of a beautiful blue sky. I exhale and exit my car. While standing, I hold the door open and look around to ensure the park is partially vacant, then lean against the driver's side of my car with the door ajar, drying my tears. I vehemently scoff. "I should have saved my brother!" I take two steps forward, listening to the sounds of my heavy feet dragging across the pavement. I stop abruptly and grunt, walking backward, then I kick my door shut with my back facing the car. Immediately, I proceed to a nearby walking trail that's adjacent to my car. Walking aimlessly, I begin to wrestle with my present and past feelings of contrition.

I wave at a Black lady and her family. Immediately after the family passes, I interlock my hands and place them over my womb just before grabbing onto the ropes of the park's bridge. I begin to cross. The rope makes me think of the time my best friend saved my life. I whisper to myself while shaking my head. "What a memory."

One day, my best friend accidentally walked on my street. I pause my thoughts to embrace the moment.

I pause to look over the bridge that holds a serene river below its heavenly structure. The park is filled with fresh trees. The scent of nature's aroma relaxes me.

While leisurely strolling along, I resume an unforgettable memory.

At least, he claimed he accidentally walked on my street. The first time we met, he walked up to me and handed me a piece of paper that contained a song I wrote. As he stood in front of my house, his complexion captivated the eyes of my neighbors. None of us were accustomed to seeing White people on our street. With the presence of a prince, he gave me a smile along with an extended right hand. "I found this in the woods," he said.

I couldn't help but notice his slightly deformed leg. During another encounter, that's when I discovered he had cerebral palsy. Despite his ailment, he is still very precious to me. The woods he mentioned earned a name: the Midnight Forest.

I pick up a nearby rock and toss it into the river. As the rock skips across the water, my mind skips back into the past.

The handsome boy stood about three inches above my own forehead, with beautiful blue eyes and blonde hair. After he handed my song to me, I asked, "How did you get my song?" I was confused because I thought I was the only one who went into the woods each night, an hour or so before midnight. I smirk. I was pretty darn smooth. My parents never heard my ninja-like footsteps.

I smile and gaze at the flowing water near the riverbank.

Our first encounter was very strange. He refused to reveal his name when I asked. "It's better if you don't know," he replied. "Bye, Sophia."

I chased him and asked, "How do you know my name?" Before he answered, my dad rushed outside.

"Sophia, get over here right now!" My father pointed his fingers at the boy. I observed sweat forming atop the boy's forehead, his small lips folded like a sandwich. His facial expression was the epitome of fear as he observed my father drying motor oil off his fingers with a rag. My dad looked like a protective tiger pointing at my new friend. "Do you know you're putting this whole family at risk by talking to that boy?"

After my dad finished fussing at me, I turned around, but Mr. Strange was gone. I spent the entire night pondering how he found my song.

At the time, it seemed improbable that someone would've known about my secret hiding place for my songs. I hid my songs in a small opening—obscurely positioned inside a tree that my boyfriend later named the Tree of Destiny. I remembered my exact thoughts as I spoke aloud in my room later that night. "Hmm. He must go into the woods each night around the same time as me." I freaked out, realizing I possibly had a stalker. But I smiled too, because I felt something during our first encounter, something I'd never experienced before. I pondered for months at a time, regarding how that strange boy knew me, as well as how he discovered my song.

We eventually became best friends several months before my brother's death.

After some time, my bestie started leaving a letter for me every Friday, a little after midnight. I often replied with a letter of my own, and I placed it inside the tree, our conduit for communication. At first, it was awkward, but eventually I began to look forward to responding to his poetic words on Fridays. Before I discovered his name, I addressed my letters to him with "Dear Mr. Mystery Man."

I developed what I thought was puppy feelings for him through our letters of endearment. His poetry was very intoxicating, and my heart still yearns for more.

While walking through the park, I yawn, and an image of my brother enters my mind. Timmy interrupts my paradise of thoughts of love with one of the sandwiches that he used to prepare for me—peanut butter and strawberry jelly, with two eggs.

I notice a wooden bench at the end of the trail, and I sit down for a few seconds. My phone beeping startles me. I sit up erect and place my left hand on my heart while quickly searching through my purse to stop the noise. It's an alarm, reminding me that I only have two weeks remaining to write the last song for my final album.

I remember when I arrived home from school on the day that sparked the end of Timothy's life. I just felt like something was off. I hate reliving the events that started it all, but I can't help myself. I was only thirteen years old when my life was turned upside down. If only I had known what I know now, my life would be painted with different memories rather than unwanted memories. I rub my forehead with my thumb as I drive my heart into the past. "I just wish I could go back in time and change my life during the summer of 1963."

Section One

Chapter 1:
Destiny Delayed:
The Trip Down Memory Lane

Summer
July 19th, 1963

The sun began to rise as I woke up in the backseat of my dad's car after crying myself to sleep. The day was dismal, and the summer air was deprived of oxygen. An air conditioner from one's car or home was the only thing that could provide a cooling reprieve in California during the summer of 1963. I opened my eyes and reunited with my unwanted fate. Slowly, I lifted my head off the backseat and wiped the morning crust from my eyes. While removing potato chip crumbs from my blue jeans, I adjusted my dark green T-shirt and my pigtail hair style, that was becoming for a child with my round face.

I stared out the back window. My heart inched farther away from my true love as my dad increased his speed. I sighed. My dad should really slow down and turn around so that I can get back to my boyfriend. Just look at him up there, he's driving me away from my man. I slammed both of my fists against the backseat as my emotions erupted. "This year is by far the worst year of my life. My day couldn't get any worse. Perfect timing, Mom and Dad. Brilliant idea! Just pack up and move two days after I lost the California State Spelling Bee. Now everyone is going to think we moved to a new city because I'm a loser!" My dad slightly turned his head to his right and side-eyed me. My mother just scoffed.

My mother and father glanced at me through the rearview mirror. As the sun radiated through my father's light brown skin, his smooth oval-shaped brown eyes accentuated his unblemished skin. He looked at my mom and she smirked while staring into my dad's eyes with a countenance of trust. I exhaled and folded my arms while rolling my eyes. I would love for my mom to do something other than always following my dad's lead. My mom turned away from him and leaned back into the car seat. My mom's perfectly symmetrical face resembled the Mona Lisa. Her long eyelashes jumped out onto an onlooker's eyes, and her lips were positioned atop a wonderful physique, one that displayed the anatomy of a perfect woman.

They continued to sit in silence while I wrestled to filter through my heart's broken thoughts. I laid back on the seat, then suddenly rose again, eager to resolve my plight. I breathed in deeply and released a boisterous sigh. My dad glances at me through the rearview mirror, raising his eyebrows. *I hated to say goodbye and leave my best friend alone, with all our secrets buried in the midnight forest. I can't believe my dad is forcing me to move away from everything I love. I wish my parents could read my mind. I'm trying my best not to think about everything I'm leaving behind as we travel across this stupid bridge.* I continued to empty out my emotions while crossing the Golden Gate Bridge from Marin County to head toward our new abode in San Francisco. Filled with rage, I said, "Dad, this isn't fair! You know I didn't want to move." My dad stared at me, but he was silent.

While listening to the luggage move around in the trunk, I couldn't help but think: *Why did my dad allow the broken community of Novato to force us into exile?* My father delivered the news that we were moving six months ago during a family meeting. I felt like I was mentally prepared to move, but as this dreaded day drew near, I realized that my heart wasn't ready to leave my best friend. My dad ran over the leg of a chair, and the bump jolted our heads into the air like a rocket. I frowned and held back the rage that was rushing toward my lips. I felt like screaming. I positioned my right foot in front of me, ready to kick the back of my dad's seat, but I changed my mind. Geesh—Dad. Why can't you see that I am in love? I really wish things could stay the same. I miss him so much already.

When my father delivered the news that we were moving, I stood up from the kitchen table as my mom and dad stared at one another. The chilling glance they gave me was too much to bear. Instantly, their stares filled my heart's eyes like a machine gun's relentless onslaught. I felt their intense disappointment in me. During that moment I discovered that the human heart is more powerful than the-all-encompassing human brain. Sammie is my addiction and my emotional high. I reacted to their stares with a sprint as my dad shouted, "Sophia, get back over here!" What a memory.

This is a bumpy car ride. I frowned while thinking of my love, looking at the back of my dad's head. *I should've kicked his stupid seat earlier.* I looked up at the wagon's ceiling before proceeding with my thoughts. *My parents aren't aware that their synchronized voices interrupted my resolve to revisit the thoughts that only the love of my life knows. I can still hear his gentle but maturing voice like it was yesterday, whispering in my heart, "Sophia, get down, don't jump!" His earthshaking voice saved my soul.* I sighed. *The reality of losing Sammie pushed me to entertain thoughts of executing an idea, one that the racist community of Novato would have been proud of. Since we are apart now, I wish he'd let me finish what I started in the midnight forest.*

I shook my head and smiled. *Exactly who was I trying to fool? I couldn't resist Sammie's piercing blue eyes; they complimented his curly blonde hair extremely well. He has the cutest little cheeks I've ever seen. I especially love how they rose whenever he used to sing to me. The night he rescued me, he looked at me like I was the most important person alive*. I placed my hand over my heart. *I never got my chance to tell him that I love him too*. My heart compelled me to stare out of the back window at the life I was leaving behind. I was grief-stricken with my first heartache.

I dried my eyes with my hand. I could feel my tears drop out of my pupils every second that my dad's car inched away from Sammie. I scoffed. My face looked like a waterfall. I rolled my right hand through my hair to feel the gentleness of my curls. *Love will make you do some crazy things. I really need my Sammie, and no one is keeping me away from him*. I screamed and pleaded for my dad to turn the car around. I forced them, especially my dad, to recall the despicable reasons why he decided it was best for us to move. Before I could say my brother's name, my dad turned around to straighten me out. We swerved into the middle lane as my dad lost focus and said, "Don't you dare accuse me of not being fair ever again! My job is to protect my family, and besides, your brother would have been a little more supportive than what you're demonstrating."

I scooted forward while sliding my butt against the car's backseat, with both of my fists clenched together like I was ready to battle. I'll regain my happiness by force. I grabbed onto both sides of my dad's car seat. "I beg to disagree, you're totally wrong Dad! You didn't know Timmy like me."

My dad immediately reacted. He lost his cool after his eardrums embraced the painful thump of my brother's name echoing throughout his memories. He slammed on the brakes and stopped the car in the middle lane of the Golden Gate bridge, turning on the emergency lights and parking his car right in the middle lane like it was a parking lot. My mother screamed.

"Anthony, what are you doing?" He ignored her.

Several people stared and passed us by, gazing with perplexed eyes. My mom placed her left hand on the glove compartment and rolled the window down to expunge the saliva that sank into her throat from an adrenaline rush. As sweat broke through her skin, she quickly observed the awkwardness of our family scene.

My mother was frantic, but she calmly asked my dad to put the car back into drive.

My dad chuckled, pressing down onto the gas to antagonize her. He politely uttered a word my mom hated to hear. My father said, "No."

In silence, we listened to the sounds of cars pass us by at sixty to a hundred miles an hour. It seemed like we were trapped motionless in time, then I heard my mom's predictable words. She placed her right hand on her heart, as though she was executing the pledge of allegiance, and stared at my father as he rubbed his hands down his face, with what appeared to me to be enough force to tear his own skin.

Then my mother erupted like a volcano. "You know, I was going to try to just move forward without addressing this with you. But now, I see that we need to have this conversation right now." My father glanced at her. "Don't give me that look like you're an innocent child. I know you very well, so I know what you're thinking." My mom shook her head. "Yes, Anthony, we're having this talk right now in the middle of this freaking bridge!" My dad looked at her with a look of reticence as she continued in a lower tone, "Yes, we're having this conversation. It's been a year since his death, and we still haven't addressed it as a family." She faced my dad, and in a nonaggressive way, pointed her finger at him. "You can't keep telling me you don't want to talk about it." My dad sighed, tapping on the steering wheel. "Anthony, you didn't even come to your own son's funeral. Why?

Because you've convinced yourself that his murder was your fault. You can't keep blaming yourself."

It was rare to observe my old man in silence. But on that fateful day, my mom was letting him have it.

They continued to argue over the next ten minutes while I recalled the final four weeks of my brother's life.

***

I used to hear a lot about the pain of death through my dad's military stories. I now appreciate death's sting. My Timmy was my first experience with losing someone close to me. I grew accustomed to waking up to the loud sounds of my big brother brushing his teeth. That fool sounded like a wildebeest whenever he brushed his teeth. Every morning I yelled out, "Timmy, can you please close your door and stop all of that freaking yacking!" My brother brushed his teeth like he hadn't cleaned them in decades. His teeth were so white and perfect, which is why I didn't get his strict regimen. He relentlessly brushed his teeth for twenty minutes every morning. I dropped my head due to despair. *Big bro, I really miss you.*

Timothy was a natural born runner. Girls loved to see him run track. He placed first in all his home meets at Winnebago High School. Timmy participated in the four-hundred-meter race, and he was good at hurdles. He always slaughtered his competitors during his hurdle races.

Every morning my brother would brush his teeth, kiss me on the cheek, and say, "Little sis, what do you want for breakfast?"

I often replied, "Jerk, you know what I want." My brother would say, "Okay. That's a peanut butter and jelly sandwich with two eggs coming your way."

Boy, I surely miss those days.

Timothy was four years older than me. He lived long enough to finish half of his senior year in high school before he was killed. He planned to become a minister if his running career didn't work out. I really miss his prayers, too. Every morning he prayed for me, Mom, and Dad after he brought me breakfast in bed. After my brother whipped up his fancy breakfast entrées, he prepared his mind for his early morning jogs before he went to school, even though we lived in a racist town. The area we lived in consisted mainly of Black folks, mixed with a few kindhearted Caucasians. My dad assumed he was accepted in the Novato community because he served a few years in the military during the precipice of the Vietnam War. He gradually changed his views during the final four weeks that ultimately culminated in my brother's untimely demise.

I remember the incident that sparked a change in my dad's views like it was yesterday.

My dad, mom, brother, and I woke up to a shattered kitchen window. I entered the kitchen, pointing to the brick that shattered the window. Attached was a note. My dad picked the note up and read it angrily as his lips quivered. "Keep that black monkey off Shelly Street."

I panicked and ran to hug my dad, wrapping my arms around him like he was a teddy bear. My dad wiped my tears as my mom followed my course, seeking comfort from him too. Then, my father approached Timmy. I felt tension developing in the air while noticing Timmy, slowly, walking backwards upstairs. Timmy tried his best to be silent, but each of his footsteps bounced off the stairs like repeated cracks of broken bones. It was apparent that Timmy was guilty of something. My dad tightened his robe and pointed his fingers toward my brother while still approaching the stairway. Timmy was standing atop the stairs at that point.

My dad placed his right foot on the bottom step of the stairs and looked up at Timmy as his voice trembled, "Timothy, what's really going on?" My dad dropped his head and shook it from left-to-right. "I told you to stay away from Shelley Street, you know that block is flooded with the Klan!"

My father signaled for Timmy to come downstairs with his index finger. Timmy was annoyed, sighing before making his way downstairs to confront my dad's gesture. He approached with caution. I miss Timmy.

My brother looked just like my dad.

Neither one of them had an Afro or any other popular hairstyle. They both had low haircuts, which complimented their high cheek bones. Their facial structures were engineered to fit their big, gorgeous, oval-shaped hazel-brown eyes. While my dad was dressed in a brown robe, Timmy had on a white tank-top that perfectly fit his chiseled physique. After positioning himself two feet away from my dad on the stairs, Timmy exploded and expressed his true emotions.

"Dad, we can't let those fake Christians take over our lives. Besides, I'm too fast for them to catch anyway," said Timothy.

My father shook his head before slamming his right fist against the rails of the stairway. "Boy, do you think this is a game? Your Black behind can't outrun bullets! You're not in some action movie." My dad squeezed his forehead. "Timothy, this is real life, and there are evil people in this world who want to lynch you, just because you're Black," said my father.

My father stepped forward and placed his hands on Timmy's shoulders. "Please, Son, you're the only son I have, please don't run on that street anymore." My father burst into tears.

While watching my father, I thought to myself. I know the real reason why Timmy likes to jog on Shelley Street every morning.

My best friend, who lives a block over from our street, mentioned something shocking to me in the midnight forest. My friend said he saw my brother exiting the back door of some girl's house. I recalled him stating that her name was Molly. He mentioned he knew Molly's dad, and that there was no way her dad was home if my brother was there—not that I cared, but Molly was White.

My thoughts were interrupted as I felt the wagon begin to move from its parked position on the Golden Gate Bridge. The engine roared as my dad pressed down on the brakes. "That's enough, Debra!"

My mom didn't respond. It was like she knew how far she could go with him. Only the sounds of moving cars coupled with my father's engine could be heard. The silence helped to drift my mind back into my thoughts of Timmy. I exhaled.

I just wish Timothy had been smarter with his decisions. My brother didn't know that I was aware of his girlfriend. I thought it was best that my brother's secret remained clandestine. Maybe I should've said something to my parents? It's not like I didn't get sick every time I pondered the likelihood of some racist prick killing Timmy. I remember Spring of 1963 like it was yesterday. Timothy's final weeks alive were both haunted and cherished memories. I vividly remember the day that started it all.

During the earlier part of that day, I walked into the hallway that led to Timothy's bedroom. His room was next to mine positioned to the left.

I was spying on him a little. I liked to spy on my big bro.

Unbeknownst to Timothy, I observed him checking his watch. After observing his focused demeanor, I walked away from his room.

The day was gloomy as hatred filled the air of our Novato neighborhood.

Later at some point, Timothy developed an urge for a late afternoon snack, so he approached me, dressed in a white jogging suit. His quadriceps protruded out of his pants like a nail that couldn't fit into a wall. His upper body was well-defined, like an Olympic athlete.

College scouts were heavily on Timothy's tail for track and field. His chiseled facial structure was at a level above a model, too. He had everything going for him.

As I laid on the couch, half-dressed in a big pink T-shirt, Timothy approached me. Although it was just approaching evening time, I already had on a head-covering in preparation for bedtime. He stood directly over me while I stared at him, my body mimicking someone inside a coffin. He asked, "Do you want to walk to the store with me, Sophia? I'm dying to get a soda."

I sat up on the couch, but before I had a chance to fully consent to going with him to pick up a coke, he turned around to greet my father. My dad worked as a part-time sales consultant, but we survived because of his military checks. "Dad, do you mind if Sophia and I walk to One Stop to grab a couple of cokes?" Timothy asked.

My dad remained seated in his lazy-boy chair, with his feet propped up while drinking a cold beer. "Yeah, that's fine son." My dad pointed his fingers at my brother. "Just remember what I told you about going on Shelley Street. Make sure you take another route, okay?" said my father.

Timothy smirked. "Dad, you worry too much. Come on, Sophia, let's bounce! You should take your new bike for a spin to the store."

"Can I, Dad?" I asked. My dad placed his feet on the floor while lifting his eyebrows.

"Yes, Sophia, just don't do that monkey bar crap." He shook his fingers at Timothy and I, delivering an engaged forewarning gesture. "You two already know that certain people in this community are just dying to call you monkeys," said my father.

For some reason, on the day we went to pick up cokes, I couldn't get my dad's voice out of my head, "Just don't do that monkey bar crap."

Despite my trepidation, the adventurer in me kicked in, whispering inside: Sophia, admit it, you love these monkey bar bike rides— they're so much fun. My internal thoughts preceded a loud outburst, "Timmy, let's roll!" Timothy and I mischievously decided to use the alternate route my father warned us not to take.

I did not realize at the time that I would vehemently grow to hate myself for disobeying my father. I still remember the joy my brother exuded.

Timmy's large, dark brown eyes stared at me as he stated, "Sophia, get off the monkey bars and come pedal. I feel like running."

My brother was hardheaded. He rarely listened to my dad. I felt safe with my big bro, though, so I often followed his lead. Timothy loved running and he wanted to be the fastest man alive. I was always impressed with his passion. He used to capitalize on every opportunity he had to run—that boy loved it.

I started to pedal faster while gallantly attempting to beat my brother to the store. Before starting my victory chants, I noticed him almost running right next to me. "Timmy, you're getting slow, you can't keep up with your little sissy," I said.

He glanced at me while turning his head to his right. "Sophia, you're on a bike, just remember that."

I put my head down and pedaled as fast as I could. "Ha-ha, excuses, excuses."

I heard my brother scoff, then a disposition of caution insidiously possessed his soul. "Sophia, look up," said Timothy.

I lifted my head to witness a massive clan of six White men standing about fifty yards away from us on a nearby sidewalk. I could tell that the men were eagerly anticipating our arrival based on the racial epithets I heard. Without hesitation, I made a sharp turn into the woods, that I knew all too well.

I pleaded with my brother, "Hurry Timmy, come on, let's go this way! I know my way around these woods."

Timmy's breaths roared like a race car's engine. He was the epitome of horsepower on two feet.

He screamed, "I'm right behind you, Sophia! Just pedal faster and don't look back, I'm right behind you!"

A violent stampede seemed imminent as the voices of the hateful men synchronized together, shouting racist names. While the men united in their broken chorus, we continued to run for our lives. I heard their chains and a few of the men saying, "I'm going to beat your monkey brains out with my bat!"

A few of the men shouted the one word that all Black folks hate.

While gasping for air, Timmy erupted, "Sophie, please—please, pedal faster!"

I knew my brother was scared. He only called me Sophie when he was terrified.

My brother continued to sprint for his life while running behind me, screaming, "Sophie, let me pedal and you get on the front of the bike." The sounds of severing leaves echoed in the woods as the blood-thirsty men continued to charge at us.

Within seconds, Timmy implemented his suggestion and swiftly placed me on the front of the bike. He pedaled like an Olympic cyclist.

One of the men managed to hit my brother in the back with a bat while we changed positions. I still remember the sound of the bat, pushing against the evening breeze, nature's friction easing the force of that racist prick's blow.

My heart is forever indebted to my brother for his heroism. There is no way I would've been able to keep pedaling at the pace I was going. I was so out of shape. I think my brother knew I wasn't going to last much longer, so he sacrificed his momentum to give me a fighting chance when we switched positions. It wasn't until later that night that my parents and I discovered his midback was broken.

During the chase, Timmy pedaled with everything he had, but those savages just kept on chasing us. Eventually, four of them stopped, but two of the younger ones from the group refused to give up. As we inched closer to a body of water, leading to our house, I realized we had to jump in the lake—to swim for our lives.

A tear fell from my face after arriving at the body of water. While panting Timmy said, "Okay Sophie, which direction? You mentioned earlier you know these woods very well." He stared at me, eagerly awaiting my response.

I can still see the fear in his eyes.

Swimming across the water was the only way to escape.

While observing him looking back, we both heard chants of hate bearing down on us like hot lava from a volcano. "Timmy, we have to swim for it!"

"Sophie, if we swim, we'll lose our momentum." He grimaced as we both panted. "Gosh, my back is really hurting," said Timmy.

I pushed my bike onto the grass while pointing at the lake. "Timmy, the lake is our only chance!"

As the men's voices closed in, my brother shouted, "Sophie, hurry—jump in the water and swim." He kissed me on the cheek. "I love you, don't worry about me."

I could feel his eyes fixated on me as I heard his voice vibrating across the water. "Swim, Sophie! Swim!"

The lake was usually deep, but on that day, the waters were shallow.

The two men were right on Timmy's tail. Once out of the water, I looked back one final time to observe my big bro charging at the men who were about one hundred yards away from him. I supplicated God to help Timmy return home alive.

I still remember how I felt once I realized I had to swim for my life. I didn't know at the time that I would name the lake I swam in the Lake of Tears. I didn't know at the time either—only four weeks later—what I thought was a lake of safety would eventually bear a deplorable name.

I swam for about two minutes in the lake before exiting the water to run home as fast as I could. My house was no more than three miles away. While running I overheard a distant voice saying, "Hey, are you okay?"

The voice sounded just like the strange boy's voice who I'd met. There was no time to clarify who was talking to me—I kept running while yelling, "Someone, please, call the police, they're going to kill my brother!"

My thoughts of Timothy were interrupted again when the car halted. Lifting my head, I observed several traffic lights, wondering which direction my father would turn. I looked through the back window as we exited the Golden Gate Bridge. My dad took a quick peek at me through the rearview mirror. It was obvious he felt remorseful about his tone with my mom. He looked dejected.

I turned my head away from him, still upset about moving. My dad turned left then I resumed my thoughts.

When I finally arrived at my house, I rushed inside to tell my dad what happened. My dad immediately called the police. The sheriff's office was only five minutes away. After waiting several minutes for the police to arrive, he lost his patience and approached me. Placing his hands on my shoulders, he said, "Sophia, take me where Timothy is!"

"Okay. It was six of them chasing us too, Dad!"

My dad instructed my mom to stay home and get a shotgun while she waited for the cops. Two weeks later, we discovered why the police never showed up during that fateful night. They were preoccupied looking for a Black man who injured a White man in the woods—the guy my brother accidentally hit in the head with a bat while defending himself.

I guess my dad intuitively knew we went on Shelley Street, because he yelled at me as we exited the front door.

Night had fallen as we ran through the woods, and the sound of crickets echoed.

My father's indignation gradually increased as he entertained thoughts of Timmy being lynched.

The crackling sounds of leaves filled the night air, then my father lost his cool. While running and pushing low hanging tree branches away from his face my father said, "I just know that my boy is hanging in one of these trees." He looked to his right at me while I stopped to catch my breath. Pointing his fingers at me, he screamed, "I told you two not to go on Shelley Street!"

While weeping I said, "I'm sorry Dad, we should've listened. I just know Timmy is dead now."

"Your brother is a fighter, but six men is a lot for him to handle all by himself. I'm sure the KKK will send more men after him." My father looked up into the night sky. "Lord, please, help my son. These woods is a perfect place to murder a young Black boy."

My dad continued to charge forward into the throes of heroism; sprinting to rescue his only son from being executed for the crime of being Black, with a pistol in his right hand and one of my brother's baby teeth in the other.

At the time, I didn't know my dad kept our baby teeth for good fortune. We both were on edge as we drew closer and closer toward the lake. It was then that we witnessed Timothy swimming.

Timmy was only ten yards away from safe and dry ground.

My dad cried out, "Swim, Son!" His voice trembled as tears drifted inside his mouth. "Your daddy is coming!"

Before my dad had a chance to jump in the lake, my brother began to crawl out of it. I briefly stared at the army of KKK members dressed in white sheets.

Thank God they were a good distance away from us.

My stare was interrupted by thunderous sounds of gunshots—then my dad increased his pace after observing my brother being struck by a bullet. I instinctually dropped on the ground. My father confirmed my fears. "Stay down, Sophia," he yelled.

Dust from the ground entered my mouth. It felt like I could taste death as I observed my brother limping toward us, then I stood up to face my family's dire situation.

My brother was struck in his right calf after jumping out of the water; bloody and scared for his life.

My father wrapped Timmy's arms around his neck and said, "I love you, Son!" His voice was filled with ardor. "Daddy is here now!" My brother limped for three miles to escape the jaws of death.

Unfortunately, this would be his only time.

As we continued running for our lives, I heard the same strange voice again, "Hey, are you all okay?"

I knew it was the same voice. What captured my attention at that time was when he said, "Sophia, are you all okay?" I turned around to see who the mysterious voice belonged to, before I was distracted by my father's commanding call.

"Sophia, let's go, we don't have time to slow down. Some of them may have swam across the lake to hunt us down," said my father.

When we arrived at our house, my mom rushed to the door and hugged my brother extremely tight while crying. "Thank you, Jesus," she said. A few minutes later, we all jumped in the car to take Timmy to the hospital.

Before we stepped into the car, Timmy hugged me and said, "I told you I would be okay Sophie. Sorry about your bike, though." He smiled.

While standing directly in front of my brother, I maneuvered my hands through my hair and smiled back at him. "I don't care about losing my bike, I'm just glad I didn't lose you," I said.

Timothy wrapped his right arm around me. "Sophie, your bike saved my life. One of the guys' shoestrings got tangled-up in it. Your bike pulled him down when he charged at me. His head hit the handlebars and the impact knocked him out. At that point, I knew I only had one of them to worry about. I managed to grab the other guy's chain when he swung it at my face." Timmy stepped into the backseat of our car. He grunted due to his injuries. "I grabbed his chain and pulled him close, then I kicked him in his knee. My kick forced him to the ground. After he fell, I picked up his bat and aimed for his knees. But he charged at me from an awkward angle, which caused me to strike him once in the head. I feel terrible, I think-- I may have seriously hurt him," said Timmy.

Timmy always thought of others, and he aimed to turn the other cheek.

A part of me knew then that he had practically committed suicide, or that he would be arrested and spend the rest of his life in prison. No one was going to believe his truthful testimony of self-defense. Marin

County was ninety-five percent Caucasian and most of them were racist. At the time, I was just very happy that my brother was still alive.

After we got back from the hospital with Timothy, I couldn't help but ponder all night over the identity of the voice that would one day name and rescue me before I leaped from the Tree of Destiny. The strange voice I heard while running through the woods during the night Timmy and I were attacked revealed its identity shortly after that.

I assumed my brother's near-death experience, fractured scapula, and his injured calf muscle would've stopped him from seeing Molly. Instead, he went right back into foolishly sneaking out to see her—just a few days after he survived our bike ride to One Stop.

That same day, I'd heard one of the Klan members on the radio with a calloused voice of darkness say, "A monkey—a freaking monkey hospitalized Billy Joe." He chuckled after completing his statement. If only I'd known that Molly would be the catalyst for guaranteeing Timmy's demise, I would've mentioned his secret to my parents.

After Timothy's death, I think that's when my dad's blood pressure issues started. He was never the same. Every so often, I used to witness my dad crying in the living room with a can of beer saying, "What kind of pathetic loser allows his only son to be killed?"

He never forgave himself. My father claimed he thought it was best for us to move because of the death threats and burning crosses that became a weekly occurrence for us.

My brother was missing for two days before we discovered his corpse.

***

Unwanted Discovery

The day my brother went missing was agonizing for me and my parents. My father reported Timmy missing after he didn't come home one night.

I woke up to sounds of my bedroom door swinging open. I rolled over on my back and lifted the comforter from over my face. I could hear my father panting like a cheetah in duress while he stood next to my mom. My mother anxiously released a shocking statement.

"Sophia, your brother never came home last night. I just know something bad has happened to him." My father walked forward and hit a nearby wall with his right hand, causing one of my baby pictures to fall onto the floor, shattering glass and scattering it about.

I wiped the crust from my eyes. "Maybe he's at a friend's house or something?"

My mother's hands were on her hips. "Sophia, if you know something—" She pointed to my father, who was pushing the broken glass into one isolated area with his right foot. She continued, "Honey, if you know where you brother is, now is not the time to be a protective little sister—you're not selling him out if you tell us where he is."

My father turned his head to his right to face me while still kneeling. He exhaled. "Sophia, please listen to your mother." He hesitated. "Does Timothy have a girlfriend or anything?"

Removing the comforter from over me, I sat up, sliding my feet into my slippers that were beneath my bed. I stood up and walked toward my parents while avoiding the broken glass. Bending down, I hugged my father. Surprisingly, he began to cry uncontrollably. My father rarely sobbed. "I just know something isn't right—those pricks have my boy!"

My mother rushed in and lifted him to his feet. We all hugged each other, uniting to embrace the possible imminent danger to one of our own.

While crying, my mother said, "Anthony, I am going to call the police."

My father responded sarcastically, "Go right ahead, but I'll be out looking for him myself. You know last time we called the so-called law enforcement squad; they didn't even show up." He aggressively pointed his fingers downward while saying, "I'm leaving right now to go search for my son!"

My mother stepped forward, placing her hands gently against his biceps. "Anthony, don't do anything crazy. You know those people will kill you," she said with endearment.

He paused briefly before facing my mother, then he turned around to face me. "Sophia, stay with your mom while I go look for your brother."

We tailed my father as he ran downstairs. He quickly grabbed his rifle by the front door and stormed out of the house. Before my mom had a chance to say something, we both heard the door slam. My mother opened the door, then I overheard my father saying, "Debra, get on back in that house and call the police like you said you were going to do!"

My mom sighed. Seconds later, I heard my dad's wagon start up—then he backed-out of the driveway as the tires squealed against the pavement.

It was only days later that my best friend and I made a shocking discovery. We were in the woods, walking and talking.

While goofing around, he said, "Sophia, let's play skip the rock across the lake." While playing his boyish game, I noticed a red shirt that stopped my rock from skipping across the water. *Oh no. That looks like a dead body. I know my brother is missing.*

I stared at my friend, he looked confused. He was standing to my right about three feet away from me. With reticence, I pointed to my left at a body of water.

My friend asked, "What's wrong, what is it that you see?" I was silent as I observed him focus his attention on the lake. He stuttered before clearly saying, "Whoa, is that a body?" After hesitating to react, my emotions took over as I panicked.

"I have to investigate if the dead body we see belongs to Timmy." I sprinted forward, rushing into the water. Once in the lake, I flipped the body over to discover my dead brother, with eight holes in his face and two obvious gunshot wounds to his right temple. Timmy's face was barely recognizable. His beautifully chiseled facial structure was gone and destroyed forever.

I overheard the sounds of my friend's presence disturbing the flow of the lake's calm waves as he rushed in behind me. "Oh God, I am so sorry, Sophia." He hugged me while I sobbed.

"Jesus, you can tell that he was shot at close range," I said with a mouth full of tears. I bent down in a shallow section of the water and held my brother's lifeless body. "Why, God, why?" I gently rested his head in my hands and kissed him on the forehead while saying, "I am so sorry, Timmy. I love you big bro." My friend tried to pull me away, but I erupted, "Get away from me!" I gasped for air as my tears distorted the smooth flow of my words. "I thought you were supposed to protect me and my family in these woods. How could you let this happen?" He was silent. I stood up and immediately apologized, "I'm sorry. I know that none of this is your fault." I sighed. He nodded his head as I said, "I just know that your dad is racist, and you knew about Molly."

He waved his hands side-to-side in front of his chest and said, "Sophia, I had nothing to do with this!"

I looked up at the sky and noticed a full moon shining brightly above us. "I just don't know what to think right now. You will never understand what it's like to be Black. All Black folks just want to be treated like freaking human beings—for once in our miserable lives!"

My best friend shed a few tears while saying, "You're right! It's a shame that this happened to your brother. I am beginning to hate my own people for mistreating Black people just because of the color of their skin." He kneeled beside me. "Look at me, Sophia, please." I stared into his now teary blue eyes as he spoke. "I can assure you that I care for you. Sophia, I had nothing to do with this. I am deeply sorry for your loss. I will be here with you every step of the way." He pulled me into his chest as I slowly released my brother's head. Timmy's deceased body drifted off with the lake's mild current. My angry sobs echoed throughout the woods, as pain unlike anything I had ever experienced filled my grieving soul.

I continued to cry uncontrollably while he held me tight. I felt dead inside as the lake's waters purified my brother's blood. The lake consumed his body like a dead fish's leftovers that floated to the top of the water. Timmy's body was hard to observe. He looked like he had been devoured by a great white shark. The lake's creatures must've taken several bites into his skin; a lot of his flesh was peeled off his face, like a mask that was unwilling to stick to its desired surface. Timmy's appearance caused even more tears to race down my face like a tropical storm. I exhaled. My brother was murdered ten times over.

Minutes later, my friend walked with me to my house, but he stopped right before we exited a section of the woods—that earned the name, the Midnight Forest.

We stared into each other's eyes, and we both now knew what would happen if anyone saw us together. So, we quietly exited the woods and went our separate ways.

During that night, I named the lake that contained my brother's body the Lake of Tears.

The only thing that kept me together was reflecting on how my best friend was there for me. I smile. *Later that night in my room, all I could do was reflect on how, just yesterday, I had discovered my best friend's name. For some unexplained reason, it brought me great joy.*

***

His Name is Sammie

At midnight one day, I entered a section of the woods near my house where I felt like I was free to be myself. I sung at the top of my lungs. My performance was interrupted by an incredible voice, joining in and starting to sing along with me.

I turned to face the unidentified voice. I stared at a familiar adorable boy. He slyly approached, stepping into my personal space. I blushed and waited for him to say more.

Silence filled the air.

I shyly turned around, attempting to run away from what I was feeling—but my heart was paralyzed. My legs were motionless as infatuation's commanding call radiated through my soul.

"I really like that one too. You sing very well." He extended his right hand, and I shook it. "To finally answer your question from a few days ago. My name is Sammie Walker."

I pretended to frown, hiding my true emotions. "Sammie, right?" I asked.

He rubbed his chin and smirked. "Correct," said Sammie. He grinned.

I placed my hands on my hips and took a few steps backwards, creating a little distance between me and his handsomeness. "So, what are you doing out here?" I asked.

Sammie waved his hands around to acknowledge where we were. "I come out here to sing, it's my escape." He pointed at me. "I usually wait until you're done before I begin." Sammie stepped forward and closed the chasm I created. He smiled while placing his hands against his heart. "I must admit, waiting almost an hour each night for you to finish up has been quite enjoyable for me."

Placing my hands behind my back, I leaned against a nearby tree to my left. Sammie approached me and positioned himself one foot away from my face, as he cornered me while placing his hands against a nearby tree. His breath was fresh; the smell of Listerine exuded from his mouth. I playfully ducked under his arms and walked briskly with my back turned toward him, before responding to his remarks. "Hmm," I said while turning back around to face him.

Sammie rubbed his hands across his forehead. "Singing is my passion too." He walked up close to me again.

I stepped two feet back. "Sammie, was that you yesterday? I heard a voice when I ran through the woods."

"Yes, that was me. Did you read my last letter?" Sammie asked.

"Maybe. But I wrote you back once regarding another letter you left for me in the tree," I said.

"Yes, you did, and that's what egged me on. Your brother needs to stay away from Molly." He pointed to my favorite tree. "I wrote the most recent letter like a week ago. I placed it in your little tree spot." He winked his right eye.

I smiled. "I haven't put anything in there lately, and I haven't checked it for deliveries either."

Boy, was I lying. I knew exactly what he was referring to.

"Okay, if you say so. But look, the Klan is out to get your brother, Sophia. I know you didn't know me at the time, but do you remember when I discussed my suspicions in one of my letters a few months ago?"

Sammie is so handsome. I love his ocean-filled blue eyes.

"Uh, yes, I read those. Do you think Molly sold Timothy out? Like maybe they had an argument and she got upset with him and turned on him?"

"That's possible, Sophia," said Sammie.

" How else do you explain the KKK knowing exactly where my house is? Remember when I mentioned in one of my replies that they threw a brick through my kitchen window?" I asked.

My arms were folded as Sammie stood in front of me with his hands inside his blue jean pockets.

"Yes, I remember, Sophia. That's a great question. I watched Molly toss your brother's jacket in his face a few days ago. It was apparent that they had a little spat," said Sammie.

I tossed my hands into the air and clench my fists. "I knew it, I knew something was up with her. I'm going to go straighten her out right now for almost getting my brother killed."

Sammie scoffed, "You don't even know where she lives."

I placed my hands on my hips while gently tapping my finger against his chest. "I don't need to know because you do."

Sammie sighed. "I'm not showing you where she lives—that would be messy."

I frowned.

"I just want to protect you from any kind of drama. Trust me, my beautiful friend-- you don't want to get mixed up with her family," said Sammie.

"Beautiful friend?" I asked.

He grinned, grabbing my right hand; I immediately pulled my hand away.

He lifted his eyebrows and held his hands in front of him to suggest that he was harmless. "Yes, you are amazing to look at," said Sammie.

I just remember blushing. It felt like my lips and cheeks had been propped open with a jackhammer as I held in place a smile that failed to dissipate.

"And don't jump to conclusions about Molly. I actually think she loves your brother," said Sammie.

"Oh, is that so?" I asked.

He placed his hands atop my shoulders, gently squeezing them. This time I didn't pull away. "Yes! Look, Sophia, my dad is the chief of police, and I can't even stop him from his hateful streaks. So, I seriously doubt that Molly will be able to stop her dad."

After our conversation, I stopped fighting the feelings I was developing for the brave young man who shouted my name in the woods. At the time, I never thought that I would've developed feelings for a White guy, not to mention someone I'd only seen once in my life at that point.

Sammie, no matter where you are, my heart will always cry out for you.

My sweet Sammie was so brave to date a Black girl, despite the horrific stories he told me about his dad. He told me that his mom didn't agree with the hatred his dad tried to foist upon him. He said that his mom was scared to stand up to his father; so, she cleverly appeared to comply with his racist views, out of fear of being beaten and removed from the widely accepted, but grossly mistaken privilege of racial superiority. Something my dad referred to as bigotry.

My painful memories of Timmy's murder are intertwined with thoughts of Sammie—when my family and I traveled toward our new destination during the summer of 1963.

After all these years, I can still vividly feel my final moments with Sammie before we moved away, just months after I learned his name.

Chapter 2:
The Midnight Forest

The Night Before We Moved
1963

I walked through the woods alone, eagerly awaiting an opportunity to experience my life's end after discovering I wasn't going to be able to see Sammie anymore. Once my heart fully grasped the reality that we were moving away, suicide seemed like the right thing to do. It was too painful to know that in just a few hours, once the sun came up, I would have to leave my one and only true love.

While strolling through the woods, I picked up a chair I'd placed by a tree I was standing near the day before yesterday. The rope was already hanging from the tree. I wrapped the rope around my neck and crept toward the edge of the chair. Before leaping, I heard desperation in Sammie's voice as he rushed forward, "Sophia, please, don't jump!" My heart fluttered as the rope continued to hang from my neck.

Sammie flashed a small flashlight in my face as I lifted my hands to cover my eyes. His eyes pleaded with me while he sang—"I Can't Stop Loving You" by Ray Charles. Sammie's voice was so beautiful I couldn't help but sing along. During that moment, I knew I was meant to be a singer.

As I continued to stand atop the chair, a few inches from death's outstretched arms, Sammie stated, "Sophia, you have an awesome voice."

I held the top portion of the rope in my left hand above my head. I perked up a little before replying, "Really?"

While distracted by his compliments and heroic romantism, Sammie cleverly cut me down from the tree, that was seconds away from taking my life. Then, I fell into his arms, wrapping my arms around his neck as he held me in a position that mimicked the execution of a professional dancer finishing a duet pose. He reminded me that Timmy's death wasn't my fault. He even attempted to blame himself for not warning Timmy about going to Molly's house.

These gentle words escaped from his mouth as he lowered me to my feet, "Sophia, a part of me knew one day that he would get caught, but I couldn't help but think of what I would do if someone tried to stop me from seeing you. I would have done the same thing as your brother." Sammie brushed his fingers against my left cheek. "I love you Sophia, and please don't think that I'm crazy. My life has drastically changed ever since we met." I looked at him with elation as my heart thumped. He continued, "After I read your song, I could hear your voice singing the beautiful words you wrote. Your song touched my heart." His voice started to tremble as he garnered more strength to open his heart while holding me with one arm while looking around in the woods. "Your singing forced me to look at life differently; it even compelled me to meditate on the monstrosities that I've witnessed in these woods." He looked around.

I hugged him, elated, as he continued to speak poetry into my heart. He positioned the flashlight to highlight the section of the woods where were located.

"In fact, I've decided to name this section of the woods where we stand, The Midnight Forest." I smiled. "Sophia, midnight begins a new day for me, and each day reminds me of the unforgettable day I heard your beautiful voice brush against the trees inside these woods. I can't believe nature hid your voice from me for so long." He released his grip, and I held my hands over my heart. "I didn't tell you that I knew you could sing the first time I heard you, because, honestly, I enjoyed stalking you." I smiled as he grabbed my hand, pulling me back into his arms.

I felt safe.

It was the scent of his breath mixed with mine, as the closeness of our faces fought the compelling force of love's magnetic field, that helped me feel secure. I slowly caressed his cute little cheeks while saying, "Sammie, why would you or anyone want to hear a colored girl sing in a town full of racists?"

He leaned in and squeezed my back, whispering in my right ear, "Sophia, I love hearing your voice. In fact, that's the reason why I discovered your heart. After I heard your voice, I couldn't help but follow you to see where you lived." He faced me face-to-face again. His voice elevated. "After I heard you sing, I eagerly sought an opportunity to meet you. I first learned of your name whenever I would guard your soul from a distance. I came out here every night because I wanted to unleash my gift too. And—" He looked downward briefly before lifting his chin again. "And it was then that I knew I had to protect you from the carnage that takes place in these woods." He accidentally dropped the flashlight, and the light shined away from us to my right and his left. "I watched over your soul as I listened with a strong desire every night." He grinned. "You were actually out here referring to yourself in third person. I could hear you talking to yourself too." He smirked.

While smiling I nudged him in his right shoulder before stepping to my right to pick up the flashlight. I flashed the light in his face to return the favor, he squinted his eyes as I said, "Just as long as I didn't answer myself." We both laughed.

Sammie blushed. "You might have, but I didn't hear you."

I handed him the light while saying, "You're so funny."

He shrugged his shoulders and playfully flashed the light into my eyes.

"Sammie, you better stop," I said jokingly. I quickly glanced at Sammie's leg.

I wonder why he walked with a limp. I noticed it every time I saw him. It was like one of his legs was slightly deformed or something. It was okay, though. He was still very handsome to me.

Sammie laughed. "I'll try." He wrapped his arms around me, and we walked for ten seconds, east of the tree that almost took my life. He flashed his light to his right and pointed to an obscure section of the woods that was compiled with farm machinery. "I managed to go unnoticed by you as I hid over there—only a few yards away from you. Every night for two months, I watched you unleash your gift into the midnight forest. It took me a while to develop the courage to bring you the song I watched you drop. I was so happy you dropped your song."

I was confused. "Why?"

Sammie squeezed my right hand while facing me. "It gave me a reason to come to your house. I used to bring my gun out here to watch over you too." I looked at him with flummoxed eyes as he stated, "I know what type of things occur out here after midnight."

I grabbed his hands while gradually surrendering to his words. Sammie rubbed my hands along the surface of his soft hands. "Sophia, I was prepared to protect you during the night that you and your brother were attacked by the KKK, remember?"

"Yes, I remember that night, Sammie."

" I withdrew my readiness for battle once I saw your dad running right next to you with his pistol."

I pondered what he meant by the things that occurred in the woods.

I spun around in a circle, tossing my hands into the air. "Sammie, what type of things happen in the midnight forest?"

Sammie rubbed his chin. "I see you like the new name I've given this cherished part of the woods."

I pointed downward to gesture that the location we stood in was important. "I think I do like the name you've given this spot. I'll be honest too—it's kind of a corny name."

Sammie's face brightened the midnight forest as his adorable and boyish smile canvased the scene. "Since we are naming things," he pointed to the tree that almost took my life. "I think I'll name that tree the Tree of Destiny, since it helped bring us to this point in our friendship."

Weirdo is what I thought to myself while remaining silent.

"I know if I hadn't heard you sing, maybe my dad's racist views would've infiltrated my heart forever," said Sammie. He stared at me like a grown man who knew what he wanted. "Sophia, your voice changed my life." He pointed to the tree again. "Hearing you sing changed my life. It helped me to view all races the same." He gently squeezed my lips together with his fingers. "I believe your voice has the power to bridge together unloving views." He placed his hands on his heart. "Your gift makes me feel that love is within my heart."

I looked around and thought to myself, the tree of destiny is the tallest tree in the forest by far. "Sammie, you're so poetic! You seem to know all the right things to say."

"Only with you," said Sammie.

We walked and talked all night in the midnight forest. He went on to tell me about the evil history of the tree of destiny.

Sammie paused during our walk as howls from a dog echoed throughout the woods. Silence continued to ruminate until I noticed Sammie's gripping of my hand increase in pressure. "Sophia, I've seen some really bad things out here in these woods." I gave him my undivided attention. "The worse was when I saw a Black man—" He gulped. "I just can't say anymore."

I was teary-eyed as I stated, "It's okay, I understand. You don't have to talk about anything that makes you feel uncomfortable."

Sammie shook his head and wiped his tears. "Thank you, Sophia— thank you!"

I squeezed his hand and replied, "You're welcome, Sammie!"

"But I need to tell you the truth about these woods," said Sammie.

He told me everything then he said, "Sophia, will you be my—" I cut him off and replied, "Yes!"

"How did you know what I was going to ask you?" Sammie asked in a happy but slightly bewildered tone, with his eyebrows raised.

I blushed and replied, "Because I read your soul."

A few hours later, I snuck into my bedroom window. My bed was still stuffed with pillows, giving the illusion that someone was in the bed—fast asleep. "Sammie, I miss you already. You were my adorable stalker." I need to be quiet, so my parents won't hear me.

I stepped into the shower and washed my hair. Because of my wonderful Sammie, the tree of destiny failed to capture its one-hundred-and-twenty-sixth victim. It was the final home for dozens of

Blacks who were lynched by hateful racists. I only know the number of victims because Sammie said that he counted the number of victims he witnessed, but we concluded that there probably were more that he didn't see. He alluded to the possibility that his dad would most likely murder me and my family if he found out what I knew. I couldn't resist the urge to ask Sammie if he'd ever witnessed his dad kill a Black person, and if he had ever participated in any of his dad's racist acts. He empathically said, "No!" He mentioned that most of the people who conducted the lynches were his dad's friends.

Sammie often walked half a mile to enter the midnight forest late at night. He sang at the top of his lungs too. I enjoyed learning that he was scared to tell anyone because his dad often called him a sissy for singing. This was why Sammie ran to the midnight forest to unleash his gift.

As I finished reflecting on Timmy and Sammie, finally, we arrived at our new abode in San Francisco.

Our new house was a different experience; I missed Sammie even more once we got there.

***

The New House

1963

I walked toward the new house, noticing that it was much bigger than our old house in Marin County. Friendly White and Black people welcomed us to the neighborhood. The open windows in the house welcomed the brightness of the early afternoon sun. While touring our new home, we heard a loud knock on the door. We were upstairs in my parent's bedroom when my mom said, "Wait just a minute, I'm coming." She tapped my father on the shoulder as she walked by him.

He was standing with his back against the entrance of the room. They walked downstairs together and then my father quickly turned around and said, "Go ahead get the door baby, I really have to pee."

I followed suit a few seconds later, after overhearing a few men walk inside. I rushed downstairs. I observed two men with austere countenances dressed in military uniforms. Both men seemed to avoid interrupting one another as they unitedly asked, "Is Mr. Smith home?"

My mother looked at the men. "How did the military find us so fast?"

A tall White man responded. "Mr. Smith informed us of his move months ago, which is a requirement."

A few seconds later, my dad rushed downstairs to the front door and saluted them. I overheard the men informing my dad that he was needed for another assignment. The two men were standing with their backs facing the front door and my mom was standing next to my dad. My dad was to the left of my mom.

My dad pointed at the men as he sighed with his hands placed on his hips, saying, "Now, you two know that I've served my country already—I'm a conscientious objector now." My dad looked at the tall man. "Come on, Alex." The shorter White man pushed his army hat down onto his head to cover his forehead a little more, as he and his counterpart continued to stand in front of my parents like assembled statues with great posture.

Alex stepped forward and the sounds of his boots bounced off the gray wooden floors. He replied, "Anthony, you must return to the base. Besides, John and I both know that you're making that up—you're no objector." He placed his right hand on my dad's left shoulder. "The psychiatrist will assess you and determine whether or not you're still fit for battle. If you don't come, you'll lose your benefits and monthly income." Alex pointed at the other man with him. "We both know you need the money to take care of your family." Alex's head moved around as he surveyed the house before saying, "And nice new house, by the way."

My dad paused before pulling my mom into the kitchen. I could hear them talking low amongst each other over the next two minutes. While my parents discussed things, I noticed the other man with Alex glance up at me on the stairway, which was positioned directly in front of the door. Then my dad walked back toward the front door while holding my mother's hand. I overheard my father saying, "I'll be there next week." He scoffed.

"Okay. You have six days to show up," Alex said.

I walked to my bedroom and left my door ajar after noticing the men preparing to depart. My dad walked them outside.

A few seconds later, he walked back inside the house, and I heard the car that the men were in crank up before they backed out of the driveway. I stepped out of my room to view my parents from the stairway while leaning on the top rail of the stairway. I looked to my left and noticed my father briefly glance up at me. I pretended to be surprised as I waved at my father. My mom erupted into a clamor, "I don't want to lose you too, Anthony." She grabbed his forearm and massaged it. They were standing by the front door, and my dad was nearest to me on the left side of the door.

My dad sighed. "Honey, I'm sure they will release me after they assess my health."

"I sure hope so, because I can't lose another one of my loved ones. I've already lost my son, so I can't lose you, too."

My dad promised my mother that he would be ok as they hugged and kissed.

***

Three months later, the same two men showed up to mention that my father was killed in the war.

"I told you all to leave my Anthony alone! Now he's gone forever!" My mom screamed.

The two men united in a sigh as Alex said, "We're sorry for your loss. You and your daughter will be taken care of." I stood next to my mom as she held me and sobbed.

The pain from hearing my mom cry her heart out was unbearable. I didn't know what to do.

Seconds later, I was overwhelmed by my heart's own tears. Subsequently, the men left and the same sound of their engine cranking up flooded my memories with images of my dad and the good times we shared together.

Over the next few hours my mom and I mourned, pondering how we were going to survive without him.

"The military will take good care of us, though," said my mom as we held one another on the living room couch.

She looked around at our house with a face full of tears. "The military will send enough money to pay for the house." She released a deep exhale. "Uh, I'll ask your Aunt Terri to come live with us so that she can help out too." She dried my tears with her fingers, pulling me into her chest as I laid my head atop her breasts. "Your dad's mom might be the better and more convenient option, though."

I looked up at my mom and smiled. "I like Grandma Pat," I said.

"Yeah, Patricia is something else." My mother patted me on my right thigh. "Oh, and the military promised to pay for your college expenses, too."

I sat in silence and listened to my mom.

The day ended, and the next few days were dismal moments in time for me and my mom. Five days later, we attended my dad's funeral.

After my dad's funeral, my mom was never the same. She started smoking and drinking all the time. She completely let herself go.

A couple of years after my dad's death, when I turned sixteen, she was admitted into a mental institution; my dad's mom looked after me. My grandmother was very lenient with her supervision.

Laying in my bed one night, I thought to myself. I am so thankful for my grandma Pat. She comes over weekly and stays with me when my aunt Terri can't come. They both really help in stabilizing my life. But I must admit, the main thing that helps to keep me afloat is thinking about something my dad said to me. "If you and Sammie are meant to be together, he'll find his way back to your heart." I turned over onto my right side and fell asleep.

Sleep was the only time I had peace.

I used to sleep so much that three years flashed before my eyes—very fast.

Chapter 3:
The Bus Ride for Star-Crossed Lovers

Five Years Later
Summer of 1968
5am

While sitting upright in my bed with a pillow behind my back, I decided it was time to catch a bus to Marin County to hopefully reunite with my true love. My legs were extended temporarily until I pulled my feet closer toward my buttocks with my knees facing the ceiling. While in deep thought, I placed my right cheek onto my lap, resting my head between my legs while thinking of Sammie.

I decided to implement the most precious thing Sammie shared with me. He gave me an address to a bar where he sang, a few hours later in my room after we hung out together in the midnight forest five years ago.

What a night that was. So much transpired before we went back to my room that night after hanging out in the woods.

I saw Sammie again in the midnight forest two days later after he saved my life from the tree of destiny.

While still sitting in my bed, I smelled the scent of my grandmother's biscuits while daydreaming about Sammie. Sammie and I snuck into my bedroom through the window. Once inside, Sammie stared into my eyes with a serious look, saying, "Sophia, here's the address where you can find me."

I looked confused. "What address? You haven't given me anything." I asked. I sat on my bed while he stood over me. With a boyish smile tattooed on his face, Sammie said, "If you ever get a chance, Sophia please come find me."

He's ignoring my question, I thought to myself.

Suddenly Sammie turned his back to me and placed his hands onto his chin. He sighed. "No matter how many years go by—" He paused and turned around to face me again. His eyes were red, but I didn't see any tears in his eyes. He handed me a piece of paper that he garnered from his left back pocket. His fitted blue jeans hugged his legs very-well. "If you come to this address around 7 p.m. on Fridays, you'll find me singing my heart out for you." He dropped to his knees and grabbed my hands. He interlocked his right hand with my left hand before placing our hands on his lips. He kissed his own hand and I blushed.

"Sammie, you just kissed your own hand and not mine—you're a little retard." We both laughed uncontrollably.

He unlocked his hand from mine and stood upright. "I'm normally much smoother than this." He chuckled once more. "Anyway, I want to tell you—I am going to be a superstar. I'm going to be a Country singer." He jumped into my bed and tickled me under my armpits. I laughed while placing my finger over my lips, signaling Sammie to keep the noise down. "Keep your voice low silly, or my parents will hear us. I know you remember how my father reacted the first time that he saw you." I raised my eyebrows.

"Yes, I'm sure he'll have a fit if he walked in and saw a boy, and not just a boy but a White boy, standing in your room." He sat at the edge of the bed to my left before leaning forward, wrapping my arms around his neck.

Sammie smelled so good to me.

I was positioned directly behind him as he kissed my hands while looking over his right shoulder, saying, "I think you're going to be a world class Soul singer, Sophia."

I stood up and sat in his lap, asking, "You really see that for me?" I kissed him on both of his cheeks, then he kissed me on my forehead.

"Yes, you have a beautiful voice," Sammie said.

I mustered up the courage to ask him about his leg, then he revealed to me that he had cerebral palsy in one of his legs.

We continued to talk for another hour before Sammie departed a little after six in the morning. Shockingly, we managed not to get caught by my parents. Speaking of, I need to go see my mom in the morning, I thought to myself.

Section Two

The Following Day
Friday July 15th, 1968

The sunlight was bright with a modest breeze. The wind continued to seep under my red T-shirt while I jogged. My blue gym shorts wrapped around my hips like an anaconda's grip. Toward the end of my jog, I started running faster as thoughts of possibly reuniting with Sammie began to enthrall my sense of reality.

After sprinting the last fifty yards of my run along the sidewalk, leading back to my house, I came to an abrupt stop, hovering over while grasping for air. While panting, I remembered I needed to visit my mother. I walked rapidly toward my house before stopping in the front yard. I placed my hands on my hips. *Geesh, I'm breathing like a moving tornado.*

I leaned over to catch my breath. I need to go visit my mom today at UCSF to sign-off on the new medication her doctor recently prescribed. I walked up the doorsteps to my house while glancing at my wristwatch. I was running behind on time. Okay Sophia, you can figure this out. I had to make time to see my mom before heading out to attempt to reunite with my true love. I glanced at a wooden rocking chair to my left on the front porch. I was glad that my grandma left for the weekend to go see my aunts. It was good that she trusted me to take care of myself while she was away.

My mom's hospitalization was going well. If she continued to progress, she would be discharged.

I turned on the shower and checked the temperature of the water with my left index finger and thumb. No matter what my mom says, I'm catching the bus at noon today to head to Marin County.

I got a whiff of my aroma. Geesh-- I stink. I need to shower.

A few minutes later after I showered and got dressed, I backed out of the driveway in my dad's old station wagon.

I pulled into the street and placed my car's gear into drive while attempting to turn on the radio. While holding my finger atop the radio's knob, I sat motionless at the stop sign adjacent to my house on the right. The engine sputtered.

While driving to visit my mom; I changed the radio. A man with a thunderous voice vibrated through the channel. "Good morning, San Francisco! Welcome to Q-107.4—where we play music for your soul." A song played on the radio. The song reminded me of a song I wrote a few weeks ago, "Bye Bye Dear Daddy." I wrote that song for my dad after he was drafted. I missed him so much while he was away before he died.

I stopped at a red light with the driver's window down, my left arm hanging out of the car. I lifted my eyebrows. I knew that I needed to explore my gift and give it to the world like Sammie encouraged me to do, but he was the only person I ever felt comfortable singing to. I couldn't audition for a singing gig without him—I needed him.

I rolled up the window and slammed my fist against the top of the steering wheel. "Enough, Sophia! Your father raised you better than this."

My self-defeating thoughts were interrupted by the following words on the radio, "Hi, my name is Duke Proctor! I'm the CEO of Cinnamon Soul Productions, and I'm looking for the next Aretha Franklin. If you think you have what it takes, show up Saturday December 17th, at my studio in Los Angeles."

I smiled as a sensation of purpose entered my mind.

The traffic light turned green as I pressed down on the gas pedal. The audition was five months away, which gave me plenty of time to find Sammie. After I found Sammie, my goal was to get him to help me prepare for the audition.

***

Unforgettable Visit *with my Mom*

Five minutes later, I arrived at the mental institution where my mother resided. A weird sensation befell me after opening the door to my car. With my leg dangling out of the wagon, I said out loud, "Ugh! I feel this way every time I come visit my mom." I was always excited to see my mom, but she didn't display the same level of reciprocity. While standing, I close my car door before peering into the window of the car to fix my hair—it looked frizzy. While addressing my curls, I observed my black sundress reflecting through the window of the car. I looked good in that dress; exercising consistently had finally paid off for me.

A few seconds later, I began my journey toward the institution's entrance. I couldn't believe my mom had been diagnosed as a paranoid schizophrenic, coupled with manic depression and bipolar disorder. She really took it hard after my dad was killed. My mother despised me for calling the mental institution to seek out help for her, but I knew she had lost her mind when I found her walking half-naked late one night.

I heard birds chirping while strolling along the sidewalk that led to the hospital. I could see the building's immense structure while glancing to my left after passing a tall, metal-wired fence.

Those fences must've been about twelve feet tall.

I paused and observed a few workers dressed in white scrubs walking around outside in the park area of the facility. Placing my hands against the fence, I sighed while observing an older Black male patient sitting on a wooden bench. A nurse attempted to administer his medication, but he swatted it away.

With my hands planted firmly against my sides, I moved forward like a robot. The entrance was about a quarter-of-a-mile away from where I parked. That place gave me the creeps. It looked more like a penitentiary if you ask me. The building looked old, and its fences were high. I could tell that the owners of the place invested a lot of money into ensuring that maximum security was a priority. Whenever I visited my mom, she often asked, "Sophia, why did you put me in this place? You know I don't want to be here. I'm not crazy, I just have a broken heart."

I approached the gate of the hospital then the guard buzzed me in and asked, "Ma'am, identification, please." I reached into my purse to comply with his request.

A heavyset, middle-aged White guard looked at my I.D. and said, "Who are you here to see?" He glanced at my I.D. card again before handing it to me.

With the wind blowing in my face, I replied, "I'm here to see Debra Smith."

While standing in front of an encapsulated booth, I peered through a square-shaped glass opening that the guard slid open when I handed him my identification card. With the window still open, I placed my purse on the countertop, placing my card back into my purse.

The guard slid the window shut, then made a phone call before walking away. He was away for about five minutes before returning to deliver surprising news. He reopened the window. "Mrs. Smith doesn't want to see you."

I grabbed my chest while scratching my chin. "Huh? Guard, you must've informed the wrong person of my visit. Did you inform Debra Smith—" I pointed to myself. "That her daughter—me, Sophia Smith, is here to see her?"

He leaned forward against the countertop, sticking his head out of the window's opening. "Yes, I informed her." He shrugged his shoulders, twisted his lips, and gently tapped his fingertips against the counter. "I even asked her if she was sure about her decision." He exhaled. "She doesn't want to see you. I'm sorry, but Mrs. Smith has declined your visit."

I stepped backwards, dropping my jaws. With my mouth wide open, I placed my hands atop my forehead, squinting my eyes while frowning. Bewildered, I wrapped my arms around my chest to unconsciously hug myself. *He must be mistaken*, I thought to myself.

As I paced back-and-forth, my crazed walk was interrupted by the guard's words, "You look just like your mom. Just be patient and maybe the next time you come to visit; she'll have had a change of heart."

I dropped my head, walking away with my heart asunder in every place—except the one spot that gave me hope.

I walked away from the hospital's entrance gate to embark upon a walk of misery. I turned around and faced the facility while walking backwards, hoping that the guard would signal for me to come back. Nothing transpired, so I turned around to walk straightforward before hearing footsteps approaching. "Hey—hey! Wait up." The guard wiped sweat from his forehead before placing a walky-talky into the front right pocket of his khaki pants. "I just received a call—your mom changed her mind."

***

A Mother's Bond:
A Unique Connection

The guard guided me through the hallway that led to the visitation room.

I couldn't help but wonder about my mom. While walking behind the guard, thoughts of why she initially didn't want to see me continued to rock side-to-side in my mind like a pendulum.

The guard came to a halt and removed a set of keys from his left hip. He opened the door to the visitation room while gesturing for me to enter. "Your mother will be down in a second," said the guard.

I waited for three minutes, then my mother entered the room, walking in my direction. I was seated as she approached. She was shaking like she had the chills. She sat down to the left of me in a chair while rocking back and forth.

With emotional pain running through my veins, I scooted forward toward the edge of the chair and tossed my hands into the air. I turned my body to face her while saying, "Mom, why did you refuse to see me?"

She was dressed in a white flowered hospital gown. Before she could answer, a female nurse approached to administer her medication. "Mrs. Smith, you forgot to take these before you left your room," said the nurse.

My mom snatched the medicine from the nurse's hands along with a cup of water. "All right!" After taking her medication, she dried specks of water from her lips. The nurse exited the room and the door closed behind her. The rash sound of the door closing made me feel like I was in a prison cell.

My mom glanced at me through the corner of her right eye, screaming, "I'm sick of taking all of these medications! And you know what—" She punched the air before pointing her hands at me. "It's all your fault!" She waved her hands around to highlight the facility along with her dissatisfaction. "Sophia, you have to get me out of this place. I'm being mistreated and I fear for my life." She turned her back to me then faced me again while holding her hands over her chest. My mother scoffed as she looked around. "How could you leave your mother in a trashy place like this?"

I was silent for a few seconds. I initially stumbled over my words with my eyebrows lifted before forming my thoughts. "Okay—okay, so what's going on, Mom? Talk to me." She stared at me with disappointment running through her veins. "Please, don't give me that look, just tell me what's going on? Like—are you being abused or something? Mom, talk to me, please."

She stood up and chuckled before walking toward the door. I followed and grabbed her right arm. She turned around with tears flowing down her face. I looked around. Just one other man was in the room, and he appeared to be waiting for someone.

My mom placed her hands over her face and wiped her eyes. "Sophia, they're beating me three times a day, and they're giving me the wrong medications too." She pointed her hand at the exit door that was positioned to her left. I was standing directly in front of her. She formed a fist and took one step forward toward me. We were approximately two feet away from each other. "Sophia, these people only feed me once a day and all of the staff, except the guard who's here today, call me racist names." My mom placed her hands on the top of my shoulders, jerking my arms. "They tell me I belong to an inferior race. And not to mention that Billy Joe's dad is the owner of this facility. Sophia, how could you let this happen to me?"

I grabbed my mother's hands, lowering them to her hips. I held her hands while saying, "Mom, I had no idea this was going on. I simply went with the nearest hospital I could find, and you needed help. I couldn't just watch you suffer."

My mom looked behind her and sat down in a nearby chair. She sighed while placing her hands over her face. She quickly stood up and positioned herself two feet away from me. "Sophia, I simply had a broken heart because of your dad and brother." She grabbed her gown and dried her tears. My mom squeezed my right hand with both of hers. "You don't know what it feels like to lose your only son. And then turn around after that and lose the man of your dreams too."

My mom's statement reminded me of Sammie. She didn't know how much I could relate to what she was saying. I tried to interject, "But, Mom!"

My mother released my hand, pushing it away. She pointed her right index finger in my face. "Don't you dare interrupt me!"

I tried to grab her right hand, but she pushed it away. "Mom—just hear me out, please," I said.

"Ugh!" My mom grunted.

I placed my right hand over my chest. "Mom, I know exactly how it feels to lose the man of your dreams."

She placed her hands on her hips then poked me right below my collar bone several times. "Hmm. Oh, is that so?"

"Mom, I miss Sammie so much. I plan to go and find him today actually."

My mom tossed her hands into the air. "I just told you that I'm being mistreated and all you can think about is that racist little brat! Sophia, don't get your hopes up—he's just like the rest of them!"

I exhaled. "Don't say that. You're wrong about him."

My mother shook her head. "You're so naïve."

I sighed. "Anyway, I'll figure out what's going on around here. Right now, though, I have a bus ticket and the bus leaves at noon today. I know I'm probably being selfish right now, but I could really use your advice. I'm in love but I don't know what to do with my feelings for him."

My mom's indignation subsided as a mother's unconditional love slowly consumed her soul. She sat down and I sat next to her. "Sophia, my dear, you haven't seen Sammie in years. What you two shared was only puppy love. You all were just kids. You actually think that Sammie is out there—" My mom lifted her eyebrows. "You think that he's just waiting around for you or something?" She chuckled.

I held my right hand up, shaking my head to signal for my mom to cease with her negativity. "Not now, Mom, not now!" Facing her I asked, "Do you think I'm wasting my time attempting to go and find him?"

She laughed. "Yes, Sophia, I do. Besides, he might be a member of the KKK by now anyway."

"Mom, please don't say that. My heart can't fathom such a thing. I know Sammie would never do that!"

"Don't be so naïve about these men, like I used to be. I failed to tell you, your brave military Dad, Mr. Anthony Smith, had an affair when he served during the war." She slapped her thighs with her hands. "And get this—he married the heifer too!"

Confused, I twisted my lips. "What? How do you know?" I thought she was being delusional.

"I hired a private investigator to find out how the affair happened. Your dad met Bich through a refugee camp that the U.S. military used during the Vietnam War."

"Huh?" I asked.

She continued, "The camp housed some of the civilians who lived in or near the areas that were under attack during the war. I had no idea your dad had done this until I went to collect the money the military pays out to a soldier's family for their service."

I was shocked. I knew my mom was telling the truth. I knew her too well. No meds of any kind could dilute her tears.

" Mom, this is a lot to take in."

She frowned. "Think about how I felt when I first found out. The investigator discovered that your dad had deceptively divorced me and married another woman." She grunted. "However, he was kind enough to leave me one hundred thousand dollars of the three hundred thousand that was owed to me. He left the rest for his current widower Bich Nyugen. Your father knew I couldn't read, which is why he called me a month before his death. Before he died, he asked me to sign some papers that he mailed to me. I had no clue at the time I was signing off for a divorce." She sighed. "Anthony told me the papers were for you to receive money to go to college. He mentioned that all I had to do was find the sections that had lines indicating a signature.

What your dad said was partially true because I hired an attorney to look at the documents after I discovered what he did to me. He did take care of your college expenses, though. So, when you matriculate into school next year, you will have a free ride. I know you sat out this semester because you want to clear your head and get your mind ready for school. Speaking of, have you decided where you want to go yet?"

I was perplexed so I stared at the ceiling for a few seconds before turning my attention to my mother. "No Mom, I'm still contemplating where I want to go. I can't believe that my dad did this to you. I believe you." I felt it was best not to tell my mom the real reason I didn't enroll into school for the upcoming semester—I wanted time off to search for Sammie.

My mom started crying, then I hugged her while saying, "Mom, I'm here for you. Everything is going to be okay."

She looked up at me as I held her in my arms. "Sophia, honey, your dad taught me how to sign papers years ago. I was getting better with reading, but my reading level was still at a first-grade level. I didn't see the word divorce in the document. He must've had his lawyers write up the document using some fancy words that he knew I wouldn't be able to recognize. I don't know why Anthony did that to me." She exhaled. "I didn't tell you when it happened because I didn't want you to hold a grudge against your father. I told the guard to ask you to leave today because today would've been our thirtieth wedding anniversary. I still love your father despite his infidelity. Baby, just move on from Sammie and be single."

I swallowed my saliva. "Why?" I asked.

"Men are no good," said my mom.

I grimaced. "Sammie is different. I still can't believe that my dad did this to you."

Isaac Samuel Miller

My mom removed her head from my arms. "Oh sweetie, don't be stupid. That boy is probably lynching one of us as we speak. It's not possible for him to grow up in a racist house and not be racist too."

"Do you remember that Timothy always quoted John 3:16? He always reminded us that God sent Jesus to die for all mankind," I said.

"Yes, I miss my son."

I looked into my mother's eyes and observed how much she had aged over the past few years. My mom looked old. "God didn't show favoritism because he loves us all! Timmy knew that hatred is taught. He used to quote Nelson Mandela, too: 'If a man can be taught to hate, then a man can be taught to love'. I think that's why Timmy had the courage to date Molly. He recognized the good within us all." I dried my mom's tears as she held my hand. "Mom, I see the same thing in Sammie. Not everyone succumbs to their environments. I am sure Sammie's upbringing has had a powerful effect on him, but I think the things he witnessed motivated him not to be like his father. He is a good person. And one day, I am going to find him, I can feel it in my heart."

My mother scoffed. "Someday, huh? Well, don't hold your breath. Sophia, be smart and move on with your life."

She was being so negative.

I hugged my mom and said, "I'm going to file a complaint about this facility and then I'll get you discharged the right way—so that your insurance doesn't drop you." I stood up. "Mom, I have to go now."

We hugged and went our separate ways.

I had a bond with my mom that never seemed to fade—no matter the chaos or dysfunction between us.

66

Before exiting the visitation room, I looked back one final time. "I love you, Mom!"

My mom shouted, "Sophia, let Sammie be, he's working for the KKK. They're probably plotting to chop your head off too." Suddenly, two nurses grabbed my mother and took her away.

I exited the building and walked to my car. Once inside, I sat in the car and meditated on the things my mother said. What if she is right about Sammie, is what I thought at the time. Sammie had alluded to the possibility one night in the midnight forest that his dad's beliefs used to influence him. I still remember his words. "Hearing you sing changed my life. It helped me to view all races the same. I believe, your voice has the power to bridge together unloving views. Your gift makes me feel that love is within my heart."

I said out loud, "Sammie, I hope my mom isn't right about you!"

I started the engine and drove home to park my car before catching a taxi to the bus station. Before heading to the station, I needed to find the address that Sammie wrote down. I thought I put the address he gave me in a small jewelry box that I kept inside my closet, behind a notebook that contained my songs.

Fifteen minutes later, I arrived at my house. I exited the car and rushed upstairs to search through my closet. The sound of paper rattling and shoeboxes sliding across the floor echoed throughout the room. While on my knees, I paused in front of my closet's door. The door was wide open. "Shoot! I can't find the paper." I grunted. Sophia, you must find this paper.

Frustration settled in as I removed twenty-one shoe boxes from the closet. Gosh, Timmy was right, I really do love sneakers. I emptied them from their boxes like a robber pillaging a home. I observed a piece of paper from the box in my hand fall slowly to the floor.

My face brightened. "Yes, that has to be it." I smiled.

I stepped forward and kneeled to pick up the paper. Standing erect, I noticed that a number was missing from the address. I sighed. Darn Sammie, you didn't write the full address. "How am I going to find you now?" I remember exactly what he said during our last encounter. "I want the name of this place to be a surprise for you—if you ever decide to come and look for me. Besides, putting in a little work always keeps things interesting." I looked back at my bed before walking near it to take a seat.

I guess he wanted it to be some type of treasure hunt for me. He knew how to intrigue and frustrate a woman. The address he left for me only had three numbers. I had a little knowledge, so it wasn't too hard. The addresses in Marin County all had four or five numbers for commercial, business, and residential addresses.

I could hear Timmy's voice in my head, whispering to my heart. "Sophia, you have to take a leap of faith, just put yourself out there. True faith is believing and seeing what you want before it happens. Faith without work is dead."

I smiled. *Okay, Timmy, I'll move to the rhythm of my heart.*

I walked downstairs, pausing on the last step of the stairway. Shaking my head, I thought out loud, "Love is complicated."

Chapter 4:
Venture into the Unknown:
A Journey of Faith

I arrived at the bus station with my ticket money in my hand, maneuvering through the line with a sense of urgency.

Just looking at the partial address was perplexing. I hoped what I had at least pointed me in the right direction. So much stuff was going on in my head during that time. I was still in shock about my dad's infidelity, and I didn't have the full address to find Sammie. I felt like I could feel Sammie's heart crying out for me. I just knew he was somewhere waiting for me. I hoped with all my heart that my mom was wrong.

As I approached the bus, a midsized Black male driver extended his hand to collect my ticket. "Bus pass." He looked behind himself while pointing his fingers. "And don't bother any of the kind White folks' on my bus, okay?"

I grimaced. Yep, he would've been a house-negro, I thought to myself. "Here you go," I mumbled under my breath, "Uncle Tom."

He squinted his eyes. "What you say there now?" The driver asked.

I ignored the driver and located a seat. I walked toward the back of the bus to find a seat since nothing was available toward the front. I couldn't believe over a decade ago, Black people weren't allowed to sit toward the front. I felt a little animosity while walking to the back of the bus. I observed a few of the White people giving me unpleasant stares. It was like most of the people on this bus were saying with their eyes, "Go to the back of the bus where you belong."

A few seconds later, I located an empty seat and sat down with my purse dangling from my left shoulder. Before I had a chance to settle into my seat, the driver said, "We are going to make three stops before we head to Novato, which is the final stop."

I glanced at my watch and the bus started to move. It was 12:30 p.m.

I removed my purse from my shoulder and placed it onto my lap. My left foot was in the middle of the aisle. I looked forward to my left while sitting on the right side of the bus. Why are those two men staring at me like they want to murder me? Lord, is this really happening, like am I going to reunite with Sammie?

I really wanted those two old White men to stop looking at me. I vehemently scoffed.

Two minutes later my heart started to pound. They're going to lynch me, and I won't ever see Sammie again. I screamed, "Jesus," before rushing to the front of the bus, pleading for the driver to stop and let me off.

I held onto the back of the driver's seat while he looked at me through the rearview mirror.

The driver looked confused. "Ma'am, I can't do that until the next stop." He quickly turned to his right and glanced at me while elevating his eyebrows. "If I drop you off right here, you'll be in the middle of nowhere."

I interlocked my hands like I was praying. "I don't care, just let me off now, please."

A crackling male voice traveled from the middle of the bus up to my post. "Let that monkey off the bus! She doesn't belong on here with our fine people anyway."

I decided not to look in the direction of the racial epithets.

Ironically, an oversized elderly White lady stood up. The lady formed a fist and pointed to the man that voiced his views. "You people embarrass humanity. You're just so hateful and ignorant. She pointed toward the front of the bus. "You hate this young beautiful lady just because she's Black!" She did a one-hundred-and-eighty-degree turn to canvas the bus. While pointing her fingers she said, "Shame on you all." She breathed in and exhaled. "You know, it's time for a change of heart." She sat down and sighed.

Everyone on the bus appeared to be taken aback.

The bus driver screamed, "That's enough! I'm not losing my job over this crap." The driver pulled over and gave me an opportunity to exit the bus. The driver looked at me and said, "Lady, since you're creating such a huge distraction on my bus, if you want to get off, then get off! But I will advise you not to—if you know what I mean." He stopped the bus on an abandoned highway and opened the door.

I stepped off the bus.

Before the driver closed the door, the nice older lady who stood up for me gently grabbed my right arm. "Sweetheart, please get back on the bus. I'll be amiss to allow you to wander into the middle of nowhere like this. You're not a vagrant or some pauper who's giving up on life, are you?"

The older lady's back was facing the bus. I was positioned directly in front of her. The driver looked on with anticipation. My eyes were watery as I said, "No, I'm not." I grabbed my stomach and vomited to my right. My torso was aligned parallel with the pavement before I dropped to my knees.

The lady patted me on my midback. "Poor thing." She grabbed my hands. "Let me help you get back up. Let's get back on the bus and you can seat with me."

I removed a paper towel from my pocket and wiped my mouth with it. The driver stepped off the bus and handed me a small bottle of water. I gurgled and spat the water out onto the asphalt. I could hear an uproar on the bus from the angry White men.

They're probably going to kill me, I thought to myself.

The bus driver stepped back onto the bus. He sat down and said, "Either you two get back on the bus or I'll have to leave you both. In case you two haven't noticed, I have a job to do." He pointed at his face. "And don't forget that I'm Black—so my supervisor won't hesitate to fire my black behind."

I overheard someone call him the N-word. The driver shook his head while looking at me and the nice lady before saying, "You see what I mean."

I turned around and grabbed the lady's hand, then we stepped back onto the bus together as a force to be reckoned with. Removing my bus ticket from my pocket, I held it in my hand for comfort. I glanced at the name of my old community on the ticket. Sammie, here I come. I have courage because of you.

If Sammie and I were still kids, I bet that he would've named this ride the bus ride of faith. I looked around and noticed something that was apparent from the beginning. My mind must've been distracted when I first got on the bus. I was literally the only Black passenger on the bus. I continued to walk to the middle of the bus as I felt the bus moving again. The older lady tailed me, then we both took our seats.

While seated, she extended her left hand. "I'm Beth. What's your name, dear?"

I looked at Beth's hand. Hesitantly, I shook her hand.

Beth detected my reluctance. "Honey, I promise you I won't bite." She gently patted my thighs. "I'm not a racist like the rest of these pricks on this bus."

I gradually smiled, extending my hand after a fifteen second pause. "Okay." I scratched the top of my head. "Uh, my name is Sophia." I placed my ticket stub atop my right thigh.

Beth smiled. "That's a pretty name. And don't worry about those racist fools. God will deal with them in his own due season." Beth glanced at my ticket. "What's in Novato?"

"Excuse me?" I looked perplexed.

"I'm sorry if I startled you but—" She pointed at my lap. "I can see your ticket stub, right there on your thigh."

I looked down and laughed. "Oh yeah, that's right. You don't want to know; you'll think I'm crazy."

"Try me. Let me guess, you're in love?" Beth asked.

"How do you know?" I asked.

"It's written all over your face," Beth said. "I've been in love before, so I think I know a thing or two about it."

Beth and I conversed throughout most of our bus ride together. An hour later, Beth arrived at her stop—the second to last stop before Marin County. We waved and said our final goodbyes. I observed her walk away as I cracked open my window, then Beth turned around and screamed, "If you can't find the missing numbers to the address

Sammie gave you, just find out three of the most popular singing venues in the area! Remember, follow your heart!" The people passing through the bus station looked at Beth like she was a crazy old lady.

I felt the bus slowly drive away as Beth yelled out the rest of her sentiments. "If it's truly meant to be, I'm certain you'll find him at one of those top three singing venues. I'm confident he'll be singing his little heart out to you."

I stuck my head out of the window and said, "Thank you so much for everything!"

After wrapping up my final words with Beth, I sat down and progressed into a timely nap. Thirty minutes later, I was awakened by the sounds of a halting bus. While stretching my arms, I stood up to walk to the front to exit the bus. Before the door closed, the driver said, "Young lady, be careful—this town is still very racist. So please, keep your guard up."

I nodded my head and walked away.

After his statement, I recall thinking, *I remember how Novato used to be years ago. I wonder if things have changed.*

There was only one way to find out. I smiled as I thought: *Yes, that is it, that's a great idea.* I looked up into the afternoon sky before searching for a taxi to take me to Sammie.

Chapter 5:
Welcome to The Blues Cafe:
The Moment of Truth

July 15th
2:30 p.m.
Sophia's First Stop

I hopped out of a taxi and faced a venue. "Hmm. Soul Flare." I walked toward a medium-sized white building. I liked the architecture of the building. It reminded me of a house. Its wooden posts were elegant, and they complimented the gray shutters. I looked toward my left and noticed a white sign that read: You must be eighteen to get in.

I pulled my sundress down from where it was entangled inside my glutes. I had forgotten my I.D., but at least I was of age—I had turned eighteen-and-a-half a year ago.

I approached the entrance of Soul Flare then another venue three buildings down to the right captivated my attention. Hmm. The Blues Café, I thought. The building should be a darker blue rather than sky blue. The Blues Café was massive compared to Soul Flare. I looked at Soul Flare, then glanced at The Blues Café once more. The Blues Café sounded more like a place where Sammie would play, so I started my search for him there.

I walked for thirty seconds before approaching the entrance of The Blues Café. Abruptly, I was stopped by the café's concierge. The vanguard immediately asked to see a form of identification. "Stop right there, Ma'am! I need to see some I.D. before I let you in."

Shoot, I forgot my I.D. I look like I'm sixteen. He won't believe that I'm old enough. I smiled and placed my hand in front of my hips.

The guard raised his right eyebrow and grinned while releasing a flirtatious sigh. *I hope he thinks that I'm cute. If so, I can flirt my way in*, I thought.

I blushed in response to the way he was looking at me. Gently tapping his arm, I said, "What's your name?"

He was leaning against the entrance door of the building with his right foot elevated, pressing against the door. "Isaac." He licked his lips and pushed himself off the door. He folded his arms as we stood one foot apart.

"Isaac, I like that name." I smiled and blew a kiss his way. "Look, Isaac, I really have to use the restroom, but I left my I.D. in the car." I wondered why his countenance shifted.

Isaac held his right hand in front of him and frowned. "Look, Ma'am, I wasn't born yesterday. Now I need your I.D. before I can let you in."

I grinned. "Don't be in such a hurry, Isaac. What's your last name?"

"Johnson, which is why some people call me Mr. John," Isaac said.

"Well, Mr. John, I promise I'm eighteen. But I can't hold my bladder much longer." I flashed my brown eyes while demurely flirting with Isaac. I lowered my voice to sound more seductive while noticing a sign to my right, near the entrance door. *Muriel Scotts is performing tonight.* I lifted my eyebrows and quickly shifted my eyes as an idea entered my mind. *Doesn't hurt to try, he might go for it.*

"Please, Mr. John, I am performing tonight. I can't have an accident on myself. In case you haven't noticed, I am Muriel Scotts." I bowed my head in a playful way. I lifted my head after bowing before winking my right eye. *I hope he has never seen Muriel Scotts before.*

He stood back and shuffled his feet. "Oh really? Sing something for me then," Isaac said.

Oh lord, I've never sang for anyone other than Sammie. Gosh, he's staring at me. "Uh, okay! If I sing, are you going to let me in?"

He chuckled, waving his hands side-to-side while saying, "Nah. If you sing and you sound good, then yes, I will let you in."

I must do this. Sammie might be here tonight. I swallowed my saliva and said a quick prayer. I sung one tag line from a song I wrote. The final two words of my tag line were Sammie Walker. I breathed heavily while staring at Isaac in anticipation of his response. My facial expression depicted someone who was waiting for a sign of approval.

Isaac clapped. "Wow, you definitely fit the sound of what I've heard about Muriel." He clapped again. "How do you know Sammie Walker anyway?"

I started to perspire. For some strange reason I was taken aback by his question. I was completely motionless for a few seconds. Just hearing his name made me nervous.

Isaac waved his hands in front of my face. "Hey, are you okay?" He asked.

I smirked. "Yes, I'm so sorry. What were you saying?"

While rubbing his cheeks and caressing his beard, he said, "You mentioned Sammie Walker in your song. Are you referring to the local phenomenon?"

"Of course," I said.

I didn't know for sure whether or not he was referring to my Sammie. I figured I would just play along and see where it went.

Tossing my hands into the air, I slapped my hands against my thighs as gravity pulled them down. "I know him well."

"That's good to know because I'm a huge fan of Sammie. He performs here sometimes with a girl named Molly too."

I placed my hands on my hips and executed a mild frown. "Oh, really?" I listened to Isaac ramble over the next two minutes. His thoughts were blocked by my inner dialogue. I couldn't help but think of the Molly that Timmy used to date.

Isaac gestured for me to enter the club by opening the door. "Come on in and use the restroom, Muriel. With a voice like yours, you might put Sammie and Molly out of business."

I entered the club, pausing after stepping in front of Isaac. "Would you happen to have pictures of them?" I asked. Before Isaac replied, I raised my left hand and said, "You know what, never mind." I decided to stop being pathetic, I thought it was obvious that Sammie had moved on.

Isaac walked into the building and acknowledged my look of worry. "Are you sure you are, okay?" He asked.

"Yeah," I said. I rushed to the restroom and cried while tossing a row of toilet paper from one side of the restroom clear to the other side. I halted, glancing at myself in the restroom. I looked so foolish. Thank God no one was in there. I dropped to my knees and ran my hands through my hair. Sammie, you better not be with Molly. I knew how to determine for certain whether Isaac was referring to my Sammie.

I exited the restroom and walked toward the front door. Approaching Isaac, I asked, "Hey, is Sammie playing here tonight?"

We walked outside the café.

He grabbed a pad out of his pocket, pointing to the itinerary on the notepad. "Yes, he is. His show starts around seven o'clock tonight."

I frowned. Traitor. I planned to wring Sammie's neck when I saw him. Sammie promised to wait for me.

Isaac interrupted my thoughts as he smiled like a lightbulb shining inside a dark room. His countenance depicted that of one who experienced a sudden epiphany. "Sammie can definitely use some more youth in his group."

I gulped. "Wait, how old are they?" I asked.

"I'm not good with guessing people's age, so I don't even try," Isaac said.

I began walking away. My backwards prance was interrupted by Isaac's voice as he stepped forward to pat me on my shoulder.

"Muriel, wait! You have to sign in with my boss, Travis. He told me to look out for you." He handed me a sign in sheet that was attached to a clipboard.

I held my hands up and said, "Okay, just let me run to my car." I pointed toward the back of the building. "I'm parked around back."

Isaac grabbed his chin and scratched his head while I continued walking backwards with a perplexed countenance. He shook his head with a bewildered facial expression and said, "I'll walk with you around back."

Immediately, I waved my hands saying, "No need for that Mr. John." I continued to wave my right hand while slowly lowering my left hand. I ceased my backward stroll then I turned to face the direction I was walking in. Looking over my shoulder to acknowledge Isaac's presence, I said, "I'll be back up front in a second."

"Alright, have it your way." Isaac turned around and walked to the entrance of The Blues Café.

I sprinted in the opposite direction toward another building. As the distance increased between Isaac and I, I heard him yelling, "Muriel! Where are you going?"

***

Sophia's Second Stop:
A Date with Destiny

July 15th
3:20 p.m.

I rushed into a venture entitled, Frank's Donut Shop.

Normally I would've been winded, but my early morning workouts were paying off. I must've jogged for at least ten minutes. I couldn't believe that Isaac thought I was Muriel Scotts. I panted. Sammie, Sammie, Sammie, you got me doing all types of crazy things, I thought.

I leaned against a wall inside the donut shop, then I walked past a trashcan before pausing at the counter for service. In a mild undertone, I said out loud to myself, "I am hungry," while staring at a glazed donut. I ordered two chocolate glazed donuts with a bottle of milk. My heart was taken aback by the perfectness of the guy that walked out from the back of the store. He was gorgeous. The guy extended his hand and handed me my donuts. I was standing directly in front of him while he leaned on the counter, resting his forearms against his muscular chest. His arms were toned; his muscular build reminded me of Timmy.

I stood frozen by his attractiveness. He kind of reminded me of Sammie, too. The main difference was that he was Black. The mystery guy stood six-feet-and-four-inches-tall; his skin was caramel colored and smooth. His eyes were hazel brown, and he had the smile of a man that was confident. He looked like he was twenty-five. I couldn't take my eyes off him, he was gorgeous. While holding my donuts, he smiled and signaled for me to pick up my donuts.

I blushed before grabbing them. "Oh, I'm so sorry. Thank you for the donuts." The way he looked at me, after handing me my donuts, was intriguing. His lips looked delicious whenever he licked them.

The handsome man removed donut crumbs from his white apron, maneuvering his large hands across his lowcut hair, as his chiseled, square-shaped facial structure gradually displayed a boyish smile. His cheeks rose as high as a mountain top, exposing his pearly white teeth. He walked from behind the counter and approached me with the stealth of a regal male lion and asked, "What's your name?"

I expelled a mild cough while clearing my throat. "My name is Muriel Scotts."

"Your name can't be Muriel Scotts, because I know her personally." He laughed. "She performs at The Blues Café this afternoon around 4:00 or 5:00 p.m."

I slapped my forehead. I was so embarrassed. I hoped I wasn't blushing too hard. I was in-awe, the man was gorgeous. I extended my left hand, tucking the donut bag into the right side of my purse. "Please excuse what just happened." I laughed while placing my left hand on my chest. "And my name is Sophia Smith."

He looked up at the clock on the wall above the cash register to his right. "Sophia, I get off in five minutes. You should stick around for a little." He displayed his perfect white teeth. "I want to talk to you for a few seconds. My name is Kyle, by the way." Kyle started walking toward the back of the store.

I didn't expect to meet Mr. Gorgeous there during that afternoon. I should've gotten out of there as soon as possible. "Kyle, look, I am sorry, but I have to go—like right now. I'm kind of in a rush too. And besides, I'm looking for someone."

Kyle turned around and stopped his pursuit toward the back of the store. "So, are you seeing anyone?" He ascertained my hesitancy, walking even closer toward me.

"Well, no not really." I am still unsure why I said that. "I'm here to find my old boyfriend. The only reason we stopped dating is because my dad forced me to move away five years ago."

Kyle laughed while holding his hands with his fingers extended in front of his chest. "Whoa, that's a lot of information." He winked his eye at me. "Save a little for when I get off. And answer this for me though, have you talked to or seen your used to be boyfriend since your move?"

I exhaled. "No, I haven't."

Kyle slyly inched closer and grabbed my hand.

My hands started to perspire.

Whenever I really like what I see, it was always obvious to well-trained eyes. I knew Kyle's eyes were well-trained, so I played the play hard to get game. I pulled my hand back after shaking his masculine hands. My enthrallment was interrupted by his words, "Wait here for a few minutes, I'll be right back."

As he walked away, I looked around, observing a vacant shop.

I probably should've left.

I crossed my arms with a guilty countenance. I felt like I was cheating on Sammie. I looked up and observed Kyle approaching. His footsteps moved to the beat of my throbbing heart. I was so nervous.

Kyle parked his face a foot away from mine, pointing to a nearby booth that was behind me, adjacent to my left. "Come eat your donuts with me over here," said Kyle. He led the way.

I hesitated while looking over my left shoulder with my back facing him. He sat down at the booth, and I smiled. "Since this will be the only time I ever see you, I guess I can eat my donuts with you," I said.

He gently tapped the table with his fingernails. "Why will this be the only time?" Kyle asked.

I turned to face him while walking toward a table. Standing next to a booth, I said, "Not that it's any of your business, but I'm only in town for one night."

"This will be the only time I ever see your pretty face?" Kyle asked.

I sat down and slid into the booth before pulling down on my dress with my hands. "Yep!"

He held his hands in front of his chest and pushed against the air while saying, "Okay, no need to be abrupt." He licked his lips. "Since you're only going to be here for one night, it won't hurt for you to tell me where you're staying?"

I stared into his eyes. "Actually, I never thought about where I was going to lay my head during my bus ride here. I was distracted by my mom, coupled with anticipation to see Sammie." I blindly planned a trip there during that time without finding a hotel. "I don't have a place to stay right now, but I'll just get a hotel," I said.

"So, that's the lucky guy's name." Kyle lifted his right eyebrow.

I glanced at him. Kyle was such a typical guy.

"By the way, all of the hotels are booked. Everyone came to see Muriel perform tonight. You'll have to catch a taxi to a motel now—and the nearest one is about thirty-five-minutes away. I doubt that you'll be well-received in that area, if you know what I mean."

"You're right. It's pretty racist here," I said.

He grabbed my left wrist and elevated my right hand as I held a donut. He lifted my hand and positioned it in front of his mouth. He took a bite and said, "I think you've already found the man you're looking for."

That was cute, I thought to myself.

I blushed. No—no, Sophia, you're here for Sammie. I quickly stood up. "I need to go! Sammie is performing at The Blues Café."

Kyle stood up and wiped his lips. "If you don't find Sammie performing at The Blues Café, just swing back through here so we can talk some more if you like. Also, you're welcome to spend the night with me."

I waved my hands side-to-side. "No thanks, Kyle." He was a little pushy.

Kyle followed me toward the door as I walked away. "Okay, but if you change your mind, I'll be waiting right here until eight tonight," said Kyle.

Once I made it to the door, I paused. A part of me wanted to stay, but I didn't know Kyle. I quickly visualized Sammie singing his heart out to me while resisting the urge to look back at Kyle, as I walked out of the donut shop. Once outside, I noticed a taxi drive by. I signaled for the taxi to stop, then I entered the car. "Please, take me to The Blues Café." I knew it wasn't far away, but my feet were hurting.

"Okay, it's just five-minutes up the road," said the driver.

"Okay." The Blues Café was my final stop on that day.

***

Sophia's Third Stop:
The Moment of Truth

July 15th
4:00pm

The taxi dropped me off at the entrance of The Blues Café.

I peered through the window of the taxi as I sat in the backseat. I observed a long line of people entering and waiting to enter the club. The crowd was going crazy. I exited the taxi and paid the driver. I approached the café while overhearing the MC saying, "Our next performer is going to kick things off a little early this afternoon." The MC introduced the performer. "Ladies and gentlemen, let's welcome Samuel Walker to the stage."

I love his full name, it's so cute. Although he prefers to be called Sammie over Samuel.

Looking at the long line, filled with excitement I screamed, "I knew it was my love!" I glanced at several people staring at me. Waving my hands, I said, "I'm sorry guys, I'm just excited to see Sammie, I'm a huge fan."

"Yeah, we can tell," Someone yelled. Several people laughed.

I paid them no mind.

I heard the singer's voice and smiled. I knew it was him. Without thinking, I sprinted toward the entrance door, attempting to skip everyone in line. I pushed my way past the guard and screamed, "Sammie—Sammie, Sammie, I'm here!" The guard glanced at Sammie singing on the stage. The guard yielded after he realized Sammie recognized me. Sammie's jaw dropped.

I noticed Isaac, the guard from earlier patrolling the stage where Sammie was performing. The new bouncer grabbed me and said, "Lady, have you lost your mind?"

I erupted. "Yes!" Sammie ceased singing, startled. He was wearing a navy-blue suit. The top button of his white-collar dress shirt exposed a patch of sweat atop his chest. He was still staring at me by the entrance door. Our eyes were locked in on one another like a magnet to electricity. I heard the sweet sounds of Sammie's voice echoing through the microphone, "Sophia, is that really you?" A medium-sized crowd was frozen in silence. Sammie looked out into the audience before reattaching the microphone to the mic-handle. Sammie rubbed his forehead and sighed, then he grinned and said, "Uh, look—I'm so sorry guys! But I have to talk to her. I'll be back on stage in just a second."

" Hey, get back on that stage," screamed someone.

As Sammie inched closer, yelling at the doorman. "Please, get your paws off of her, right now!"

Before I had a chance to fully behold the magnificence of the man I love, I observed a beautiful blonde step in front of Sammie.

Who the heck is this heifer? Why did she just grab ahold of him like he's her man or something? Sammie didn't appear to be shocked. What? Then, she just kissed him right on his lips.

I pushed the guard out of my way, sprinting away with a heart full of shame. I cried. I guess my mom was right. I'm so stupid.

I heard Sammie running behind me. "Sophia, wait! It's not what it looks like!"

"Just let me be," I screamed.

I ignored his calls while creating distance with my strides. I thought my dad was the most honest man alive. If my dad was a cheater, then why should I believe Sammie? I paused and turned around after faintly hearing the club manager screaming at Sammie. "You're embarrassing this family. If you don't get back on that stage, you'll never sing in this town again!"

Ahh. That's right, I forgot that Sammie's uncle ran the club he told me about.

I paused and thought to myself for a few seconds. I turned around to face the direction of Sammie's voice. Sammie was nowhere in sight. I placed my hands on my hips and pondered. *He's not the same boy I fell in love with back in the midnight forest.* I lifted my head and began walking toward Frank's Donut Shop.

Along my stroll, I listened to cars pass by. The compacted sounds from the vehicles fused with my rage like a crescendo. Should I really be mad with Sammie? I mean, it has been five years. I guess my mom was right. How foolish of me to think that a man would wait around for me. I'd planned to give him the note that contained the address he left with me. I was going to finally tell him that I love him too. I scoffed while walking along the darkness of the streets. I just wanted him to see that I'd held on to his note. I practically guarded it with my life. I wrote my new home address on the note that I was going to give him tonight too. Originally, I hoped that he would come search for me just like I did tonight. But obviously he's moved on.

Three minutes later, I arrived in front of Frank's Donut Shop. I pulled the door open and synced my broken heart with the sounds of the bells on the door. Yep, that's about how my heart feels—noisy and confused. I entered the shop and observed Kyle walk from the back after he heard the bells. I know my face probably depicted a depressed soul. I breathed in then exhaled.

Kyle smiled when he saw me walk in. He increased his walking pace as he approached me.

My eyes were watery.

Kyle placed his hands on my shoulders. "I can tell that you're bothered by something." He stared into my eyes and his eyebrows elevated into the sky. "What happened? Did you find Sammie?"

I turned my back to him; he walked in front of me, placing his hands on my shoulders again. I quickly grabbed his hands, removing them from my shoulders. I grunted as I tossed my hands into the air while saying, "I found him alright—I found his cheating behind kissing another woman. I should've known Sammie was using me. How stupid of me, to think that a White boy could actually love a Black girl."

Kyle looked perplexed. He scoffed and said, "Wait—wait, wait, what!" He frowned.

I held my right hand up. Kyle and I were face-to-face. "Kyle, please save your pro Black demeanor."

He scoffed again. "Nah, it's not even like that. So, you're telling me that Summie is White?"

I sighed. "It's Sammie, not Summie! And yes, Kyle, he's White." I took a deep breath. "The love of my life is White." I thought it was foolish of me to date outside of my race after I saw Sammie kiss another woman.

"Uh—" Before Kyle had a chance to voice his thoughts, he yielded to me falling into his arms. He held me as I cried like a baby.

I made a fist, repeatedly tapping his chest with my right hand. I looked up at Kyle as he held me. "I really don't know why I'm being this open with a complete stranger."

He rubbed my back and held me tight. "It's okay." He reached behind himself and grabbed a napkin to help dry my tears. "I can take you back to my place since you don't have a place to stay tonight." He yielded to my unfavorable stare. "I know how that may have sounded, but I promise you—I won't try anything. I just want to make sure you're safe, and that's it. You can stay a couple of nights with me, and then I'll drop you off at the bus station on Sunday."

Huh, where did he get Sunday from?

"I never mentioned that I was staying a couple of nights."

Kyle seemed so anxious. He must've really liked me.

"Oh, my bad," said Kyle.

I attempted to walk away but Kyle cut me off at the entrance. "Sophia, I'm so sorry how that came out. Look, I just want to help you make it through the night, okay."

I stared at him for a few seconds as my emotions ran wild. "Ugh!" I was too broken to think clearly, so I didn't resist his charm.

We exited the shop and walked around toward the back of the store. Kyle held open the passenger door of his car. I lowered my head and paused before entering his car. I turned my head to the left while pointing my fingers in a flirtatious way as I said, "Now, don't you try anything."

Kyle smiled and closed the door after I was inside. He walked to the driver's side and entered the car. We departed into the streets of Marin County, arriving at Kyle's house about thirty minutes later.

Chapter 6:
Life's Changing Seasons:
When Love Surfaces

July 15th
1968

I observed Kyle wrestling to open the door of his modest home. Looking around, I noticed the pristine nature of his front porch, then I was taken aback by a bag full of empty beer cans in a clear plastic trash bag underneath one of his chairs. He was obviously a drinker. I was used to that because my dad drank a lot, so that didn't bother me. I loved his white wooden posts. Wooden houses are so beautiful to me. Kyle was taking a mighty long time to open the door, though.

Kyle opened the door and walked inside. He left the door wide open and observed me in a frozen disposition. He pointed toward his couch to his left, signaling for me with his hands to come inside. He softened the tone of his baritone voice. "Come on. I told you, I don't bite." He pointed toward his couch again. "Sophia, you can sleep right here on the couch if you want. Or you can sleep in my bed, and I'll sleep on the couch."

I chuckled as I stepped inside his house. "Kyle, I don't want you to give up your bed for a complete stranger."

"You know, normally I would agree with you, but I know you feel the electricity between us firing off within your heart," said Kyle.

I halfway smiled, lifting my right cheek while showing some of my teeth. I felt like Sammie wouldn't have liked me being here with Kyle, and I longed for an opportunity to tell him—I couldn't wait to tell him, too. All I could think about was Sammie having fun with Molly. Sammie was letting a complete stranger outwit him.

After I walked inside, Kyle slyly walked toward me.

I quickly tried to smell my breath by placing my hands over my mouth. I thought he was going for a kiss. At the time, I thought about kissing him just to get back at Sammie.

I closed my eyes and puckered up to embrace his lips, but when I opened my eyes, I was shocked that he wasn't standing in front of me. I was so embarrassed. Kyle held a vase in his hands. He was simply trying to catch the vase that I bumped while preparing for what I know now was an empty kiss of shame.

Kyle balanced the vase on the coffee table. "I'm sorry Sophia if my abruptness startled you. Are you okay? You look confused." He looked at the vase while repositioning it.

With my hands behind my back, I twirled my fingers while fidgeting. I was so embarrassed. I held up my left hand and said, "Nah, I'm A-Okay."

"Great!" Kyle pointed at the vase again. "This vase is very precious to me, so I had to save it—it's the only memory I have of my mother before she died. All of our pictures were burned when the KKK set our house on fire five-years ago." He slowly bridged the gap between him and I. He walked up to me as I stood about five feet away from the front door.

I guess he didn't notice my blunder. Kyle was so beautiful. I felt like Sammie would've been jealous, or would he?

Kyle interrupted my thoughts by grabbing my hands. "Would you like to proceed with that kiss I noticed you were eagerly anticipating?" Sweat from his hands moisturized mine.

He noticed I was puckering up. Guys don't like easy girls, so I should redeem myself and politely pretend like I don't want to kiss him. I remained silent, looking at the floor to convey shyness.

"Sophia, you don't have to be so demure, I know you're feeling something toward me in this moment." He placed his finger underneath my chin and gently lifted it.

I blushed. I let go of his hands and quickly walked near the coffee table in front of me to my left. As I moved away with my back facing Kyle, I said, "Boy please, I don't even know you. I'm just looking for a place to lay my head tonight."

Kyle took a few steps in my direction. He walked in front of me on the other side of the table. We were face-to-face. The table served as our separator. "No, you're looking for a place to lay your broken heart," Kyle said. I smiled. "I can repair your broken heart with my favorite dessert."

I rubbed my lips and laughed like a kid that heard his favorite joke. "Dessert!"

"Yes beautiful, I bake a mean sweet potato pie."

How does this man know that sweet potato pie is my favorite dessert?

I walked around the table to my left and asked with my hands whether or not it was okay to sit on the couch.

"Yes, make yourself at home, Sophia."

I sat back, crossing my legs. Kyle turned to face me as he continued to stand. "What happened to your mom if you don't mine me asking? How did she pass away?" I asked.

He finally sat down next to me; he was positioned to my left. He sighed. While looking straight ahead at the television positioned in front of him, he said, "Normally, I don't like talking about what happened to my mom, but since I like you, I'll tell you."

I placed my left hand on his lap, and he cut his eyes at me while blushing. I quickly removed my hand.

Our interactions seemed so natural.

"Kyle, I don't want you to talk about your mom if it's going to force you to dig up old painful memories."

He tilted his head to the right. "I really appreciate you considering my feelings, Sophia. Right now, though, I'm going to head in the kitchen and get started on your pie." He playfully squeezed my left thigh.

I politely removed his hand. He shrugged his shoulders and smiled as I asked, "Can I help?"

Kyle placed his left hand on my thigh again. This time he brushed his hand gently over my kneecap. He winked at me and said, "Of course."

A few minutes later, we were laughing and talking in the kitchen. We were sitting at the breakfast table, and Kyle offered me a glass of red wine. I'd never had any alcohol, so I didn't know what to say. I decided to decline his kind gesture. I didn't want anything to happen that night that I would regret. I was saving myself for marriage. I wanted Jehovah God to be proud of me. A part of me felt like Kyle was trying to seduce me, though. But I wasn't offended. He was such a cutie.

Kyle smiled.

He continued to wave a glass of wine in front of me. I held my hand up to decline his offer again. This encounter forced me to think about Sammie. Sammie never made me feel uncomfortable or like I was a piece a meat. I had told Kyle no already, but he was being so darn insistent. Sammie shared my views and we both were saving ourselves for marriage. Most importantly, we were saving ourselves for one another. Well, at least I thought we were saving ourselves for one another; it was obvious that he had moved on.

Kyle placed his glass of wine down and started on the pie. I glanced at him. My mom was right. When I get back home, I'm going to tell her everything. "I'm going to get her out of that hospital and bring her home with me or she can go to Los Angeles with my aunt." I hope that she's able to get along with Grandma. I shook my head. I was talking out loud to myself.

Kyle turned around to face me with a sweet potato in his hand. "Your mom is in the hospital?"

I rubbed my forehead out of frustration for speaking out loud. "Yes, but she's going to be okay. Thanks for asking." Kyle wasn't aware that the question he just asked me, redeemed him from being judged as a man that uses women. My dad always told me to be on the lookout whenever a man offers you a drink. I see why my dad had so much advice because he understood the games that men play. I crossed my arms and observed Kyle cut several sweet potatoes. I began humming a song. I couldn't believe that my dad cheated on my mom, and then had the audacity to exploit her because he knew she couldn't read.

Kyle put the pie in the oven. "Sophia, is your mom from the Los Angeles area? I heard you mention something like that, and you were humming "Sing Me Back Home" by Merie Haggard. You know that song is about living in Los Angeles, right?"

I grimaced. Shoot.

Kyle set the oven temperature to three-hundred-and-twenty-five-degrees. "Your humming sounded pretty good. Can you sing, Sophia?"

I waved my hands in front of me like he just asked a loathsome question. "No—no! I can't sing at all." I only wanted to share my singing with Sammie. I started to cry as Sammie sprinted through my mind.

Kyle heard me sob and rushed to check on me. "Sophia, what's wrong?" He pulled a chair out from the breakfast table, scooting his chair closer to me.

I scooted away. "Stay back! I don't want to discuss what's bothering me."

He held his hands up and moved his chair about a foot away from me. "Okay! My intuition tells me that what's bothering you involves Sammie?"

Handsome and smart I see. "Correct!"

Kyle sighed as silence inundated the room over the next minute, before I mentioned that Sammie's father was a member of the Klan.

Kyle looked perplexed. "What? Really?"

I exhaled. "I don't want to talk about it."

I should've focused on the negative things about Sammie to help me get over him.

"I'm thinking about Sammie, Kyle. You know, maybe this is a bad idea. I shouldn't be here. I'm leaving." I stood up.

Kyle immediately administered an appropriate amount of space between us. "Nah, that's nonsense. Hold on for a second." He took the pie out of the oven. "The pie is almost ready. And where are you going to go at this time of night anyway?"

I pointed my fingers at him. "I see what you're doing. First, you offer me my favorite pie, and then you offer me some wine. Look here, nothing is going on tonight or tomorrow in this house if I were to stick around. I know guys like you all too well. You're just like my cheating father."

He contorted his face to express a slight degree of irritation. "I understand that you're hurt and all, but you're not going to stereotype me." He frowned. "How dare you anyway? You're in love with a White guy whose dad was a prominent leader of the KKK! And now you're attempting to judge me for expressing my sincere interest in you?" He scoffed while tapping on his chest. "I'm the one that should be questioning your motives. I am just trying to have a nice night and get to know a beautiful woman."

I crossed my arms. "Oh yeah? If that's the case, then why didn't you just take me to the nearest hotel by your house as opposed to bringing me back to your place?"

He leaned against the kitchen sink, then glanced at me to his left and said, "Hey, I didn't make you come here with me. I even told you that the hotels were booked."

"How do I know if that's true?"

Kyle tossed his hands into the air before pulling a knife from the kitchen drawer. He placed the knife on the counter and elevated his voice. "Go find out for yourself!"

I started to rub my forearms with an apprehensive countenance. What is he going to do with that knife, I thought to myself while slamming my fist on the breakfast table. "I know your kind! None of what you're saying is true. I remember your exact words, 'You won't be able to find a hotel for miles'. But I noticed one on the way that looked vacant. Liar!"

Kyle's hands were resting atop the edge of the sink. The tip of his palms were firmly pressed against the sink. "If that's the case, then why didn't you just ask me to stop and take you there?" He scoffed. "That's because you wanted to come with me back to my place." He picked up the knife and cut the pie into triangles.

"Boy please, don't flatter yourself."

"Don't flatter myself, huh?" Abruptly, Kyle charged at me, and I stepped back quickly, creating distance between us. I thought about Timothy. Is this the type of fear that Timmy felt during his last moments alive? Kyle appeared to have violence filled within his eyes.

What is he going to do with that knife in his hand? Scenes of Timmy's mutilated body flashed before my mind. I visualized the holes that Timmy had in his face. "Please, don't stab me in my face!" I placed my hands over my face, shielding it while turning my head to the left.

***

When Love Finds You:
Don't Run Away

I rushed toward the front door to escape but Kyle cut me off. I attempted to run upstairs, and he chased me.

Kyle was panting. "Sophia, stop running, I'm not going to harm you!"

While running up the stairs I screamed, "Please, don't kill me! I just want to go home!" I managed to make it to one of his bedrooms. Before I could shut the door, Kyle pushed the door in with his massive strength. He entered the room and observed my trepidation. He looked down at the knife as pie crust fell from the edge of the blade.

I dropped to my knees and visualized my blood dripping from the knife. I drove my face into my hands as tears fell from my eyes. Looking up at Kyle I said, "Just get it over with already—go ahead and kill me."

He released the knife and sounds of a blade dropping to the floor compelled me to open my eyes. "Kill you? I don't want to kill you, Sophia. I just want you to relax and calm down."

I stood up and pointed at the knife on the floor. "Why were you holding that knife in your hand then?" I asked.

"Sophia, you actually thought that I was going to stab you?"

"Yeah, duh! You were the one holding the blade."

"I was cutting the pie and I got upset with you. So, I approached you to look you in the eyes to let you know that I have your best intentions at heart." He bent down and slid his hands across the blade, scraping up a sample of the pie. He approached me and gently grabbed me with his massive hands.

The way that Kyle pulled me into his arms was the way that any man should grab and hold on to a lady.

He extended his hands as a sample of pie rested atop his right index finger. "Here taste this."

"Boy, I don't know where your hands have been. I'm not licking that off your fingers. You must be retarded!"

"Very well then." Kyle licked the pie from his own hands while attempting to exit the room. He paused at the entrance of the room. "Sophia, just come downstairs and taste the pie. I apologize for scaring you. I must admit, I should be a little more sensitive and understanding."

I hesitated. "Okay, but if you look at me funny or try anything, I'm going to karate chop your behind like Bruce Lee."

He turned around and smiled. "Oh really, please do." He licked his fingers again. "I think I might enjoy that." He gestured for me to follow him downstairs. I followed a few seconds later.

Kyle was already in the kitchen when I walked in.

"Sophia, here is a piece of my famous sweet potato pie." He handed me a slice of pie atop a white plate while pointing at the kitchen table. "Let's sit at the table and talk." I smiled and took a seat. "As I tried to mention earlier, I normally don't talk about my mom, but you make me want to open up to you. You remind me of my mom, that's why I'm so drawn to you." He dropped his head out of despair. "I really miss her."

"Kyle, I understand. I lost my dad a few years ago during the Vietnam War. I think about him all the time."

"Sophia, may I ask you something?"

I nodded my head. "Yeah, go right ahead."

He lifted his head. "What happened to your father?"

"Uh, he served in the military. He was killed by a landmine." I squinted my eyes while shaking my head. "Ironic, I know. But yeah, he accidentally stepped on a landmine."

"I am sorry to hear that. Your dad was a true hero to serve our country. Personally, I would have never fought for this racist country."

"I guess you have a point," I said.

If only Kyle had known that the hero, he was referring to was a deceitful cheater, then he wouldn't have called my dad a hero. I unknowingly spoke out loud. "What am I saying?" I glanced at Kyle's disturbed look, realizing that I spoke out loud again. "Excuse me, I'm sorry. I promise you I'm not crazy. I'm just deep into my thoughts." I finished my inner dialogue as Kyle stared at me with admiration. My dad wasn't a man who lacked character, he was just a man who couldn't control himself.

I looked up at Kyle. "You know, you're right. My dad was a true hero." I sighed while rubbing my hands against my thighs. "I can't help but recall the night my dad came to my brother's aid to save him from the KKK. My dad was definitely fearless and brave."

"That's awesome," Kyle said.

I sat up erected in a chair. "My father had his flaws, though. A lot of men during the sixties had trouble staying faithful to their wives."

"I don't need to know his personal flaws unless you just want to mention them. I mean, he is a dead hero," said Kyle.

"I don't believe that the dead can harm you or that we dishonor someone that's dead by simply speaking the truth." I leaned forward. "He was a cheater, and regardless of what other men were doing my dad knew better." Timmy would have been so disappointed if he knew our father's sins. "I've spilled the beans about my dad. So now, are you going to tell me what happened to your mom?"

Kyle drunk a glass of wine—very fast, then he stood up and cut two slices of pie. Afterward, he walked toward the breakfast table and sat down.

Why is he staring at me so strangely? He had lust in his eyes. "Kyle, I feel it's necessary to remind you that just a few minutes ago you were chasing me upstairs with a knife. So please, stop giving me a serial killer's stare."

"Ha-ha. I was thinking about my mom. Sometimes, I get lost in my thoughts whenever I think about my hero. My mom was such a great woman." He massaged his lips. "I can't believe I'm getting ready to tell you what happened to my mom."

***

Scintilla of Chemistry:
The Art of Falling in Love

I observed Kyle preparing himself to share his story.

All I knew so far was that the KKK burned his house down. I couldn't help but notice Kyle was shaking. He was nervous.

"Kyle, am I making you nervous or is it the thought of talking about your mom?" Kyle remained silent.

"Kyle?" I asked. He still didn't respond.

I didn't know what his problem was. What I did know was that my heart was throbbing. I placed my hand over my heart, observing a beautiful specimen of a man displaying his softer side. It was amazing. During that moment, Kyle reminded me of Sammie. Kyle didn't know when he heard me humming while he prepared the pie, I was on the verge of singing. Only Sammie made me feel comfortable enough to expose my gift. I observed Kyle's silence along with a countenance that depicted deep thought. A thought flashed through my mind. How am I going to audition for the singing gig? I don't have the confidence to do it without Sammie. I glanced at Kyle's handsomeness. I don't know if Kyle or anyone else will ever make me feel the way Sammie does.

Kyle scoffed and lowered his hands from under his chin as I said, "Okay—"

I cleared my throat, lifting my hands as Kyle glanced my way. "I hate to stop you before you get started, but I have a stupid question to ask you." I needed to know his interests in music. I just had to know— it couldn't wait.

"What's your question?" Kyle asked.

Good, he's talking again, I thought. "What's your thoughts on music? Can you sing?"

He laughed uncontrollably. "Sophia, you're quite the lady, aren't you? What does singing have to do with me and my mom?" I shrugged my shoulders in a flirtatious way. "Ha-ha, but uh, no I can't sing. However, I do appreciate the art of music," Kyle said.

I exhaled. Oh no, this man can't sing, I pondered. But I felt my heart compelling me to let my guard down for a stranger. My gift of music was the only thing I had that gave me hope. Maybe I should sing for Kyle and see how it makes me feel, I thought.

"Don't sigh. I wish I could sing but I can't. However, I can do other things extremely well." He gently slid his right finger across my lips and smiled. "Sophia, I have to ask why do you want to know if I can sing? Are you sizing me up and comparing me to Summie?" Kyle asked.

I tilted my head out of frustration. "Summie! Really? Again, his name is Sammie, and you know that, Kyle!"

Kyle chuckled. "Oh yeah, I'm sorry."

I ran my fingers through my hair. "Yeah—yeah," I said. Kyle stared at me with a gigantic smile. Kyle was right about one thing; I was sizing him up to see if he had the potential to make me feel like Sammie did during our special night together in the midnight forest. I was trying my best to find the strength to sing for Kyle. I wanted to tell him about my gift, but I couldn't for some unexplained reason.

"Sophia," said Kyle. I acknowledged his call with a smile.

That moment validated why Sammie was so special to me. I planned to provide Sammie four months to find me; if he didn't come looking for me then I was moving on with my life.

"Sophia, are you okay?" Kyle asked.

"Yes." My thoughts of missing and leaving Sammie were interrupted as I felt around in my pockets for the piece of paper that contained my address. Where is it? Did I give Sammie my address? That's right, I dropped it when I got out of the taxi. I'll just go back tomorrow morning to The Blues Café and leave my address with one of the clerks to give to Sammie, I thought to myself. I glanced at my watch—it was 10:30p.m. "Uh, Kyle, I have a huge favor to ask you."

"You know, I'm starting to think that you don't want to hear about my mom, because every time I get ready to tell you what happened you interrupt me," Kyle said.

I rubbed my hands together. "I apologize. But I think I dropped something that's very important near The Blues Café."

Kyle stood up. "What did you drop?"

"I don't know." I can't tell you that, just in case things don't work out with Sammie. I must be honest with myself, I hope I run into Sammie so that I can make him jealous when he sees Kyle. I'll give Sammie a taste of his own medicine. And why is Kyle still standing in front of me with his arms crossed?

"Come on. Just tell me what's going on," Kyle asked.

I smiled. "You really want to know what I misplaced, don't you?" *I can't believe I'm just now about to ask this.*" How old are you anyway?" I asked.

"I'm twenty-seven." Kyle grinned. "How old are you?"

"Now, you know, you should never ask a lady her age." I turned away from him while looking for the bathroom. "I need to use your bathroom before we leave. Where is it?"

"Wait, I'm still deciphering whether or not I want to take you back to the cafe." He pointed to his left and said, "It's right over there, right outside the kitchen. And I'm not taking you anywhere, since you won't tell me what you left behind. Feel free to catch a taxi."

I frowned and turned around to face him. "Thanks a lot!"

"You're welcome," said Kyle with a playful and frustrated look on his face.

I walked away and entered the bathroom.

If I don't see Sammie or find the paper I dropped, I'll just drop by later and leave my address for him. I wrote the lyrics to a special song on the piece of paper as well. I wrote the song a few years ago the day after I unpacked my things when we first moved to our new house in San Francisco.

I had to find that paper because it was the only copy of the song—the song was special too.

I plan to sing that song for my audition in December. Sammie is going to love my song, and I know he is going to love that the song is about him, I thought.

I exited the bathroom and observed Kyle moving from the kitchen table to his living room couch.

I approached him while observing an appearance of someone who was in deep thought. His feet were resting on top of a table in front of his couch. "Kyle, I know it's super late, and I know you're sleepy, but can you please take me back to the café?"

Kyle looked up. "Uh, I was thinking to myself while you were in the bathroom, and I realize that I'm being a little too aggressive. I really just need to mind my own business." I nodded my head to show that I agreed with him as he removed his feet from the table. He sat up erect and said, "So yeah, sure, I don't mind."

I blushed. "Thank you. Also, since it's a thirty-minute drive, you can tell me all about your mom and more about yourself along the way too."

Kyle stood up and smiled. He gave me a handshake, saying in a joking tone, "Alrighty then, we have ourselves a deal, now, don't we?"

I nodded my head.

Kyle looked so cute to me.

***

The Revelation Ride:
Love Lost, Love Found

Kyle and I exited the house to head to The Blues Café.

Kyle began entering his car, and the right side of his body was inside the car before he halted to the sounds of my voice. "Hey, I need to use the bathroom again," I said as I stood on the passenger side with the car door open. We stared at each other for a few seconds.

He laughed. "Again?" He finished getting into his car.

"Yes, again. Don't even try to make fun of me either," I said.

He grinned. "Okay, go right ahead."

I leaned in through the passenger side of the car and he handed me his house key. "Here is the key. Don't forget to lock the door behind you," Kyle said.

I smirked. "Of course."

I walked inside, rushing into the kitchen to take down the rest of the sweet potato pie. I didn't want to look like a fatty in front of him in the kitchen, so I only nibbled on a small piece of pie. "Man-oh-man, this pie is good." I washed the pie down with a cold glass of water before saying a silent prayer to God. *God, please, let Sammie still be at the café.*

"Amen. Okay Jehovah, here goes nothing." I wiped pie crumbs from my mouth then walked outside to observe Kyle's blue 1967 mustang. For a few seconds, I was taken aback by his beautiful car, coupled with consternation, since I thought Kyle was just as beautiful as his car. A very hot guy in a hot ride was something very special to watch.

Maybe God meant for Sammie and me to break up. If we were meant to be then why is this process so hard? I glanced at Kyle. My brother used to share Proverbs 18:22 with me, "The one who finds a good wife has found something good and he receives God's favor." Yes, that's right, it's Sammie's job to come and find me.

I didn't know what to do.

Kyle backed out of the driveway, putting his car in drive while asking, "Sophia, why are you just standing on the porch staring at me? Come on, let's roll." He tapped on his watch to indicate that time is ongoing. "The clock is ticking."

I didn't realize I was in a trance. I looked at Kyle. "I'm sorry, I didn't hear you."

"Really! Um, that's interesting," said Kyle as he stopped his car in the street, waiting for me.

I walked down the steps.

Kyle honked his horn and then I strolled toward his car. "Kyle, I'm coming, don't pay my antics any mind. I was just having a weird moment." I got inside his car.

Kyle grinned while staring at me with endearment running through his eyes. He pointed toward his head. "I hope you have all of your screws intact up there because you're too beautiful to be crazy."

I shook my finger from side-to-side while playfully saying, "Stop while you are ahead." Kyle smirked.

Seconds later, we drove away into the darkness of the night.

***

The Ride to The Blues Café

"Tell me about your mom. What happened to her the night the KKK burned your house down?" I asked.

He looked sad. "Are you sure you're ready to hear my story?" Kyle asked.

"Of course."

He rubbed his chin and licked his lips. "Uh, where should I start?"

Those are some tasty looking lips, I thought to myself.

"Just start wherever if you still feel up to it. I mean—we have at least thirty minutes before we arrive at the café, right?" I asked.

"Correct," said Kyle.

Kyle stopped at a red light and turned his attention on me. "My mother was the kind of person that believed in humanity. She had a lot of idyllic views that just didn't fit into how the world we live in works. I loved how optimistic she was, but she just didn't know how to see the worst in people. My mom truly believed if we focused on being better people then we could uproot the racism." He started driving again after the light turned green.

"Kyle, you're a very intelligent man. I can tell based on how you're speaking and the views your mom had."

I had never heard Sammie speak the way Kyle spoke, but maybe that was because Kyle was much older than Sammie. I've always been attracted to intelligent men.

Kyle interrupted my inner thoughts as the breeze from the wind brushed against my face. "Sophia, I want to say something to you that's coming from my heart."

"Okay," I said.

Turning left onto a street, Kyle gripped the steering wheel tightly. "Don't worry about Sammie. If he was truly the man for you, he wouldn't have let you get away. No man in their right mind would let a beauty like yourself escape their arms. If he really loved you, the girl who you saw kissing him wouldn't have been able to get within ten feet of him." I listened attentively while crossing my legs. Kyle glanced at my legs, licking his lips. "She would have known better than to attempt to stop a man from reuniting with his queen. Trust me, Sammie has something going on with that girl. I'm a little older than the both of you, so trust me I know."

I crossed my arms and fidgeted a little. I could feel my heart falling to pieces. "You think so?" I asked.

"I know so. If you give me a chance, I'll show you how a real man searches and finds the woman that he wants."

I blushed. The way Kyle was articulating himself forced me to think of Proverbs 18:22 again. Maybe Kyle is right, I thought. If Sammie truly loved me, he would be looking for me. But I couldn't help myself—I still had to search for Sammie, to at least give us another try. I looked at Kyle and smiled. He placed his right hand on my thigh as we cruised across the interstate. Kyle was amazing but he still wasn't Sammie.

I kindly removed his hand away from my thigh. "I appreciate those kind words, Kyle. You're quite the smooth talker, aren't you?" He smirked. "Not to change the subject, but please, finish telling me about your mother," I said.

He massaged his face and stretched his neck. "Oh yeah, I just got caught up with my thoughts of you." He winked his right eye at me.

I laughed with joy. "Stop it. You're too much."

Kyle scooted over toward me, placing his right hand on my left thigh again.

I was surprised, I didn't move his hand that time. A part of me really wanted to embrace his strong hands. I was mesmerized by his manliness.

"So, where did I leave off with my mom? Oh yeah, I mentioned how my mom was like a visionary, right?"

My neck started to sweat as Kyle gently massaged my thigh with his hand. I stuttered. "Yes-- you did," I said.

"The night the KKK set our house on fire was a result of my mom walking into a White-only store. She demanded the same service as everyone else. But those racist idiots had no interest in accommodating my mom." He exited the interstate and stopped at a red light.

Kyle drove off after the light turned green. "There aren't a lot of true Christians anymore. Everyone seems to be a hypocrite nowadays. My mom felt the same way and that's what really led to her demise. My mom would get into a lot of trouble whenever she walked into an all-White venue. A part of me knew that she had pretty much signed her death certificate on the day she stood up for what she knew was right. I believe if my mom influenced my thoughts, then maybe she could've influenced a lot of people to change their ungodly ways too."

I looked straight ahead then twisted my neck slightly to my left, locking my eyes onto Kyle's sadness. "Whoa! For real?" I asked.

Kyle's hands started to shake as he repeatedly placed his right hand on his lap, and then back onto the steering wheel. Poor thing, I could tell that he was trying his best to hold back his tears.

"Yes, for real." He quickly brushed his right hand across his eyes, wiping his tears.

I placed my hand on his lap to console him. "Aww—Kyle, don't cry." He pulled over on the side of the road.

Silence filled the car for a few seconds before he started to sob. I caressed his back while saying, "It's okay."

He was forthcoming with his emotions. I really liked that he was open. However, it was a little weird, because I was still like a stranger to him.

Three minutes later, he put the car back into gear and resumed driving. "Thanks for consoling me. I just really miss my mom." I leaned in and wiped his tears with my hands.

Maybe it was just me, but I felt like we should've kissed, because he was definitely eyeballing me like he wanted to.

We briefly stared at each other, with the temptation to kiss him intensely tugging at my heart. Suddenly, Kyle regained his composure and said, "We only have about fifteen more minutes before we arrive, in case you were wondering."

"Okay." I cleared my throat and wiped the sweat from around my neck. "Kyle, I'm not worried about what time we arrive, I'm just trying to hear your story and be here for you."

"Sophia, I'm sorry you had to witness me crying like that, but I feel so comfortable with you." He gulped while glancing back and forth between me and the road. "I'm enamored by your presence." He removed his right hand from the steering wheel and looked straight ahead. "My heart just knows there's something special about you." He lowered his right hand onto my left thigh, gently tapping it.

I looked down at his hand and smiled. "You're such a romantic, Kyle." It was getting a little steamy. "Uh, continue telling me about your mom?"

He removed his hand. "Well, one night, about a week after my mom started receiving death threats, we woke up to a cross burning in our front yard. She told me to go hide in the closet after she realized what was going on. She rushed to the front door but was met by three men who told her to go and get me. They called me a black gorilla. After my mom called for me to come out of the closet, I ran and stood next to her. They told my mom it was either her or me. They opened the door, and my mom said, 'Kyle, run, go get help, baby.'" He gripped the steering wheel with force, dropping his head to express his pain. He hesitated. "When I returned, my house was in flames—I just knew my mom was still inside." I placed my hands over my mouth as Kyle pressed down on the gas pedal. He increased his speed to sixty miles an hour.

I placed my hands on the dashboard, then checked to ensure that my seatbelt was fastened. "Slow down a little, please," I requested.

He sighed. "I'm sorry, Sophia."

"It's okay. I'm so sorry Kyle."

Kyle's tears dropped onto his shirt as he slammed the steering wheel with his fists. He looked up at the ceiling like a lost soul. I started rubbing his shoulders as I said, "I could even smell her flesh burning. I got a whiff of the scent of her perfume when I approached the front door." He lowered his head again. "Then, I ran into the street because I knew an explosion was sure to follow, and I was right." He vehemently sighed and gasped for air after more tears flowed down his face like a waterfall.

I continued to console Kyle. Seeing tears flow down his face as he expressed himself was turning out to be a defining moment. He reminded me so much of my dad. My father was a big marshmallow, too. He only outwardly appeared to be a tough guy. During that moment, Kyle reminded me of my dad—a lot. Sammie reminded me of true love, but people say, 'a girl ends up marrying a man like her father.'

"Wow Kyle, those are some vivid memories."

He lifted his right hand. "Yeah, I can't talk about it anymore, it's too much for my heart to bear. I hope you understand."

"I do," I said.

"I would love to share the rest of what happened on the day she was murdered, but right now I just don't think I can. Why are you going back to The Blues Café, again?"

" Remember, I mentioned that I dropped something very important."

"Oh yeah. What is this important thing you're referring to, though?"

He was so nosy. "Oh, it's nothing." He asked a lot of questions. "How much longer before we arrive?" I asked.

Kyle stretched his neck. "Maybe another five minutes."

I started to daydream. *"Sammie, I came out here to find you, and I've found you."* *We hold hands and kiss. I've cried many nights waiting for this special day. Sammie begins to cry.* *"By the way, your voice sounded so beautiful to me. I see you are a professional singer now too."* *We lock lips and kiss behind the café. As our lips separate, I say,* *"Sammie, I really missed you."* *I hand him the note that I dropped. "I would love for you to come visit me at this address." Sammie smiles. "I'm only an hour or so away from here."*

Sammie leans in, grabs my hands, and gently kisses them. My heart explodes as he says, "Sophia, I'm so happy you found me. I've been dreaming about this day too. I didn't think that you would come and find me though. I've agonized over what I would say if I ever saw you again. And now I know there aren't any words that a man could even begin to express that can adequately convey the way I feel for you." I blush. "Sophia, you are my sun and not having you was like a dark storm with loud thunder all the time. Every time the thunder sounded-off its roar, that was my heart crying out for you." I smile and tear up while staring into his blue eyes. "Don't even get me started with the rain." Sammie pulls me in closer and wraps his arms around my waist. "The rain represents all of the tears I've cried for you." He looks up into the midnight sky. "Sophia, my love for you reaches the ends of the earth and back. If this moment is true, then there is a true God who believes in the coming together of two."

Suddenly, my fantasy was interrupted by Kyle clearing his throat and saying, "We're here!"

Startled, I twitched my eyes. "Okay."

I hoped for my fantasy to come true.

We approached The Blues Café; it was apparent that the café was closed. No lights were on, in or around the building. The raucous crowd that was there earlier was gone. I opened the passenger door before Kyle stopped his car.

"Dang, girl, you must really want whatever you dropped. You're obviously trying to kill yourself in the process. Close the door, we're almost there," said Kyle.

We pulled up near the entrance, and I asked Kyle to stay in the car while I searched outside the café for the paper I dropped. He refused. "Nah, I'll help you look. Besides, two eyes are better than one," Kyle said.

I really didn't want him to know that I was looking for something pertaining to Sammie. "Just stay in the car, please," I said.

"Okay, no need to be so aggressive." He opened his glove compartment and handed me a flashlight. "Here use this since it's dark outside," said Kyle.

"Thank you," I said.

I stepped out of the car and walked toward the area where I thought I dropped the paper. Kyle parallel parked next to the café. I walked about two yards to my left, away from the café. I kneeled and looked over my right shoulder. I could see Kyle from that angle. I looked back at him, flashing the light in the car. He winked his right eye at me. I stood up and looked through the drainage well on the curb to ensure that my note didn't fall under the earth. Whew! I don't think it fell here. There was a chance that it could've still been on the ground. A minute later, I stood fully erect, then I looked around some more near the café's vicinity. I was standing at the entrance door of the café. I hope the wind didn't blow it away.

My thoughts were interrupted by Kyle saying, "Looks like you need some help."

He was so persistent.

I turned around to face him. "Okay, come on and help out. I guess you're right."

He exited the car, then we both searched for the missing paper that I desperately wanted to find.

Kyle walked to my left with me, a few feet away from The Blues Café. I zoomed in on the ground with laser beam eyes. A middle-aged White drunkard yelled as we passed. "That's a fine piece of negro tail you got there, my man!"

Kyle frowned and said, "Say punk, show this fine Black lady a little respect before I—" I politely pushed Kyle away from the guy.

"Kyle, please, I don't like violence," I said.

Kyle scoffed then executed a three-hundred-and-sixty-degree spin. While facing the street he started punching the darkness of the air like he was shadow boxing. He stopped abruptly, then faced me. The White guy quickly walked away. Kyle walked up to me and watched the guy walking in the opposite direction of the café. He grunted as he observed the guy intently.

"Look, I'm just trying to protect you," Kyle said.

I walked directly in front of Kyle to face him. He was really upset. The light from the flashlight created a spotlight for us as it beamed off the ground. "Kyle, I've seen what some White folks are capable of, so please just don't engage." He stepped forward like he still wanted to pursue the guy. I quickly grabbed his arms and pulled him in the opposite direction of the drunkard.

He sighed. "Okay, okay! I'll let that idiot slide this time, just for you."

"Thank you, Kyle."

He exhaled and attempted to distract himself. "Uh, so, Sophia, what are we looking for again?"

I remained silent while walking in the late-night breeze. The wind covered every inch of my skin. I glanced at Kyle as he strolled along, positioned to my left side.

"Are you ignoring me?" Kyle asked.

"No! And it's nothing—it's just an important song I wrote."

I looked along the walkway near the café. Kyle was walking behind me. "You can sing, I knew it," said Kyle.

I stopped and faced Kyle, then I playfully pushed him in his right shoulder. "No, I can't sing. I just write from time to time, okay?"

"Yeah sure," said Kyle.

"I'm telling you I can't sing. But anyway, I was saving the song for a great singer to sing. However, I do want to be a famous songwriter." I leaned against the café's wall near the front of the building. Kyle took the flashlight out of my hands and shined it against the wall. The light exposed my face. "You have the most amazing eyes, Sophia," Kyle said.

I blushed.

"And a famous songwriter, huh?" Kyle asked.

I crossed my arms and legs while continuing to lean against the wall. Kyle was standing about two feet away from me, he was slightly diagonal to my left. "Yeah, I plan to major in some type of literary arts when I enter college next semester too," I said.

He positioned himself directly in front of me. "Wow, that's great Sophia."

"I still don't know what school I want to attend, though." I held up my finger. "That's going to be my first order of business when I return to San Francisco."

Kyle poked his lips out and nodded his head to acknowledge my ambitious goals. We resumed walking around, and I continued to stare at the payment as we walked.

Where is the note?

"Uh Kyle, I really look forward to starting college too."

He nodded his head. "That's good. I'm almost done with law school."

"That's cool, I thought you worked at Frank's Donuts for a living?" I asked.

"Obviously I work there, so duh. However, I attend the University of Marin County. I only have one year remaining, then I am going to take the bar exam," Kyle said.

I lifted my eyebrows and we faced each other. "What type of law do you plan on practicing?"

"Criminal law coupled with Civil Rights," said Kyle.

"Why Law instead of being a doctor or something?" I asked.

"I want to be a Civil Rights Activist to help my people receive justice. You know, Black people are grossly mistreated in this country. I want to help do something about it."

My face lit up. I loved it. "Sammie!" Shoot—shoot. "I mean Kyle—that's impressive." I quickly walked in front of Kyle.

Kyle ran in front of me and shook his head before grabbing my hand, signaling for me to stop. "Hold up." We stop walking. "Sophia, that note you're looking for, is it connected to Sammie?" Kyle asked.

"No." Not that it's any of your business. Kyle looked perturbed.

It was obvious I wouldn't find the note, so I figured it was best to be more relaxed with Kyle. I thought my Sammie was gone forever. On the bright side though, it looked like I had an educated and very attractive man who stood before my eyes. I grabbed his hands. "Kyle, let's go." He turned the flashlight off. I quickly canvased the area once more. "Ugh!" I couldn't find what I was looking for.

We walked back to the car and Kyle leaned against his truck. I paused in front of him. He sighed. "Sophia, you're obviously withholding something from me. Look, if we're going to be close friends, this isn't how you want to start our friendship."

I rubbed my face and positioned myself next to him, to his left. He turned his head to his left then I turned mine to the right. "I never said I wanted to be close friends with you. For an older man, you surely live in a fantasy world. And we can go now, because I'm done looking."

We both laughed. "Fantasy world, huh?" Kyle asked.

I playfully tapped him on his arm. "Yes, you live in a fantasy world, so just relax a little. Besides, I barely know you, remember? You don't want to scare a girl off by coming on too strong."

He laughed and tossed his hands into the air. "I am living in a fantasy world simply because I'm being up-front with my feelings?" He contorted his body, placing his right hand on his hip. "I am sorry sweetheart, but there's nothing I can do about your inability to recognize a real man." He stood erect and scooted over to his left, bumping me with his hip. Kyle tapped his chest then pointed to his head to draw attention to his brain. "I think you may need to check your thinking on this matter."

I chuckled.

He tapped his chest again. "If you were a man, you would go after you too." He waved his finger side-to-side, positioning himself directly in front of me as I continued to lean on the car. "I can see it all in your eyes—that note you're looking for has something to do with Sammie, doesn't it?" Kyle asked.

"You're being a little too nosy right now, aren't you?"

" One day you're going to learn how to accept the uncertainties in life. I know you think your romance journey should unfold a certain way, and maybe it will. Meanwhile, there's nothing wrong with keeping an open mind to other romantic adventures in your life." He shrugged his shoulders. "And maybe you're right, maybe I am being a little too pushy." He grabbed my hand and I yielded to his handsomeness. He licked his lips. "It's like this, Sophia: I am from the old school, and we believe in going after what we want."

That was smooth.

"I know how you old men are, but you can't always rush the things you want. Patience is a virtue, right?" I asked.

He smiled. "Right!"

I gently pulled my hand away. "Besides, I have my whole life ahead of me to focus on love."

"True! So, are you ready to go now?" Kyle asked.

"Yes, I'm ready. I mentioned that a while ago, before you started your thirty-minute dissertation on romance. You just gave a whole sermon on how I shouldn't pass up my opportunities to find new and exciting paths for love."

He laughed. "I see someone has jokes," Kyle said.

"Ha. I'm just saying, Kyle, you were rambling on-and-on about life and romance. Even though you're a guy, you really are open with your feelings."

He stared at me. "All real men are open with their feelings."

"Well, if you're going to deliver a sermon, I'd rather you wait until Sunday. So maybe don't be so open with your feelings."

"You're talking a lot of trash, Sophia, especially since you haven't found the note you're looking for. Don't forget, I'm your only ride back to my place."

"Boy please, you wouldn't leave me out here, and I know that for sure. Besides, it's obvious you can't keep your mind silent to resist the urge to think about me," I said.

He stepped backwards, rubbing his head while smiling before saying, "I concede. You're right. I wouldn't leave you out here. Now, enough of the small talk, sweetness. If you're finished looking for your note, then let's bounce."

I laughed. "I see you're hard of hearing," I said.

"Oh yeah, you said that a while ago, right?" Kyle asked.

"Yes, silly, I surely did." I looked at Kyle and smirked.

His swag was slightly arrogant, but it was extremely cute. Kyle had no clue that he was filling my emotional vacancy. *I really wish I could have found that darn note, though.*

He walked me to the passenger side and held the door open while I got in. Then he walked on his side and started the engine.

Kyle looked at me while I put my seatbelt on and asked, "Do you want to grab some donuts from Frank's while we are in the area?"

"Aren't they closed?" I asked.

"Yeah, they close for a few hours after eight or nine most nights, then they reopen at midnight." He glanced at his watch. "They open in like five minutes."

That moment made me think of the midnight forest. Sammie was the only other man that I'd been out with until midnight. "Yeah, that's fine." That moment seemed so ironic. I came back home looking for Sammie, but I was spending my weekend with Kyle.

We drove to the donut shop.

While driving to Frank's, Kyle resumed talking about his mother. "You know, my dad really didn't love my mom," said Kyle.

I positioned my body to face Kyle with my back pressed against the passenger door, as I pushed my hair over my shoulders. "Why do you say that?" I asked.

Kyle only had his left hand on the steering wheel, his right hand was resting in his lap. "My dad was seeing another woman. I caught him cheating with different women a couple of times. My dad didn't know I used to sneak in through my bedroom window some days while my mom was out shopping. I knew my mom's schedule like a book. Sometimes I would get bored at school, so I wanted to come home and chill in my bedroom. At the time, I loved laying in my bed, staring at the ceiling to clear my thoughts." He scratched his nose. "I guess my dad thought the house was empty whenever he cheated on my mom, but he was wrong. I didn't know how to respond to the things I saw him do, so I just kept it to myself. The messed-up part, though, is that one of his women was my Aunt Sue."

My eyeballs opened wide. "Whoa," I said.

" I was shocked when I discovered that my father was sleeping with my aunt. I watched my dad engage in his deeds for six years prior to my mom's death. I'd planned to inform my mom of his infidelity, but I just couldn't find the courage to tell her. My dad was a huge man, and I was too scared to confront him or my aunt. I know all of this reflects the cowardly feelings that exist within me." He glanced at me. "I really wanted to tell my mom, but I didn't want to break up my family."

I folded my arms. "Kyle, no one has the right to judge you."

"I don't like talking about my mom anymore. I can't help but feel guilty, and partly responsible for her death. Maybe if I had the courage to tell her that her beloved husband was sleeping around, then maybe she would have moved out or something." He sighed. "She might still be alive too. I miss my mom, and it's sad that she died with deceitful memories. She never found out the truth. Before I had a chance to confront my dad, he committed suicide. He held himself to high standards. He wasn't perfect, but I think my mom's death opened his eyes to who he really was. He enjoyed his fleshly and temporary gratifications from his adulterous lifestyle, but he didn't like the demeritorious self-guilt that was finally lodged in front of his eyes after my mom passed."

"Demeritorious? I see you're showing off that law school education."

"No, that's just how I talk, Sophia."

"I love it! You have to forgive yourself and recognize that you didn't make your dad do any of those things," I said.

"You're administering some really wise counsel for a youngster," Kyle said.

I smiled. "Don't let my age fool you, I am a big thinker too. I put a lot of thought into understanding the pros and cons in life."

"That's good. But uh, that's the rest of the story about my mom. No one knows, but I used to spit on my dad's grave every week for a few months after he was buried. I blamed and I still blame him for my mom's death. I feel like he abandoned me by taking the easy way out of life when he killed himself. Although, I'm still angry with him, I wish he was still here because I need him for guidance in so many ways."

"Kyle, I've never met a man like you. It sounds like you need a friend and a shoulder to cry on. I'll be that shoulder for you." He parked the car. "Come on, let's get out and order these donuts, we can finish talking inside," I said.

"Sophia, I really appreciate you telling me I can count on you. I'm going to hold you to that, too."

I smiled and winked my right eye. "Please do."

"Sophia, are you flirting with me?" Kyle asked.

I shrugged my shoulders. "That's for you to determine."

We walked inside Frank's and ordered donuts, then we sat down at a nearby table.

"Wow, these donuts are good, right?" I asked.

"Yes, they are." He wiped his mouth and took a sip of his orange juice. "What kind of donut places do you have back in San Francisco?" Kyle asked.

"Good ones, but definitely not like the one's we're eating right now," I said.

"What a shame. I guess everything is better in Marin County," Kyle said.

"I wouldn't say that, but these donuts are amazing. So, I didn't know if I wanted to leave this morning or tomorrow, but I think I'll stay until Sunday now."

He blushed. "Maybe we can hang out tomorrow for the whole day before you leave on Sunday."

I twirled my donut in my hand. "That sounds fun. I need a day of relaxation after a weekend like the one I've had."

"I'll surprise you with some cool stuff." He bit into his glazed donut.

I smiled and took a bite of my donut. "Okay, let's see what you come up with before I depart on Sunday." I playfully tapped him on his hand as he rested his forearms on the table. "I hope you make tomorrow a memorable day—Mr. Romance." I smiled in a flirtatious way.

He sipped his orange juice then licked his lips. "Don't worry, I will."

I laughed. "I just have to ask, why in the heck do you lick your lips so much?" I asked.

"I don't know, but I know you like it." Kyle bit his lips.

"You're quite confident, I see."

Kyle shrugged his shoulders and squeezed his lips together like a crushed soda can. He placed his glass of orange juice on the table. "Let's just say, I know how to make a true queen like yourself very happy."

I took a deep breath, crossing my legs while squeezing my thighs together. "That's good to know." I stared at Kyle, twirling my feet from side-to-side under the table. I extended my donut to Kyle while gesturing him to take a bite. He quickly bit into my donut. "It's good, huh handsome?"

A few minutes later, we exited Frank's and drove back to Kyle's place to rest our sleepy eyes.

My true love appeared to be lost, but maybe a new one had been found.

Chapter 7:
Changing My Last Name

Seven Hours Later

I heard gentle knocks coming from Kyle's bedroom door as I woke up from a distressing night of misery. Kyle slept on the couch, as any gentleman would have done. I didn't sleep well because I was thinking about Sammie and Kyle all night. While lying in bed with my hands over my chest, I continued to listen to knocks on the door. The knocks increasingly got louder. I removed the comforter from over my body, exposing my smooth, brown legs. As wind blew in from a partially open window, I realized that Kyle's white T-shirt wasn't enough to keep me warm.

I replaced the comforter over my body. I can't believe I'm only in my underwear with another man's t-shirt on. Reaching over to my left, I turned a lamp on that was atop a nightstand. I heard a few more knocks before Kyle stated, "If you don't answer me, I'm coming in."

I jumped up, quickly grabbing a pair of blue jeans from my luggage bag. "Wait, I'm coming out in a few minutes. Do you have an unused toothbrush?"

Kyle spoke loudly from the other side of the door. "Yes, it's in the bathroom underneath the sink. There's toothpaste and mouthwash in there too."

In my raspy morning voice, I replied, "I'm sorry. I forgot to pack my toothpaste and a few other things for my trip."

"It's okay, I got you covered. I'll see you downstairs whenever you finish up," said Kyle.

"Okay, thanks," I replied.

While brushing my teeth I stared into the mirror, then thoughts of Sammie kissing the woman from the café flashed through my mind.

I felt like my heart was slipping into a hole. If Sammie had showed up at that moment, my next words would have been "bye-bye, Kyle!"

I sighed, washing my face with warm water before gargling mouthwash to rinse away the stench of morning breath.

I exited the bedroom and crept downstairs, dressed in blue jeans and a red t-shirt. I heard noise coming from the kitchen as the aroma of fresh food filled my nostrils. What Kyle was whipping up smelled delicious.

Kyle stepped into the hallway and observed me creeping down the stairs. Holding a white dishtowel in his hand, he laughed. "Why are you creeping down the stairs like a ninja? Did you sleep, okay?" He stood dressed in a black t-shirt accompanied with gray jogging pants. He smiled as his slippers slid against the floor, uniting with the creaks from the stairway. He started to take steps toward me.

I laughed. "I obviously failed at that since you heard me. I'm no ninja, but I slept okay. However, my head hurts a little."

Kyle extended his hand to guide me down the remaining stairs. He pushed his hands into the air to dismiss my concerns. "No worries. I have the perfect remedy for your headache. First though, I'll finish preparing breakfast. Um. How is a peanut butter and jelly sandwich with two eggs, along with cheese grits?"

My legs quivered while I grabbed my forehead. While rubbing my forehead I realized that my headache's tension was improving. I attempted to respond as my voice crackled with shock coupled with heartfelt surprise. Several thoughts flooded my mind. This is so unreal.

How did Kyle know? I smiled, shaking my head in a playful demeanor. "How did you know?"

He guided me into the kitchen while holding my hands. He paused and asked, "How did I know what?"

I looked into his eyes, contorting my cheeks while squeezing my eyes together until they were slightly ajar. I tried to ascertain if I mentioned that I love peanut butter and jelly sandwiches. I couldn't remember telling him anything. "This is my favorite breakfast. My brother used to make it for me all the time."

"Aww, Sophia, don't cry." He pulled me in close, giving me a firm hug. His affection temporarily blocked my tears.

A few seconds later, my heart was overwhelmed, compelling me to cry out. "I miss Timmy." I swiftly exited the kitchen and sat down on the living room couch.

Kyle rushed to the bathroom to garner tissue paper. After exiting the bathroom, he sat next to me. I laid down and he laid next to me. I started to rub and cover his muscular chest with my tears. He started caressing my shoulders and massaging my head while I filtered through my thoughts. How could Kyle have known that I like peanut butter and jelly sandwiches for breakfast? Sammie's favorite breakfast was biscuits, eggs, and pancakes. Maybe my love with Sammie was just 'kid's play', like my mom said back at the hospital. I knew how to find out if Kyle was the man of my dreams: if he used the same type of jelly I use for my sandwiches, then he might be worthy of me paying him another visit someday.

I love strawberry jelly, and if we have this in common then maybe some things are meant to be. Time to get up now Sophia, because cuddling can lead to other things.

I tapped Kyle on his chest. "Let me up." I got up and dried my tears. "What type of jelly do you like to use?" I asked.

He exhaled while sitting up on the couch. "I keep a stash of grape, strawberry, and raspberry jelly."

Okay, moment of truth. "But which one is your favorite?" I anxiously stood in front of Kyle with my fingers interlocked behind my back.

Kyle scooted forward on the couch until his rear end hung off. I intervened as I held my hand out, saying, "Before you stand, answer my question, please."

He smiled. "Okay, okay—since jelly is the hot topic this morning. If you must know, I actually like them all equally."

Ugh. "So that means you don't have a favorite?"

"No, I do," Kyle replied.

I tapped my right foot against the wooden floors. "Well then, spit it out. You still haven't answered my question." I approached him and sat down while pulling him back onto the couch as well. I sat to the left of Kyle.

" Dang, have some patience. I'm about to answer."

" Also, before you answer my first question, answer this for me too: If you just had to pick a jelly, which one would be your favorite?"

"Ha-ha, Sophia. You do recognize that you're literally asking me the exact same question?"

I smirked while scooting closer toward him. "I wouldn't have to repeat myself if someone, would just answer my question." I lifted my hands.

"Okay, calm down." He licked his lips. "Look, my first option would be you."

Whoa now, calm down tiger. I stood, adjusting my shirt. "Okay, Kyle, let's go eat breakfast now."

He stood to make his way toward the kitchen while saying, "You got it Ma'am. I'll play along as you continue to fight against our chemistry."

I took a deep breath. "By the way, what's your last name?" I asked.

"My last name is Coleman. What's yours?" Kyle asked.

We ceased walking before entering the kitchen near the stairway. "If you must know, my last name is Smith," I replied.

Kyle grabbed my hands. "Sophia Coleman sounds really good." He licked his lips while winking his right eye at me.

I dropped his hands and stepped back. "Wait. Kyle, you're freaking me out now," I said while lifting my hands in front of my chest.

He looked worried. "I'm just saying, the two names flow together, that's all."

I stared at Kyle, observing his perfectly square chest beneath his broad shoulders. They rested perfectly above his chiseled biceps. His fit-looking veins reminded me of my brother's athleticism. *Sophia Walker or Sophia Coleman? Hmm. Both names sound good together. I must admit that Sophia Isabella Coleman sounds better than Sophia Isabella Walker. Oh Lord, this man somehow knows how to read my heart; he just knows the right things to say.*

Kyle tapped me on the back and guided me into the kitchen. "Let's eat breakfast now. I can't wait to bite into my peanut butter and strawberry jelly sandwich," said Kyle.

Yes, Lord. I lifted my left foot, curling it toward my glutes. We have something in common. "I love the sound of that."

He pointed to my lifted leg and smirked. "So strawberry jelly must be your favorite kind of jelly?"

I blushed. "That's correct, and don't you ever forget that!" I sat down at the table while Kyle prepared breakfast.

He looked back at me. "Are you admitting that you're planning to stay in touch with me?"

While sitting at the breakfast table, I styled my hair into a ponytail, wrapping a hair tie around it. I grinned. "I didn't say all of that."

"You said, 'Don't you ever forget that.' So, you apparently plan on seeing me again," Kyle said.

I dismissed his confidence with a playful hand gesture before shrugging my shoulders.

***

My Memorable Day with Kyle Coleman

After eating breakfast Kyle suggested that we go see a movie. While at the theatre, he mentioned a picnic at the park afterwards. He stated something that activated my interest. He offered to show me around Marin County University's campus. While conveying his plans, I observed his arms, wrapped around my shoulders as the thrill from the movie increased.

I still hadn't told Kyle that I'd planned on attending Marin next semester. My arms were folded.

An hour later we exited the theatre. While walking side by side in emotional bliss, Kyle asked, "Hey, did you enjoy the movie?"

I looked in his direction. "The storyline was intriguing."

"Agreed! Are you still okay with my picnic idea? Also, we can go see Bonnie and Clyde later as well. If you want to?"

I looked confused. "You want to go see another movie? That would be twice in a day."

He grinned. "Is that a problem? I love going to the movies."

"Me too." I faced him while pointing toward my surroundings. "Kyle, what's all of this? I'm not trying to start a relationship or anything, I'm just trying to get to know you. Geez, I just met you yesterday." I sighed and walked away while saying, "Like I mentioned before, I think you're coming on kind of strong."

Kyle followed me. "Sophia, wait up!" He increased his pace until he was pedaling backwards in front of me. He lifted his hands in front of his chest. "I apologize, but I can't help myself.

I shook my head. "Why?" I asked.

He looked his lips. "I've never met a lady like you. I thought you said you were looking forward to your day with me."

While tapping my feet against the pavement, I looked in the opposite direction of Kyle's face. Kyle wasn't as wise as I thought. If he was, he would've known that sometimes women can be emotional and erratic. He should've understood that women may say one thing and then do another. I scoffed. A man who has a woman's heart is the one who has true power. I still missed Sammie.

Facing Kyle, I said, "I truly appreciate your flattery, but you're going to have to control yourself, because that's the only way you stand a chance at seeing me again." I rubbed my fingers through my hair. "I'll go ahead and do this picnic thing with you today, since I'm leaving soon. Where is the picnic going to be, anyway?"

He looked excited. "Thank you. I was thinking of going to the park that's around the corner from my house. I normally jog there every day. If you haven't noticed, I like to exercise."

He was so handsome, but arrogant with it. I sighed while shaking my head. "Yeah, yeah. I noticed, Mr. Conceited."

Kyle looked me up and down with his eyes. "Ha, I can tell that you keep yourself together as well." He twirled me around.

I liked the attention he gave me during that moment. "Yeah, I have a regimen I follow but I haven't done it today."

"Well, I don't want to help you make a habit of missing your workouts. So, let's exercise together before we have our picnic. What do you think about that?" He jogged in place while trying to make me laugh. "Come on, you know you want to."

I gave in and laughed. "Actually, that's the best idea you're mentioned today so far."

He stopped jogging in place and leaned over with his hands on his thighs, pretending like he was tired. He faked like he was panting. "Oh really?"

"Yep!" I smirked.

We walked back to the car and drove away.

***

Love in The Park

A few minutes later, we arrived at Blossom Park. We exercised and shared a picnic together. During our blissful picnic, I smiled and bit into a sandwich. While eating my sandwich, I looked up at the sun while we sat atop the greenness of the grass. The entire park looked pristine. Kyle was seated to my left with his legs extended as he leaned back, holding himself up with his hands. I glanced at Kyle as he stared into the sky. His side profile captivated my attention. I was enthralled by his attractiveness. Blushing, I thought to myself, *Love is crazy.*

Kyle and I leisurely strolled through the park as we talked.

While passing a beautiful tree along the sidewalk, Kyle asked, "Sophia, what happened to your brother? Based on the tears you shed yesterday, I just know something ominous happened to him. His name was Timmy, right?"

I stared at the pavement for a few seconds. "Right. He was murdered by the KKK."

Kyle formed a fist and frowned. "I hate those racist pricks'."

I nodded my head. "Me too."

"What happened?" Kyle asked.

I gulped. "I really don't want to go into detail about what happened, but he was shot in his face and head." I grimaced. "After those monsters' shot my brother, they tossed his body into a lake not too far from my parent's house. I really miss my brother. He was such a sweet guy. And he loved Jehovah God, too. My brother taught me the importance of developing a relationship with God, which is why my relationship with Jehovah is so important to me."

Kyle said, "I feel that!"

I stopped and sat on a nearby bench while gesturing for Kyle to take a seat, too. He obliged my overture as I faced him while he squinted his eyes; reacting to the sunlight beaming into his face. "Kyle, my love for God is why I don't want to put myself into a compromising situation with you. I don't want any kissing or anything else that could lead to something else. I am saving myself for my future husband, so please respect that, okay?"

He looked concerned but engaged, as he leaned forward to display that I had his undivided attention. "That's a very nice thing you're doing. I encourage you to keep that up." He held up his finger to crack a joke. "However, I do want to kiss those precious lips at least once." He leaned forward and tried to kiss me. I immediately placed a finger against his lips.

I released a deep exhale. "Men really have a problem with listening," I replied, standing up.

"Maybe! And just admit it, you want to kiss to me too, right?" Kyle asked.

I sighed while waving my hands from east to west. "Let's change the subject, Kyle."

He extended his legs in front of himself, before standing up. "I see you're playing hard to get."

I really wasn't. I was slightly frustrated. "Kyle, I'm leaving tomorrow, and we will never see each other again."

We both continued to stand while staring into one another's eyes. "Sophia, I'll come visit you, I promise. What's your address?"

"I'm sorry, but let's just enjoy the rest of our walk, and please let's talk about something else." I turned my back to him. Geez, I wish he would stop.

"My heart tells me that you're still worried about that Sammie guy." He gently grabbed my arm, turning me toward him. "Why don't you just give that Sammie guy up and move on, it's clear he didn't have enough sense to realize a perfect angel when he saw one. You can defy me all day, but one day you'll be mine."

Kyle was relentless.

Maybe if I give him a little feedback he'll stop. "I guess we will have to wait and see."

He blushed. "I bet that I can outrun you back to the house," Kyle said.

"No, you can't," I replied.

Kyle smiled while stretching his legs. "If you lose, I get a kiss."

I chuckled. "In your dreams."

We sprinted toward his house. I noticed as we got closer to his house that Kyle started to fall behind. As sweat poured out of my skin like a tropical storm, I pondered: *It seems like he's falling behind on purpose.* After we arrived at his house, Kyle acknowledged his defeat.

He leaned over, his hands resting atop his kneecaps, breathing like a cheetah running at maximum speed. "You are super-fast! I'm disappointed, though—I was really looking forward to kissing you."

I wasn't stupid, he lost on purpose. I liked that he did that.

I smiled. "You just refuse to give that up," I said as he smiled back at me.

A minute later, we entered his house, sweat dripping off our bodies like a waterfall. Kyle walked upstairs to take a shower while I took a shower in the bathroom downstairs. After we got dressed, we met up in the kitchen to grab a quick snack.

"I love honey buns." He wiped his mouth. "What's the verdict on Bonnie and Clyde?"

I hesitated. "We can go to the movies again, I guess."

We exited the house and Kyle asked me, "Do you want to drive?"

I thought you would've asked that a long time ago boy, I love hot rides. "I would love to drive your Mustang." Kyle opened the car door and looked back at me while winking his left eye. I entered the car then closed the door. Kyle acts just like my father, I thought to myself.

***

Love at The Movies

We drove to an outdoor theatre and Kyle parked his car. He looked to his left and noticed a car driving up next to him. "Lord, I hope that isn't John," Kyle said.

I looked to my left. "Why, who's John?" I asked.

"Just a quaint friend of mine. He's a little unraveled."

"Hmm. Well, I love watching movies outside," I said.

Kyle looked to his left again after hearing the crackling sounds of John's voice.

I leaned forward, glancing at John. "Um."

John lowered his passenger window and said, "Hey Kyle, who's that pretty young girl you have in your hot ride?"

Kyle waved at John, lowering his window too. John was a Black male; he was dark as midnight as he held a cheeseburger in his hands. John's orange short-sleeve-shirt exposed his thick biceps. He curled a burger in front of his square face for another bite, his yellow teeth ruining his handsome image. His hair added two inches to his height, and his light brown eyes shined forth from the light of the theatre's screen.

Kyle rested his hands on the lower portion of the steering wheel and scoffed. "What up, John!" Kyle pointed to me. "This is my friend, Sophia." I waved and smiled.

John wiped his mouth and spoke with a mouth filled with bread. "I've never seen her before." He smirked, biting into his burger. He chewed, his lips moving around wildly like a bear. "Uh, does Nancy know about her?" He chuckled.

I opened my eyes wide and frowned. Huh? I hit Kyle on his right arm. "Nancy! Kyle, you have a girlfriend?" I asked.

Kyle exhaled while looking at the theatre screen. Both my eyes and John's were glued onto Kyle. John had a smirk on his face as Kyle replied, "Not really."

"What do you mean—not really?" I asked.

Kyle was silent for a few seconds, then we suddenly observed John drive away in his white Mustang.

The way John was laughing, I could tell that he wasn't a true friend of Kyle's. But the way Kyle reacted was still suspicious too. I felt obligated to investigate whether or not John was telling the truth. I shouldn't have even cared, but I did.

I crossed my arms while staring at the movie screen. Men.

Kyle broke his silence while looking frustrated as he looked at me and stated, "Sophia, Nancy and I broke up a few weeks ago." He tossed his hands into the air. "We are not together anymore. I know this doesn't look good, but I just need you to trust me on this one."

"Kyle, I don't even know you that well, so why should I trust you?" I turned my head away from him and looked out the window. My hair quickly bounced from right to left as I turned around to face him again. "I'm not your woman anyway." I pointed toward the theatre screen. "Let's just watch the movie. Don't say another word to me, okay?"

He gently tapped me on the shoulder. "Sophia, please don't be like that."

I administered a serious stare, forcing him to comply with my request. While sitting in the car, it increasingly became more difficult for me to focus on Bonnie and Clyde.

My arms were still crossed as I cut my eyes at Kyle through my peripheral vision.

I couldn't help but think, just a few days ago, I found out my dad was cheating on my mom. Maybe my mom was right. You can't trust men.

Kyle attempted to say something. "Sophia, I like you."

I cleared my throat, cutting him off. "Kyle pump your brakes. Look, just pay attention to me and stop worrying about yourself. If you haven't noticed, I already had a heartbreak the other day with Sammie. So, I really don't trust you right now." I opened the car door and stepped out. My eyes were teary, but Kyle couldn't see them. I leaned over the middle of Kyle's car with my forearms resting on top of it while looking into the sky. God, can I just have a breakthrough with love, please.

I heard Kyle's door open. Here he comes. I quickly reentered the car, then he stepped back inside too. After the movie ended, Kyle attempted to talk to me again. "I'm not interested in what you have to say." I gave him the silent treatment.

We drove back to his house, then I entered the living room to go to sleep on the couch—without saying anything to Kyle.

***

Home Sweet Home

The Next Day
Morning Time

I woke up from another restless night as the sun shined through the living room window. Placing my right forearm against my forehead, I laid with my legs extended on the couch.

I refused to sleep in his bed after finding out about Nancy. I was unsure about what went on in his house. All I knew was I needed a man who respected God's laws. I didn't know if Kyle was sleeping around with Nancy out of wedlock, but the thought of it was a major turn off for me.

I sat up, stretching my arms. Sammie said he would save himself not just for marriage, but for me. I removed the morning crust from my eyes, then I stood up and walked to the bathroom. After I wash up, I'll fix a peanut butter and jelly sandwich.

After preparing a sandwich, I ran upstairs to pack my luggage, then I heard a couple of knocks on the door before Kyle entered the room.

Kyle wiped his eyes and stood in front of me with black underwear on. His shirtless body left me speechless for several seconds. Before I responded I thought to myself, *Lord, this man is too fine.* "Uh, put some clothes on. And I'm taking a taxi to the bus station," I said.

Kyle turned around and exited the room. He quickly reentered with a pair of pants on. He held his hands in the air, signaling for me to wait for him. "Sophia, don't leave just yet."

I walked away and went downstairs. "I'm not interested in being around a deceitful spirit like yours anymore."

He chased me downstairs, the creaks from the stairway echoing throughout the house. "Sophia, please, just let me take you to the bus station."

Kyle's endeavor was interrupted by a loud knock on the front door. We both paused on the last step of the stairs, embracing a rowdy voice saying, "Kyle Coleman, you open this door right now!"

I turned around and faced Kyle. He stood atop the stairway as his chiseled abs cut through my eyes. A sexy dog. That's all you are. I sighed and pointed toward the front door. "Is that Nancy, Kyle?"

He shrugged his shoulders and poked his head out like a confused toddler. "Uh—uh. Uh, yes, she lives a few houses down from me." He lifted his eyebrows. "But it's not what you think!" I rolled my eyes and walked away. He positioned himself two feet away from me. We were standing by the front door as Nancy continued to knock.

"She must've seen us together, so she's probably just jealous," said Kyle.

143

Jealous, huh? I crossed my arms, letting go of my luggage. "You're a real jerk you know that. Ugh! I'll be catching a taxi for sure now," I said.

We both yielded to the slow sounds of a key engaging the front door. We watched the knob turn slowly, then the door swung open. Nancy rushed in. She was dressed in blue jean shorts with a white tank top on. Her beautiful physique looked like a slim built runway model. Her light green eyes rested neatly atop her caramel complexion. She stood about the same height as me. Her red lipstick protruded from her medium-sized lips.

She was gorgeous.

I attempted to exit through the door, but Nancy grabbed my left arm. "Come back here! What are you doing in this house with my man?"

I jerked my arm away. "Girl, you don't know me like that!" I stood back in my legs and formed a boxer's stance to prepare for a potential battle. My back was facing the door that was wide open. Kyle was standing directly in front of me, and Nancy was to my left near the living room, ready to throw down.

I released my luggage again, then Nancy balled up her fists, stepping forward to strike me. I grunted, dodging a single blow. Kyle intervened, grabbing Nancy's arms from behind her. Her back was facing Kyle as he said, "Nancy, I'm not your man anymore! We broke up weeks ago."

Nancy aggressively pulled away from Kyle. She stared at me before facing Kyle. While pointing her right index finger at me, she looked back. "Kyle, get your little whore before I bust her up real nicely."

I would love to see that. I stepped forward and said, "Oh, I got your whore!"

Nancy repointed her fingers at me while Kyle forcefully held her back. She took off her shoes and hit Kyle in his head with one of her sneakers.

He stepped back, rubbing the right side of his skull. "Ouch, woman, that hurt," said Kyle.

I held up my hands, grabbed my luggage, and walked outside while saying, "I don't have time for this crap." Once I was off the front porch, I was forced to turn around and observe a scene full of drama.

Nancy and Kyle walked outside as Kyle continued to restrain her by holding her arms.

"Nancy, we are over," said Kyle.

"Oh yeah, you think we are over?" Nancy asked as she fell back into Kyle's chest. She lifted her legs to throw Kyle off balance, trying to break free of his grip.

I think she wanted to charge at me again. I was glad Kyle was restraining her, because I was going to swing back that time.

Suddenly, I overheard Nancy crying. "You proposed to me three months ago, and now you want to bring our love to an end. Just let me go, I promise I won't do anything."

Kyle gradually released his firm grip, then Nancy faced Kyle, she was standing to my left.

Kyle rubbed his forehead while glancing at me, then he refocused his attention on Nancy. "Yeah, because you cheated on me with John!"

I glanced over my shoulder and saw him looking at me as I walked toward the sidewalk. "Sophia, wait," said Kyle. I heard his footsteps approaching as I turned around again. He was standing in front of me, we were near the mailbox at the edge of the street. "Look, Nancy and I were engaged, but she cheated on me with John—the guy you met at the movies." Nancy was still standing on the porch with her arms folded across her chest. Nancy stood with a calm disposition.

I squinted my eyes to ascertain if he was telling the truth. "I think I believe you."

"Please do," said Kyle.

After I understood the background of what was going on, I realized that Kyle was the victim. I tended to jump to conclusions without giving someone a chance to fully explain themselves. I didn't want to have a repeat of what I did with Sammie a few days ago at the café.

Nancy walked forward and Kyle turned to face her to his right. "Look, Nancy, you need to go now before I call the police."

Nancy rolled her eyes, stomping her left foot against the pavement. Then she bent down to put her shoes on. After standing erected, she said, "Go right ahead and call them." Nancy waved her hands around to form a-one-hundred-and-eighty-degree-circle. "They'll probably shoot all three of us. I don't care, Kyle, so let them come out! You all need to die anyway." She pointed at me. "Especially this little mistress you have here!"

I frowned while walking forward, clenching my teeth together. I'm going to destroy her. "Who are you calling a mistress?" I asked.

Kyle lifted his hands and approached Nancy, creating a wall between us. He looked at me and said, "Sophia, stay out of this." He stared at Nancy. "I'll handle this crazy woman." He tossed his keys in my direction. "Just get in the car, here are the keys. I'll take you to the bus station, and you'll never have to worry about seeing me again."

I observed his keys fall to the ground like raindrops. *Oh no he didn't, just toss his keys to me like I'm some dog or something.*

Kyle picked Nancy up and carried her into the street, forcing her to walk away. Then he whispered something into her ears. *What's that about?*

Nancy looked at me and frowned before walking away.

I looked on. Whatever he told her must've worked.

Kyle turned around and faced me as I stood near his car with my luggage. He approached at a rapid pace. "Sophia, I am sorry about all of that. I totally understand if you don't want to say anything to me. I'll just focus on getting you to the bus station."

"No, I want to apologize for jumping to conclusions. Kyle, you remind me so much of my dad. I found out recently that my dad divorced my mom illegally. He was cheating on my mom before he was killed in the Vietnam War. I guess because of how highly I viewed my father, and then only to find out that he wasn't the man I thought he was—it just makes me lack trust in men."

Kyle grabbed my hands and stared into my eyes. "Sophia, I'm not a cheater. I'm just a man trying to live by God's righteous standards like you." He pointed in the direction where Nancy was walking, she was no longer in sight. "Nancy cheated on me because I refused to have sex with her before marriage. We were only four months away from the wedding date, so she definitely could've waited." He took a deep breath. "John is just a scumbag who I thought was my friend. Now that I think about it, he's always slyly tried his hardest to ruin my life."

We both leaned against the trunk of the car, like we did back at The Blues Café. He looked to his right as I stood with my arms beside my thighs. I looked straight ahead. "I'm sorry you had to go through all of that. You deserve better than that, Kyle."

He nodded his head. "Yeah, I realized that the moment I laid eyes on you. Please don't forget about me when you're back in San Francisco." He pointed to his house. "You know where to find me. You see where I live, where I work, and you even know what university I attend. But I don't have a way to contact you. Can you please provide me with a way to contact you?"

I gulped, then scoffed. "I just don't see a future for us Kyle. I'm sorry, but I'm still in love with another man."

He rubbed his chin. "Okay, I can respect that. Well, I hope you're able to find Sammie again someday. However, if you don't find him, I'll be right here in Marin County if we ever cross paths again."

I shrugged my shoulders. "No one can really say what's in store for the future," I said.

"True that. Just at least allow me to take you to the bus station."

"Okay," I replied.

Kyle walked inside his house to put a shirt on, then we departed. During the ride, silence filled the car.

Kyle and I must say our final farewells, I thought to myself.

A few minutes later, we arrived at the bus station. We exited the car and hugged one another, with the urge to taste each other's lips. Kyle grabbed me by my waist, pulling me in close as he asked, "May I?"

We kissed for the first time, and my eyes rolled into the back of my head as I lifted and bent my right leg behind me. Kyle gently slid his hands down my backside, squeezing my buttocks. I smiled while holding his face. We kissed like we were madly in love.

Several seconds later, our lips slowly pulled apart, then they were pulled back together like a magnet. We shared a passionate kiss once more. I pulled away and walked to my bus, waving goodbye as I stepped onboard. I sat down and watched Kyle stand alone as he appeared to hold back his tears, while leaning against the hood of his car. He blew a kiss at me, and I read his lips, "I love you."

Wow, he's shaking a little. I just don't know if Kyle and I have a future together, even after a passionate kiss like the one we just shared. It wasn't enough to stop me from thinking about Sammie. The bus drove away. Somehow, I know Kyle is telling the truth. I guess he fell in love with me in just three days. My bus ride back to San Francisco is going to be full of excitement and sadness. I'm happy I met Kyle, but I'm sad I didn't get a chance to talk to Sammie. I hit my forehead. I should've turned around when I heard his voice calling my name. He looked so good, and his voice is even more beautiful than when we were kids. Why didn't I just turn around and run toward him rather than run away from him? I really hope he picked up the note I dropped.

Chapter 8:
Don't Fight What You Feel in Your Heart

While sitting on the bus, I began to daydream about being back home. I visualized myself taking a warm shower, waking up in the morning to the scent of my home. Suddenly, I snapped back into reality after ascertaining that the bus may have had a problem. Someone was checking under the engine.

Engulfed in daydreaming, I pondered. I hope my bus ride back to San Francisco is peaceful. Meeting Kyle was worth the experience, despite the fact my encounter with Sammie didn't go as planned. If I don't see Sammie again, the thought of what if I'd handled things differently will torment my mind forever. There was no way Sammie could catch up with me with his cerebral palsy.

I sighed. If I had to grade who was better looking between Sammie and Kyle, if I'm being honest, maybe Kyle is aesthetically more attractive. But he doesn't have Sammie's heart. They both are tall with broad shoulders just the way I like my men. But Sammie's gift of music is what united us.

While staring through the window, I observed someone pull up in a white pick-up truck. Seconds later, a guy stepped out of the vehicle, wearing a hat that obscured his face.

It looks like he resembles Sammie.

My face filled with joy.

Is that who I think it is?

I couldn't tell for sure, because I only saw his side profile. I wish I knew what kind of car Sammie drove. That info would've really helped me identify who I was looking at in the car.

The bus started to move.

I stood up to get a better look, but the speed of the bus pushed me back down into my seat. "No!" I missed my clear view of the front of his face. Two silent tears fell from my eyes.

Thirty minutes later, the bus's engine started to sputter.

Oh no, I hope we aren't breaking down.

The bus pulled over, smoke coming from underneath its hood. The driver immediately ordered everyone to get off the bus. Grunts and sounds of frustration from several passengers were rampant. The driver phoned for help.

Finally, after waiting around for an hour for a new bus to arrive, we started driving again. Thirty-five minutes later, we arrived at the bus station in San Francisco.

The bus driver opened the door. I stood up, yawning with outstretched arms. After stretching, I grabbed my luggage then glanced to my left, observing the same white truck from Marin County's bus station.

Is that the same vehicle and guy I saw back at the other bus station?

I observed with intense concentration, noticing what appeared to be Sammie leaning against his car. *Is that my Sammie? He's in the same pick-up truck I saw earlier, too. If he wasn't like seventy yards away, I could see better. That stupid red hat he has on is getting in the way too. I smiled, glancing at the lady in front of me as she looked back at me. If that's him, why is he just standing around looking at his watch? He must be waiting around for someone. I rocked side-to-side while peering over the shoulders of the people in front of me.* "Come on, come on, hurry up people," I mistakenly whispered out loud. *I wish my seat wasn't at the back of the bus. I placed my luggage on the walkway then rubbed my hands across my head. I can't wait to exit this bus.*

The line started shifting forward.

Maybe Sammie found my note? I indicated on the note when I was headed back home. Sammie could've easily tracked down the bus station.

I peered out of the window and notice the unidentified guy removing his hat. My face lit up. "That's him!" My smiled expanded from one end of the earth all the way to the other end. My body began to stiffen as nervous feelings attacked my soul.

The line moved forward a little. I looked out of a different window near the front of the bus, smiling as the remaining passengers continued to exit the bus.

My arrival was delayed by an hour or so because of mechanical issues. So, either Sammie was waiting for someone else, or he stuck around just for me. My heart was pounding out of control. I dried sweat from my hands by using my shirt. I wanted to find out what really was going on a few days ago at The Blues Café.

I took a few steps forward and noticed that only five more people were in front of me. Those people were taking way too long to exit this bus. I stomped on the walkway like an irritated toddler. I couldn't miss my chance to talk to Sammie again. I peered through another window. What is Sammie doing? Is he looking at the paper I dropped? I slapped my forehead. I grunted, tossing my head back to express my frustration with the wait on the bus. I attempted to push through the remaining three passengers in front of me. An older white lady turned around and said, "Ma'am, just wait your turn!" I ignored the lady in front of me, continuing with my pursuit.

It dawned on me that I wrote the old address to my old house in Marin County on the paper. I looked upward. Thank you, God. You must've arranged for Sammie to be here at the bus station since you knew he wouldn't be able to find me otherwise. I sighed. I can't believe I wrote the wrong address down like an idiot.

Before I was able to exit the bus, I watched Sammie repeatedly looking at his watch. Sammie shook his head like he was frustrated before placing his hat back onto his head.

Hold on, Sammie, I'm coming.

I could tell he was growing impatient. He did that thing where he placed his hands on his hips while squeezing them together with his free hand whenever he was anxious. I was next in line to exit the bus. If Sammie was waiting for me, he had been waiting for almost three hours, and he was about to leave. He must've thought I wasn't there since my bus was a few hours late. It didn't help that I was the last person to get off the bus. It also didn't help that another bus was slightly obscuring his view of me too. I could tell Sammie couldn't see me. The bus right next to me was blocking his view of the middle and posterior sections of the bus I was on. Finally, I stepped off the bus, but Sammie entered his car. "No! Ugh!" His car was facing the street away from me—so he couldn't see me.

I dropped my luggage and ran behind Sammie's truck. I screamed, "Sammie, please don't go!" I sprinted as fast as I could. My cheetah-running instincts kicked into high gear. But my legs were still sore from my workout yesterday with Kyle. Sammie dissipated out of sight as I leaned over to catch my breath. "Whew!" I breathed heavily.

"No—no!" I dropped my head in despair before standing up to look around. Several people were staring at me with strange countenances.

I turned around, searching for my backpack. I left my luggage behind. I canvased the area and located my luggage. I wrote the address where my mom was residing in my note as well. Even if Sammie didn't have my new home address, maybe he would try to find me through my mom. I decided to keep her admitted for at least four more months, in case Sammie couldn't find me at my house. I knew it was selfish of me not to grant my mother's wishes, but I had to leave a conduit for Sammie to find me.

I looked up and observed a police officer standing near my luggage. It looked like he was waiting for me. The White officer stood six-feet-tall, with a build like an NFL linebacker. The officer spat in my direction. "Hold it right there." He scratched his head and looked back while pointing toward the bus. "A few people on the bus accused you of attacking them," said the Officer.

My mouth opened as wide as an alligator. I waved my hands in front of me, saying, "No—no, that's a bold-faced lie."

"Ma'am, that's not what several eyewitnesses' told me," the officer said.

I was in shock. It was weird, the officer kind of looked like one of the men who chased Timmy and I during our One Stop encounter. I looked around and observed some of the people that were on the bus with me. A lot of them were now standing outside the bus station. The older White lady from the bus yelled while pointing her fingers at me. "That's the rude Negro girl right there that assaulted me!" The lady walked forward. "Officer, arrest her for assaulting a White woman."

As ridiculous as her claims were, I knew the officer believed and agreed with her. I never assaulted her—I just pushed her a little in order to get by her.

The officer picked up my backpack and tossed it over his right shoulder as he said, "You're under arrest for assault. Hands behind your back now!"

I pulled away as the officer wrestled me to the ground. I screamed, "I haven't done anything wrong! You're lucky I can't see your face because of that stupid hat you have on." I exhaled. "Your sunglasses are hideous by the way. If only I could see your ugly face, I'd look you right in the eyes and spit in your face—you bigot!"

He uttered the one word that all Black people hate. "I know you didn't just call me a—" I turned on my stomach as I desperately tried to roll over so that I could spit in his face. "You racist fool! I can't wait to spit in your face!" My speech was interrupted by the sudden pain I felt in my back. I erupted into a clamor. "Ouch, get your knee off of me!"

"Shut up, you monkey!" The officer pressed his knee into my back. "Stop resisting or I'll blow your black little brains out." He pulled out his handcuffs.

I breathed heavily before I started to cry. "I'm not resisting anymore. Please, just don't shoot me. I'm not resisting you."

He handcuffed me and picked me up then escorted me to his car. A few seconds later, we drove away. While in the backseat I said out loud, "This isn't right what you're doing." The officer looked back at me and smirked.

"You and your whole race aren't right, that's what isn't right," said the Officer.

I observed the officer looking at me through the rearview mirror. He chuckled and said, "And you better hush up back there before you end up in a lake, you little gorilla!" He laughed.

I was shaking and my makeup was washed away by my tears. *I'm going to die, just like Timmy*, I thought to myself. "God, please help me."

"Shut up back there—I won't say it again," yelled the Officer.

***

The Interrogation Room

When we arrived at the police precinct, I immediately asked for a lawyer. I sat inside the interrogation room, then the officer who arrested me proceeded to uncuff me. As he exited the room he said, "I'll be right back. And you'll get your low-grade public defender. I know that's all you can afford." He chuckled, then I jumped as I heard the door slam.

"Good. Some type of defense is better than nothing," I said. I twisted my hands in the air to enjoy the liberty of free hands. My mom and dad instilled the importance of understanding that there isn't any Black privilege in the world, especially in the justice system. What a poor job the officers' did in searching for my brother's killer. My thoughts yielded to the sounds of the door opening as the officer reentered the room.

He approached me and spat in my face. He slammed his hands on the table while saying, "Little black monkey, you are done!" He breathed heavily as I wiped his spit from my face.

I leaned forward with my voice trembling while attempting to speak. "Please, just get my attorney," I said in a low tone.

" Speak up, monkey," said the Officer.

"You heard me," I said.

He chuckled and stood up straight. "You people are so dumb." His footsteps inched closer, with the sounds of his boots tapping against the floor, which lifted the hairs on the back of my neck. His hot breath bounced off my skin. "Sophia, I know who you are." He walked in front of me. "You probably don't remember me, but I most certainly remember your black butt. I requested a transfer to San Francisco after I found out your mother was institutionalized out there." He frowned.

Before the officer finished articulating more racial epithets, someone who appeared to be a lawyer entered the room.

I stared at the guy that entered. *I recognize him.* I raised my eyebrows. I was taken aback by the sheer coincidence of him showing up to represent me. I looked at his dark brown hair. His front teeth were rather large, just like the guy I was thinking of. He had the same build too. I glanced at his stomach. *His belly looks a little bigger than what I remember as a child.* Man, he had to be almost seven-feet-tall. His green eyes reminded me of the color green inside a rainbow. His double chin was rather unusual for someone that's not significantly overweight.

As the guy approached me, sounds from the heels on his black dress shoes tapping against the floor echoed in the room. I observed his ensemble as the officer that arrested me attempted to walk out, but the guy angrily said, "Officer, stay!"

The guy seemed upset with the officer. *He must be a lawyer,* I thought.

The lawyer extended his hand, glancing at his hand while I twirled my left index finger. I hesitated before saying, "I think—I know you?"

The attorney smirked, pulling his hand back to his side, then he exhaled. He started speaking but his words were blocked from being processed by my brain. I was distracted.

It was a lot to take in. I continued to internally entertain if I knew him for certain. "Have you figured out who I am yet?" The guy asked.

I squinted my eyes. You're one of the military men who delivered the bad news about my dad's death. How did he know I was detained? Maybe it's just some random coincidence.

The apparent lawyer pulled out a chair and sat next to me. "Okay, since you're still struggling to figure out who I am, I'll just tell you." He looked me up and down. "Sophia, you're all grown up now." I stared at him with a countenance of distrust. "You don't remember me? I served with your dad."

I nodded my head to gesture that I remembered him.

He exhaled. "Okay, good. I decided to pursue my passion as a defense lawyer after I was honorably discharged from the military three years ago. I've been practicing law for two years now. It didn't take much for me to get my career going, since I'd already finished most of my curriculum whilst I was in the military."

I exhaled. *Mister, I don't care.*" Uh, how did you know I was arrested?" The officer that arrested me reentered the room.

He grinned and turned around with an indignant countenance while facing the cop that arrested me. While staring at the officer with bloodshot eyes of rage, the lawyer said, "I'll tell you later how I found out about you being unjustly arrested."

The attorney turned his attention back to me. "Sophia, I need to have a serious talk with you." He pointed while focusing his attention on the small interrogation room. "You can't afford to end up in a place like this again. These racist fools aren't playing with you. They'll lynch you, and not think much of it." I swallowed my saliva. "The laws are on White folks' side. Although the policemen took an oath to serve and protect their communities, I hate to say this, colored people were not on their list of people to protect."

I turned my head to loosen the tension in my neck. "Yeah, I reached that conclusion after my brother's death," I said. I took a deep breath.

"Smart girl. I can assure you I hate the things that kind Black folk like yourself have to go through. I've been looking after you and your mom for a while now."

His statements compelled me to cross-examine his sincerity. I think this guy has an ulterior motive. Why is he practically stalking me and my mom?

Then, it dawned on me—the officer who arrested me was Billy Joe. Ahh. Billy Joe is the guy Timmy accidentally almost killed a few weeks before he met his tragic end. I jumped up out of the chair and attempted to run out of the room while saying, "Billy Joe is going to kill me!"

The lawyer whose face I couldn't match with a name, quickly stood up and his chair fell to the floor. The sound of a chair bouncing off the floor frightened me. I paused and gasped for air, which gave him enough time to grab my arms as he said, "Wait—wait!" He frowned at Billy Joe. He pointed his clenched fist at him and said, "Wipe that smirk off your face, have a little class."

Billy Joe patted the handle of his gun that was inside his holster. "Yeah, yeah, we'll see about that," said Billy Joe, his calloused and baritone voice echoed through the room.

The lawyer sighed while turning his attention back to me. I fell to the ground in a desperate pursuit to free myself from his commanding grip. "Calm down. Billy Joe won't be able to harm you now." I looked up at him from a subdued position, his height overwhelming my fears of Billy Joe.

He gave me reassurance while saying "Sophia, I'm protecting you now. And besides, I have a lot of evidence connecting Billy Joe to over fifteen lynches of young Black males." He looked at Billy Joe with fury and agitation. "Billy Joe will be going to jail soon."

My survival instincts were fully activated as I observed Billy Joe pull his gun out of the holster. He slammed his gun on the table and violently charged in my direction. Oh no. I hid behind the lawyer, his long arms kept Billy Joe at bay.

With saliva flying from his mouth like stinging mosquitos, Billy Joe screamed at the lawyer. "You monkey loving traitor!" They started wrestling and Billy Joe seized his opportunity, spitting in my face. The barrister started to quote laws, then three officers rushed into the room because of the raucous. The officers detained Billy Joe, taking him into custody after they were threatened with lawsuits and prison time by the counselor. It was kind of weird that they seemed so afraid of the lawyer. I guess that was a good thing.

One of the officers', short with blonde hair and light blue eyes, assisted with escorting Billy Joe out of the room. The officer that was escorting him stopped at the door of the interrogation room, then turned his fragile physique in the lawyer's direction. His murderous eyes pierced the counselor. "Don't worry, Billy Joe will be exonerated from whatever little crimes you think you have on him!"

The lawyer glanced at me as I shook uncontrollably. The counselor responded to the officer, "Look here, you bigot, Billy Joe is a serial killer. The people he killed only committed the crime of being Black.

If you have sympathy for a scumbag like Billy Joe, then I feel sorry for your soul." The lawyer waved his fists in the air. "Whatever God your nation of racist pricks professes to serve can't stand in the way of true justice. You might as well quit now. You and Billy Joe don't serve the God of the Bible. I really hope you look at the work you're doing and change your wicked ways."

Billy Joe's devotee spoke out again, replying with a statement that sealed his fate. "Billy Joe and I love to kill Black monkeys. We will kill some more Blacks as soon as he gets off."

The lawyer pulled out a small rectangular device and squeezed it. A few seconds later, an army of FBI agents dressed in navy blue FBI jackets rushed in to arrest Billy Joe and his accomplice.

I rubbed my hands across my face while trying to ascertain what was unfolding in front of my eyes. I didn't realize he was baiting them. However, something was still fishy about everyone there. It was like the lawyer was more concerned about Billy Joe rather than starting the process of doing legal work for me. I was slightly confused.

After the arrests were solidified, the lawyer turned around and looked at me while saying, "I know you're probably confused about what you just saw," said the lawyer.

I quickly chimed in. "Yes, I'm definitely confused."

"No worries, I'll explain. I work with the FBI to help protect African Americans from mistreatment. What those racist monsters' were doing is illegal. Also, while it's on my mind, you should listen to your mom more, she's right about the staff at her facility. I know your mom is mentally sick, and I can't objectively prove everything she told me. However, I wouldn't put ill intentions past any of the people who are caring for your mother. You really need to look into getting her out of that hellhole that she's in."

I took a few steps back and exhaled. "Uh, what's your name, anyway?" I asked.

The lawyer glanced at the agents, signaling for them to leave him alone with me. He extended his right hand, then I finally shook his hand. "My name is John Proctor." He sighed. "I am so sorry, I thought I'd introduced myself when I walked into the interrogation room earlier."

"You did. Informally, I guess. You just didn't mention your name." I scratched my head. "Tell me more about your relationship with my dad?"

John picked up the chair that fell on the floor, then he sat in it while gesturing for me to take a seat too. I rejected his offer. "Your dad and I got really close after he went back to serve in the Vietnam War. He accidentally saved my life too. The landmine that killed him was really destined to end me. Your father placed his foot on the landmine before I had a chance to step on it." I turned my back to John.

John stood and walked toward me. He placed his hands on my shoulders after I started to sob. I shrugged my shoulders and said, "Please, remove your hands, I'm fine." Through my peripheral vision I could see him executing inappropriate facial gestures. Why is he smirking? I faced him. Seemed odd. I took a deep breath. Something is up with Mr. John Proctor.

John lifted his hands and poked his lips out while tossing his hands into the air. "Alright! Anthony mentioned I was a good Christian man, and that I had more to live for than he did. He asked me to look after you and your mom. Although your dad had sealed his fate once he stepped on the landmine, I could tell a part of him felt like maybe a miracle would happen."

"Um," I uttered, turning around to face him while wiping my tears.

"Sophia, why were you arrested? Every time I attempted to ask that knucklehead Billy Joe why, he got an attitude and asked, 'Why are you helping that black monkey?'"

I scoffed. "I'm just sick and tired of racism. Billy Joe arrested me for no reason—for no reason at all!"

John exhaled. "Give me your version of what happened at the bus station? Because Billy Joe has a very believable story regarding why he arrested you."

I was too embarrassed to tell him what happened. Staring at the walls, I conjured up a story. No one will believe that a Black girl was trying to get off a bus to chase after her White soulmate.

John continued to look at me with anticipation. The sounds of his shoes rubbed against the floor. The noise from his shoes added to the intensity of my delayed response.

I pointed my fingers at my complexion. "I did nothing. It was simply because I'm Black."

John shook his head while staring into my eyes. "I see why you would feel that way. When we came and took your dad back to the base a few years ago, he told me why he moved and what happened to your brother. I'm not going to have a problem getting you out of here. I'm sure this community doesn't want to be all over the news like Marin County was when the KKK shot your brother to death a few years ago." He abruptly walked toward the door and elevated his right hand, signaling for me to hold my thoughts. "Hold on Sophia, I'll be back. I'm going to get you out of this place."

" Thanks, Mr. Proctor."

Five minutes later, two new officers entered the room, releasing me. This whole encounter is interesting but odd too. One of the new officers stated, "Ma'am, you're free to go." I stood up and exited the room.

Mr. Proctor paid for a taxi to take me home. He handed me one of his business cards and said, "Call me if you need me. Meanwhile, I'll continue to look out for you and your mother."

I looked back at him through the backseat of the taxi as the driver slowly drove away. Mr. Proctor waved at me as I stared at him. Something about Mr. Proctor, just didn't seem genuine to me.

***

Unforgettable News

The Next Day

Staring at the ceiling in my bedroom, I started cogitating the events that transpired over the past few days. While crossing my feet I continued to lay on my back while twirling my fingers. Nothing went as planned. I picked up a pillow and placed it over my face while screaming. "I feel so stupid for even attempting to find Sammie. Nothing ever goes my way, anyway. I've lost Dad, Timmy, and now Sammie too. Not to mention I was harassed by a racist cop as well. And on top of that the one that my brother was involved with." I started to cry then I wiped my tears and said out loud, "Every time I allow myself to love someone, I lose them."

I like Kyle a little, but why would I even waste my time trying to develop something with him? My mother is practically out of my life as well. She's mentally unstable. Timmy and my dad were such brave men. I need to be more like my brother and father. "Ugh! Why do I always talk like a defeatist?" My brother used to tell me that negative thinking will produce negative results. Maybe I keep losing because I'm expecting to lose.

I moved around in my bed. I am made in God's image, and Timmy used to remind me of this. The real reason I sat out my first semester of college is because I felt guilty about surpassing Timmy. I don't think it's fair for me to go to college since Timothy didn't get his chance to go. I also sat out because I wanted to search for Sammie too. I exhaled. I must get ahold of myself. I sat up in my bed like someone that was resurrected from the dead, bracing myself by placing my hands behind me, where they sank into the mattress.

Why didn't I just tell my family about my gift in music? I really don't know why I was so afraid to tell someone other than Sammie. Well technically, I didn't tell Sammie he discovered my gift in the midnight forest. I smiled. "I am in deep thought this morning." My mom used to tell me that my only hope for being successful was to find a good Christian man who could take care of me. But I never saw myself the way my mom saw me. I am more than just a housewife.

I lifted my right hand, rotating it in a circle to stretch my hand from the pressure of pressing down on my wrist. I placed my hands back on the mattress. I've always felt like I have something special bubbling within me. I placed my hand on my chest. "I can feel it in my heart." I just know that there is something special for me to do in this world. I'll never be happy until I manifest the musical gift that God placed inside of me. This is one of the reasons why I'm so connected to Sammie. He's the only person who makes me feel like I can do anything. He encouraged me to use my gift and to share it with the world.

I positioned myself toward the edge of the bed. "When I start college next year in January, I think I'm going to major in music." I need to nurture my gifts. I stood up and reached for my toes, with my knees locked to stretch my lower back and hamstrings. Do I feel like exercising this morning? I twisted my neck to the left and right while reaching for my toes. I probably should drive back to Marin County later today so that I can register for my classes for the spring semester. While standing fully erect I spoke out loud, "I have so much stuff to do." I'll just jog this morning. I miss my grandma. She called last night to say that she's staying a few more weeks in California. I got dressed and walked outside for a morning jog.

While jogging at a moderate pace, more thoughts flowed throughout my head. I only have a few months to prepare for my audition on December 17th, in Los Angeles. I need to find a job, too, since my dad's funds are starting to run low. I started to breathe heavily as my jogging pace increased like the speed of a gazelle. I'm going to need a way to pay for food, taxes, electricity, water, and gas. I need to work on getting my mom out of that place, so she can go stay with my aunt.

After I finished jogging, I took a quick shower. A few minutes after, I freshened up, then walked past a picture of Timothy that was hanging on the living room wall, I stopped to stare at it. I remembered how Timothy used to pray to God every day. He used to mention that King David asked God to direct his life, even though he disappointed God on more than one occasion. Timmy used to feel like God didn't love Black people until he had a revelation. My brother had a way of explaining things that would make me feel differently about White people. That's another reason why I love Sammie, he gave me hope.

I walked away from Timothy's picture and my inner thoughts continued to accelerate. *I'm going to need a lot of courage if I'm going to become the next Aretha Franklin in December. Sammie said this to me a while back, "Why would God give a Black girl such a beautiful voice if she wasn't my equal?"*

I entered the kitchen and poured a glass of orange juice as thoughts of Sammie's blue eyes brighten my day.

My gift drew our hearts together, and that's why I'll never stop hoping for us to meet again. I swallowed a portion of my juice too quickly, which caused me to choke a little. I placed the glass on the countertop with my fist over my mouth. I coughed then exhaled before speaking out loud, "Whether or not I have Sammie in my life, I am going to go after my dreams." It's my only way to honor Dad, Sammie, and Timmy.

I peered through the kitchen window with the sunlight shining through, glancing at the kitchen's illumination while coughing. It's time for me to head out and go visit my mom.

I exited the house in a black one-piece jogging suit, entered my car then backed out of the driveway. While driving I started to reminisce over my weekend and the moments I shared with Kyle. I stopped at a stop sign in my neighborhood. Two seconds later, I pressed on the gas, but I slammed on the brakes as a young child suddenly appeared in front of my car. "You crazy little kid, I almost hit you." I smiled while experiencing a flashback of playing with Timothy as a little girl. I miss my brother.

After the boy crossed in front of me, I looked to the left and right before resuming driving.

I gripped the steering wheel tightly then entered onto the highway. I've suppressed my gift. I should've still been practicing. Sammie obviously didn't allow the fact that I wasn't in his life stop him from living his dreams.

While rotating my neck I pulled my hair from underneath the hood of my hoodie. I turned on the radio and sang along to a familiar song. Just hearing myself sing again fills my heart with joy, like the scent of a beautiful rose. After exiting the highway, I pulled over onto the shoulder of the road. My chest throbbed as the pain from not using my gift flowed throughout my soul. I punched upward, striking the ceiling of my car. A few seconds later, I drove back onto the road, pausing at a stop sign for several seconds. My tears were interrupted by a honking horn behind me. "Okay, okay," I yelled. I pressed down on the accelerator.

A few minutes later, I arrived at my mother's facility, parked the wagon, then exited the car, filled with emotion. I showed my I.D. to the guard, and she gave me the okay to enter. I walked inside the facility like a tiger, staking out the scene. *Hmm. The way they're looking at me is creating a fear in my heart. I feel like something bad has happened.* I approached the window to fill out the paperwork to visit with my mother. The attendant at the window said, "The doctor wants to see you."

While lifting my eyebrows, I scanned the pristine hospital, with its freshly painted cream-colored walls. *That's interesting.* "Uh, is my mom, okay?" Before the guard replied I immediately turned to my left, facing the direction of heels piercing into the hospital's floor. Like a sharp needle, the continuous sounds of heels dug into the facility's surface. I caught a glimpse of a white coat before facing a tall, middle-aged White woman with short blonde hair.

Oh, that's just Dr. Peterson.

Dr. Peterson halted and said, "We need to talk." She pointed her fingers toward the end of the hallway. "Sophia, let's go to my office."

I grabbed the doctor's arms, stretching her coat's sleeve then we paused in the middle of the hallway. "I just know something is terribly wrong," I said.

Dr. Peterson looked dejected as she sighed. *Something's wrong.* I started to cry while helplessly staring into her eyes. My emotions exploded as I fell to my knees and said, "I just know that something terrible has happened!" I looked around as my tears fell on the floor. "Did you all kill my mom?"

She exhaled. "No, Sophia," replied Dr. Peterson.

I stood up with tears falling onto my jacket. "I recall my mom saying that she was being beaten. I just attributed it to her mental illness."

Dr. Peterson politely removed my hands from her jacket. I hugged her then placed my hands atop her shoulders. "Maybe she was right, maybe Billy Joe's dad does own this facility." John Proctor alluded to this as well back in the interrogation room. But my mom never mentioned anything about John Proctor. I wonder why?

"No one here harmed your mother. However, I'm saddened to inform you that your mother passed away," said Dr. Peterson.

"Wait, what?" I shook my head out of disbelief. "None of this makes any sense! When?" I asked. *Why are the other staff members looking at me so strangely? Too many of them are walking around, it's never like this. It's like they're planning to do something to me or someone else. I don't know, but I've never seen so many White people dressed in white scrubs. Even the guards have on white shirts and pants today. It kind of looks like a KKK meeting just ended—just without their dresses and head-coverings on. I don't trust the vibes I feel here.* I turned my attention back to Dr. Peterson.

Dr. Peterson stepped forward and said, "She hung herself Friday. We tried to notify you, but no one was home when we dropped by."

Lies. I contorted my wounded soul like a baby in a fetal position. "Oh no, this can't be true. Dr. Peterson, please tell me you're lying!" I stared into her eyes while desperately anticipating a different reply. "Please, tell me this isn't real!" My sobs echoed through the hospital like a lion's roar. I turned my back to her, placing my finger and thumb over my forehead. My head started to slowly sink into my shoulders. As my head continued to drop in despair, I turned around to face Dr. Peterson. "I just—" I stuttered. "I just—I just saw my mom a few days ago."

" Yes, we know." She pulled out a note from her coat pocket then handed me a piece of paper. "Your mother left this note for you." I snatched the note and immediately read it. Dr. Peterson continued, "We didn't think much of it when she asked to see you a few days ago. Your mom asked me if I would write a letter for her, addressing it to you. I didn't know your mom was illiterate."

With the note in my hand, I frowned and said, "That's bogus! How could you not have known that?"

"I didn't know." She exhaled. "Your mother said she always wanted to share her thoughts on paper. She mentioned, whenever you came to visit her again, she wanted to write something for you that showed remorse for when she refused to see you the last time you were here."

I reread the note before balling it up and tossing it at Dr. Peterson. While pointing my finger at her I said, "You all killed my mom—I know you did." Dr. Peterson attempted to hide a smirk.

"Since you're going through a lot, I'll forgive you for throwing that paper at me. And by the way, a young gentleman came by looking for you yesterday. He was a young White boy. I think his name was Samuel or Sammie." Dr. Peterson squinted her eyes. "What are you doing fooling around with my kind anyway?" She grinned. "I could tell that he cares for you, though."

While looking startled I replied, "I really don't have time for this today." Wait, she just said Sammie. "Uh, what did you just say?" I asked.

Dr. Peterson sighed. "Since you're dealing with a little pain, I won't make an issue out of your tone with me. But he came in with a piece of paper. It was a letter you wrote to him I think," she said.

I was bewildered. *A little pain? Something is off here. I should probably be cautious.*

Dr. Peterson crossed her arms. "The guy said he tried to find your house, but you left out the street name on your address or something like that. The Sammie guy may have even mentioned that you wrote down an address to a house that your parents had in Marin County too." She shrugged her shoulders. "Anyway, you mentioned in the letter where your mom was hospitalized." She pointed down the hallway in front of her toward the area where the front desk was. "He also left a note for you, the guard has it at the front desk."

I was shocked and completely silent as I scratched my head. Then, I noticed an ink pen on Peterson's coat. I grabbed the pen without her permission.

She scoffed. "Excuse you," said Dr. Peterson.

" Sorry," I replied. I picked up the piece of paper I tossed at her. While picking up the paper, I dissected the note I read. My mom's final words to me were, "I love you and do well in life." Seems like my mom should have said more. I turned my attention back to Dr. Peterson while quickly looking around at the unusually high volume of workers. I probably should put more emphasis on Sammie to distract them from thinking that I'm suspicious of my mom's death, just in case these people are up to something. I hate to say this, but I just can't trust certain White people, especially after all that I've seen. I glanced at

Dr. Peterson as she looked at some of the workers walking by. *Dr. Peterson has no empathy and that's very alarming.*

I wrote my correct address on the paper. "Dr. Peterson, please give this paper to Sammie if he comes by looking for me again." She took the paper and walked away without saying anything.

I didn't pay Dr. Peterson any mind. Instead, I headed toward the front desk to pick up Sammie's note. After I arrived at the front desk, the guard chuckled and said, "Hey, I ripped your note up, you black monkey." Leaning forward, the guard stuck her head out of the glass opening. "You don't deserve to date anyone in my race."

I tensed up. Dazed in a fearful silence, images of my brother's blood, gushing out of his right temple and flooding the lake of tears, flashed through my mind. While still backpedaling, I turned around and walked in the opposite direction.

"I don't want to die!" She's a new guard who obviously believes that mixing races leads to a mongrel-breed. Due to trepidation, I started to run. While running, I overheard a woman yell, "Be sure to cremate your mom! That's what she wanted!"

Huh?

After storming out of the facility I charged toward my car, looking back over my shoulder as my pace increased. I know Dr. Peterson heard that woman. There's no way my mom asked to be cremated. I continued to run toward my car like a wild horse. I'm so saddened by my mom's suicide, but at least my mom wrote me a letter. Or maybe she didn't? I had no idea my mom was contemplating suicide. I stopped my pursuit and leaned over to catch my breath. I looked behind me before restarting a rapid walk to my car. *There's no way I'll be able to drive to Marin County now. I just don't have the energy.* "I just can't believe my mom killed herself!" Thoughts of the midnight forest rushed through my mind. Thoughts of the night when I attempted to take my life froze my brain's capacity to think.

I unlocked my car then rested my hands atop the roof. I scoffed. "I need to find out what really happened to my mom." Or maybe she committed suicide? I'm on a collision course but I don't like where I'm headed.

I stepped inside my car and drove away. After I arrived home, one of my aunts called to inform me that my grandmother had a heart attack after she found out about my mom's death. The institution called my aunt in California after they couldn't reach me or my grandmother at home.

Lord, this is too much.

I dropped the phone, leaving the cord dangling from the wall. I sat at the kitchen table and sobbed while saying out loud, "First my mom and now my grandmother too."

This is too much.

***

The Day of the Funerals

A Week Later

I drove into my driveway after attending my mother's and grandmother's funerals. It was best to have them together. My black dress was smeared with me and my family's tears. I remained in the car, reflecting on my mother's well-done makeup. My mother looked a little better than my grandma. My mother's face looked so good. She looked like she was finally at peace with her life. She laid in the casket like a soul filled with life. I know people say rest in peace, but I believe that the dead are conscious of nothing, so only the living can rest in peace. The dead are not aware of rest nor peace. Still, for my mom I would say she's finally at peace.

While peering into the rearview mirror, I noticed some of my family members drive up. My mom's side of the family is small, she only has two sisters. My aunts, Doris and Dorothy, both have two kids.

My cousins stepped out of their cars.

Everyone was dressed in black. I hadn't seen my cousins, Janet, Victor, Travis, and Lonnie, in a very long time.

I jumped after hearing a knock on the window, on the driver's side of my car. Looking to my left, I noticed Aunt Doris. I rolled my window down then Doris said, "Sophia, are you going to be okay? You're all by yourself."

I hesitated before I replied, "Uh, I think I'll be fine."

"Okay," said Doris. She walked in the direction of the rest of my family.

My left leg hung from the car as I watched my aunt walk away. For being on the older side, Aunt Doris looked amazing. Her figure is astonishing, and her skin is flawless. I love the freshness of her long hair too. Her hair just seemed to ride her behind like a horse's saddle. It's the longest I'd ever seen in my life. Her cute little pie face is pudgy, though, unlike my mother's.

I stepped out of the car, signaling for Doris to come my way. "Aunt Doris, come here please." Doris approached along the pavement like a runway model.

While standing near my car Doris said, "Yes."

"I know, I answered you earlier, already. I just want to express myself a little more to help ease your concern. Again, I think I'll be okay." I exhaled. "It just seems like life is happening to me all at once. First Timmy, then my dad, and now my mom. I just don't know if I can take any more losses." Sophia shook her head.

Doris pulled me into her arms, we both shed tears. While hugging each other, Doris said: "I can only imagine what you're going through right now. I remember how your mom and I felt the night we lost both of our parents. You never got a chance to meet your grandparents, Sue and Bill—you didn't miss anything, in my opinion."

I leaned against my car, listening to Doris bash her parents over the next two minutes. I met my grandparents on my dad's side, but I never met or knew the names of my grandparents on my mom's side. My mom always said she didn't want to talk about them, it was too painful for her. My dad never met them either, my mom's parents were dead, long before my mom and dad crossed paths.

I intervened while Doris was in midsentence. "Auntie Doris, can I ask you something?"

"Sure," said Doris.

"If I ask you, will you tell me the truth?" I observed other family members walking up toward my house. I held my hand up, signaling for Doris to stay put while I unlocked the front door to my house. My family entered my house. After unlocking the door, I walked down the steps and walked over to Doris. I stood in front of her, then we reversed positions. She was leaning against the car.

"To answer your question, of course, Sweetheart. What do you want to know?" Doris asked.

I gestured for my aunt to move to the left then I opened my car, hopping inside whilst inviting her to do the same. After we were seated, I sighed. "What happened to my mom's parents?" I asked.

Doris faced me on the passenger's side and placed her hand on my thigh. "I'm sorry your mom never told you what happened." She took a deep breath then stared out of the window. With her head turned away from me, her face was filled with tears as she uttered, "Sophia, are you sure you're ready to hear what I'm about to disclose?"

I placed my right hand atop her shoulder then I tugged at her shoulder, inviting her to face me. My face was a pool of tears.

"Yes, I'm ready. I feel I'm missing a lot of pieces in my life because I don't know my history," I said.

Doris nodded her head. "Your grandfather wasn't the greatest man in the world. Your grandpa Bill was a molester. He molested all three of us. Your mom, although she was the youngest of us three girls, was the only one who had the courage to stand up to him."

"I didn't know my mom was molested by her own dad," I said.

Doris sighed. "Not just your mom, but me and your auntie Dorothy too."

I lifted my right leg to a partial Indian-style posture, my left leg hanging below the surface of the car's seat. "What happened to my grandparents?" I asked.

Doris held her hands up, gesturing for me to be patient. "I'm going to get to that part in a second," she said.

" Okay, I'm sorry."

"It's okay, Sophia, considering everything you're probably feeling right now."

"Thanks for being here for me," I replied.

Doris tapped my thigh. "Any time." While looking straight ahead away from my face, she said, "One day when your grandmother was out shopping for groceries, your Grandpa Bill decided to take advantage of me and Dorothy. That was how we found out he was doing the same thing to the both of us. At first, Dorothy and I thought he only violated us separately. Neither one of us knew he was engaging in his despicable behavior with the both of us." She shook a little. "We both were terrified. While in the middle of his perverted acts, your mom walked in with your grandpa's gun. She closed her eyes and fired several shots at him. A ton of bullets pierced his flesh but none of them were fatal."

I lifted my eyebrows and rubbed my right calf.

"When your Grandma Sue returned home a few minutes after his shameful conduct, she learned about what he did to us." Doris started to cry. "I hate to even mention what happened next." Doris dried her tears with a napkin. Silence filled the car for several seconds. I locked my eyes onto my aunt while waiting for her to finish revealing the details. She looked at me and asked, "Are you sure you want to know the rest?"

I placed my hand on hers. "I need to know everything," I said.

Doris lifted her hands to convey the trauma she was experiencing from reliving the events. "I guess my mom lost it. She grabbed her shotgun, shooting my father several times. Later that night, after everything settled down, I guess, she had a chance to process the reality that she had killed her husband. I don't know if it was the pain of knowing my dad molested her daughters, or if she felt guilty about shooting him in the heat of the moment. All I remember hearing was a loud gunshot. We ran to my mom's room and found her lifeless body on the floor. She had a massive hole in the left side of her head."

I put my hand over my mouth. I was in shock.

"Your mom used to say, 'If only I hadn't picked up that stupid gun, then maybe my parents would still be alive'. Your mother felt like, although our dad wasn't a good man, she still would have rather seen him alive and in jail rather than six feet under." Doris sobbed.

"Auntie Doris, I'm glad you're sharing this with me. But can we stop here? This topic seems to be a lot for you now."

"Thank you. Uh, and it just crossed my mind. Do you need any financial help with anything while I am here?" Doris asked.

"I think I'm okay, thanks, though. My mom's life insurance will cover my expenses for some bills I need to pay. I plan to use the remaining funds for school and my singing career."

Why did I just say that?

Doris looked elated—but puzzled. She cleared her throat. "Singing career?"

"I meant my college career!"

"Oh ok, I thought for sure I heard you say, 'Singing career?'"

"No, I can't sing to save my life." Without any warning I opened the door and got out of the car. That was a close call.

While still sitting in the car, Doris said, "Well—don't let me hold you back my dear, go talk to your cousins. They all really miss you."

I smiled. "Thanks for talking to me, I love you." I walked away only to be struck deeply with grief. Doris stepped out of the car and approached me. "I've never felt a pain like this before," I said.

She grabbed my hand and caressed it. "Auntie, I need some time to myself. Can you just let everyone know I'll be in to mingle with them in a little?" I said.

We held hands and entered the house a few seconds later. Once inside the foyer area, I decided to go to the bathroom. While walking to the bathroom I observed that about fifty people attended the funeral. Most of the attendees were friends of my mom and grandma. Before entering the bathroom, I paused to observe my dad's two siblings, Uncle Jake and Uncle Troy. I look forward to chatting with them after I pull myself together. I entered the bathroom, then closed the door.

A few minutes later, I exited the bathroom and approached my four cousins that were sitting on my living room couch. When they saw me inching closer, they stopped talking amongst themselves. "Hello."

While standing in front of my cousins I removed my heels. My feet were hurting. While holding my heels in my hands, I said, "I'm so happy to see you all, but today really isn't a good day for me to catch up with y'all. Please understand."

My cousins looked around at one another. Then, one of them said, "No problem, we totally understand."

"Thank you," I replied. I walked forward and hugged them one by one. My cousins scooted over to the left and right sides of the couch, making room for me. I sat down and glanced to my left and right. I smiled. "I promise, girls, I'll come visit you all in a few months. You all are the best cousins in the world. I really appreciate y'all more than you know. Thank you for coming out to support me. I know I broke tradition by coming home first before I buried my mom and grandma.

But I just needed a few minutes of familiarity to get my head together. Now it's time to head back out to bury them."

My cousins looked at one another while nodding their heads to respectfully acknowledge my needs. They all hugged me in a spirit of unity, as their arms formed a wall of love around me.

A few minutes later, my family and I were guided by policemen to Cella Gardens, the burial site. I drove myself to the burial site. While driving in the car, I thought to myself. *I need some type of solace right now.* A few minutes later, I exited the car, then my family and I approached the burial site. We unitedly walked together, like a crowd of silent protesters. After everyone gathered around, Minister Boykins said a few words before ending with a word of prayer. After finishing his prayer, he stated, "Does anyone have any last words to say?"

I was taken aback after observing a large figure step forward, embracing Boykin's invitation.

I thought to myself as a cool breeze blew underneath my dress. Aunt Dorothy has gained so much weight. Her black dress looks more like a gigantic comforter. I sighed. Aunt Dorothy can be so superficial at times too.

Standing over my mom's casket, Dorothy delivered her last words to her sister's lifeless body.

I exhaled. Right after this, we're going to do this again for my grandmother; at least we are getting everything out of the way in one day.

My entire family cried while Dorothy expressed her final words. A clamor of despair erupted because of the pain of our losses; our cries for comfort sounded like an orchestra of emotional pain.

Chapter 9:
Rebirth:
The Key to a Life of Adventure

As Dorothy progressed further with her sentiments, I thought, *she's speaking from the heart today.* Listening to her endearing words softened my spirit.

While focusing on her words, I noticed a familiar looking man to my left glide across the cemetery like an angel of life. He looked so handsome in his gray suit. God must've heard my prayer. I smiled while looking up into the midday sky. He's walking toward me. Yep, here he comes. I held my hands over my mouth, blowing hot air into my hands. I smelled my hands to check the status of my breath. I hope my breath doesn't smell, because it's been a long day. I pulled my dress down then adjusted my hair as he inched closer. *Lord, what's his name? I guess I'm so surprised to see him, I can't even remember his name.*

I stood up then walked a few yards away from the burial site, creating an obscure distance between the approaching male and my family. While walking, I looked over my shoulder to see if the man of interest was pursuing my trail. I smiled. Here he comes.

He increased his pace as his walk progressed into a light jog. He yelled, "Wait up, Sophia!"

I discreetly checked the status of my breath once more, before turning around, controlling an urge to smile. I can't let him see that I missed him.

He stared into my eyes as we met each other halfway, closing the distance between us. "I've been looking all over for you."

I swallowed my saliva. "My mom passed." Tears wet my face.

We hugged. With a saddened look on his face, he replied, "I'm so sorry to hear about your mom. I haven't been able to stop thinking about you. I just had to come and find you. I wasn't going to stop until I had one more chance to see you again." He looked around. "I didn't think we would meet again under these awful circumstances." He held me tight.

Leaning back, I stared into his eyes as we held hands like a married couple on our honeymoon. I looked at him like it was the first time I'd ever laid eyes on him. I didn't expect to see you again, I thought to myself.

He created a foot of distance as he stepped back, releasing his firm grip. He looked perplexed while stating, "You haven't said anything to me yet. Sophia?"

I blushed. "Yes?"

He pressed his hands together to form a hand sandwich before positioning his hands underneath his chin like he was saying a prayer to God. "Well, say something already," he said.

I stuttered, "Uh, I'm just shocked that you're here."

He smiled.

"Uh." I fanned myself off with my hands as my body heated up. "Is this moment real, like are you seriously here right now? How the heck did you find me?"

He smirked. "I followed you to the bus station in San Francisco, before losing sight of you somehow at the bus station."

I hope he didn't see me get arrested.

"Look, I know, I'm a stalker. I found your address by looking it up in the phone book. I went back home after I lost you at the bus station. I came back a few days later when I had a few days off from work. I stayed at a hotel around the corner from your house." He exhaled. "I could tell something was terribly wrong after you left your mother's hospital. I saw you running like a bull. I called your name, but I guess you didn't hear me."

I playfully punched him in his right shoulder. "Basically, you've been stalking me?"

He executed a three-hundred-and-sixty-degree turn while jokingly tossing his hands into the air. "Didn't I say that earlier?" He laughed.

Why didn't Sammie show up to rescue my heart?

" Kyle, you're too much." I lowered my chin and smiled in a flirtatious way. "I'm sure you know that, right?"

"No, I don't know anything." He licked his lips. "Hopefully, I'm not too much for you."

Oh Lord, what he is doing. I started to walk in the direction of my family. "Kyle, I can't thank you enough for being here for me during this tough time in my life." While walking, I paused and looked over my shoulder, before lifting my hand, signaling Kyle to follow me. He walked forward, we stood facing one another, motionlessly. I pinched his left cheek and said, "I want you to hang around for a little while, if that's okay?"

He jumped and landed with a skipping motion as he propelled his body forward like a slingshot, then he leaned in to hug me. "You got it Sophia."

Before replying, I turned around to embrace the sounds of leaves being crushed. My cousin Janet walked up, pointing to Kyle. "Who is this, Sophia?"

Why does she have that skintight dress on? Her butt is so much bigger than mine too. She's never had negro hair like me because she's mixed. She's so beautiful. I hope Kyle doesn't meet my cousin and forget about me. I glanced at Kyle. Good, his eyes appear to be fixated on me. I pointed to Kyle as he shook Janet's hand. "This is my friend Kyle."

Kyle and I were side by side, and Janet was standing in front of him.

Janet stood back in her legs, twisting her body to display her rear end. She perked up her full lips. "Wow, he's a cutie."

Kyle blushed. "Janet, thank you for the compliment. And, nice to meet you too."

I grimaced. Did he just blush?

While fiercely staring at Janet with an indignant gaze, I rotated my eyes to my left, in Kyle's direction. "Don't blow his head up Janet, it's already big enough," I said.

"Kyle, do you mind if I borrow Sophia for a second?" Janet asked.

Kyle waved his hands to gesture that he didn't care. "No, go right ahead," said Kyle as he placed his hands inside his pockets.

Janet pulled me aside and said, "Sophia, you can tell me if that's your boyfriend?"

He's mine, Janet, so stop asking about him. I tossed my hands into the air then placed my hands on my hips while my legs shook like I was having a seizure. "Nah, he's not my man Janet."

"If you don't want him, then I'll get to know him," Janet said.

I knew it. "Heck no!"

Janet twirled her unmatched physique in front of Kyle. She bent over and pushed her hips out while looking back at Kyle. Then, she stood up while looking at me. "I think you like him more than you're willing to admit."

Before I had a chance to respond to her statement, I observed Kyle approaching. "Sophia, I need to go but I wanted to show you something first. It'll only take a second or two," Kyle said.

I stared at Janet and smiled with a feeling of vindication. "Okay, what do you want to show me?" Take that, heifer.

He nodded his head in the direction of his car. "It's in my car. Do you mind walking to my car with me?"

"No, I don't mind." I blushed. "I can use a little walk to clear my mind anyway."

We walked toward Kyle's car. Along the way I looked back and winked at Janet. *That's right heifer, keep them arms folded, I'm winning him and not you.*

***

My Mind Spoke Too Soon:
Your Heart Usually Corrects Your Mind's Errors

I stood behind Kyle as he opened the door of his Mustang. Subsequently, he reached inside of the backseat to grab something.

I tried to peek over his shoulders. I couldn't see what he grabbed, but whatever it was, it seemed intriguing.

Kyle handed me a gift that was neatly wrapped.

Surprised, I asked, "Kyle, what's this?" I opened my hands as he placed the gift in my hands.

Kyle squeezed his lips and leaned against his car. "It's just a little something I put together for you."

I smiled and asked, "Can I open it now?"

He waved his hands side-to-side, saying, "No—no, wait until later when you get back home."

I shook the gift and placed it to my ears. "Okay! Are you going to stick around?"

He pushed his body off the car. "No, I can't. I'm sorry, I really want to stay but I need to get back to Marin County. And your family is in town, I don't want you to be distracted with trying to entertain me."

"You aren't a distraction, Kyle. I'm really happy you're here," I said.

He blushed. "Thank you, but I really need to leave soon. I have some things to address back home. Nancy did some crazy stuff and I need to help her out."

I dropped his gift and frowned. "Nancy! I thought you were done with her?"

He picked up the gift and attempted to hand it to me, but I pushed his hand away.

"I am done with Nancy," Kyle said.

I held my hands up and sighed. "If you're done with her then why are you trying to help her?"

"Sophia, none of that should concern you right now. Besides, you and I are just friends anyway. So, why are you jealous?" He extended his gift to me again.

True. I snatched my gift away from Kyle while rolling my eyes. "I am not jealous." He doesn't know my blood is boiling on the inside. *I can't believe he would come to my mom's funeral and then leave to go help Nancy.*

Kyle placed his right hand over his mouth and coughed, indicating that he was still waiting for my reply.

I held my finger up to indicate that I was thinking, then I walked toward the front of his car. I shouldn't be jealous, since I was frank with him when I said there was no future for us. I don't know if I'm just vulnerable because of my mom's death, but I'm really feeling something special for Kyle right now. I placed my gift on the hood of his car. "Kyle, be safe on the road."

Kyle grabbed me, pulling me into his arms. I surrendered to the scent of his cologne as he massaged my upper arms. The gentle pressure from his touch gave me goosebumps. Without hesitation, Kyle leaned in and gently kissed me on my right cheek. *That was smooth.* I blushed.

Our bodies detached as the chemistry I felt fought to pull me back into his arms. He reached into his pocket to grab a small piece of paper. "Here's my number. Make sure you use it," he said.

I grinned while looking back to see if Janet was still within the vicinity. Good, she's gone. I looked at Kyle and said, "Okay, I will."

Kyle entered his car and held the door open, in a seated position he said, "Promise me you won't open your gift until later tonight."

I glanced at my gift. "You're really serious about me waiting to open this gift, aren't you?"

He winked at me while licking his lips. "Yep, that's correct, beautiful."

Kyle started the car, then drove away as the engine roared. A part of me felt empty watching him disappear into the sun.

After a minute, I turned around and walked back to my mom's grave, only to witness my aunts' staring at me with big smiles.

Doris approached me, showing all her pearly whites. "Girl, looks like you have a keeper."

I stood in front of them in silence. I really wanted to discuss Sammie. Now, I don't know what to think.

"Is that the boy who you wanted to get my advice on?" Doris asked.

"Uh, don't worry about it now," I said.

She twisted her lips then crossed her arms. "Are you sure?"

I nodded my head. "Yes, I am. I think God just answered my question."

An hour later, we wrapped up everything at the burial site as we said our final good-byes. Minutes later, we returned to my house for the repast. Everyone was eating together and socializing.

I looked around at the repast.

A few hours later, my family started to depart. My dad's two brothers said goodbye with hugs and kisses. I thanked everyone for their support before escorting my final guests to their cars, then I reentered my home and closed the door. While leaning against the door, I said out loud, "I can't wait to open Kyle's gift." After I freshen up, I'm going to prepare a peanut butter and jelly sandwich with strawberry jelly, and then I'll open his gift. I rubbed my hands together. "I can't wait!"

I entered the bathroom and prepared for a hot shower.

Chapter 10:
Unwrap Your Gift

I turned the water off then stepped out of the shower. There's nothing like a hot shower. I know it's going to be an uphill battle, but I'm going to try my best to cope with the loss of my mom. I dried off with a towel then put a nightgown on.

After exiting the bathroom, I walked into the living room, picking up Kyle's gift. I stared at it for a few seconds. Stop the foolishness and just open the gift. I sat down, then slowly unwrapped my gift's decorative pieces. As the blue ribbons fell to the floor, the box's opening was exposed. I glanced at the lid of the box, hesitating to open it. A few seconds later, I finally removed the lid to look inside. I carefully removed each item. Hmm. A long letter, Bible, and a box of chocolate. I smiled as my teeth shined brightly like the rising sun.

I can't wait to read his letter. I'm really impressed with the Bible. It has my name embroidered on it. I unwrapped the box of chocolate then tasted a piece. This piece of chocolate is pretty darn good. While smiling, I leaned back on the couch, placing Kyle's letter over my heart. He remembered that I have a sweet tooth. I held the letter in front of my eyes as I thought, *time to read this letter.*

Dear Sophia,

I really enjoyed the weekend we shared together. I wish our weekend together could've lasted forever. You are the first person to make me feel new inside. Simply put, you force my heart to embrace my sensitive side. If you recall the moment when I began to tell you everything about my mom during our ride to The Blues Café, it was then I knew I didn't want you to leave or go away. If I could have done anything to convince you to stay, I would 've done it repeatedly—until I convinced your heart to stay with me forever—and all day.

I paused, then tears formed in my eyes. His words are beautiful.

Before I met you, I was somewhat enlightened but now I am truly free. I see a future with you, a future that beholds true love between you and me. I know you may not see what I do right now, but if you give me a few months, I 'll change your mind—one kiss at a time.

I know you 're attached to Sammie but believe me Sophia, your presence impacted my heart and foisted upon me a double whammy. You might think that true love for you is inseparable without Sammie, but I can promise you that 's a myth. My heart is crying out for you right now, it 's you who I miss. My heart is eagerly but shyly amiss as it cries out for just one more kiss. You are my new sensation that give 's my heart true bliss. I pray my letter isn 't emotionally dismissed.

I laughed. "He doesn't mention what the double whammy is, I guess he just thought that that part sounded good." I smirked. "I like the rhymes, though."

If you 're experiencing any doubts about me, please allow me to assist your heart in unlocking your heart 's fist. You 're so guarded Sophia until I can 't find any room to enlist my vision into your loving hands. I promise you if you give me a real chance, I 'll take you up high to a heavenly romance. If you would be so kind to give Kyle and Sophia a chance, your thoughts of another man will only be that of a dissipating glance.

I truly adore who you are and there 's something very special about you, I just know in my heart you 're going to be a star. You have a way of raising the bar to a status that leaves a permanent imprint like a scar. No matter how far away you are, no one in their right mind would remove a moment shared with you from their mind. My heart is glued to getting to know you. I feel you are necessary like someone's spine. I have to say this though: You are the one who has drawn the line.

Sophia, just this once can you please erase your boundaries by coming to see me this weekend. I am not going to even pretend like I don't like you; I want you and it's as simple as that my friend.

Love Kyle,

The End.

Call me anytime (666) 666-6666.

I scanned over the letter again while propping my feet onto the coffee table. "That was really beautiful." I'm in total shock. I didn't know Kyle could write like this. His words were so profound. I felt his heart beating inside my brain after reading his words. I placed my feet back on the wooden floors while staring at my home's foyer, allowing my guilt of liking someone other than Sammie to exit my heart's door. I stood up and adjusted my bra, then shook Kyle's letter while looking at it. "This letter has earned him a surprise visit from me."

I stood, paralyzed by Kyle's creativity. "Kyle really is a romantic guy." I'm trying to figure out why he feels so strongly about me when we barely know one another, though. I do feel something different about our chemistry, but I still barely know him. I reread the last sentence in his letter, then my heart of love expanded inside my chest. Is it possible to like or even love two guys? I know I can't be with both, so I must decide which one I want to be with. I slapped my forehead. "I sound so stupid." Sammie isn't pursuing me like Kyle is, he isn't going the extra mile to be with me in the same way. I moved around in a circle. Sammie did try and find me at the hospital, though. Maybe Sammie and I aren't meant to be.

I put Kyle's items back in the box, before placing his gift on the coffee table. Subsequently, I walked upstairs and prepared for bed.

While lying in bed I thought to myself. Kyle has most certainly earned a visit from me this weekend. Hmm. What should I wear? I'll surprise him with my red dress that I bought a few weeks ago. I still haven't had a chance to wear it. I might introduce my red dress to the world this weekend. Kyle doesn't know we're going to attend the same university either. I'll complete my registration process for college Friday morning, then I'll go visit Kyle. Today is Wednesday, so I have a couple of days to get myself together.

I rubbed my stomach and thought to myself, I should be able to lose these two pounds of fat by then. I've accumulated a little extra weight from my bad eating since my mom passed. It's so hard to eat healthy when you're depressed.

***

Kyle, Here I Come

The Next Day

I woke up from my alarm clock sounding off, then rolled out of bed, feeling restless. While stretching my arms, I reached for my toes, loosening the stiffness in my lower back. After stretching, I sat down, running my hands through my hair. Despite my current emotional state, I must admit the thought of going to visit Kyle is really getting me excited. I stood up and twisted my torso, rotating my neck like a steering wheel. Then, I opened my blinds, the sun rushing in like a tsunami. While holding my hand over my forehead to help block the sun's beaming rays, I spoke out loud: "I'm calling Kyle right now."

I turned around and headed to the bathroom to prepare myself for the day. After I finished, I walked downstairs to the kitchen and paused, then walked into the living room to pick up Kyle's letter. I reentered the kitchen, lifting the house phone from the kitchen wall. While the phone cord dangled like a slinky, I looked at Kyle's letter, entering each digit of his telephone number with growing excitement. My fingers started to perspire as I envisioned Kyle holding me inside his muscular arms.

My heart boiled like a pot filled with hot water. I eagerly listened to his phone line ring. Each ring increased my heart rate like I was walking up a flight of stairs.

"Hello, who is this?" Kyle asked.

I twirled the phone cord, wrapping it around my right index finger. "Don't act like you don't recognize my voice, silly," I said.

"Ha, okay. You're right. I know this is you, Sophia."

I smiled, placing my hands over my mouth to contain my excitement. "I opened your gift, and I read your letter. You're quite the poet."

"That might be true, but only when I meet the right person," Kyle said.

My fingers stroked the telephone cord. "The right person, huh?" I blushed while leaning against the wall.

He breathed gently into the phone. "You know we all have a side to ourselves that only the right person can draw out."

"I hear you. Well, I just called to let you know I read your letter. I might come visit you this weekend. I plan on coming to Marin County tomorrow. I have some business to address in Marin anyway."

I listened to him chuckle. "Sophia, you don't have to pretend like you need to come back here for some business. You can just tell me that you are coming to visit me."

He probably just licked those luscious lips. "Nah—I really have some business to address tomorrow in Marin County."

"Oh okay, what type of business do you have to address tomorrow?" Kyle asked.

I uncrossed my legs while using my left hand to run my fingers through my hair like a lawn mower. "You're a nosy little fart, aren't you?"

"I see someone has jokes," Kyle replied.

I grinned. "I like to joke sometimes, you know."

"No, I don't know. But you can educate me in person."

Smooth. "Sounds like you're begging for me to come see you?"

"Correct! I am definitely begging for you to come see me this weekend," Kyle said.

"If it's meant to be, I guess it'll happen, right?" I have to play the game.

He breathed softly then replied, "Oh, it's meant, believe that!"

"Okay, we shall see, Mr. Confident." His voice sounds so sexy.

"It's not confidence, baby, I just know what I know. By the way, how are you feeling anyway? Are you holding up, okay?"

"Thanks for checking on me. Yeah, I am holding up the best way I know how."

Kyle softened his tone. "I've been praying for you, too. When you come to visit me this weekend, you will have a chance to take your mind off a few things."

"You meant if I come. I need to go now, my friend. I have some things I need to get back to."

"Okay, you're welcome. I hope to see you soon," Kyle said.

"Okay, bye-bye," I said. I hung up then faced the wall while placing my hands on the kitchen wall near the phone. Images of Sammie trying his hardest to run normally by my side, suddenly overwhelmed my mind. I envisioned his contorted limbs, pushing against the breeze of the midnight forest. I smiled. Sammie always looked so cute with his little limp-leg.

I pushed myself off the kitchen wall then poured a glass of orange juice, sipping on it as I thought out loud. "I think I did a good job of building anticipation for our visit this weekend." I can't seem to get his melodious words out of my heart. Kyle's a very talented writer. I bet he can probably write me a beautiful song to sing.

I sat down at the kitchen table to reread Kyle's letter. I really need to start practicing and focusing on my audition in December. I also need to write a song that I plan to sing for the audition. What should I write a song about? I got it. I'll write a song called, The Blues Café. But what will The Blue's Café be about? I could write a song about my experience at The Blues Café when I saw Sammie. I think I will do that. I stood and shuffled my feet like a Latin dancer. "The Blues Café will make people want to dance."

I danced my way out of the kitchen then walked upstairs to grab a pen and notepad. I sat down on the edge of my bed. I can feel it right now—this song is going to be a major hit. While holding a notepad in my hand, with a clean sheet of paper awaiting my touch, I said out loud, "Okay, 'The Blues Café,' where do we begin?"

The words to the song began to flow into my soul. I scribbled on the paper to ensure the pen had ink in it.

The Blues Café

My best memories are trapped inside his scent. My heart felt like we were meant to be.

If only I'd known our moments shared together weren't meant to last forever. I thought our coming together was meant to be forever. I know your presence was heavenly sent. I can't stop thinking about when we were together.

What happened to the times we never spent? I didn't know one day we would find each other again the same way we did when we were friends. We both just seemed to blend-in with the rhythm in our hearts.

I owe it all to a special day that brought us back together at The Blues Café. I should've known the day I saw my love again with a new friend, that our past was no longer his heart's home. What do you do when your feelings aren't gone, and someone else fills your love's zone.

How do you cope when your future is your past and your feelings are stuck moving fast through your heart's future, that doesn't seem like it will last. The night I saw my love again at The Blues Café, I watched him dance his way into another woman's heart while throwing mine away.

It's the music in your heart that feels the spark. Dance to the rhythm of love the moment it starts. Just let love show you the way, the same way it did with my heart at The Blues Café.

I owe it all to a special day that brought us back together at The Blues Café. I should've known the day I saw my love again with a new friend, that our past was no longer his heart's home. What do you do when your feelings aren't gone, and someone else fills your love's zone.

Music was our spark, it united us in the forest when we first met. I knew then that our love was set. I didn't know a special café would one day place a bet that we would one day reunite through music, to dance our way back together through the music within our hearts. I owe it all to one special day that brought us back together at The Blues Café.

You were my air, I was your vent, we needed one another like a clue does to a hint. I wish we could run together again in the forest where we first met, where true love was set on catching our love in its net. I still love you the same way I did when we first met.

I owe it all to a special day, that brought us back together at The Blues Café. I should've known the day I saw my love again with a new friend, that our past was no longer his heart's home.

What do you do when your feelings aren't gone, but someone else has filled your love's zone?

I dropped my pen. I was teary-eyed after finishing my song, and my tears dropped on the paper like a slow drizzle. I was exhausted from working on The Blues Café and singing its beautiful melody. Within seconds, I quiescently fell backward onto the comfort of my bed; less than a minute later I was fast asleep.

***

A Few Hours Later

I opened my eyes as the sun beamed on my face. I sat up and stretched my lower back once again.

"I can't believe I was able to stay asleep as long as I did, especially with the sun shining in my room."

While standing, I started to meditate on the things I needed to do.

I really need to get back into reading my Bible daily. Besides, there's nothing stopping me from doing my Bible reading right now. I walked toward my bedroom window, peering through the lens of nature. "What a beautiful day outside."

After I finished reading the Bible, I brushed my teeth, washed my face, and packed my clothes. I can't wait to take a shower and go visit my mom's gravesite. I want to see if they have put her tombstone down. I still feel like I should have her purported suicide investigated. I should call John Proctor; I still have his card. I bet he will be able to get to the bottom of what happened to my mom. I exhaled. Dr. Peterson's behavior—along with everyone else at the facility—was kind of suspicious. The fact that Billy Joe's father might own the facility really bothers me too. I must seek justice for my mom, which will most likely lead to justice for Timmy too. I can't believe the police department didn't even try to find my brother's killer. I just know Billy Joe killed my brother. If it wasn't for Mr. Proctor looking out for me, I don't know what would have happened to me. Maybe I shouldn't be wary of Mr. Proctor, he's just trying to help me out.

A few minutes later, I searched for Mr. Proctor's card. It should be in my purse. "I can't find it anywhere." I must've misplaced it. I probably dropped it in the taxi during that night.

Chapter 11:
Committed Decisions

An Hour Later

After I took a shower, I cooked green beans with a small chicken breast. Caught up in my thoughts about my mother, I pondered: I can't help but think of the many times when my mom used to say, "Sophia, you're going to make a guy really happy one day." I placed the chicken inside the oven.

Despite the adversities my mom and dad experienced together as a couple; I still believe their problems came from not putting God first in their lives. My brother used to study God's Word with me once a week. He learned a lot of information from this elderly couple. They came to our house once a week to study the Bible with him. My parents were impressed with Timmy's decision to study the Bible. The people who studied with him were Jehovah's Witnesses. My mom used to attend, but she stopped, and she never said why. She never became a witness, even though the Witnesses' were always so nice and pleasant.

I always wondered why they took such a sagacious interest in preaching to people when people were so mean to them in return. I don't think I could have dealt with the ridicule and harsh treatment they endure. I have always respected the Witnesses' for their evangelic spirit. They really helped Timmy to understand the Bible, which is why I asked him to study the Bible with me. I wanted to be wise and smart, like my brother, so I started to play close attention to some of the things he did.

While stirring green beans in a skillet, I continued to cerebrate. Some things I noticed were that he exercised, read, and monitored his associations. I paused while unsuccessfully attempting to thwart a single tear drop from falling. I burned my right elbow after accidentally bumping into the skillet. "Ouch!" I quickly pulled my arm away like a released trigger.

I sighed while running cold water from the faucet onto my elbow.

***

The Next Day

I exited through the front door of my house, then locked the door. My sky blue warm up suit blended in with the earth's morning sky. While walking to my car, I thought, *I was going to travel to Marin County via a bus, but I think I'd rather take my car instead.*

I drove to a nearby gas station to fill up. While there, a group of White guys started to yell from a black pick-up truck. "Hey, little lady in that red dress, you're looking mighty fine," said a young man in the passenger side. He was a blonde haired, chubby guy.

I looked over my left shoulder. Guys are so predictable. "Thank you. I'm just trying to pump my gas and hit the road."

Another guy approached. His walk dragged as his ego shined through in his body language. He leaned on the trunk of my wagon then stepped forward and said, "Oh no, sweetie. Step aside, let me pump your gas for you." He smiled. "You're too gorgeous to be pumping gas."

These men are something else. "Okay, have at it," I said.

After he finished, he asked, "Do you have a pen and paper?"

I displayed a perturbed countenance. "Why?"

"I want to give you my number, so you can call me sometime."

No way. "Do you live in San Francisco?" I asked.

"No, I live in Marin County." He placed the pump back on its latch, then tightened my gas cap. "My name is Ronnie by the way."

I pretended to be disappointed through my facial expression. "That's just too bad because I was going to ask you out on a date tonight." I walked around toward the driver's side of my car.

He opened the door for me, then I got inside. "Thanks. I have to get out of here, though." He tossed his hands into the air, shrugging his shoulders before walking away.

As the men departed, the driver honked the horn. They're so obnoxious.

Less than a minute later, I decided to walk into the store to purchase a coke. I liked to drink a soda while I drove, it relaxed my mind.

After I exited the store, I walked back to my car to observe John Proctor pumping gas. I was shocked to see him. "What a coincidence." I was elated to see him. I never found his card.

While John's back was turned away from me, I approached, then tapped him on his right shoulder. He turned around, slightly startled. "Hello, Mr. Proctor, how are you?" I asked.

"Sophia, it's so good to see you." While still holding the gas pump, he hugged me with his left arm while patting me on the back. "I am fine. Uh, it looks like you're headed out of town?" John asked.

"Yes, I am. How did you know?" I asked.

He shrugged his shoulders while reattaching the pump to its station. "I can just tell."

I hesitated. "Uh, okay." I should just tell him about my concerns while he's here with me right now. I took a deep breath. "You know, I'm still suspicious Mr. Proctor."

"About what?" he asked.

"About my mom's death. Uh, I am glad I ran into you, because I lost your card. Can we chat right now, if you have a moment?"

John faced me with his midnight black suit, crumbled in the shoulder area. "Yes, I have a few minutes." He reached into his left coat pocket to hand me another card.

I took the card. "Thanks."

John held his right hand as a shield over his forehead while the sun flooded his face with brightness. He pointed to his left while walking forward. "Follow me, there's a park about two minutes away. That way, we won't be as compromised," said John.

"Okay, that's fine." While following Proctor, I contemplated my suspicions.

I noticed something different on my mom's medicine sheet when I looked at it the last time the doctor changed her medicine. I had some time to research the medicine. The medicine had some bad side effects, such as suicidal thoughts. My mom was trying to tell me that she felt like they were giving her some medicine that was harmful for her, but I just didn't listen.

Less than two minutes later, we arrived at the park. I pulled up next to Mr. Proctor, positioning my wagon to his right. John rolled the passenger side of his window down, signaling for me to get inside his car. "Hey, Sophia, come hop in my car."

I killed my engine. The sounds of my engine ceasing its spark faded into the serenity of the park's atmosphere. While the birds chirped, I opened the door, then walked to John's car. "Here I come." I opened the passenger side of his car and got inside.

John placed his hands on the steering wheel and asked, "What suspicions do you have regarding your mom's death?"

I glanced at John, then looked straight forward. "A few days before my mom passed away, I went to visit her, and she mentioned that the staff at the hospital was trying to harm her. She said she wanted to leave the facility because she didn't feel safe there anymore. I didn't think much of it at the time. I just thought that maybe she was experiencing one of her psychotic spells. But she insisted she wasn't crazy. She was adamant about the doctors misdiagnosing her on purpose. She told me she was just sad about my dad and brother's death. My mom also mentioned that my dad was having an affair, which did gravely affect her. I think that was the real reason behind her misrepresented emotions."

John scratched his chin. "Interesting … continue."

I sighed, adjusting my posture in order to face John. "During our last visit, my mom told the guard she didn't want to see me." John lifted his hand, attempting to intervene. I countered and said, "Wait! So—so, she changed her mind right before I left, though. It was very strange, Mr. Proctor."

He rubbed his left eyebrow. "Sophia, where are you going with all of this? What exactly are you trying to insinuate?"

"I think the doctor changed my mom's medication to make her have psychotic spells. I think the doctor cleverly coerced my mom into suicide. I think she gradually increased my mom's dosage to a point where she would experience suicidal hallucinations that seemed real—forcing her to interpret death as a viable option to escape her misery."

John listened intently.

" Also, I overheard one of the workers' yell out to me, telling me to cremate my mom when I ran out of the hospital, after Dr. Peterson broke the news to me. The worker that yelled out to me said, 'That's what she would have wanted'. I remember my mom telling me that she never wanted to be cremated."

He twisted his lips while nodding his head. "That is strange," said John.

"I would like an autopsy done on my mom to see if she had medications in her bloodstream that weren't necessary. Whenever someone hangs themself, it normally breaks your neck, but I didn't see any wrings around her neck when I went to I.D. her body. So, I'm interested to know if there's any evidence supporting that. I want to know my mom's official cause of death. I wouldn't be surprised if it wasn't from hanging herself." I vehemently sighed while staring at John.

He looked forward then turned his attention to me. "Normally, I would say your suspicion is a bit much. I think I believe you, though. That facility has been accused of mistreating African Americans for a while now. Also, there have been five other suspicious deaths of you colored folks at that facility over the past five years." He frowned. "I'll start on this investigation right away. I'll have to contact the FBI too. I think this is something they will be interested in."

Hmm. That's kind of strange, the way he just said colored folks. For a second, he sounded kind of racist. I'm sure he didn't mean anything by his words, though. "Thanks, Mr. Proctor. I really appreciate all that you're doing for me and my family."

"I am really sorry that colored people have to experience so much injustice, simply because of the color of their skin. It's pathetic how evil some people are in this world. It's unimaginable for me to even cogitate doing some of the things I've witnessed," said John.

"Do you think you can convince the FBI to investigate one of their own, regarding my brother's death as well? His killer was never brought to justice. The police didn't even try to find his killer. Rumor is, the person who killed my brother worked for the police department back in Marin County, and it's the same person that arrested me."

"Who, Billy Joe?" John asked.

"Yep!"

"I'll look into trying to contact the right people to reopen your brother's case. I can't make any promises on your brother's case, though, since it's out of my jurisdiction. However, I know some people here in San Francisco who are interested in taking down the facility where your mom was. I will send her body to another lab in another state to ensure no bias is involved. It's going to take a little money to get these projects done, especially exhuming your mom's grave. I have to get permission from the governor in order to execute that process. That shouldn't be a problem, though. The governor is a good guy, and I know him personally." Abruptly, he turned his attention to my dress. "And what are you all dressed up for?"

I smiled. "I'm going back to Marin County. I'm registering for college today. And I'm going to see a guy I like—his name is Kyle." I blushed as my voice elevated. "He claims that he likes me a lot."

"I think you like him, too, if you're willing to drive an hour and some change to see him. Where are you going for college?" John asked.

"The University of Marin County."

He slapped his forehead. "Duh, right! Ha. That makes perfect sense. Have fun and be safe. Uh, let's meet up one month from now on Wednesday. I'll have an update for you then."

He extended his right hand, and I shook it. "Okay, sounds good. Thanks so much, Mr. Proctor."

" You're welcome."

I walked to my car. I feel like I am finally about to receive justice for my brother. I don't really know what to think of my mom's situation, because I don't know if I have a valid point just yet. I have to wait until Mr. Proctor completes his investigation. It's interesting that five other Black families had one of their loved ones die in a mysterious way at the same facility.

Mr. Proctor drove away as I slid down the driver's door of my car. As soon as my butt hit the pavement, tears fell onto my face. If only I had listened to her, she probably would still be alive. Seconds later, Proctor returned and parked in the same spot. I guess he saw me wallowing in my misery in his rearview mirror.

"Sophia, are you alright?"

"I'm good, don't worry." I looked up at him and asked, "Do you think I made my mom feel like she couldn't talk to me?"

"I don't know, Sophia. I think it's best if you don't speculate." He exited his car and approached me. He extended his hands and said, "Sophia, let me help you up."

I got up, drying my tears. "I do need to hit the road. I have a lot of stuff to do before 3 p.m. What time is it right now?" I asked.

He glanced at his wristwatch. "It's almost noon."

I dusted residue from the pavement off my buttocks. "Thanks, Mr. Proctor. I'll see you in a month."

"That's correct, my friend. I feel like you need a big hug. Come here, let me give you one." John said.

"Yes, I could use a hug right now. Thanks."

While we hugged, memories of my father running through the woods during the night Timothy was shot raced through my mind like a stampede of wildebeests.

A few seconds later, Proctor stepped into his car and drove away, then I entered my wagon and meditated for two minutes before starting the engine. *Kyle and Marin County, here I come.*

***

Life is Unpredictable

While driving on the interstate, I mulled over the things that had recently transpired.

I felt like my conversation with Mr. Proctor was productive and necessary. I glanced at my watch. I'm about forty-five-minutes away from Marin County. I should practice on The Blues Café a little while I am driving. I don't know all the words just yet, but I know the chorus. I pushed a dangling strand of hair away from my eyes. I wonder what Kyle is doing right now? I smiled. If we had kids, what would their names be? If I had a little girl, I want her name to be Isabella. Izzy would be her nickname. Hmm, Isabella Coleman or Isabella Walker? I laughed to myself, contemplating having a baby with a man who wasn't even my boyfriend, let alone my husband.

Forty minutes later, I arrived at Marin County University. "Wow, the school is really nice." *I love the modern appeal of the buildings.* I drove around, observing the university's beauty. *I can't wait until January, when I can start investing into my future.*

While driving through the campus, I saw a sign pointing toward the visitors parking lot and followed the arrows. After parking, I pulled out my makeup kit and looked into the mirror, redoing it. Look at this.

A few minutes later, I exited the car, then looked around like a lost child. I wonder where the admissions office is located.

I observed a middle-aged, White male approaching in a golf cart. Maybe he can help me. I stepped in front of the cart. "Excuse me. Do you know where the admissions office is?"

He sat back in the cart with sunglasses on while caressing his Santa Claus-like beard. A soft-spoken frequency exited his mouth. "Yes, it's right over there." He pointed toward his right. I looked in the direction where he pointed. "It's right over there by that gray building to your left," the man said.

"Okay, thank you."

I happily proceeded toward the building. While walking, I started to sweat around my forehead. I can't wait to see Kyle's reaction when he finds out I'll be going here too.

***

Life is Full of Surprises

After meeting with a college adviser, I scheduled my courses, then made my way to the cashier's building. While walking, I enjoyed the pristine look of the campus along with its horticultural appeal.

I look forward to the times when I can experience the full college experience. I'm taking eighteen credit hours this coming semester. I entered the building and sounds of several college students flooded my eardrums like a train crossing over railroad tracks. I walked around in the building, observing a crowd that was predominately White. *I have to get used to this.* I located my destination. *There's the line to pay for my tuition.* I entered a medium-sized line. I couldn't help but notice the guy at the front of the line. I stood on the tip of my toes to achieve a better view. His back was facing me, but he looked kind of familiar.

My thoughts were interrupted by someone bumping into me.

"Hey, watch where you're going," said a tall, young White man.

I turned around to face him. "I'm sorry, I didn't see you," I said. Suddenly, I'm struck by his broad shoulders, blonde hair, and blue eyes. Wow, he looks a lot like Sammie. He's just a little shorter. I glanced at his posture as he aggressively stepped forward into my personal space. He even has a similar limp-leg like Sammie.

"What do you mean, you didn't see me? Are you blind?" He asked.

I remained silent.

As the guy continued to make a big deal out of our incident, a White security guard walked up, asking, "Hey, is everything okay?"

The guy I bumped into pointed at me and said, "No sir! This rude woman bumped into me, and she did it on purpose."

I was afraid and confused as I held my hands up and said, "That's not true!"

"This is why segregation is a good thing." He formed a fist then pointed it at me. "We don't need people like her at this school anyway. Her kind doesn't have home training," said the young White male.

"Wait, what are you trying to say?" I asked.

He chuckled while frowning like an evil snake. "I said exactly what I mean!"

Through my peripheral vision, I noticed the guy that looked familiar walking my way.

The unidentified man approached. "Sophia!"

I glanced at the White guy I was debating with before turning around to the familiar voice. "Kyle!" *I love that red short-sleeve shirt he has on. He looks like the American flag with those blue jeans on. His jeans even have a touch of white in them.*

Kyle stepped in front of the guy who was harassing me. Kyle frowned as he bit his lips. He clenched his fists with a readiness to strike, spit flying from his mouth. "Hey dude, I don't know what your problem is, but I would back off if I were you!" Kyle looked at the vanguard. "Mr. Security, are you just going to stand here why this bum continues to say racist things to her? She's trying her best to diffuse the situation, but this clown is adamant about continuing a petty argument," Kyle said.

The White guy fostered forth more bigotry, pointing at Kyle while saying, "Here is another one. Let me guess, you got into this school because of some special laws for negros?" He chuckled. "I don't know why you all are so insistent on coming to places where you don't belong!"

Kyle charged at the guy, but the guard grabbed him and said, "Son, don't let this fool ruin your career."

The guard was able to calm Kyle down. The guard turned toward the White guy and said, "I'm going to have to ask you to leave! Just come back during another time."

"I am not going anywhere! I'll have you fired if you try to make me leave," said the young, White man.

The guard replied, "Son, I can assure you that my job is secure. However, I don't know if you'll be attending this school if you don't listen to me. I suggest you get out of this line and walk away now."

The rude guy walked backwards as several onlookers stared. He tossed his fists into the air and said, "I'll be seeing you Blacks' again, or should I say colored folks?" He laughed. "Do you have a preference?"

The guard grabbed him by the back of his right arm. "That's it, you're coming with me young man! I can guarantee you—you won't be attending this university next semester."

"Oh yeah, we will see about that since my father is the University's President."

"Well, you might be able to wiggle your way out of this situation, but we have a crowd of witnesses in here," said the guard.

He waved his arms around like a machine gun hitting all its targets. "You think my fellow Americans are going to turn on me and be witnesses for these two monkeys? You might want to readjust your thinking, Mr. Security Guard. I bet you only have a tenth-grade education, anyway, from some lower-class school."

One of the faculty members walked up with a police officer and another guy.

A strong manly voice filled the auditorium. "Jimmy, what's your problem? Why are you acting like this with these students?" Jimmy looked surprised. "Jimmy, you're embarrassing me. Where did you learn such hatred from, anyway? I didn't raise you to be a racist!"

"Dad, you're a sellout," said Jimmy.

Jimmy faced his father, a man about the same build and height as him. "My grandpa told me you were a big wimp—and now I believe him. Dad, can't you see that these colored people' are trying to take over all of the things that were meant for us fine White folks to have?" He spat in Kyle's direction.

Kyle held me and frowned.

Jimmy's father looked around then placed his hands on his son's shoulders while saying, "Son, apologize to these kids right now. Or, I'm going to have to expel you from the university for good."

He laughed. "What! Are you serious? Dad, I am your son for crying out loud," said Jimmy.

"Yes, and you obviously need some help. I love you, son, but you're out of line right now. I'm going to call your grandpa today and tell him to keep his poisonous ideologies to himself."

Jimmy was angry. "They're bad people, Dad, and you know I'm right!"

"Son, do you believe in God?" Jimmy's father asked.

"Yes, I do. I believe that God loves White people more than any other race!"

"Son, Acts 20:35 says, 'God is not partial but the man that fears him and works righteous is acceptable to him'. 2Peter 3:9 says, 'God isn't slow respecting his promises but he's patient with us because he doesn't desire anyone to be destroyed. God desires us all to attain to repentance.'" Jimmy's dad removed his hands from Jimmy's shoulders. "John 3:16 says, 'God loved the world so much that he gave his only begotten son and whoever exercises faith in him might not be destroyed but have everlasting life'. God loves us all the same. The Bible doesn't say that Jesus died only for White people. God's Word says that Jesus died for the whole world'."

Jimmy scoffed. "If God looked at us as equals, then why does the majority of the world feel the way that I do?"

"The world is twisted. Now tell this kind young lady here and her friend that you're sorry." Jimmy's father turned around to face Kyle and Sophia. His father extended his hand to Kyle. "Hey, I am Micah Sullivan. I'm the President at this university. What's your name, young lady?"

My lips quivered as I stuttered. "My name is Sophie." I'm shocked, another White man is standing up for me.

"You mean Sophia," said Kyle.

"Yes!" I glanced at Kyle then looked at Micah. "Thanks Kyle. I'm sorry, my name is Sophia, Mr. President."

"Nice to meet you two." Micah looked at Kyle. "And your name is obviously Kyle." Kyle nodded his head. "What are you two majoring in?" Micah asked.

"I'm finishing up law school soon. I plan to become a Civil Rights lawyer," said Kyle.

"That's awesome young man. We obviously need a lot of that as you can see." Micah glanced at his son.

Micah turned his attention to Sophia. "What about you, young lady?"

"I'd rather not say, if that's okay," I said.

"Okay, I respect that." Micah looked over his right shoulder. "Jimmy, son, it's your turn to speak now."

Jimmy stormed toward the exit of the building, growling like an angry hyena. Before exiting he turned around and screamed, "Dad, you're a traitor and a nigger lover!"

***

A Date with Destiny

I walked away from the registrar's office thinking about the type of day I was experiencing.

What a day. I looked around to locate Kyle several feet away. Oh, he's finishing up his conversation with the President. Kyle looked in my direction and performed a hand gesture, indicating he wouldn't be much longer. I waved my hand in acknowledgement.

Seconds later, Kyle turned around to head my way. His height is to die for, and his muscles are crying out for me. I want Kyle to flex his biceps so I can touch his big muscles.

While standing near the exit door, I turned my back to Kyle while he continued walking my way. I quickly checked the status of my breath, then pulled a small towel out of my purse, patting my face to ensure that my makeup looked perfect. I reached into my purse to grab a mint, then tossed it into my mouth. Before I had a chance to process my thoughts, I felt a playful tap on my shoulder.

"I see you must really have a crush on me." Kyle smiled.

I fumbled my purse, dropping it on the floor. "Why do you say that?" I bent down, but Kyle intervened. He beat me to my purse. He handed it to me as I smiled.

"You followed me all the way to Marin County to attend College with me. There are a lot of universities you could've attended in San Francisco, but you just had to come here," said Kyle.

I laughed. "Kyle, I'd already planned to come to Marin University before we met. I didn't tell you the first time you told me you attended school here because—" I smirked. "Honestly, I don't know why."

Kyle placed his hands on my shoulder, guiding me in the direction he wanted to walk. "The lies you tell yourself. Just admit it, you wanted to be close to me," said Kyle.

I followed his lead while playfully slapping him on the right shoulder. "Boy hush, you are not all that."

"I beg to differ. I must be something, because you came down to see me."

"Correction, Mr. Cocky, I came down to take care of my errands and register for school."

"What errands? You just registered for school, so what other errands do you have to address now?"

I lifted my hands, bouncing them around like I was weighing something on a balance beam. "Just some other things I need to do, like catch up with some old friends." I should try and find Sammie while I'm out here. No, Sophia. You came here to spend the weekend with Kyle.

Kyle waved his hands in front of my face. "Sophia, snap out of it. You have been in a trance like stare for several seconds now. Are you okay?"

I shook my head and cleared my throat. "I'm sorry."

We paused our stroll then faced one another. I noticed a bench then sat down. "What was I saying again? Oh yeah, so I just need to run a few errands, then we can hang out."

While standing over me, Kyle said, "Sounds good to me. What a show earlier, huh? Jimmy was being rude to you. I was going to set him straight for you, but his daddy intervened. I'm happy he did, too because if he hadn't, I would definitely be in prison."

I smiled. "Let me guess; you were going to beat him up for me?" I asked.

"Yes, of course. He was being very rude to you," said Kyle.

Kyle sat down next to me—to my right.

"Oh yeah, is that so?" I asked.

Kyle smiled, placing his hands on my right thigh. He squeezed my thigh and said, "Yep!"

I crossed my right thigh over my left one. "How are you, Kyle?"

"I'm great. I didn't think you were going to actually come and see me." He looked me up and down. "You look very nice in your red dress. I didn't realize you had such a great body. Your body looks amazing, I was wondering why you dressed like a tomboy at first."

I giggled. "I can be a bit of a tomboy, but I do like to put on high heels, makeup, lipstick, and dresses sometimes too."

"You look great. You should dress like this all the time." He licked his lips. "I mean, you look amazing. Oh, and I cleaned up for you." He nudged me with his left hip. "I have the guest room ready for you."

I faced him. "Let me stop you right there, I'm getting a hotel. I think that's best."

"I am totally okay with you staying at a hotel, in fact I support your decision. I will just follow you back to your hotel after our date, just to make sure you made it back to your hotel safely."

"No way." I stood up then pulled my dress down while observing Kyle devouring me with his eyes. "I know what you are trying to do, and it's not going to work."

"Sophia, I don't know what your mind is thinking right now, but I'm definitely only interested in getting to know you. Nothing more." He pushed off the bench with his hands before standing upright. "What are you majoring in, by the way?"

"Music." I looked at him and replied while holding my purse across my left shoulder.

"Where did you park?" Kyle asked.

"In the visitor's parking lot."

"Do you want me to walk you to your car?"

"You don't have to. I'll just meet up with you later at your place." I tensed up while glancing to my right. I think I just saw someone walk past that reminds me of Sammie. Maybe it's just Jimmy? Seconds later, I started walking in the direction of the guy I observed.

"Okay, Sophia, sounds good." While standing behind me, Kyle grabbed my right hand, then said, "You're walking the wrong way."

That's because I'm walking in the direction of the guy that looks like Sammie. But it's not Sammie. He wouldn't be here.

Kyle pointed to his right. "Visitor's parking is over this way-- to your left."

"I know."

Kyle smiled. "Girl, get it together. I'll see you in a bit."

"Okay." I went north and Kyle walked south.

I leisurely strolled along toward my car.

I wonder what my specialty in music should be? I'm going to have to master a few instruments. I look forward to learning about the flute, violin, and guitar. I jumped, tensing up. I heard someone call my name. "Sophia!" Huh? Sounds like I heard someone calling my name. I turned around. From a distance, I saw a guy who appeared to be Jimmy. He looked anxious, like he wanted to tackle me or something. I don't want to end up like Timmy. I started walking faster. I was panting like a tiger as I created a bigger gap between me and my imminent threat. He probably wants to harm me from the incident from earlier. I looked back as my hair bounced from left to right. I saw him limping as I faintly heard him saying, "Sophia, stop!" Looks like he changed his clothes too. Maybe he's trying not to be recognized or confuse people that saw him earlier, after he kills me. I looked behind once more. Oh Jesus, he's getting closer.

I removed my high heels then pushed my dress up. I started to run like a serial killer was chasing me. A few seconds later, I jumped into my car, tossing my heels into the backseat. While driving, I created a comfortable distance between us, before looking in the rearview mirror. I observed him running behind my car. Jimmy kind of runs like Sammie. Sammie's cerebral palsy made him run funny. Maybe Jimmy had something similar. I gripped the steering wheel with force. "Whatever though!" You're not lynching me.

I pressed down on the gas, speeding away like a street racer. A few minutes later, I entered the highway. I turned the AC on to embrace a cool breeze. The air conditioner's fresh air bounced off my sweaty face. I looked in the mirror. "Now my makeup is all messed up."

Chapter 12:
Birth of Forever

While driving, I observed the natural beauty of my former town. *It has such a homey feeling here. I just love our well-kept roads and the newness that's everywhere. Marin has always looked like an ongoing place of new construction sites.* I took a deep breath.

"The way Jimmy ran behind my car was definitely scary." His demeanor was weird. I was the only person in the parking lot, so he could've easily attacked me and gotten away with it. I sighed. Jimmy still reminds me of Sammie, they look a lot alike. His running style is like Sammie's, too. Maybe I'm just seeing things, since a major part of me still misses him. I removed both of my hands from the steering wheel, placing my right hand back onto the wheel while resting my left hand atop my head. "I could really use some Frank's Donuts right now." I exited the highway onto Richie Road. I'm only two minutes away from the shop, I might as well stop there.

A few minutes later, I pulled up to Frank's. I parked and fumbled through my purse, looking for small coins, then I noticed Kyle approaching my wagon through the rearview mirror.

He knocked on my driver's window with his fist. "Hey, I guess great minds think alike." He flashed a small white paper bag outside the window, donut crumbs fell from his fingers. "I figured you would want some donuts, so I thought ahead." I rolled my window down, then Kyle smiled and said, "Do you want to eat theses donuts in your car or inside Frank's?"

He always understands me so intuitively. I grinned as my cheekbones rose high as a mountaintop. "It's up to you, Kyle. I think we should definitely eat them while they're hot, though."

"You're right. Do you mind walking with me to my car, and eating them in my car?" Kyle asked.

"Kyle, what's wrong with eating them in my car? Are you trying to insinuate something?"

Kyle looked inside my car, lifting his eyebrows to indicate my car was junky. He smirked. "Ha-ha. I'm just saying, we can eat the donuts in my Mustang or in your wagon. It doesn't matter to me. However, I know a pretty young thing like you would look great eating a hot donut in a hot ride." He glanced at his car, parked a short distance behind mine.

I blushed and shook my head. "You're so corny." I laughed. "You say some pretty smooth things most of the time, but you're definitely not saying smooth things right now." I opened my door and attempted to step out of the car.

Kyle gently halted my movement, pushing my door inward. He held the bag to my face, then leaned in toward my neck, sniffing my scent. *I hope I don't stink.* Kyle kissed me on the cheek. We both stared into each other's eyes. "Actually, let's just eat the donuts in your car," Kyle said.

He jumped inside my wagon, pulling out a glazed donut. He broke off a tiny piece and fed it to me. I complied, accidentally licking his fingers. *I can't believe I just licked this man's fingers.* Kyle glanced at me, tilting his head to his left while rubbing my face. *I really want Kyle to come over here and kiss me.*

Kyle turned his head to a neutral position. "How are the donuts?" Kyle asked.

"They're delicious. Thanks for getting them."

"No problem. Are you ready to follow me back to my place to hang out for a little before we head to the art museum tonight?"

My eyes lit up like a blazing fire. "Art museum? That sounds fun. I'll just meet you there. What's the address?"

"Sophia, that's nonsense. Let's just ride together."

I stared at him with a flirtatious smirk on my face. If only Kyle knew the real reason why I don't want to ride alone with him. I exhaled. I want to jump on him, like right now. He's so handsome. I'm feeling vulnerable right now.

I repositioned myself, lifting my left leg onto the seat and placing it underneath my right thigh. While gently rubbing Kyle's thigh, I said, "How about we do this—can we go to a shopping mall, and I just park my car there? We can hang out at the mall then ride together to the museum."

Kyle acknowledged me rubbing his thigh by blushing. "Okay. Do you plan to wear what you have on to the art show? If you don't want to change, I guess we could do what you're suggesting," said Kyle.

"Nah, I don't need to change."

"I didn't plan on changing my clothes either, so we can do what you're suggesting."

"What kind of shopping malls are near here?" I asked.

"There are a lot of areas where you can go shopping. It really just depends on what you're looking for."

I continued to caress his thigh. "Well, I'm a simple girl." I shrugged my shoulders and smiled. I'm getting way too comfortable.

Kyle licked his lips, wiping the moisture from his bottom lip. "Oh, is that so?" He leaned in for a kiss, and I immediately pulled away.

Kyle pulled back too. "Okay, have it your way."

"Ha-ha." I crossed my arms. Men will be men. "I would like to find some nice pursues and clothes. I need to find a gift shop so I can purchase my cousins and aunts some nice gifts, since I plan to visit them soon. You know, you should come with me, Kyle. They all seemed to like you." Did I really just invite this man to go with me to visit my family? He's going to think I'm nuts.

Kyle faced me. "Sophia, I would love to go with you to visit your family. When?"

I raised my eyebrows while placing my feet onto the floor. I glanced at him. "Did you really just say you would love to go?"

Smiling, he exited the car. Kyle walked away saying, "Just follow me."

I started up the engine while waiting for Kyle to drive in front of me. I tailed him like a wildcat following its prey.

Ten minutes later, we arrived at Novato Mall. We parked next to one another, then stepped out of our cars. "Wow, this mall is so beautiful, Kyle. To say I used to live here, I've never seen this mall before. I guess my parents didn't explore my old town as much as they could've," I said.

We looked both ways as we crossed the parking lot, approaching the sidewalk of the mall. Kyle grinned while looking at me. "This area was notorious for lynching and mistreating Black folks."

"I heard." We paused then I removed his arm from around my neck.

Kyle raised his eyebrows. "You remember the eight men who went missing four-years ago near the Shreveport Gas Station?"

"Yeah," I replied.

Kyle was silent. *I guess he gets the point.*

I shrugged my shoulders as images of Timothy's body in the of lake of tears flashed inside my mind. The topic made me feel uneasy.

We entered the mall, and my perpetual silence prompted Kyle to do something nice. He took me inside a store. Once I placed my items on the countertop in front of the cashier, Kyle stepped in front of me, saying, "Girl, don't be silly. I couldn't let you pay for your own things after you came out here just to see me."

I smiled, placing my wallet inside my purse. "Correction, I came out here to register for college." I poked him in his shoulder. "You just happened to live here."

He laughed. "Still playing hard to get I see, just don't do that tonight."

Huh? "Wait, what are you talking about?" What does he mean by that?

He smirked while gently smacking his lips. "You know."

"No, I don't! What are you referring to Kyle?" I frowned.

He exhaled. "Let's just get out of this mall and make our way to the car," Kyle said. He paid for my items then led the way out of the store.

I followed him, staying a few feet behind. "Are you going to tell me what you were referring to?"

He turned around and sighed while saying, "It's nothing, so don't worry about it."

He seems upset, suddenly.

After arriving at the cars, Kyle pushed me against the door of my wagon while grabbing my waist lambently, but in a firm way, too. He looked me in my eyes. "I want to kiss you all the way into a future with me."

Hot.

We kissed. Kyle wet my lips with his, then I pushed against his chest, trying to push him away, only surrendering even more to my desires.

Two minutes later, Kyle escorted me to his car and opened the door for me. While inside his car, we looked at one another in silence. That was steamy.

He put his car into drive, then turned the radio on as we drove to the art show. After the art show was over, I decided to go back home with Kyle rather than getting a hotel. Once inside his house, he entered the kitchen to prepare a peanut butter and jelly sandwich along with a tall glass of red wine for me. Meanwhile, I got comfortable in the living room on the couch.

As I sat on the couch in my red dress with my legs crossed, Kyle glanced at my exposed right thigh as it slid through my dress. He approached, handing me the sandwich along with a glass of wine. "Here, taste a little of this wine."

I obliged while clearing my throat. The strength of the wine made me gulp. "This is my first time drinking, so I don't know my limits." I coughed.

He sat down next to me and said, "Really, this is your first time?"

"Yes."

Throughout the night I drank three more glasses of wine. As my awareness faded, I noticed Kyle picking me up. He carried me upstairs to his bedroom while sounds of an old stairway echoed throughout his house. Once inside his room, Kyle placed me on the bed, tucking me in. I faintly heard him walk toward the door to exit—but he didn't. The room was dark, and I was relaxed. Suddenly, I heard sounds of a button unfastening, along with a zipper being pulled down; then clothes dropping onto the floor before I felt the warmth of Kyle's body lay next to mine. Seconds later, we started to cuddle.

We kissed, then I gradually surrendered to the romance during that moment as I thought to myself: We really shouldn't be doing this.

***

I woke up the following morning next to Kyle. While sitting up in the bed, I noticed Kyle lying next to me shirtless. I grabbed my chest— I only had a bra on. While opening my mouth wide, I thought. *I hope that what I remember us doing was just a dream.* My confusion transitioned into shock as I raised my eyebrows while lifting the comforter. I noticed my underwear was on. *Thank God.* While the comforter was still elevated, I glanced at Kyle as he laid peacefully on his back. He only had on a pair of blue underwear. I grabbed my face with both of my hands, screaming within. I hope we didn't have sex.

I turned my attention to Kyle; I picked up a pillow and attacked him. He woke up then jumped out of the bed. "Woman, what's your problem?"

I frowned. "Did you date rape me?"

Kyle clenched his fists then aggressively threw them downward toward the floor. "Heck no! I gave you exactly what you wanted."

I sighed. "I thought I was better than this! Please just leave me alone right now, okay."

Kyle walked out of the bedroom, and I observed his chiseled body. Who am I fooling? God sees everything, I can't blame the alcohol. "God knows what I wanted to do." I capitulated my motive to blame Kyle for my conscious transgression. To be honest, I kind of remember everything that happened.

A few minutes later, Kyle and I shared a silent breakfast together. After our hiccup, I completely lowered my guard. Later that night we talked, and Kyle promised to make things right between us. The things he said made me feel like I could fix my relationship with God. I felt torn up after committing a sin. As the night progressed, I fell prey to my own desires again. Kyle and I were intimate once more.

Before leaving to head back home on Sunday, I thought to myself: I should have just followed my first mind and got a hotel. None of this would have happened if I'd simply done that. I felt terrible.

A few hours later, I attempted to drive back home. While in my car I pondered, the conversation we shared last night was helping me to start the process of redemption. I hope that Kyle marries me so that we can make this right. "I need to make sure he's serious about being with me." A few minutes later, I drove back into his driveway then knocked on the door. Kyle opened the door and we reconvened in the living room. I sat down on the couch, sighing with tears falling from my face. "Kyle, we need to talk some more. I just feel so terrible about what happened."

Kyle patiently waited for me to express my feelings, as I thought to myself. If you were a gentleman, you wouldn't have even hinted toward trying to get me to stay with you in the first place, since we aren't married. You've been offering for me to stay with you since we first met. Maybe sleeping with me was a part of your big plan all along? I scoffed.

Kyle stood over me, half dressed in a white tank top, accompanied with white underwear. "Sophia, I am sorry about what happened." He kneeled in front of me, placing his hands on my thighs. We were eye level. While looking at me with sincerity, he said, "I assure you, I'm in this for the long haul." He gently squeezed my thigh. "I have no plans of leaving you."

I dropped my head between my legs and sobbed. "You don't get it!" I lifted my head. "You don't get it, do you Kyle? I told you I wanted to save myself for marriage and you took advantage of me." I exhaled. "You should have forced me to go back to my hotel." But instead of doing the right thing, you lured me to my romantic demise. I screamed, "You served me alcohol in order to get me tipsy so you could get into my pants." I aggressively rubbed my hands across my eyes. I growled while tossing a pillow from the couch at Kyle. "You are a dog—you will never be like Sammie!"

"No need for you to play the blame game, sister. And remember that you are a Black sister while you're walking around all enthralled by some White guy! He probably doesn't give a rat's behind about you anyway." He vehemently exhaled while pointing his fingers at me. "No one made you come visit me. You wanted to come here, and you knew what you were getting yourself into. So rather than blame me, we need to focus on what should happen next." He stood up. "Look, I want to be with you Sophia." He placed his hands on his chest. "The intimacy we shared means a lot."

I chuckled and stood up while Kyle stared at me. Placing my right hand in his face, I said, "Oh yeah, then I expect you to marry me. I refuse to be a woman who sleeps around with a guy out of wedlock."

"I have news for you, Sophia. You're already guilty of that, and that's your problem. You try way too hard to uphold all these religious teachings. I hope you realize now that you're no better than the rest of us. You're imperfect and you make mistakes too."

I charged at Kyle and punched him like a lightweight boxing champion. He shielded himself by holding his hands up. "You little jerk. How dare you!" I fell to my knees and cried like a two-year old. My temper tantrum continued, then I struck him again. He dodged my left jab before grabbing my arms to subdue me.

My back was facing him; his arms were firmly pressed against my hands.

Kyle turned me around then I spat into his face. He removed my saliva from his cheeks and angrily said, "You're welcome to leave anytime you want!"

"Fine, I am out of here! I never want to see you again. In fact, when you see me on campus, just keep walking, you jerk!" I flinched at him like I wanted to hit him again. Kyle jumped back like he was bracing himself for impact. "I see why Nancy was yelling at you. I should've known then that you were a total waste of my energy. I made a promise to my God, and I broke it with a man that's never going to even be my husband."

I stormed out of the room, but Kyle followed me as I skipped down the stairs at maximum speed. "Sophia, wait, let's talk!"

Chapter 13:
A Blessing in Disguise

1968
September
Two Months Later

I woke up early in the morning to go to the bathroom. While holding my stomach, I said out loud, "I feel like crap." I rushed into the bathroom, stumbling onto the floor. I crawled to the toilet then lifted the seat, vomiting with the force of a suction cap. I've had much better nights than my past two nights. I don't know why I keep vomiting. What a way to start my new fall job today. "I might have to call-in on my first day." After hanging over the toilet for a few minutes, I pushed away from the toilet, positioning my back against the toilet as vomit fell from my mouth.

I pulled my right leg into my body, forming a right triangle with my left leg outstretched. *I have a few hours before I start my new job, so maybe I can drop by the doctor's office. It's only five minutes away. I should call before I go in, just to make sure he has an open slot to see me.* I slowly stood up, dragging my body downstairs into the kitchen before I called my doctor.

I picked up the phone, then leaned against the wall for support. The phone line rang.

The receptionist answered. "This is Dr. Morgan's office; how may I help you?"

"Hello, my name is Sophia Smith. I am calling to find out if Dr. Morgan has a slot open this morning to see me?"

"What's the purpose of your visit with Dr. Morgan today?" The receptionist asked.

I grunted. "I'm experiencing some really bad stomach pain, and I'm nauseated. I've been experiencing some bad headaches as well. I just feel sluggish."

"Thank you, Ms. Smith. I am sorry to hear that you aren't feeling well. After checking Dr. Morgan's schedule, I see that he has an opening in about thirty-minutes. Can you make it to his office within the next twenty or thirty minutes?" The Receptionist asked.

I grimaced. "Yes, I can."

"Okay, I'll see you then."

We hung up, and while still leaning against the kitchen wall I pondered. I don't know why I am having these bad stomach pains. I just haven't felt well over the past few days and it's getting quite frustrating.

I grabbed my keys off the kitchen table then walked upstairs to brush my teeth. Five minutes later, I exited my house and drove to Dr. Morgan's office. Six minutes later, I arrived at his office.

Once inside, I walked up to the receptionist, then she instructed me to fill out a few papers. After completing the paperwork, a White nurse checked my blood pressure and sugar while asking several questions.

This feels like an interrogation. It kind of reminds me of Billy Joe and his flagitious colleague when they interrogated me a while ago. I need to check-in with Mr. Proctor to see how my mom's investigation is coming along. I'll call him later today or tomorrow to get an update.

After answering the nurse's questions, she escorted me to a waiting room, instructing me to remain seated. "Dr. Morgan will see you in just a minute," said The Nurse.

A few minutes later, the receptionist called my name. "Sophia Smith, Dr. Morgan is ready to see you now."

The same nurse from earlier walked into the waiting room, instructing me to walk through the double doors that were in front of me. I followed her instructions, then I was kindly embraced by another nurse, who instructed me to take a seat inside the patient's waiting room.

"Hey, Sweetie, I'm Nurse Betty. We are going to help you feel better today. I just need to ask you a few questions before Dr. Morgan completes his assessment. Are you a virgin?" The Black nurse asked.

I am so embarrassed. My mom and dad would be so disappointed in me for having intercourse out of wedlock. I nodded my head. "Yes, I am." I am such a pathetic excuse for a Christian. I'm nothing but a classless lady.

The nurse lifted her eyebrows. "Well, uh, okay! Uh, I guess you haven't found the right guy yet?"

"Yeah, and I'm saving myself for marriage. I want to please my God." I'm not even worthy of mentioning God right now.

"You know that's commendable, you're such a beautiful young lady. I am certain that all of the guys are after you."

Not the one I really want. "Just a few. The guy I really want to marry, we just can't seem to live in time—at the right time together."

"You just have to be patient. I'm going to need a urine and blood sample from you to complete our assessment today. Dr. Morgan will be in right after we run these samples through our systems."

Why does she need all of that? "Uh, okay, thanks."

While waiting for Dr. Morgan, I pondered: *This is taking way longer than I expected.* I looked at the clock on the wall. *I've been here for an hour now.*

Ten minutes later, Dr. Morgan entered the room. I glanced at the clock again. I am going to be late for work, but I need to know my results.

"Hey, Dr. Morgan, can I use the telephone?" I asked.

"Hi to you as well, Sophia." Dr. Morgan smiled.

"Sorry for being rude, but I need to call my new job to inform my boss that I'm going to be a few minutes late."

He placed his clipboard against his chest and crossed his arms. "Sophia, how are you? I haven't seen you since you were about fifteen, and that was three or four years ago. You have a birthday coming up soon, right?"

"I do, in three months. My birthday is in December."

He pointed to a telephone outside in the lobby. "Go ahead and make your phone call to your job, then we will talk about your results."

"Okay, thanks for letting me use your phone," I said.

"No problem, Sophia. How is your mom by the way?"

I dropped my head, sighing as I walked pass Dr. Morgan. "I'll tell you what happened after I finish my phone call."

I phoned my job.

The phone line rang. Someone answered and then I said, "Good morning, may I speak to Mr. King?"

The person on the other line asked, "Who's calling, please?"

"This is Sophia, I am scheduled to start work in thirty-minutes, but I'll be late today."

"Okay, I'll go grab him right now," said the person on the other line.

I have a funny feeling this conversation isn't going to go very well.

Less than thirty seconds later, a man picked up and said, "Hello!"

"Hey, Mr. King. Uh, I probably won't be able to make it in today. I'm at the doctor's office right now, I'm not feeling well."

He exhaled. "Sophia, you do realize that this is your first day of work, right?"

"I know."

"Just keep me posted. I hope you feel better," said Mr. King.

"Thanks for understanding."

"No problem." He hung up.

After hanging up, I walked back into Dr. Morgan's office. "Sophia, let's talk about your results." He sat down in a rolling chair then scooted my way with a serious look on his face. "I have a question to ask you, but I need you to be absolutely honest with me. Are you sure that you're still a virgin?"

I squinted my eyes while staring at the floor to avoid eye contact. "Yes, I am sure."

"Well, your test results show that you are four weeks pregnant."

I shook my head. "Can't be, your results must be wrong!" My eyes were watery. God, no.

"Sophia, I can assure you that the test is right." He pointed to the test results. "You see this little line here; it indicates the percentage of pregnancy certainty. Your results are one hundred percent. We tested it four times to make sure. You don't have to be embarrassed." I started to cry, as he patted me on the shoulder. "Look, bringing a baby into the world is a beautiful thing. Since you're going to be a mother, it's best to accept this weighty responsibility. You should start preparing for the journey that's ahead you," said Dr. Morgan.

I stood up. "I told you, I'm not pregnant! Now stop trying to force your stupid results on me!" I sprinted out of the office with tears rolling down my cheeks. I overheard Dr. Morgan saying, "Wait, come back, please!"

I ignored him and exited the clinic, slamming the office door. It echoed as loud as a fire alarm. A few seconds later, I angrily sped away in my wagon.

After arriving at my house, I stormed into the kitchen, staring at the phone for several minutes. How am I going to break this news to Kyle?

I said a silent prayer to God before calling Kyle. While holding the phone to my ear, I pondered: I couldn't have imagined that my life would turn out this way.

"Hello, this is Kyle."

My tone was sad as I spoke softly, saying, "Hey Kyle, it's Sophia. Uh, can we talk?"

"Of course! I've been looking forward to hearing from you. I've tried to call you almost every other day for the past month or so. Every time I called—you hung up after you heard my voice."

"I apologize for doing that, but we really need to talk. In fact, do you think it's possible for us to talk in person? Can you drive to San Francisco today? I'll be home all day today."

"Sophia, is everything okay?" Kyle asked.

My voice trembled. "No, but I think everything will be okay at some point."

"Can you tell me what this is about over the phone? I'm still going to come to your house today to talk, but I want to know what's going on."

"Kyle, please, I'll tell you once you arrive. Please, just respect my wishes for once, okay?"

"What are you trying to insinuate, Sophia?" Kyle asked.

I screamed, "You know exactly what I am saying! You're the reason why I am in this predicament anyway. You just couldn't be a gentleman and respect my wishes. You just couldn't keep your stinky hands to yourself. I'm pregnant, and you're not going to leave me alone to care for this baby!"

"Wait, Sophia, are you telling me you're going to have my child? This is exciting, I am so happy. I love you! I couldn't think of a better woman to have a child with. How many weeks are you now?"

That's not what I expected to hear. My voice toughened up a little as I replied, "I'm six or seven weeks, I think," I said with a distressed tone.

"Are you absolutely sure that you're pregnant?"

"Yes, I went to the doctor today. I was feeling nauseous and vomiting everywhere, so I went in. They took a urine and blood sample then conducted four tests, confirming I am pregnant."

"I just have to ask, have you been with anyone else since me, Sophia? I haven't seen you in a month," said Kyle.

Jerk. "No, I haven't! And, after this experience, you're going to be my first and last."

"I understand why you sound stressed. Remember this, though: It's a new experience for the both of us. So, don't feel like you're alone. Sophia, I am hitting the road now. I'll be at your house in about an hour or so. I promise to take good care of you and our baby."

"Don't worry about me, just help me take care of this baby." I pulled a chair near the phone and sat down.

"I've always wanted to be a father," he said.

"Kyle, please just get to my house."

"Okay, I'll see you soon."

After my phone call with Kyle, I dropped to my knees and fervently prayed to God for his guidance for over an hour. *God, I am afraid of how my future is going to transpire. I don't know if I'm going to have a boy or a girl. Whatever I have, please help me to be responsible. In Jesus' name I pray. Amen.* I stood up and sat in the kitchen chair for an hour, meditating. My thoughts were interrupted by loud knocks on the front door.

"Hold on, I'm coming! Give me a second!" That must be Kyle. I hurried and spruced up the house while continuing to hear loud knocks. Ugh! Why is he rushing me? "He's such a jerk sometimes."

I rushed to the door, only to discover that it wasn't who I expected. I looked through the peephole. "Huh, Mr. Proctor." I opened the door.

"Mr. Proctor, how are you?" I asked.

He was dressed in casual clothes with a pair of black gloves covering his hands. He looked around then asked, "Sophia, are you in a rush? We need to talk about the things I have discovered about your mom."

I signaled for him to come inside. "Are my suspicions true?" I asked.

He stepped forward, walking inside, then he yielded as we both heard a car pull up into the driveway. John looked to his right. "Uh, that's what I want to discuss."

Our conversation was interrupted by a loud engine. I stuck my head out the door and noticed that it was Kyle in his blue Mustang. His engine created an obstreperous sound.

Kyle exited his car, then walked up.

John glanced at Kyle, then refocused his attention on me with his left foot still inside my house, while his right foot was stationary on the porch. John placed his hands inside his pockets and asked, "Sophia, is this still a good time to talk? I can come back tomorrow if you prefer?" He glanced at me and Kyle. "It's urgent. Uh, based on the looks you two are giving one another, I feel like you all have some pressing issues to resolve," said John.

I waved at Kyle as he stood a few feet behind John, gazing at Mr. Proctor with eyes of suspicion. I looked John in his eyes and said, "Yes, we do, but I really want to know what's going on with my mom, too."

John looked back at Kyle again, with his hands glued inside his pockets. Then, he refocused his attention on me. "Uh, let's do this. I'll go grab lunch, then I'll come back in maybe an hour or so." He nudged his head in Kyle's direction. "Since thi-s guy is your guest, I'll give you two some privacy to handle your business."

Kyle stepped forward and extended his right hand. "Hi, I'm Kyle."

John removed his right hand from his pocket, quickly shaking Kyle's hand.

Kyle pointed at John, gesturing for him to stay. John looked at me then removed his left foot from inside my house; he walked down the steps.

I waved bye to John as he stared at Kyle in a weird way before exiting off my steps. I shouted, "Okay, thanks Mr. Proctor. I'll see you in a little while."

John tossed his hands up and waved goodbye.

I glanced at Kyle as he held a grocery bag in his hand. I watched Kyle as he attentively stared at John before entering his car. After John drove away, Kyle walked up the steps and said, "Hey, Sophia." He hugged me.

I pulled away then I pulled Kyle into my bosom, kissing him. We kissed for several seconds. Gasping for air, I said, "Are you ready to have this conversation about our child?"

He licked his lips and grinned, swiping his right thumb across the edge of his nose. "Yes, I'm actually excited about this whole process." He walked inside. "Something seems off about that John guy, though—I think he might be an undercover racist."

I raised my eyebrows. "You do? Um … this is the second time since I've known him that I've felt like his spirit was off, too. I am glad you showed up, when you did, I felt like something bad was about to happen. I don't know if I am feeling this way because of what happened to my mom, or because I feel like he came to harm me."

"Yeah, I saw a gun in his pocket. And—those black gloves didn't help him not look suspicious either," said Kyle.

We sat down on the living room couch, then Kyle placed his bag down in front of his legs. "John is a lawyer, but I think he investigates crimes too. I think he's a private detective," I said.

Kyle faced me, shaking his head. "Sophia, how many people do you know that're a lawyer and a detective?"

"I see your point. I didn't look at it like that. I feel like he genuinely wants to help me. He's the same guy who came to inform my mom that my dad was killed in the war."

"Did you talk to him yourself, when he showed up to inform your mom?"

"No, but I remember seeing him."

"Seems like we have a lot of stuff to talk about today, Sophia."

"Before we talk about all the things we need to address, I think that we should—" Kyle interrupted, nudging me on my thigh while pointing toward the stairway. Wow, really? I sighed. "Don't even go there, that kind of behavior has put us in the current predicament we are in," I said.

"What? No, you're misunderstanding me." He reached inside the grocery bag, removing a few items. "Sophia, look at the things that are in my hand."

I slapped my forehead. "Oh! Okay, sweet potatoes, butter, sugar, and pie crust. Just tell me Kyle, because my mind isn't functioning right now—I have too much on my mind."

"I understand. I want us to bake a sweet potato pie before we talk. Sweet potato pie always relaxes my mind. And I know you love sweet potato pie too, so I picked up the ingredients from the grocery store around the corner. I think it's called—"

"It's called Kugan's Grocery Store, don't slaughter the name of my favorite grocery store. Speaking of, I need to call my boss and inquire about when I'm scheduled to work again."

"Okay, but let's go in the kitchen and start baking this pie," Kyle said.

While in the kitchen Kyle stood behind me, gently rubbing my arms as I cut the potatoes. I paused and leaned back into his chest, then I kissed his left bicep.

"We are going to get through this difficult process together. I am almost done with law school. My Uncle Jermaine has already put a good word in for me at the law firm where he works. I will definitely have a good job, so I'll be able to take care of you and our baby," said Kyle.

I turned around to face him. "How many uncles do you have? And just focus on taking care of this baby—I don't need you to take care of me."

"I have two uncles. I'm going to take care of you and the baby— both of you are my babies." He grabbed my butt, swatting it like a fly.

"Ouch! Don't grab me like that anymore, who do you think you are?"

He wet his lips. "Your future husband."

He's so smooth. "Hmm—"

He rubbed the top of his skull. "Sophia, I'll take your heart where it really wants to go."

I grabbed his hands, wrapping them around my neck. Kyle participated, pulling me in close as I asked, "And where does my heart really want to go, Mr. Prophet?"

He looked at his arms to bring attention to what we were doing. "Obviously, into my arms," Kyle said.

We both laughed.

Corny. I placed my fingers inside my mouth. "Yuck, you're so corny."

I laughed then he lifted me up, tickling me underneath my armpits. "I'm not like most men, Sophia." I stared down at him as I embraced the feeling of being conquered by his massive level of strength. *Wow, he's so strong.* Kyle smirked at me. "Just keep watching my channel, and I'll show you better than I can tell you," Kyle said while putting me down.

"Your channel?" I asked.

He held my hands. "Yes, my channel. Life with me is exciting; it's like watching Bonanza." He hit his chest. "With me, you'll always be on a journey." He pulled me back into his arms, kissing my forehead. "I'm a real cowboy, baby."

Here we go again. I stomped my feet and laughed. "Kyle, stop! There you go, you're being corny again. Come on, let's go sit down in the living room while the pie bakes." I playfully waved my right index finger side-to-side. "Now, we can finally discuss the baby."

Kyle and I walked into the living room. We held hands while walking. While sitting on the couch cuddled up with Kyle, I pondered: I wonder why Kyle thinks something is off with John? I felt something strange, too, when we were in the park that day. I started to reflect on the niceties of my brother's death. I glanced at Kyle, noticing that his eyes were glued to the television. With my legs outstretched and my head positioned atop his lap; I resumed my inner thoughts. In retrospect, during the night my brother and I ran for our lives, I ran like I'd never run before. I only faintly remember seeing two men after we made it to the lake, but maybe a third man was out there. I sat up as Kyle continued to watch TV. Yes, there was a third guy, and he was older than the other two men. I think the two younger men left him behind, maybe the third guy wasn't in great shape. I do remember seeing a man far away when my brother told me to jump into the water, now that I'm walking down memory lane. But when I looked back to see my brother after I swam across the lake of tears, I only saw two men.

There definitely was an older man who saw my brother defending himself well. He turned around like he was on a mission and disappeared. When my dad and I went back to get my brother, he got shot in his leg. Immediately after that, we saw a slew of hateful KKK members dressed in their white robes, yelling racial epithets. Hmm.

"Oh my God, Kyle!" I stood up. "That's it, I knew Mr. Proctor's voice sounded familiar to one of the men's voices who was out there the night my brother managed to escape. I think Mr. Proctor might be a part of the KKK!"

Kyle powered the television off then he stood up. We looked into each other's eyes as my intuition kicked into high gear like a launched rocket. Kyle gulped. "Sophia, I have a funny feeling, we need to leave this house—like right now!"

First my brother and now me. "Timmy!" I fainted into his arms. I woke up a few seconds later to Kyle gently tapping me on my face. "Sophia, wake up!" While kneeling, Kyle held me as I looked into his eyes. Abruptly, my face refilled with fear. After I fully regained consciousness, I screamed. "John's going to kill me!"

Kyle helped me to my feet then guided me into the kitchen, pouring a cold glass of water for me while I sat in a chair.

"No, he won't! I won't let him," said Kyle. Kyle paced back and forth, then paused while looking at me. "Did he call you before he came? I mean, how long were you home before he showed up?"

I leaned forward in the chair, shaking uncontrollably as I pondered thoughts of death. He came here to finish me off earlier. I looked at Kyle. "I was home for at least an hour."

Kyle frowned. "I think I may have deterred his intentions since he wasn't expecting to see me. My intuition is rarely wrong. Let's go, Sophia. Let's go now!"

I stood up, clenching my hands together to control the chills of death that were running through my body. "Kyle, I am trusting you with my life—" I looked down at my belly. "—and our child's life, too."

He caressed my forearm. "I got you girl. Now go pack some clothes and other necessary things. We need to take our cars and park them around the corner. I got lost a couple of times when I was trying to find your house. I noticed that you can still see your house from the other block. I think John has something ominous planned. When we leave, I want us to park around the corner, so we can see if he comes back. I just feel like we need to see what he does.

I nodded my head. "Okay! I want to see if what you're suspecting is true, because if you're wrong, then I still want to know if John can help with resolving what happened to my mom."

Kyle sighed. "I know this isn't the smartest thing to do with our baby, but I just have to be sure so that you won't be vulnerable to him again. And you'll also have your own peace of mind about him, too, if you see it for yourself," said Kyle.

Kyle continued to talk to me as we walked up and down the stairs while I packed. My heart was racing like a motorcycle as my survival instincts progressed into a different gear. After I finished packing, we exited the house. I jumped into my wagon and Kyle hopped in his Mustang. I followed Kyle around the corner, we parked our cars on the next block. About fifteen minutes later, we witnessed several cars drive up to my house.

***

Kyle and I parked next to one another. I was positioned to his right; he was stationed to my left. We glanced at one another as frogs echoed their sounds into the late-night sky. Subsequently, we witnessed eight men get out of their cars, dressed in white sheets. The men huddled together before stationing a massive cross in front of my house. I placed my hands over my mouth while glancing at Kyle, then two of the men emptied several gallons of gasoline onto the cross.

Tears ran down my face. *It's time for me to leave San Francisco forever.* The cross went up in flames. The men broke into my house as well. I could almost read their lips, "Let's kill these black monkeys for Billy Joe." I knew something was off about that Proctor guy. If he wanted me dead, then why did he wait until now? It's obvious to me now that my death must've been a part of an elaborate scheme. Now I am wondering about my dad's death, and the story of him cheating on my mom with some Asian lady. Mr. Proctor deceived me. This whole time, he and the Klan were carefully planning an attack to eliminate me—and perhaps, my mother too. Maybe the story about my father is just a made-up story too?

John was dressed in a white sheet, leaving his head covering off his head before placing it on. I watched in disbelief as the men raided my home. This is happening because Timmy almost killed Billy Joe.

Kyle looked at me through his car, both of our windows were down. I looked to my left and said, "This is crazy! That could have been you and my baby if you didn't—" Kyle's words were interrupted by my house exploding.

Immediately after the explosion, I got out of my wagon and jumped into Kyle's car. While panting, Kyle grunted due to shock and frustration. "Ugh!"

I grabbed Kyle's hand to help calm his soul. I bet he's shaking like this because it reminds him of what happened to his mom.

I stared at him and asked, "Kyle are you okay?"

He ceased shaking as tears fell from his face. "I hate these racist pricks! Sometimes I wonder if there will ever be justice for Black people. What makes this acceptable? I lost my mom to a fire just like this. What makes me super angry, is that—that could've been you burning in that house tonight." He stepped out of the car, slamming his door. He placed his head inside the driver's side of his car. "I am putting a stop to this tonight!"

Kyle popped his trunk and pulled out a gun. I jumped out of the car, trying to stop his pursuit by grabbing his hand. He turned around and held his hand up. "Sophia, don't try to stop me. I am about to eliminate all of these low-lives!"

"Don't do anything stupid. If you go over there, you will be outnumbered." I jumped into his arms. My tears wet his trigger finger. "Kyle, I love you. I need you to be here for our baby."

Kyle looked at me. "I love you too."

We held each other, then Kyle suggested that we get married at the courthouse in Marin County. I was taken aback by his suggestion. After considering our circumstances, my heart agreed that marrying him was the right thing to do.

A few minutes later, after holding each other as we watched my house burn, we got back into our separate cars, driving in the opposite direction of the KKK. We drove to Marin County. After arriving at Kyle's house, we walked inside and chatted in the living room.

As we sat in the living room, Kyle smiled, asking, "Is tomorrow still going to be our big day?"

"Yes. We should call the authorities and tell them what happened at my parent's house too," I said.

He elevated his eyebrows as waves formed in his forehead. "I don't think that's a good idea. We don't know who to trust anymore. You mentioned during our ride here that you told John about me and where I am from. He probably informed the authorities here about me. Sophia, did you tell him my last name or give him my address?"

I nodded my head to acknowledge his point. "No, I didn't. You're right, we have to lay low."

He placed his hands on my thighs, caressing my broken spirit. "Sophia, I wouldn't be able to live with myself if I'd come to your house—and saw that something had happened to you and our baby." He stood up and grabbed my hands, lifting me up from the couch. We hugged and kissed. He placed his hands on my belly before his left ear touched my tummy too. Kyle's ear was glued to my stomach like super glue. "By the way, do you want a boy or a girl?" Kyle asked.

I smiled, emptying out more tears. "I want a little girl. What about you?" I asked.

"This might shock you, but I want a little girl too. I really miss my mom. If I have a girl, it will fill a large hole that's in my heart. Sophia, I can't wait to marry you tomorrow morning."

"I just thought my wedding day would be different. I wish all of my family could be there," I said.

"We can still have an official ceremony on another day. I know all of this is happening so fast, but I know in my heart it's the right thing to do." Kyle's eyes lit up like the morning sun. "I have a nice amount of money saved, too. I got most of it from my mom's life insurance policy. I have a nice policy on myself as well. I will add you to my policy today, as one of my beneficiaries," said Kyle.

I feel so secure in this moment. "Kyle, I love you." My eyes started to close like a nail filling a punctured hole. "Oh boy. Kyle, I am very sleepy." I laughed, and he did too, because of my lack of coherence.

"I love you too, and I am whipped myself." He looked toward the stairway. "Go and rest while I make a phone call to my life insurance agent. Once I'm finished with my call, I'll finish planning everything for our big day tomorrow."

"Sounds good, baby," I replied.

"I look forward to sharing my life with you," said Kyle.

***

From a Smith to a Coleman

The Next Day

I woke up a little earlier than Kyle. I was nervous about getting married within a few hours, so I laid in the bed, thinking.

Hmm. Maybe I should tell him I don't mind waiting a while longer before we get married. Wait, I don't have a place to live anymore. Since I'm going to be living with Kyle, I will face the temptation to sin again. Maybe it's best to marry him so we won't live in sin. I need Jehovah to guide my thoughts. If I marry Kyle, that'll cancel any opportunity for me and Sammie to be together. We probably should get to know each other a little longer before we make such a huge commitment.

A few minutes later, I walked downstairs in my nightgown and ate my favorite type of sandwich. Subsequently, I got dressed for a jog. While getting dressed, I thought to myself: When I get back, I'll surprise Kyle with some breakfast when he wakes up.

I prepared to open the front door to depart for my run, then I heard Kyle rushing down the stairs, saying, "Wait up! Don't tell me you're leaving me already? We haven't even married yet." He smirked.

I replied, "Well, technically it makes more sense to leave before we get married rather than leave you after wedlock." I smiled while standing in front of the door.

Kyle walked forward, positioning himself directly in front of me. "Ha, that's true. Where are you headed?"

I playfully jogged in place. "I'm going for a jog in the park. I feel like I need to clear my head."

He played along, jogging in place with his shirt off. "Me too, especially after everything we witnessed yesterday," said Kyle.

Kyle walked to the stairway and sat at the edge. Suddenly, he looked bothered. *He's probably having second thoughts.* I stepped forward and said, "Kyle, don't give me that look. I know that getting married is a huge decision," I said.

While still looking worried, Kyle replied, "That's not what's bothering me." He stood up. "I really appreciate you, Sophia." He sighed. "I have a confession—" He dropped his head and exhaled. He looked up at the ceiling. "Okay, I've slept with three women prior to you."

Liar!" What? Three!" I frowned. "Really, Kyle?"

He took a deep breath. "Yes, really," said Kyle.

I folded my arms while slightly bending my right leg. "Who are they?"

Kyle rubbed his stomach and reluctantly said, "Nancy, Jill, and Mira."

I was furious but I decided to maintain my composure. "Uh, well, thanks for finally being honest with me."

" No problem. Uh, when you get back from jogging, I'll have a nice surprise for you."

Please, God, help me not to knock this fool upside his head with my fist. He had the temerity to reply to me with a cocky statement like that. I took a deep breath. "Okay. I'll go for my jog now." I quickly exited the front door.

Thirty minutes later, after finishing my jog, I returned home. I freshened up, then waited for Kyle to return. I wonder where he went, I thought as I sat on the couch. I'll go look for him, then pick up some donuts from Frank's along the way. Two minutes later, I stepped inside my car and departed.

About twenty-five minutes later, while driving up to Frank's, I was appalled by a ghastly scene. Wow, smoke is everywhere. Whoever is involved in this car wreck must be dead. Glass is everywhere. A lot of people were on the scene. Everything looked like a milder comparison of the aftermath from World War II. Wait, nah it can't be. I looked closer as the smoke began to fade. Is that Kyle's car? I drove slowly past the scene, just across the street from Frank's. I placed my hands over my mouth. " No! Jesus, that is Kyle's car." I observed a few cops arrive on the scene. They couldn't get to the driver's side because of the massive damage. One of the officers walked on the passenger's side, opening the door. I could see food scattered atop the passenger's seat. *I guess he went out to get us something.*

I cried. Getting us breakfast was his surprise. I hope he's okay. I looked around. I didn't see him anywhere. *Maybe he's in the back of the ambulance? God, please let Kyle be okay.*

After my prayer, I jumped out of the car with my engine still sputtering in the middle of the street. I looked to my left and noticed a black body bag with someone inside. *I hope that's not him.* I lost feeling in my legs.

I'm surprised that no one has instructed me to stay back yet. I looked closely as a man who appeared to be a detective walked up, pulling the zipper down to the body bag. From my vantage point, about twenty yards away, I could see that it was Kyle. I placed my hands over my mouth and sobbed. "His whole face is filled with blood!" Oh my God, his face is full of glass too. I quickly ran to my car and got inside.

I panted while moving wildly in my seat. *I wonder what happened because I don't see another car out here.* Abruptly, I jumped out of my car to sprint toward the man who I thought might've been a detective. While gasping for air I asked, "Sir, what happened?" I pointed to the body bag. "The man inside that bag is my husband."

The officer pulled me aside and said, "I'm sorry for your loss." I cried my heart out while falling to my knees as I listened to the officer, "He was killed instantly by a drunk driver that ran a red light. Some maniac pummeled into him head-on. It's a hit-and-run vehicular homicide," said the officer.

I erupted into a loud outburst, "Kyle was going to travel with me to Los Angeles in a few months—to visit my family!" The officer tried to console me.

Chapter 14:
A Lover's Finale:
My Audition in Los Angeles

December
1968
Several Months After Kyle's Death

I arrived at a hotel in California and checked in with the concierge. I stared at the golden countertops and the amount of glass the hotel had as a part of its design. *Wow, I didn't realize that a five-star hotel looks like this. I have the money to pay for it, though. I've collected so much money from my mom's and Kyle's life insurance policies.* I looked down at my belly. My belly is starting to show. I stepped onto an empty elevator. *I can't wait to get this baby out of me in April.* I pushed the button on the keypad that corresponded with my room's number.

I leaned back against the elevator wall, observing the pristine nature of its glass ceiling. I feel confident about my cadence and the flow of The Blues Café. I glanced at my wristwatch. I need to hurry to the Coliseum right now or I'll be late. I placed my luggage in my room and then exited, walking to a nearby elevator and clicking the first floor on the keypad. I exited the elevator then reported to the front desk. "I need a taxi," I said to the concierge.

"We keep drivers available at all times for our guests," said the concierge as he pointed to a taxi through the open glass windows of the hotel.

I smiled. "Thanks. This is five-star service at its best." I exited the building, stepping into the taxi. I pulled out an address on a sheet of paper and handed it to the driver. Fifteen minutes later, I arrived at the venue. The coliseum reminded me of the Yankee stadium. *What a fun trip that was, when my dad took me to a baseball game there.* My eyes opened wide. "Wow, this place is amazing."

Upon entering, I was guided by personnel to the proper location. *I don't know what to expect today but I feel like my audition will go well.* I looked around and noticed a few of the girls, after exiting the registration room. They were all slim and trim. I awkwardly avoided looking at my stomach while numerous potential contestants stared at my belly. I gained a decent amount of weight with this baby.

I walked forward in a line before entering a waiting room to wait until my number was called, taking a seat in one of the chairs that was located inside. I heard several voices colliding as people practiced.

Despite my few extra pounds, I really like my outfit. My purple dress and my black boots look really nice. I think I look like a star. I probably should run to the restroom and double-check my makeup. I placed my hand on my lower back as I stood up to exit the waiting room to locate the nearest restroom.

I entered the restroom. I could feel my baby kicking inside of my stomach. Maybe my future queen or king is telling me to relax and have a little more faith in myself. I looked around, then bent down to check under the openings inside the stalls to ensure that no one was in the restroom with me. I probably should practice a little while I have this space to myself. I sung the chorus of The Blues Café. I sounded pretty good.

After I finished rehearsing, I exited the restroom to instantly embrace thousands of girls screaming as Duke Proctor walked by. I turned my head in the direction of his masculine footsteps. This was my first time seeing Duke up close and in person. *I must admit, he's very attractive and tall.*

Duke paused and turned to face the crowd as hundreds of women stampeded around him. He smiled as his light purple suit sat atop his golden shoes. His blonde hair complemented his ensemble, and his snow-white teeth brightened the background of the hallway. "Ladies, I hope you all are ready to showcase your skills. Some of you will be on the road to stardom after today." Duke walked in the direction opposite of the preliminary audition rooms.

While standing outside the restroom, I said out loud to myself, "I hope that I'm one of those girls."

With my back against the wall, I glanced to my left at a nearby audition room, overhearing the judges call ten girls into the room. While the audition room door was ajar, I overheard one of the judges saying, "Everyone will have thirty seconds to sing. However, you must make it to the second round to be seriously considered. Everyone that makes it to the second round will have an opportunity to audition for Duke, where you'll have one minute and thirty seconds to showcase your abilities. Most importantly, the final round will be tomorrow. Only ten contestants will have the privilege of performing during the final round."

I walked closer to the door, then I started to perspire as the realization of my dream captivated my emotions. I walked back into the waiting room adjacent to the audition room. I could hear my number getting closer. I looked at my shirt, reading the label that was attached to my dress. I could be up next—at any moment now.

Finally, my number was called. I entered the audition room, and everyone was instructed to fill out a worksheet that asked one question: Why do you think you are a superstar? I filled in my answer. I think I am a superstar because singing and writing music are two of my passions. I handed my worksheet to one of the judges. Subsequently, I walked toward the back of a short line, waiting for my name to be called. Six minutes later, I heard, "Sophia Smith, we are ready to hear what you got," said one of the judges.

I stepped forward as several eyes gazed upon me. I approached the judges with my hands glued to my hips. I was stiff as a robot. *Jehovah, please be with me.*

One of the judges, a middle-aged White man, asked me about my response on the worksheet. "My name is Duke Proctor, I'm one of the judges for round one."

I elevated my eyebrows. Proctor! I clenched my fists.

" Sophia, your response was kind of bland and generic. Can you express why you want to be a singer again please?"

I took one step forward with my right leg then crossed my arms. I looked up at the ceiling before refocusing my attention on Duke. In a nervous voice I said, "Singing is who I am. If I'm not singing, I don't feel complete." *I should've said something more profound.*

The same judge spoke again. "Your paper also indicated that you are in college, correct?"

"Yes," I said.

"You are aware that we specifically said no college students? We are only looking to sign a serious artist that doesn't have outstanding obligatory deeds," said the judge.

I squinted my eyes. How did I make a mistake and put that down?

The same judge continued, "Are you prepared to drop out of school if you had to? If you're a full-time college student, then most likely you won't have time to record songs and go on tour. If you are received well today, we may ask you to consider stepping away from school, so that you can grow your fanbase."

"I am prepared to do whatever it takes!" I stepped back and sung my heart out. I clenched my fists together, tossing my hands into the air, as my emotions flowed throughout my musical soul. Singing like a professional, my vocal cords produced melodious sounds, like the calmness of birds humming. The judges were taken aback; they stood up after I executed a high note. I could hear their chairs sliding against the floor as they stood. I held my note for several seconds then the judges administered a loud standing ovation.

I heard one of the judges scream, "You're definitely going to the next round." Another judge clapped and said, "Absolutely brilliant! We don't need to send you to the second round—" The judges looked at each other and nodded their heads. "—in fact, we just decided you will be a finalist. Congratulations, you're that good!"

I smiled, rushing toward the judge's table like an excited little puppy. I shook their hands. "Thank you all so much!" *I can't believe this.*

The judge who asked me questions earlier spoke. "Wow, you were really impressive. Out of the thousands that auditioned today, Sophia, you have what it takes. Even though you're pregnant, I can really see your potential. Be sure to come back tomorrow as one of our finalists. Come at 10 a.m. tomorrow. We'll get you in and out."

"Okay, thanks so much Mr. Proctor for the feedback. I will definitely be back tomorrow."

As I walked toward the door I overheard, "Next up is Lucy Beth!"

Whew. *I need to use the restroom.* I exited the audition room to head to the restroom. While strolling along I noticed someone who looked familiar. *Is that who I think it is?* I stared at an attractive woman through my peripheral vision.

I entered the restroom, then another woman walked in a few seconds later.

I looked into the mirror. *That is her.*

I faced the woman and asked, "Nancy, is that you?"

Nancy glanced at me with a confused look displayed on her face. She squinted her eyes and replied. "Yes, my name is Nancy, but who are you?"

"You don't remember me from Kyle's house?" I walked closer to Nancy. "Remember, we met several months ago?"

Nancy frowned and responded. "Oh yeah, you're the little girl that took my man."

" I'm not trying to start anything," I said.

Nancy crossed her arms. She faced me, placing her left hand behind her hip. She lifted her purse to adjust it atop her right shoulder. "I don't have any interest in talking to you. And what are you doing at this competition anyway?" She laughed. "You must be here volunteering or something."

I shook my head and scoffed. "Look now, Nancy, I was just trying to speak to you and say hello. I thought maybe we could grab some coffee or something since we both really cared about Kyle," I said.

Nancy lifted her eyebrows then wrinkles formed in her forehead like cracks in an asphalt. She twisted her neck like a giraffe and said, "We both really cared about Kyle?" Nancy adjusted her purse again. "Actually, I loved Kyle." She placed her finger within one inch of my face. I pushed her finger away. Nancy chuckled. "You interfered with us getting back together. I just don't understand what he saw in you, anyway. You're just a little girl, and I'm a grown woman," said Nancy.

I could really smack the taste out of her mouth right now. "I am definitely a full-grown woman," I replied.

Nancy laughed. "Are you auditioning for this contest or something?" She crossed her arms, rocking back and forth and awaiting my reply.

I stepped forward, positioning myself within a foot of Nancy's face. Then, another girl entered the restroom. I glanced at the newcomer then turned my attention back to Nancy. "Yes, and I auditioned already."

Nancy executed a full circle, erupting with hysteria. "Ha, girl, you might as well quit while you're ahead." She pointed at herself. "There's no way you're beating me. If Kyle didn't mention it to you, then I will." She patted her chest. "I am the best singer in the world, and I've been waiting for a break like this for a very long time."

So arrogant. "No, Kyle never mentioned that you were an incredible singer. In fact, he never mentioned your name at all—he was too busy thinking about me." Take that.

Nancy smacked her lips. "I see you have jokes." She put her right hand up near my face. "But anyway, I can tell you right now—you're not going to win this competition." She pointed at my stomach. "Especially not with that fat little belly that you have."

I frowned. "I am pregnant with Kyle's baby, so that's why my stomach looks a little large right now."

Nancy stepped back, making a fist. She screamed, "You know, you ain't even worth it, you heifer." She chuckled. "I can't believe—" She pointed at me. "I can't believe he got you pregnant when I practically begged him for a baby."

I really don't like this chick. "I've had enough of this. I'll see you around, and just for your information, I was invited back for the final audition tomorrow morning."

"Good for you, but it won't matter after they hear me sing. You should stick around for a few more minutes." She lowered her tone. "That way, you'll hear how a real singer sings."

I tossed my hands into the air while observing a few ladies exit the restroom. "Whatever, Nancy. I wish you the best on your audition."

Nancy placed her hand in my face. "I don't need you to wish me anything. I just wish that you would stop talking to me."

I'll stick around to see what you can do.

A few seconds later, we exited the restroom, then Nancy entered the waiting room. I placed my back on a wall near the restroom. *She did a lot of bragging, and I bet she can't even back it up.*

I walked toward the waiting area before Nancy walked out of the waiting room. One of the judges called her number. *I can't wait to hear what you can do.* I placed my right ear onto the door of the audition room. The judges were asking her similar questions. *She's doing a better job than me, because I sucked at answering mine.*

"My name is Nancy Bright. I'm singing an original piece I wrote entitled, Rhythm. Without you only loneliness is projected through my eyes. It's only because of God's supervision I'm able to survive. I wish for you to grant me life again. I've put my pride aside. I'm letting you know I need you. I'm off track, off beat, so please on these words don't sleep. I want my rhythm back, that's a fact. I need you back, you're the rhythm of my heart."

I placed my back against a wall, slamming my fists into it. I sighed. All I heard was loud clapping. *She's going to the next round. She sounded amazing. That's a beautiful song she wrote, too. Well, that's if she wrote it. She probably isn't as good as I am when it comes to writing.* I placed my right ear against the door to listen in again. "Wow, Nancy we really loved your enthusiasm. That song was well-written. We would love to hear the full version. We've seen a lot of girls audition today, and only five other girls stood out to us. You're definitely standing out in your own unique way," said one of the judges.

"Thank you. I do have the rest of this song prepared and ready to perform," said Nancy.

" Okay great, we will see you tomorrow. And you don't need to audition for the next round just come back tomorrow for the final round."

"I'm shocked, this is such a privilege to be placed in an elite group," said Nancy.

After overhearing the judges' commentary, I removed my ear from the door, storming into the restroom to gather myself. A few minutes later, I exited the coliseum. *I need to start practicing as soon as possible.* I bumped into Nancy before I made it to one of the exit doors. The impact of our collision pushed the both of us backwards. While off balance, I erupted and said, "Watch where you're going!"

Nancy chuckled. "You might as well quit while you're ahead. After what the judges just told me, this competition is mine."

I turned my back to Nancy then exited the building. While trying to catch a taxi, I pondered: I think Nancy is right. I was received well, but they didn't respond to me like they did with her.

A taxi pulled up, then I entered the car. I instructed the driver to take me back to the hotel. While in the backseat, I prayed to God. *Oh Jehovah, how am I going to beat Nancy?*

***

The Big Day

I woke up and stretched my arms while sitting up in the bed. I quickly removed the comforter away from my body after glancing at the clock on the nightstand. "It's 3 a.m." *I still don't feel comfortable the way I would like to with The Blues Café.* I was supposed to come back and practice yesterday, but instead, I went to sleep like a loser. I only have seven more hours before my audition time.

I stood in front of the mirror with just my white bra and panties on. *I look so fat. I can't wait to have this baby.* I turned the lights on then sung in front of the mirror. A few minutes later, I stopped rehearsing. *Sophia, if you mess up one more time on your notes, I'm going to strangle you.* I chuckled. "Yeah, I'll strangle myself."

I freefell backwards onto the bed. While lying in the bed, I stared at the ceiling. *Why am I letting Nancy get into my head like this? A part of me feels like she is better than me.*

What will I do if I lose to Nancy? I slapped myself. *Shut up mind, I'm not losing to Nancy.* I rubbed my belly. I just know I'm going to have a girl. I'm going to name my baby girl Isabella Smith. I'll call her Izzy for her nickname. " Little Izzy, I can't wait until you're out of my belly."

Within a few minutes I was fast asleep.

***

Hours later, I woke up and noticed I fell asleep half-naked and uncovered. I jumped up in a panic, after staring out of the window.

After looking out of the window I turned around and looked at the clock. "Shoot, it's 12:30pm." I beat the floor with my fists. "No! I missed my audition. I can't believe this—" I took a deep breath. "I missed my audition, and now Nancy is going to win my record deal!"

I stood up and walked outside onto the balcony outside my room. I looked down and observed ongoing traffic. I started to visualize my blood splashing against the pavement, crying profusely. I really had an overwhelming urge to revisit my thoughts—the same thoughts that Sammie saved me from years ago in the midnight forest. I glanced at my growing belly. My thoughts of never meeting my child motivated me to stay alive.

With my fingers interlocked, I leaned against the balcony with my forearms. With my head hanging low I spoke out loud, "This is truly one of the worst days of my life." *I am not going to even waste my time trying to find Duke since my flight departs in a few hours.* I walked back inside my hotel room to put my clothes on. While packing my luggage, I thought to myself. It's time for me to get back to the real world. I need to get to the airport and head back to Marin.

Thirty minutes later, I arrived at the airport.

***

The Plane Flight of Defeat

I rushed through the airport to board my flight on time. I looked up at the monitor to check my flight status. After checking my flight's status, I noticed Duke. *Is this my chance? Looks like he's waiting at the gate for his plane.* Duke was only about thirty yards away from me.

I overheard an announcement. "Calling all final passengers to board flight number two-three-four-seven. Our doors will close in thirty seconds," said the flight attendant.

Darn that's my flight number. I've flown with Southwest before. I know they're serious. If they say, 'forty-five seconds', they literally mean forty-five seconds. I sighed. I can't miss my flight home. If I risk it all and go talk to Duke, then maybe he will understand why I missed my audition. He'll probably give me another opportunity to audition too. I started to walk toward Duke, but I stopped in the middle of the aisle. My hands started to perspire as I held onto my luggage. I'll probably just make a fool out of myself. He probably already signed Nancy anyway.

I stared at Duke then looked back at my gate. *This is a tough decision. I only have about twenty seconds.* I *need to make up my mind—like, right now.* I stared at Duke once more as snippets of the judges praising Nancy harassed my confidence. I pinched a small portion of my belly fat. *No one wants to see a pregnant lady with love-handles as their next superstar anyway.* I turned toward my gate, racing to get in line to board my plane. While standing in line, I panted and held my hands over my mouth to restrain my tears. A young man behind me asked, "Ma'am are you okay?"

I need to pull myself together. I looked over my right shoulder and replied, "I'm fine, thank you."

A few minutes later, I boarded the plane then located my seat near the back of the airplane. After I found my seat, I sat down. How fitting, a loser who gives up on their dreams is sitting at the back of the plane. And it doesn't help that I'm Black. I'm such an embarrassment to my race. I just don't have the boldness that Timmy did. I scoffed, peering out of the window before laying my head back.

Ten minutes later, the plane sped off along the tarmac. I braced myself against the seat as a future mom while flight two-three-four-seven took off into the clouds.

Section Three

Chapter 15:
Meet Isabella:
Izzy

Los Angeles, California
January
1986

While sitting at the breakfast table of my home, I stared through the kitchen window at the sunlight that illuminated my house. I held a coffee mug in my hand as the scent of warm coffee beans opened my nostrils. I rubbed my flat stomach. *I can't wait to go jogging, I have to stay fit.*

I placed my right leg atop my left, dangling my right foot while looking around at my house. "If only I'd had the courage to pursue my dreams, maybe I wouldn't be in this small crappy home." I lived in the inner city rather than in Hollywood with the stars, where I belong. I chuckled while sipping my coffee. I rubbed my forehead, touching the smooth skin of a wrinkleless lady in her mid-thirties.

My gray jogging suit fit my body like a glove. A few seconds passed then I placed my right leg back onto the wooden floor. My mind briefly reflected on my past as I listened to Nancy's latest song debut on the radio. My mind still hurts, eighteen years later. I didn't have the courage to risk it all to make my dreams come true. I felt in my heart that if I'd taken the chance to risk everything, Duke would have appreciated my willingness and given me a shot to redeem myself. I placed my mug on the kitchen table. *I will never know now, because I didn't have the courage to go for it.*

I overheard keys dangling at my front door, then the door unlocked, sounds of squeaks entering my home as it opened. My reminiscent thoughts were interrupted by Isabella walking in. I stood up and walked into the living room to embrace the spitting image of my younger self. My baby girl is all grown up. I wish I could go back in time. I should've gone to college; I thought while staring at Isabella. She has a booty just like her mom, but mine was a little bigger when I was her age. Her hair is shorter too, but her eyes are just like mine. Her face and ears are just like her father's. She has his chiseled facial structure too—just with a model-like feminine tone to it. Her skin is flawless, and unfortunately for me, she's two inches taller than me. I've always wanted to be a little taller. Isabella must've gotten her height from Kyle. I smirked. *Look at my baby in that red dress.* Although not as dressy; it's like the dress I wore the night I lost my virginity to Kyle. I smiled while staring at Isabella.

Isabella placed her bookbag on the floor near the couch. She laughed as she faced me and said, "Mom, stop staring at me like a weirdo."

Isabella was standing directly in front of me. I laughed and asked, "Isabella, honey, how was your first day of college?"

Isabella walked to the couch and sat down. She moved her backpack near her legs. "Uh, it was pretty good."

I held my finger up and said, "Hold that thought sweetie, I'll be right back." I walked into the kitchen to grab my coffee cup then I reentered the living room. Standing a few feet away from Isabella, I leaned against a section of the living room wall that was adjacent to her. "Sorry, I had to get my coffee." While drinking my coffee I said, "That's great, Izzy. I'm glad you enjoyed your first day." I approached her while sipping my coffee. "Baby, you're getting so big." She looked disturbed. I placed my mug atop a table. Standing directly in front of her, I said, "You're an adult now, so stop being rude." I extended my outstretched arms. "Come here and give your mother a big hug." We hugged and I whispered in Isabella's right ear, "I'm so proud of you."

She affectionately squeezed me, then gracefully untangled our arms. "Mom, are you trying to say that I look fat or something?"

"You don't look fat—that's certainly not what I meant. I'm saying it's been amazing to watch my little girl grow into a young woman."

Isabella grinned. "If you say so. But, uh, I have to leave. I just wanted to drop in and say hello before I go hang out with Mark."

"Mark? What kind of lame name is that?" I asked.

"Mom, be nice. I like him a lot. I plan for the two of you to meet soon."

I folded my arms. I don't want her to get pregnant too early like I did. "Izzy, you're only eighteen. Are you sure you have to start dating right now? You have your whole life ahead of you. You'll have plenty of time to date boys and have fun. You know I had you at a young age. I was only eighteen."

Isabella tapped her feet against the floor. It vibrated with creaks of its own. "Mom, don't lecture me right now, please."

"I'm just trying to help out." I took a few steps forward and placed my hands atop her shoulders while staring into her eyes. "I never got a chance to finish school or pursue my dreams the way I wanted too. I'm just looking out for you; I don't want you to get caught up. Just remember, no sex before marriage." I elevated my tone while pointing my finger at Isabella's face. "I'm telling you now, don't disappoint God like I did. I've already experienced a lot of failures in life for you." I squeezed her shoulders. "If you listen to me, you will be successful."

Isabella dropped her shoulders, dragging her speech out of irritation as she replied, "Mom!"

She's just like me when I was her age. She's so headstrong. I held my hands up, signaling for Isabella to cease speaking. "Don't depend on your own knowledge, Isabella. Remember, mankind's inability to acknowledge his own flawed viridity always produces bad results."

She sighed. "Viridity? Mom, really? You had to use a big word like that? You're trying to show off, huh? And when did you become such a philosopher?"

"Come on college girl, what are those professors teaching you at Marin? You should know a simple word like viridity."

Isabella smirked. "I'll be careful, Mom, I promise. I'll even save myself for marriage too." She walked toward the front door.

I escorted Isabella toward the door. We stopped in front of the door. "Don't fall for those boys' tricks. They're sneaky." I opened the front door. While standing on the porch I said, "If Mark offers you sweet potato pie or a peanut butter and jelly sandwich, run, because he's only after one thing."

She faced me. "Mom, you're hilarious. But we both know you're the one who has a weakness for peanut butter and jelly sandwiches. I don't really like either one of those things that you claim are a girl's weaknesses." Isabella tilted her head and grinned. "However, a nice tall glass of red wine, on the other hand, might be kind of hard to turn down, if you know what I mean."

I stepped forward, folding my arms. "Izzy, just make your mommy proud." I pushed my hands into the air, signaling for Isabella to leave. "Now go and have a good time."

She smiled. "Okay, Mom. And I'll be back around 7 p.m. And don't forget that you mentioned that you were going to tell me about the gift that you wanted to pursue when you were my age."

I did say that. But I'm embarrassed now, especially after seeing her come back from her first day of college. She will look at me as someone that's a quitter if I tell her. It's probably best if I recant. "Actually, I don't like talking about what I wanted to be. The reality that I never achieved my goals really bothers me. I hate being reminded of the poor decisions I made," I said.

Isabella looked confused. Her hands sat atop her hips. "Okay, but you still haven't told me about this mysterious guy that made you go to The Blues Café before you met my dad either."

"One day, when you're in love, you will understand. I just can't say his name right now, it brings me too much grief."

"Is Sammie his name?" Isabella asked.

I raised my eyebrows. "What? Where did you hear that name from?" I rubbed my chin. How does Isabella know about Sammie? I've never mentioned his name to her.

Isabella smirked. "Mom, I don't know if you know this, but you mention a guy's name in your sleep, almost every other night. You always say, 'Sammie, I tried, thanks for saving me in the midnight forest. I love you too, Sammie, please come back to me'."

I walked down the steps, looking into the sky, then I waved at my neighbor across the street. I refocused my attention on Isabella. "Sweetheart, I'm sure I was just having a dream." I wonder if Izzy found the song that I wrote with Sammie's name in it.

She walked toward her car, a four-door silver BMW. After she sat down in her car, Isabella held the door open and said, "Mom, is writing your gift that you are hiding from me?"

That's one of them. I smiled. "Sweetie, writing is one of my lesser gifts."

"Mom, I don't want to keep Mark waiting too much longer, so I really need to go now."

I stepped back in a playful manner. "Well, excuse me." I waved bye as Isabella reversed out of the driveway. Isabella looked to her left once she was in the road, then she looked at me and waved bye.

I waved back. "Take care!"

While walking up the steps to reenter my house, I decided to pursue my singing career again. I walked inside and closed the door. While leaning against the front door, I started to cry while singing. "My baby girl just inspired me!" *I can't keep living my life vicariously through my daughter.* My tears turned into joy as I ran up and down the stairs. I reenacted scenes from the musical Grease, singing at the top of my lungs. Minutes later, I was panting, sitting on the couch with sweat pouring down my face. *I need to be brave and go after the things I truly want out of life.* I stood up and sung the chorus to "The Blues Café." I applauded myself for a few seconds then wiggled my hips. "Looks like I still got it."

I looked around at my house while walking back and forth throughout the living room. *I am finally in a position where I can honestly say that I'm not willing to live another day without chasing my dreams. After Izzy turned thirteen, I knew she would be okay staying at home by herself.* I sat down on the couch and placed my fists underneath my chin. After Izzy demonstrated that she was responsible and capable of holding her own; I started performing at The Blues

Café. I smiled. Friday nights at the café has been my personal spotlight for the past five years. *I'm twenty-four years behind.* I stood up and looked upward at the ceiling. "Before I die, I vow today to give my dreams one final shot."

I walked upstairs to enter my bedroom. I laid across my bed and thought to myself. I plan on revealing to Izzy the music within my heart once I've achieved some type of success. It doesn't have to be a record deal, but I need something for my daughter to be inspired by. I caressed my forehead. I'll be completely out of money in two months. I won't have any money remaining from the life insurance policies. I need a job, but if it's not a job in music, I don't want it.

I stared at my bedroom ceiling, counting the various line distinctions. I didn't have the courage to be who I was called to be at eighteen, but now, I finally have the courage to be who I truly am at thirty-six. I have the perfect song I am thinking about using for an audition in six months at The Blues Café. I saw an ad that a famous music producer was going to be there for the audition, too.

I wrapped my arms across my chest, giving myself a big hug. I'm glad I kept up with my exercise regimen in honor of Timmy. I'm thirty-six, but I look like I'm only six years older than my daughter. I laughed. I'm glad my daughter decided to stay at home with me rather than on campus. I sat up. She keeps me company when I get lonely. The university's campus is only twenty minutes away from my house. I lodged at the edge of the bed. Since Izzy doesn't get home from class until the afternoon now, that means I'll have to practice late at night while she's asleep. I can't let her find out about my gift just yet—at least not until I've produced some results that will inspire her.

I stood up and said, "My daughter is my true inspiration. Isabella deserves to know that her mother is a winner too." I clenched my teeth together. Izzy doesn't realize it just yet, and I haven't proven it either, but she gets her tenacity from me. "Izzy reminds me so much of Timmy."

Chapter 16:
Chase Your Dreams:
Isabella is Unstoppable

ISABELLA

That Sophia is something else, but I love my mom to death.

I arrive at Mark's residence. While sitting in my car outside his place, I briefly reflect on a secret I'm withholding from my mother. I put my car in park then look in the mirror to ensure that my makeup is perfectly structured. While painting my lips with red lipstick, I playfully sing a short and melodious sequence. "Mark, I can't wait to see you baby." I laugh to myself. *My voice is becoming powerful. I'm so happy God blessed me with the ability to sing like a superstar. I know being a singer is my true calling.*

I smell underneath my armpits and smirk. *Good, I'm not musty.* Reaching into my purse, I extract a bottle, then spray a feminine fragrance on my body. The scent of fresh strawberries fills the car. I polish the edges of my hair with a small comb. *If only my mom knew that I can write too. I want to be a singer and a songwriter, but my mom doesn't know. I don't want her to know that I'm going to move away soon to pursue my goals and dreams. I exhale. I hate that I have to do this to my mom, but I have to live my life and do what makes me happy. I don't know why my mom just won't spill the beans about her gift that she claims is so powerful. I shook my head. I'm going to be the next Chaka Khan or Whitney Houston. I wish I could tell my mom I have an audition coming up in six months at The Blues Café. How ironic. I'll be auditioning at the venue where my mom went looking for the love of her life nearly twenty years ago.*

I exit the car. While closing the door, I notice Mark through my peripheral vision. I look over my left shoulder and observe him peeking out of the window with the blinds wide open. I smile, my vision filled with his radiant smile. *He looks like a celebrity on the cover of a magazine.* I turn around to face Mark's house, adjusting my red sundress. *I hope he loves my dress.* The day's breeze blows my long curly hair into the wind. My light caramel complexion complements the beige colors of Mark's house.

While walking, I lift my bra, adjusting the straps. I smile like Marilyn Monroe when I see Mark open the door. My hazel brown eyes draw energy from the sun as the sunlight shines across my face. The light exposes my long eyelashes, perfectly positioned beneath my long and pristine eyebrows. I lift my eyebrows and my medium-sized forehead forms a few wrinkles as I stare at Mark walking down the steps to greet me.

Mark's walk resembles that of a military man as he strolls along, commanding the scene. His unmatched attractiveness is ready to do battle with any willing contender. His vanilla complexion is a perfect fit for his long blonde hair. As he walks, his hair bounces, and he pushes his hands through it. His orange T-shirt blends in with the sun. The sun's radiance illuminates his swimmer's body, his broad shoulders captivating my eyes. While walking, he gracefully adjusts the belt on his blue jeans. His long torso sits atop his shorter legs. Mark's height could make him a point guard in the NBA.

Once Mark positions himself within a few feet of me, he pauses and glances at me with his light gray eyes. He winks his right eye at me. His wide eyebrows convey a flirtatious countenance as he lifts his round cheeks. His face is short, but it complements his small skull. Mark's ears protrude more than usual, especially on the average male.

When he's a few inches away from my face, I think: He's so tall and handsome. I just wish he didn't have those jumbo looking ears. But he's still my baby.

I rub my lips together to ensure that my lipstick looks pristine. I halt and embrace the fresh scent of a clean man. He smells like he just stepped out of the shower. We hug for several seconds, then Mark lifts me into the blue sky like a teddy bear. I smile while flying in the air. After Mark puts me down, I say, "Hey, Mark. Sorry I'm late for practice tonight. I was talking to my mom." I smile while pointing my fingers at him. I gently nudge him in his right shoulder. "And I finally told her about you too."

Mark rubs his chin. "Awesome, baby, just awesome." He grabs my hands and stares into my eyes.

"It's so cool having my boyfriend as my manager. Hopefully, this will be to my advantage once my singing career takes off."

He squeezes my face. "It's to your advantage." He squints his eyes. "So, what did she say when you told her about me?" Mark asks.

I squeeze his hands then we hold hands while walking toward the front door of his house. I am walking to his left. As we continue to slowly walk, I make eye contact with him. "Uh, she didn't really have much to say—she just told me not to have sex with you." I laugh.

Mark tosses his head back and laughs like a comedian in tune with his jokes. "Your mom is something else I see."

We pause along the sidewalk, facing one another. We kiss, then Mark guides me into his house. His kisses are always so refreshing.

Mark's home looks like a medium-sized massage parlor. His mancave is neat. It looks like a maid cleans up his place at least five times a day. His light blue walls complement the red and white glass furniture scattered throughout his home. He's a man of beautiful human artwork, I think to myself while looking around at several pictures hanging from the walls. He guides me around the points to the dining room table. I place my hands over my mouth while pointing as I smile and say, "Baby, is that a candlelight dinner I see over there by the window?" Mark nods his head in a playful demeanor and smiles. "I was wondering what smelled so good." I look down at the kitchen floor. "Oh wow, I didn't notice the rose pedals on the floor either."

I grab his hand tight and kiss him on the cheek. This is very nice. "I'm so excited to be here with you tonight. I didn't think you were going be so romantic today. I thought we were meeting up to practice for the audition in six months, remember?"

Mark scratches the side of his head to gesture that he forgot about my audition. "Don't be mad, but it slipped my mind." He looks dejected.

I'm slightly disappointed. I sigh. "It's okay."

"Baby, we're going to practice for your audition tonight for sure." He looks toward the dining room. "Meanwhile, how about we get your creative juices flowing first? With a nice, delicious meal that really hits the soul. I look forward to meeting your mom soon too. To be honest, I've been kind of worried whether or not she will like me, since I am a White boy."

"Ha, ha. Don't be silly, Mark." I laugh. "We aren't living in the fifties anymore. And besides, my mom isn't like that anyway." I playfully punch him in his right shoulder. "I still haven't met your parents yet either."

He rubs the back of his head and says, "Uh, about that—"

We quickly turn around to embrace the front door opening. I glance at Mark while observing a strange man entering his abode. The man looks about fifty years of age, and he's a few inches shorter than six feet in height. His belly protrudes out of his black, long sleeve dress shirt, resting atop his belt. His jet-black slacks perfectly complement his all-black ensemble, which uniquely suits his Caucasian complexion. The man looks a lot like Mark, minus the laziness of his left eye.

I look at Mark once again, then glance at a lady standing to the right of the identified man. The middle-aged woman exudes happiness. She is about five-foot-two-inches-tall, with short hair that sets off the brilliance of her brunette hair color. Her facial structure resembles that of a Native American. Her physique is fluffy like a filled-out buffalo. Her plus-sized dark blue dress blends in with her freckled complexion.

With cluelessness glued atop my face, I look at Mark and lift my hands up while attempting to speak, as Mark walks toward the lady and man. Mark hugs them.

Mark places his left hand on the lower back of the lady and guides her in my direction. Confused but anticipating, I lift my eyebrows as Mark smiles.

"Hey Izzy, meet my mom and dad," he says. He points to his father and mother. "Meet my dad and mom, Joseph and Terri."

Terri steps forward and extends her right hand. With the voice of a soft-spoken angel, she says, "Hi Isabella, I'm Terri. We have heard so much about you. Mark wanted to surprise you tonight. He asked us if we would be willing to come meet you." Terri points at Joseph and he waves. "Joseph and I are music teachers." Terri looks around at the studio. "This is our studio as well. We have worked with tons of artists over our careers. Mark mentioned how talented you are." She gently touches my right shoulder. "We would be honored to see your skills."

I didn't know who they were at first. I sigh and remove a tinge of sweat from my forehead. I smile and shake Terri's hand as both of her hands continue to rest atop mine. "That is so awesome. It's so good to finally meet you Mrs. Clay," I say while making laser-sharp eye contact.

I shake Joseph's hand. After shaking my hand, he places his hands back into his pockets, rocking his pelvis back-and-forth. While glancing at his son to gesture his stamp of approval, Joseph winks at Mark then turns his attention to me and says, "So, Isabella."

I smile. "Yes sir, Mr. Clay?"

Joseph playfully hits Mark on the shoulder before asking, "How is that boy of mine treating you? I taught him to be a gentleman and to respect women, is he doing that?"

Mark grimaces. "Dad, don't embarrass me."

With his hands open Joseph glances at Mark and I as he says, "I'm just asking this fine young lady a question, Mark." Joseph chuckles. "Calm down."

I place my hands over my heart, and I speak with endearment. "Mr. Clay, Mark is a beyond a gentleman to me. I really love that you all are here tonight. Since you all have worked with a plethora of artists, uh, maybe the two of you can give me some pointers."

Terri replies, "Of course, my dear." She grabs my hands. "You are such a beautiful girl." She points at her son. "Mark looks at you the way Joseph used to look at me."

Joseph quickly twists his head in Terri's direction. "Used to look? Oh no, baby, I still look at you the same." Joseph grabs Terri's hand and she pushes it away. "Come over here and give your hubby a big kiss."

Terri frowns and whispers, "Not in front of our new company, Joseph. Don't start! Now you know how you get when you start drinking. I told you not to drink those glasses of wine until after we ate." She rolls her eyes at him before turning her attention to me. "Isabella, are you ready to eat?" Terri asks.

I smile. "Yes of course." I glance at Mark. "Hey Mark, can we talk for a quick second? It'll only take a minute."

"Okay," says Mark.

Joseph places his hands over his mouth to hold back his laughs. "Son, sounds like you're in trouble already." Joseph smirks. "It's never a good sign when a woman says, 'can we talk'."

Terri hits Joseph in his shoulder and says, "Don't you start, you've obviously had too much to drink already." She sighs.

While Mark and I walk toward the front door to talk outside, I think: Why didn't he tell me his parents were coming tonight? I would've fixed up a little more if I'd known. He knows how I feel about first impressions. I frown. Guys can be so clueless sometimes.

Mark opens the door like a gentleman and escorts me outside.

Once outside, he grabs my hands and pulls me close to him. "Izzy, what's going on?"

I bend my left knee and cross my arms while raising my eyebrows. "This is all kind of shocking to me. I didn't expect to meet your parents this way. Why didn't you tell me they were coming tonight? I would've dressed up a little." I look down at my red dress. "This dress isn't appropriate enough. It's very tight, so I feel like a slut in front of your parents. You get what I'm saying, Mark?"

He exhales. "Isabella, I totally understand." He smiles. "You look great to me; I don't see a problem with your dress." He licks his lips.

Lord, he's so fine. Maybe I'm just being a little too self-conscious. "Mark, you're funny."

He shrugs his shoulders and smirks.

"I just want us to have a good understanding of one another, that's all," I say.

Mark nods his head in agreement as we make our way back into the house. The surrealness of the moment pushes my heart into nostalgia.

While slowly trailing Mark, I ponder how we met. I've been going out with Mark for three months now. We started dating over the summer and we met at a local library. He walked up to me while I was looking at a new book. "What type of things do you like to read?" Mark had asked.

I blushed without even receiving a compliment after I realized how gorgeous he was. "Hi there. I like romance novels and biographies."

He mentioned that we like the same genre of books. We hit it off right away. We talked for an hour at the library before he asked if I wanted to go get coffee and talk some more.

After we arrived at the coffee shop, he asked, "What do you want to do with your life? Are you going to college?"

I laughed and reflected on the frankness of his questions. "I'm going to Marin County University. I want to be a singer."

He placed his coffee down after taking a sip. "I'm going to Marin County too. I want to be a music producer." He licked his lips then stared at me. His gray eyes lit up my soul. "You know, I can be your producer."

I blushed. "Okay."

There's no denying those eyes of his, and it's good that we both have a love for music. Mark wants to be a music producer and I want to be a singer, and we're enrolled at Marin County together too. I know that we are meant to be together.

I'm shook back into the present moment as Mark squeezes my hand while we stand in the living room. Mark starts talking to his parents. I glance at him and his family. He releases my hand, then they walk into the kitchen. I remain in the living room area for a few seconds before following them. I lean on the counter while observing Mark converse with his parents. He's so adorable. I look around. I guess their studio is just another house that they have.

Terri glances in my direction. "Come on boys' the food is getting cold, and we have a lot to talk about. I am so excited to learn more about you, Isabella, and your upcoming audition."

Joseph says, "I hope you're ready to taste the best cooking you've ever had in your life, Isabella. I don't know if Mark told you, but I can make some really fine dishes."

I smile and nod my head. "I really like the way that Mark cooks, so if your cooking is better than Mark's, then I know you are an excellent cook."

Joseph points at me and replies, "I like this girl, son. You should keep her around, so don't mess this one up."

"Yessir, I'll try my best not to."

After the food is ready, we prepare our plates before walking into the dining room to eat. Terri and Joseph sit down and observe Mark pull out my chair. I sit down and embrace Mark's hands atop my shoulders. He gently squeezes my shoulders while I glance over my right shoulder and smile at him.

Terri exhales and places her hands over her heart. While looking at Joseph with disdain she says, "Joseph, our boy is such a sweet gentleman—you could use some pointers from him. You didn't pull my chair out for me." She smiles for a few more seconds before saying, "Son, can you say a prayer over the meal?" Joseph scoffs.

Mark walks to his chair and sits directly across from me. Mark extends his hands and I grab ahold of them. He glances at his mother and says, "Yes Ma'am, I surely can." While holding my hands, Mark transitions into saying a prayer. Mark smiles at me before he starts. "God, thank you for this special evening tonight. We thank you for bringing us all together for this great feast. We pray that you help this small gathering to be memorable as we enjoy the experience of getting to know one another. We pray that you give Isabella the courage and strength to perform the gift you have given her tonight with boldness and grace. Prepare her heart to embrace her destiny in six months as well. We thank you for the food we are about to eat, and we offer this prayer in the name of your son, Jesus Christ, Amen."

Everyone joins in and says, "Amen!"

Terri starts to gobble down her steak and potatoes, then she wipes her mouth with a napkin and says, "I can't wait to hear you sing, Isabella."

I smile at Terri while gracefully chewing my food.

"Where are you from, Isabella?" Terri asks.

"My mom and I are from Marin County."

While holding a silver fork to her mouth, Terri asks, "What about your dad, where is he from? What type of work does he do?"

I sigh as the remembrance of death attacks my spirit. I lower my voice and hesitate before saying, "My dad is dead."

Terri places her fork atop her plate. The sound effects of a fork tapping against a glass plate echo through the room. She wipes her mouth with a paper towel and says, "Aww … forgive me, I'm sorry I asked."

I wave my hands to signal that it's okay. "It's okay, I never got a chance to meet him. He was killed while my mom was pregnant with me. He got into a deadly car wreck; he was killed by a drunk driver."

Joseph chimes in, placing his hands over his mouth to cough. "I guess that water went down the wrong pipe. Isabella, my grandfather was killed by a drunk driver as well. I'm named after my grandpa; his name was Joseph too." He points to his wife. "He was killed way before I married Mrs. Clay here. I was ten or twelve at the time."

" Thanks for sharing. I'm sure that was pretty traumatic for you."

Terri intervenes and says, "It was!" Joseph gives Terri a stare to show his annoyance but remains silent for a few seconds.

Joseph clears his throat and says, "While it's fresh on my mind, back in the day, men couldn't really pursue their dreams the way you all can today. My dad worked for an oil company. Men from my generation were taught to do industrialized work. We were molded to focus on taking care of our families. We were taught to do everything with our hands. Now don't get me wrong, some people's gifts involve their hands. During my time, a lot of people had other gifts that went untapped because of the conditions of society. It's interesting how the generations have refined their concepts, though, and despite the hard work of our ancestors." Joseph looks at me with fatherly ardor. "Make no mistake about it, Isabella, it takes courage to pursue a singing career."

Joseph sips some of his water. "If you two stick to your guns and work hard to perfect your craft, you will succeed." He glances at his son. "This is what I have instilled into Mark here. If you haven't noticed yet, he's a go-getter."

"Mr. Joseph, that was very motivational. I can see where Mark gets his determination from." I scoot my chair back and ask, "May I excuse myself? I need to use the bathroom."

While holding her fork in her right hand, Terri replies, "Go right ahead, sweetheart. Joseph and I don't care." She glances at Mark. "And Mark doesn't either."

"That's correct, Mom." Mark smiles at me. "Go right ahead baby, we will be at the table waiting for you until you come back."

I stand up. "Thanks everyone, I'll be right back." While walking to the bathroom, I ponder: This is such a great dinner. Seeing everyone laugh like this is making me feel comfortable about performing in front of Mark's family. They're really down-to-earth-people too. I raise my eyebrows. I hope my mom receives Mark the same way that his family is receiving me.

I enter the bathroom and close the door. My mom just doesn't seem happy. She keeps mentioning this guy, Sammie, in her dreams. She won't disclose a lot of things about her life to me. I exhale. She won't even tell me what her gift is. It's like I know my mom, and then I don't know her. I know she can write because I discovered some of her work. I rest my hands beneath my chin as my elbows serve as table legs for my hands. But she refuses to elaborate on why she used to write songs. I am beginning to wonder if my mom has a gift in music like I do.

I'm ambivalent about discussing my dreams with my mom, since she told me that she wants me to be a doctor, lawyer, nurse, or a schoolteacher. She always says, "That's nonnegotiable." I sigh. I have to move out because I can't be free in my mom's house. She won't let me be who I truly am on the inside. I often wonder if my mom is jealous or envious of me because her life didn't turn out the way she wanted it too.

I stand up, flush the toilet, and then wash my hands. I look at myself in the mirror. I just can't put my hands on why she thinks and feels the way she does about life. I'm going to have to stand up to my mom soon. I'll force her to come clean about her past.

I turn the faucet off and dry my hands on a towel that's hanging from the wall. Music is my gift and without it, I'm nothing. I polish my makeup in the mirror then I hear two loud knocks on the bathroom door. Mr. Joseph interrupts my erumpent emotions by saying, "Hey, it's Joseph!"

"Uh, yeah—"

"Hey, can I call you, Izzy? I like that name. Mark revealed your nickname at the dinner table."

I look confused while continuing to fix my makeup. "Yes, you can call me Izzy. Do you need to use the bathroom? If so, I'll be out in a minute."

"I'm an old man, so I can't hold my bladder much longer, so yes," says Joseph.

I open the door. "Ha, okay, Mr. Clay. I am coming out now." Joseph is rocking side to side. His all-black attire makes him look like a ninja prancing around.

Joseph smiles then enters the bathroom. He pauses next to me, patting me on my right shoulder as he says, "You remind me of my wife's smile when she was a young lady like yourself."

I smile and say, "Thank you." A few seconds later, I rejoin Mark and his mom. Three minutes later, Joseph walks into the dining room as I prepare to perform for Mark's parents. I stand up at the table then position myself at the front of the dining table—so that everyone has a clear view of me.

***

The Rehearsal

I turn my back to them and lower my head, saying a silent prayer to prepare my mind. Izzy, you have to really bring your A-game. I would hate to embarrass myself and Mark. I'm sure his parents have some valuable connections that may be of good use to me. Maybe they want to see the diversity of my skills before they start promoting me to other people. I've been practicing a song I found inside my mother's room, inside a shoebox. The Blues Café, I really like it. I think it's beautiful. I clear my throat. Okay, here goes nothing.

I turn around to face my audience like a world class performer, twisting and moving my feet like Michael Jackson. I clench my fists together. "Okay, so the song is entitled, The Blues Café. My mom wrote this song." I smile. "And without further ado—here's how it goes." I step back, tossing my head back into the air as melodious sounds escape through my mouth. My voice sounds like I've been singing as a professional my entire life. I start to clap, snapping my fingers as I sing. I add flare to my style through the continuation of finger snapping coupled with a cadence. I walk forward, holding a high note, just as long as an average person holds their breath. Then, I cease singing while panting. I ponder while smiling and perspiring. *I can tell that Mark and his family really like my voice as well as the song. They're still clapping for me like I just finished a grand performance or something. Wow, they just gave me a standing ovation too.*

Mark runs up to me and kisses me on my cheek. "Wow Izzy, that was great!" He stands in front of me with his arms wide open, smiling like an excited newborn baby. "I'm so happy you're my girlfriend. You're definitely going to be a superstar with a voice like that," Mark says.

Terri chimes in. "Yeah, I agree. Your voice is unlike anything that we have heard before." While standing near the dining table, Terri signals for me to come her way. "Isabella, come here and give me a hug." We hug for a few seconds. "You sounded amazing, and what a well-written song by your mom. She has a true gift herself. I guess music just flows through your family's veins. I honestly don't know if I am more impressed with your voice or the song. Do you know what the song is about?"

I glance at Mark and notice him playfully conversing with his father. They're a few feet away near the pantry. I turn my attention to Terri and say, "Not really, but it's obviously a love song."

"Do you know if your mom can sing, Isabella? I really like the song your mom wrote. I think she could have a real career in song writing, if she wanted to. What does she do for a living?" Terri sits down at the dining table and gestures for me to sit down with her.

My mom is such an embarrassment. I scratch my eyes, my elbows resting atop the table. "Uh, she doesn't work." That sounds extremely lazy, what should I say now? "She has just enough money to get by with the life insurance settlements that she received after my dad passed away."

With a face reflecting the image of a concerned mother, Terri says, "That must've been really hard for her." She exhales. "I would like to meet her one day soon."

"Thanks, Mrs. Clay. I really appreciate your kind words. You've helped me to confirm that I should stick with The Blues Café as my audition song."

" You're welcome sweetie." She turns her attention to her husband. "Joseph, let's head home." Joseph acknowledges his wife as he smiles and hugs Mark goodbye. "I have to get up early in the morning to meet Sabrina and her mom for breakfast at The Golden Café."

A few seconds later, everyone walks toward the front door, then Mark's parents exit their studio home. After everyone walks outside, I reflect on the visit. Feeling Mark's mom's soft hands brush across my face as she says goodbye makes me feel like she adopted me as her own. Mark's mom is so nice, and his dad isn't far behind. I really liked their visit. I need to get home as well. I think I will leave with Mark's parents.

Before Mark closes the front door, I say, "Mark, I think I'm going to go ahead and head back to the house before my mother gets worried. She doesn't like when I stay out too long, you know."

Mark grabs my hands and holds them as he says, "I totally understand baby. I'll see you on campus tomorrow. Uh, we can do lunch during one of our class breaks. I'm going to go clean up the studio, and then I'll head home too."

"I am sorry, I totally forgot about that. I'm being rude, I'll come help you clean up."

He grimaces and waves his hands side-to-side. "No, don't worry about it. Besides, I don't want your mom disliking me before we meet. You told me she wants you to be home by a certain time tonight."

"You're right, that would be a bad first impression. Especially with how my mom is currently thinking. She just doesn't seem happy." I lift my eyebrows. I shake my right index finger. "However, she does seem to be happy on Fridays for some reason—I just haven't put my finger on it yet." I'm curious to find out why she's always so excited on Fridays, now that I think about it.

Mark shrugs his shoulders while wiping the kitchen table with a towel as he says, "Who knows."

I unconsciously tune Mark out as he continues to speak while I stand back, observing him.

I've always wondered what my mom does at night on Fridays. I used to think she was a stripper when I was younger, but I know better than that now. My mom is a devout Christian woman. There's one thing she did well, she instilled God's Word into my heart. She taught me to have a healthy fear of God. I smile. "Mark, I'll see you tomorrow."

"I thought you were going to help me?" Mark asks.

I glance at my watch. "Oh, I'm sorry, but I think I really need to go."

"It's okay," says Mark. He blows a kiss at me as I step backwards toward the door. "Okay, bye baby. Oh, and Isabella, I have a question however, I need you to answer it right now, please."

I cease stepping backwards. "Okay, what's up?"

"I was wondering if I can have another one of your delicious kisses." He licks his lips and smiles.

I love when he licks those juicy lips of his." I'll give you a kiss on the cheek for now. Beggars can't be choosers. I think I'll make you wait until tomorrow. I'll give you a kiss tomorrow if you behave yourself." I grin.

Mark drops his head and pokes his bottom lip out, conveying the look of a sad puppy. "Yes Ma'am." He grins.

I laugh then Mark puts the towel down and walks me out. "Bye, silly." He's so stinking cute.

I get into my car and drive away, Mark watches me drive away from his heart. While driving I think about my mom. *I need to help my mom realize she's sitting on a gold mine with her writing abilities. I'll tell her that two music professors are interested in meeting her. My mom will want to know how they know about her, though.*" I'll have to tell her that I performed her song." I sigh and rub my eyes. *I think it's time for me to be open and honest with my mom about how I really feel. It would be so nice if my mom realized that there's more to life than drinking and temporary excitement on Friday nights.* I exhale. With the radio volume set to low, I nod my head and listen to jazz music while I drive. "I have a lot to learn about you, Sophia Smith, and you're going to tell me everything I want to know." I probably should have moved into the dorms on campus, so that I could have more freedom. But I wanted to keep a close eye on my mom, and I didn't want her to be lonely. I may have to reconsider some things if our talk doesn't go well, because she is a little possessive with me at times. I have my own life to live, and I'm an adult now.

Twenty minutes later, I arrive home and walk inside to freshen up before preparing for bed. I rush upstairs and prepare a bubble bath, then I walk out of the bathroom with the water running to see if my mom is home. *I don't hear any noise in the house.* I knock on her bedroom door, but I hear nothing. I enter her bedroom, turning the lights on, only to witness a well put together bed—one that is undisturbed. "I guess she must be out again, doing her secretive stuff that she does on Fridays." I shake my head while walking back to the bathroom to get inside the tub.

Chapter 17:
Inspiration from the Soul

With bubbles forming inside the decadent 80s tub, I lay my head back and ponder as the water encompasses my nude body. It feels good to be home after a long night of fun. Soaking in the tub is one of my favorite things to do. I wonder what time Mom is going to be home. I smile as I sit up, cleaning underneath my armpits. Mark was smooth tonight.

I place a washcloth over my back and the water runs down my spine like a waterfall. Still thinking. I wonder if my dad had a gift in music as well. I can't wait to audition for Duke Proctor in six months. Duke has been around for a while. He's worked with artists like Nancy and Draketa. Every time I play Nancy's music, my mom goes crazy and tells me to turn off the radio. I can't figure out why my mom dislikes her so much. When I asked my mom why, she always says, "I just don't like her, and there are much better singers than her anyway." I clean my chest and wipe my neck. I'll hop out of the tub now and get ready for bed. I probably should look over my syllabus for school and double check to make sure I have everything I need. I step out of the tub and dry off with a towel. After drying off, I tie a medium-sized purple towel around my head to help dry my hair. Seconds later, I enter my bedroom to turn on a lamp near my bed, before putting on a pajama set.

While sitting upright with my legs stretched out in the bed, I look over my syllabus, confirming that I have everything I need. I look over my professor's names and notice that I have five: Sammie, James Allen, Burrick Miller, Brittany Coles, and Elana Miles. Hmm…I don't see a last name for Sammie. *Sammie is the name of the guy that I think my mom had a crush on or something back in the day. He has the same name as my mom's crush.* I smile. *I know this is absurd, but it'll be crazy if one of my professors is the guy my mom whispers about in her sleep.* I reposition my body, scooting down toward the edge of the bed near the nightstand. *I just know my mom's dreams are based on a real person. I can tell by her emotional response whenever I question her about Sammie. You don't get emotional over a fictional character from your dreams unless you're missing some marbles, and I know my mom isn't crazy. I just want my mom to be happy, even if I have to create a hoax. Or maybe it's him? Regardless, I think it will make her smile and give her hope.* I sigh. "I don't know anymore; I just know that I want my mom to be happy."

I lay down in the bed, crossing my legs as I place a pillow underneath my head. I wonder what I need to do to get my mom to sit down and have a decent conversation with me about her life. My mom is a great communicator. She will talk your ears off. But when it comes to her personal life, she just doesn't want to entertain the topic.

A few minutes later, I fall asleep.

***

The Blues Café

1986
Sophia

A crowd of about two hundred people erupted into a loud chant.

"Sophia…Sophia…Sophia!"

My blue dress was accompanied by white high heels, which complemented my pearl necklace as I moved from side-to-side on the stage. I grabbed the microphone, maneuvering it around like a racket hitting a tennis ball. My moves were calculated and smooth as I twisted, twirled, and shook my thick hips. I moved like a dancing machine to the sounds of a saxophone and drums. I skillfully held the microphone away from my mouth while blowing melodious sounds into it. As the crowd listened to the excellence of my voice, they screamed. "You're the best! Sophia, you're the best!" I smiled as my teeth gave a face to my voice's mystic. With sweat running down my face, I performed like a superstar. I had the stage presence of Diana Ross.

After I finished my performance, I bowed before the crowd then exited the stage. I walked toward the back of the café to The Singer's Lounge. "I love this chill spot." It's so peaceful after a performance. I'm glad that I usually have this space to myself. I sat down on a red leather couch. I love to hear the crowd chanting my name. I feel free when I am performing. I smiled. I'm almost ready to perform my final song. My goal still is to perform the song I started working on a few weeks ago before the year ends. And then, I'll retire from singing at The Blues Café. I have been coming here for five years now, every single Friday. I had high hopes to see Sammie, but I haven't seen him in about twenty-years. I'm sure Sammie is married now with kids by now. I just thought that maybe he would eventually show up here again—like he did back in 1968.

I lifted my right leg then fully extended it on the couch as I continued to think. I'm just so disappointed with how my life has turned out. I never became a renown professional singer, I don't have a job, and I have survived off the deceased my whole life. I don't have an identity and it's really affecting me. I'm almost forty years old, and I haven't done much of anything with my life. I have this amazing gift God gave me, and yet, I won't even share it with my beautiful daughter. Hopefully everything goes well for me during the audition that's coming up right here at the café. This is my second chance to make things right.

I placed my left leg onto the couch. "I'm just trying to protect her from my past." I placed my right hand over my forehead. Squeezing my forehead, I exhaled. "But maybe I'm harming myself in the process." I stood up and grabbed a cold bottle of water from the refrigerator, immediately opening it and drinking the water. I have one more song to sing before the night ends. The club manager is finally paying me to perform every Friday. *I just hope that one day I will see Sammie here again. Hopefully, I'll get a chance to talk to him before I die.*

I changed into another outfit, I put a red dress on. "Okay, it's time to get back on stage and give the crowd another great show." I walked out on stage to perform The Blues Café. The crowd went crazy, screaming as the spotlight shined brightly on me. I looked out into the crowd. I would love to experience this all the time on the road.

A few minutes later, I finished my last song, then thanked the crowd. I took my heels off and exited the stage. "Whew!" Now it's time to head home. After I left The Blue's Café, I drove by what used to be Frank's Donuts. Frank's is a hair salon now. Looking at the hair salon brought up nostalgic memories of how I met Kyle.

I parked my car outside of the salon. *I wonder what Kyle would be doing with his life right now. I'm thirty-six, so Kyle would be forty-six and Timmy would be forty.*" Life really does fly by." *If I don't see Sammie by the end of the year, I'm going to start performing somewhere else.*" I need to move on with my life." I don't think I really want to retire. I think it's more the reality that my heart can't handle performing at the café anymore without seeing Sammie. *I have to leave the café soon, or I'll never heal my broken heart's wound. I feel like I'm still living inside our memories inside the midnight forest. I was only a kid when I met Sammie, but I do believe that kids can fall in love too.*

I've been asked out by a lot of men, but I don't want to go out with anyone. The only man who was able to temporarily distract me from

Sammie was Kyle, but he's dead now. I still don't really know for sure if Kyle took my mind off Sammie, because I still thought about Sammie when I was with him. I placed my left hand over my heart. "Sammie was like the battery to my heart; he was always able to jump start me." *That boy made me feel like I was needed. I really want that feeling again.*

I looked at the time. "It's 10 p.m." I've been sitting in my car reflecting for about thirty minutes or so. Isabella is probably worried about me. *I think I'm going to reveal everything to my daughter tonight. I am going to be upfront with her about everything. She has been asking me for a while now to share my past with her.* I sighed then cranked the engine, driving off into the heat of my reflective night. While driving, I started to tear up while thinking about my relationship with Izzy and how my life would have been with Sammie.

✳✳✳

The Letter of Intended Separation

Isabella

I wake up a few hours later after falling asleep. I notice my mom still isn't home. She's pulling another all-nighter. This defeats the purpose of not staying on campus. I thought we would be spending more time together. I take a deep breath and exhale. I turn the television on and start watching TV in my room. I am sitting in an upright position with pillows behind my back to create a cushion. I'm not waiting to move out any longer. Seeing Whitney Houston on TV just now confirms that I need to be free so I can live my dreams. I can't keep living my life this way. Our relationship is dysfunctional anyway. My mom had a responsibility as a parent to teach me my history, and she hasn't. I'm going to write her a letter explaining everything, then I'll call Mark and ask him if it's okay if I lay my head at his parents' studio for a while. I glance at the clock on my nightstand. Who knows what she's out there doing at this time of night? I cross my arms over my chest, frustrated. "Anywhere is better than my mom's house of misery."

I jump up and grab a notebook along with a pen. I start writing my mom a letter.

Dear Mother,

As I start writing my letter, I overhear my mom walk inside. I pause writing the letter. I'll just tell her in person. I put my letter aside to rush downstairs. Once downstairs I discover my mom sitting on the living room couch, drowning inside her tears.

I rush to my mother's aide, wrapping my arms around her like a comforter of hope. "Mom, what's wrong?"

My mom wipes her tears as she hugs me. "Sweetie, I just want to hold you and tell you I'm sorry for not being the type of mom you needed. I know you have a lot that you want to know about me." My mom exhales. "Every time I attempt to share my past with you, it hurts me to my soul. You remind me so much of myself. Talking to you about my past makes my past feel like it's the present. Isabella, I lost the only man I've ever truly loved." My mom erupts into a clamor, her tears fall onto my pajamas. "I miss him so much."

I gently pull away from my mom while placing my hands on her shoulders. I look into my mother's teary eyes and say, "Mom, I'm here for you. And I miss my daddy, too, even though we've never met. I wish the two of you were together right now. I have always wanted to experience what it would be like to have my father in my life."

My mom shakes her head as snot runs down her nose. "That's the problem, sweetheart!" She sighs. "After all this time, you think I've been referring to your daddy, and I haven't. The man whose name you hear me mumbling in my sleep sometimes—that's who I'm referring too."

I elevate my eyebrows. "Sammie?" I ask. I knew it.

My mom places her hands over her heart while looking at the ceiling. "Yes, and I miss him with all of my heart," says my mom.

"You don't mention him sometimes, Mom—actually, you mention his name every single night."

My mom asks, "I do?" My mom smiles as happy tears rage war with her sad tears.

"Yes, you do. I just knew you were in love with a man name, Sammie." I should tell her about my music professor. "My music professor's name is Sammie too," I say.

Her eyes light up like a bright lamp. "What's his last name sweetheart?" My mom asks.

"I don't know, it wasn't on the syllabus for some reason," I say.

My mom smiles and grabs me before kissing me on my right cheek. My mom's pearly white teeth are widely displayed for the first-time in many years. "Oh my God, how does he look?" She asks.

"He is tall with blue or gray eyes, I think. And he's White with blonde-hair too," I say.

My mom crosses her arms and drops to her knees. She kisses the wooden floor and looks up then forms a big two-handed fist with her hands. "Thank you, Jehovah! Oh my God, I have to go see if it's Sammie."

I place my hands over my mouth and stare at my mom. *My mom is tugging at my heart. Whoever Sammie is, she still hasn't gotten over him, even after all these years.* I start to cry while trying to help my mom to her feet. "You should come on campus next week to find out whether or not my professor is the Sammie that you adore," I say.

My mom eventually stands on her own accord. With a look of complete happiness, she says, "Please, Izzy, let's do that. It would mean the world to me." She holds her hands up. "However, I don't want you to mention anything to him just yet, because if he isn't Sammie, I'll make a fool out of myself. Your professor—is his left leg kind of deformed?"

Why is she asking me about that? I look perplexed. "No, his legs look normal to me, and he looks like he's about forty-five-years-of-age."

My mom turns her back to me and places her hand underneath her chin as she engages with her thoughts. "Hmm … maybe Sammie had a rough life without me, because he should look like he's in his late thirties," says my mom.

I walk in front of my mom. "Mom, don't trust my opinion. You all are much older than me, so all of you look like you're in your forties from my perspective."

My mom points her finger at me and grins. "Hey, watch it now young lady. I feel like you're trying to call your mom old."

I'm glad she's laughing a little. "Ha, I'm not trying, Mom, you are an old fart."

Seconds later, my mom starts chasing me throughout the house. We start to laugh and play while throwing water on one another from the bathroom sinks. I really wish we could have this type of connection every day. I really love my mom, and I'm going to share my gift with her soon. I don't think that tonight is the night, though. She is excited about my professor possibly being the love of her life. I don't want to shock her with too much all at once.

While in the bathroom downstairs we both take deep breaths before sitting down on the edge of the tub. "Mom, what are you going to do if my professor is the Sammie Walker?" I face my mom to her left and wait for her reply.

My mom looks at me and says, "I'm going to punch him then ask him why he didn't put forth more effort to come and find me?" My mom smirks.

"What if he has moved on with his life?" I ask.

My mom drops her shoulders in despair, then she frowns and erupts with an emotional outburst, "Why are you being so negative all of a sudden?" My mom scoffs.

Oh lord, here we go. "Mom, I was just trying to help you prepare for the possibility that Sammie might have moved on with his life." I place my hand on her thigh as we continue to sit on the tub.

"No, you don't tell me when I should move on. You have a life and you're dating someone. I never had a chance to really live. Besides, you are the reason why I lost out on my opportunity to live my dreams."

What's her problem? I hate when she acts like this. I stand up and scream, "Mom, I didn't ask you to have sex and give birth to me." I point my fingers at my mom's chest. "I was going to share something with you tonight about me that you don't know. You don't know me, Mom. And it's because you keep living in the past, I've had enough!" I walk toward the door to exit the bathroom. I pause, turning around. "Tell me, where do you go on Friday evenings' anyway?"

My mom slams a large brown bath towel against the floor. "None of your business!"

Yep, she won't ever change. I frown and scream. "I'm moving out! And I'm leaving tonight."

My mom crosses her arms. "That's fine with me."

I scoff as my mom gets into my face, placing her forehead against mine. Like two bulls going head-to-head, I push forward. "I'm glad that's fine with you because it's perfectly fine with me too."

My mom removes her forehead away from mine and points at the door of the bathroom. "Get out of my house right now Isabella!"

I shake my head. "My pleasure, I will get my things right now. But first, I need to call Mark."

"Don't touch my phone, just leave right now. Come back after you've learned some manners," says my mom.

"Get over yourself, Mom."

I exit the bathroom and pack a bag before storming out of the house.

***

Sophia

I sat on the toilet seat in the bathroom, reflecting on the events that transpired over the past few minutes of my life.

I heard Isabella exit the house. "We were having such a good time." *I can really see myself in Isabella, she's superior to how I am in a lot of ways.* I stood up then exited the bedroom. While standing in the hallway, I spoke out loud. "I guess, I'll just try to get some good rest." I changed my clothes and got into bed without taking a shower. *I'm going to say a prayer to God and leave the rest in his hands.* Subsequently, a thought entered my mind after praying to God. "Hmm." *I think I have a good song idea.*

While lying in the bed, I think to myself. I'll start writing it soon. When I think about Sammie and Isabella, I know now that they are the music within my heart. I hope Izzy understands that I truly do love her. I really hate that we have these nasty fights so often. I just want the best for her, and I don't want her to make the same mistakes I've made. A lightbulb went off within my mind. I perked up a little. "That's it! That's going to be the name of the song I perform at The Blues Café for my audition in a few months." The Music Within My Heart. I like it already. I think the title sums up how I have been feeling all my life.

Regardless of what happens after my audition, I'm going to bury the thought of being with Sammie after I sing my heart out for him one last time during my audition. I have to move on with my life at some point, and I know that that time is fast approaching.

A few minutes later, I closed my eyes and fell asleep.

***

Chapter 18:
Rediscovery of a Love that was Lost:
Love's Treasure

Two Weeks Later
Isabella

I wake up in Mark's bed at his studio. I hate that my mom and I fight so much. I get out of the bed, stretching my arms. I walk up to the bedroom window, pulling the curtains back. I peek through the window. "The sunshine is so bright today. What a beautiful day it is outside." I still feel a little tired, though. I get back in the bed, laying there a little while longer. Whilst in the bed I think out loud. "It's been two weeks since I've seen my mom. I just can't see her right now." She knows where I go to school, so she can find me if she wants too. I am just tired of my mom making me feel like I'm just this cumbersome pest to her.

Mark enters the room, dressed in a blue T-shirt with gray gym shorts; he brings me breakfast in bed. I glance at the bacon, two boiled eggs, a piece of sweet-glazed ham, and a glass of orange juice. "Wow, that looks delicious." We kiss and hug.

" Good morning," he said softly. "Are you okay? I overheard you talking to yourself when I was walking toward the room. I really think you should call your mom, or maybe we can go and see her together," says Mark.

I shrug my shoulders. Maybe. I start to eat my breakfast, sitting upright in the bed. "Good morning. I appreciate you trying to help, but I have already tried all of that with my mom ten times over. She just doesn't get it, and I'm not going to drive myself crazy." I lift and point my piece of ham at him before devouring it. "Mark, that woman is set in her ways."

He holds his hands up. "I'm going to stay out of your business. However, if you need someone to talk to, just let me know. I love you and I want the best for you."

"I just don't know why my mom hates me, Mark. All I have ever done is try to be a good daughter and make her proud." I sip some of my orange juice then I share some with Mark. He sits down on the bed to my left.

He scoots closer to me. "I don't think your mom hates you. She might have really experienced some traumatic things in her life. I really think that maybe you should go to your mom and try to talk to her—like, today. I'll go with you if that makes you feel a little better, my love," says Mark.

I peel my eggs and start to eat them. I exhale with my morning breath colliding with Mark's nose. Mark smiles as he pinches his nose. "What if she doesn't want to see me? She might yell at me like she normally does. I can't deal with the thought of that happening right now. I think it would break my heart in half. Besides, I don't want to make the situation worse. So, I think I'm going to wait a little longer." My eyes light up. "Whoa! I think I have an idea. Remember we're going out of the country in two weeks on that trip to Spain, to study various features of music, right?"

He nods his head and says, "Right!"

"Maybe I can inform my mom that I would like to spend some time with her before I leave."

He pushes his left leg back onto the bed, resting his arms on it. He squints his eyes. "Wait, you still haven't told your mom about the trip to Spain?"

I know, I know." No, I haven't! I just haven't found the right time."

He lifts his right leg on top of the bed as well. "What about inviting her to go on the trip? I think that would be a great idea. My parents are coming as well. That would give us a chance to get to know one another, and my parents would really enjoy that."

"My mom doesn't have the money. Heck, I barely had the money. My mom has never had a job. She has survived from life insurance policies her entire life. I am not saying that to say anything disparaging about my mom, but it's the truth."

Mark places his hands on my thighs as he feeds me a piece of bacon. While I eat the bacon from his hands, I mistakenly lick his fingers too. Mark smiles and says, "Don't you go starting nothing now."

He always makes me laugh. I smile with a mild giggle.

He stares at me and licks his lips. "I'll pay for your mom Isabella, and that isn't optional, I'm insisting or I'm breaking up with you." He smirks.

I lift my eyebrows and push my plate aside. "Mark, you pick the worst times to crack lame jokes. Now we both know that you can't live without me, so why are you tripping? You know that we are inseparable."

Mark grins. "Dang, you saw right through my facetiousness. You know me all too well. I don't want to break up with my beautiful queen. I love you and everything about you." He gestures for me to get up and get dressed. "Let's get you out of this studio. I'm sure your mom doesn't like the fact that you left her house. She probably thinks you just wanted to leave so that you can live an immoral life with me. Based on the things you told me about your mom, it sounds like she's only trying to protect you from a lot of mistakes that she made."

"Mark, you're so good with insight." I walk into the bathroom to freshen up. Mark follows me and we continue talking.

"I think you should go see your mom this week, since it's been about two weeks since you two saw one another. Uh, since today is Monday, maybe you can get your thoughts together sometime between today and Friday, and then go talk to your mom."

I glance at him through the mirror while brushing my teeth. With the faucet running I say, "I'll go on Saturday."

"Okay, sounds good. Meanwhile, let's get out of this studio and head to class," says Mark.

Mark has so much wisdom. I really like that about him. He's right about one thing, though, we both need to get to school. I don't want to flunk my first semester of college. I exhale. *All of my professors seem so nice too. I had a chance to meet them at a get-to-know-your-professors-orientation that my university does each semester.* I start the shower, then Mark walks up to me, giving me a hug and a kiss. I blush. "See you on campus, baby."

Mark pauses at the door, gently tapping his knuckles against the door as he says, "Let's do lunch today too. We can finish this discussion then if you don't have to study for anything."

"You got it baby." I step into the shower after Mark walks out. I embrace the warmth of the water as it hydrates my body. I position myself in the shower, allowing the water to cleanse my backside. Man,

I have so much stuff going on. I wonder what my mom is doing right now.

***

I Found You:
The Hunt for Love

1986
Wednesday
Sophia

I miss my Izzy.

While sitting in the living room at my house, I watched a little TV before putting on a gray jogging suit. I grimaced as I reflected on my life. When I really thought about it, I have a few things to be happy about. God is still waking me up in the morning, and I have been able to maintain my physique through regular exercise. I love to meditate in the morning before I jog. While reflecting, my meditation was interrupted by an advertisement on television. I heard an announcement on TV then I increased the volume. I stared at the screen. "It's Sammie!" Sammie is having a concert in London next week and I have to go. I guess that clears up any possibility that Sammie teaches at Izzy's university. Maybe she thought it was him because her professor just happens to have the same name as Sammie. I jumped up and danced. While dancing I dropped my butt low to the floor, then I stood up, looking around as I received a sudden epiphany. Maybe that's why I haven't heard from Sammie, because he lives in London!

The commercial didn't say that he lives in London, it only mentioned that he's having a concert there. However, I do recall Sammie saying that he planned to move out of the country at some point once he got to a certain age. He said that when he was a teenager.

I don't know how much of that was true or how much of it he meant. I used to tell him, "There will be hatred no matter where you go," and he would say, "That's true, but there's less hate in other parts of the world."

I had to figure out how to find him in London. I didn't have the courage to talk to Duke decades ago, and I didn't won't to repeat that same mistake with Sammie. I didn't have anything to lose since my daughter wasn't talking to me anymore. I exhaled. "I hate that we aren't talking, though."

My Friday gigs had been really paying off. I booked my flight that day. I only had six thousand dollars remaining in my savings account. I'm going to use about three thousand dollars to find Sammie in London, so hopefully it would only take me a few days to find him. I think it's time for me to accept the rest of the money that Travis owes me for my singing gigs at The Blues Café. I wondered if he'll let me perform on some additional days as well, so I could make some extra cash. Anyway, jogging time now.

While running I thought to myself. *Oh, God, what I would give to see his smile again in the midnight forest.*

Thirty minutes elapsed after I finished my run. I headed back to the house in order to purchase a plane ticket, risking everything. I'm glad I decided to get my passport a few months ago. It's handy right now. I'd planned to take a mini vacation out of the country to clear my mind. I loved Paris and how it looked on television. Going to London with the hope of seeing Sammie again was a great replacement for Paris.

A few minutes later, I booked my flight.

***

The Following Day
Thursday
Sophia

While walking through my house I thought to myself, My flight leaves tomorrow afternoon. I have time to get myself together. I need to inform Travis that I won't be able to perform this Friday at The Blues Café. I'll call Travis after my shower to inform him that I need someone else to fill in for me—and for a while.

A few minutes later, I took a shower, before calling Travis. While sitting on my couch in the living room I waited for Travis to pick up while the phone line rang. He answered. "Hey Travis, I know I'm scheduled to perform tonight, but I won't be able to fulfill that obligation. Something urgent has come up, and I really need to address it. I am leaving tomorrow to handle it."

"It's okay, Sophia. I always keep an artist on standby. I like to give other artists opportunities to shine and thrive, anyway. I have a funny feeling where you might be going. I was thinking to myself the other day, where do I remember Sophia from? I knew I'd seen you somewhere before I hired you to perform at my club five years ago. That's when it dawned on me that I saw you when you were a teenager. You were the young girl that interrupted Sammie's show eighteen years ago." He chuckled. "I fired that boy after he pulled that stunt on my stage. I told him to get back on the stage, but he refused to because he tried to chase you, after you sprinted out of my bar that night."

That's such a painful but good memory, too. I love anything that involves Sammie. I smiled and stood up as the phone cord got tangled around my right arm.

Travis continued, "When Sammie returned from chasing you, he just couldn't pull his performance together. He was dysfunctional, so I pulled him off the stage, then fired him. I remember that moment vividly because it cost me a lot of money. I did Sammie a favor by firing him. After I fired him, he started receiving invitations to sing at other places. And now, he's a superstar. He has a concert in London soon. You might be wondering how I know all of this?"

I laughed. "It's obvious how you know, you saw his commercial on TV."

"Ha, no, that's not how I know. I am Sammie's uncle. My brother never supported Sammie's singing career. After I discovered that Sammie was serious about singing, that's when I tried to help him out." He stopped abruptly, "Hey, can you stop by today?"

I wonder why he wants me to stop by. "Yeah, because I want to finish this discussion," I said.

"Good! I have some more stuff to tell you about Sammie too," said Travis.

I rubbed my face while sitting on the couch. "I think he lives in London now, but I'm not sure. Can you find out for sure by asking his dad?"

"Hey, Sophia, I have to go. Just drop by at some point today. We'll finish our conversation then."

"Okay bye, and thanks." I smiled and made a fist. I pulled my right arm into my side and screamed, "Yes! I'll definitely be headed to The Blues Café to speak with him." I wonder where that note is that I wrote for Sammie back in 1968, when I ran into him at the café? He's sentimental, so if I do manage to find him, I'll show him that I still have it. It'll really convey the agony I've felt without him, as well as how much I've missed him.

Over the next hour, I searched for the note with my address on it while pulling out clothes from various rooms inside my house.

I sighed and stood up in my bedroom with my things everywhere. *I'm such a hoarder. Look at the mess I've created. If I wasn't so messy, it would be easier for me to find things around this dump.* I rushed up and down the stairs to gather my luggage situated for my trip to London. *I just want to be able to steal his heart away even if he's with someone else now.* The thought of Sammie being with another woman set my heart on fire. I continued to search for the note, but I couldn't find it. While ransacking my house, I remembered an important detail. "Oh, I forgot—" I slapped my forehead and laughed. I dropped the note outside The Blues Café right before I met Kyle.

I sat on the floor and started to think about Isabella. *I'll write her a letter if I don't see her before I leave on Friday. I might even stay at a hotel near the airport tonight to ensure that I don't miss my flight.* I knew that I probably should go try to find Isabella, but I just feel in my heart that going across the world for Sammie is what I should do. I sighed. "Love makes no sense!" Many people would think that I'm crazy. I'm so glad I don't have any friends to talk me out of this.

An hour later, I jumped into my car, my luggage packed inside as I drove to the café. While driving, I remembered that I forgot to write Isabella a letter informing her that I was leaving the country. I squeezed the steering wheel while running my right hand through her hair. "Ugh! I forgot to say goodbye to Izzy." *I'm on a timed schedule though. I'm going to miss my daughter, but I trust that she'll be okay. I must do this, since my chances of seeing Sammie again are looking good. I just can't miss this opportunity.* I teared up. Travis might even have an address for Sammie or something.

A few minutes later, I exited the interstate.

I will find you, Sammie. I don't care if you're in this country or another one. I took a deep breath then exhaled slowly. One way or another, I'll find you.

***

Missing Heart Beats

Isabella

Mark is so cute. I smile. While sharing a cup of coffee together with Mark at The Hot Coffee Shop, I lean forward inside the booth. "Hey Mark, I think I'm going to drop by my mom's house. Like right now."

Mark glances at his watch. "Okay."

"It's midday, so I know she's there because she doesn't work. She has slowed down a lot with her volunteer work, and she only goes out on Fridays now."

He nods his head. "Let's head out to go see our Mom," says Mark.

"Our mom?" I ask.

He smiles. "Yes! Your mom is my mom because I'm going to marry you soon."

I lift my eyebrows and twist my lips. "Look now, don't get any ideas from all those love stories you're watching. I'm only a freshman in college and so are you. We need to focus on school and getting our careers established," I say.

Mark scoots closer to me, placing his hands on my rear end. "I agree. But we also need to focus on getting our romance established, too," says Mark.

I frown and push his hands away. "Mark, as much as I want you to keep your hands on my butt, I don't think that's a good idea right now. I don't want this to lead to other things. I am living with you now, and we are by ourselves at your place." I take a deep breath. "I really don't want to do anything that will upset God." I stare at him. "Now, I see why you want to get married so soon." Mark sighs. "Mark, please, just be patient. Our time will come. Besides, if you really love me, you'll support me by helping me to keep my relationship with God strong. You should be focusing on this too. Just as a reminder, I love you, but I want us to be married before I lose my virginity."

Mark sips his coffee and wraps his right arm around me. He winks at me and says, "I am definitely going to marry you. However, I don't think God will hold it against us forever if we lose our virginity together."

He's really starting to annoy me with this. My mom was right. "Mark, can you please just respect my wishes?"

"I do! Look, I'm being teased for being the only guy with a girlfriend in my fraternity that's still a virgin," says Mark.

I scoff and poke him on the shoulder with my left fingers extended. "Has it ever crossed your mind that maybe some of the guys who are claiming to be so great with women are lying to make themselves look good?" I ask.

Mark doesn't reply, he places his hands atop the table and frowns while looking away from me.

He's really being selfish right now. "Uh, just lie and tell them we are doing it, okay?" I sigh. "I don't care!" I glance over at Mark's facial expression. He's irritated. "Look, if you can't respect me then I'll have to move in with Jill and stay on campus with her. Or maybe I'll get my own place. I'm not saying I want to break up with you, but I am saying I don't want to mess up and sleep with you. In order to safeguard my wishes, I don't mind keeping my distance from certain situations." Mark grunts. He's totally being a jerk. "You can look at me like that all day, but this is one thing my mom drilled into my head, and I agree with her on this." I really do.

"Well, why kiss me and tease me then?" Mark asks.

"That was me compromising and working with you. Being away from my mom is making me think about the things she taught me. So, maybe we should stop that too. You go to Sunday worship Mark, so I know that you know what I'm saying is right." I rub his thigh to cheer him up.

Mark playfully shakes his head and faces me as he smiles and says, "I apologize for being inconsiderate."

Finally. I didn't know he was this stubborn. "That's all I wanted you to say. Now, let's head over to my mom's house."

Mark and I get into his red 1986 Corvette, and we drive off into the west coast sunshine. The drive to my mom's house is silent. Mark seems a little embarrassed about being rejected.

At some point during the ride, I glance at Mark while he drives. I think he's taking it personally.

A few minutes later, we arrive at my mother's house. We pull up in the driveway and Mark's engine roars with the power of several hundred horses. I look at the driveway. Hmm. That's interesting, her car is gone. We walk inside and the lights are on. What the heck happened in here?

Mark glances at me and says, "It looks like she ransacked the house looking for something, or something sinister happened," says Mark.

I hold my hands over my mouth. "Mark, should we call the police? Something doesn't seem right about this. My mom is always home around this time." I look worried with my arms crossed before I start to pick up my mother's clothes, placing them on the couch.

Mark shrugs his shoulders as he looks at the items scattered about. "I don't think it's a bad idea to be safe rather than sorry."

I walk to the phone by the couch and dial 9-1-1. I hold the line as it rings. I observe Mark looking at me with annoyance. I swear, if he says anything to me after his little show at the coffee shop, I'll just lose it. A second later, a calm female's voice echoes through the phone.

"9-1-1, what's your emergency?"

I clear my throat. "My mom might've been the victim of foul play! Her house looks ransacked, and she isn't home."

The dispatcher replies like a nurturing mother. "What's your name?" The dispatcher asks.

Mark approaches me, placing his hands atop my shoulders and comforting me as he stands behind me. "My name is Isabella Smith."

"Isabella, we are going to put our best foot forward to try to find your mom," says the dispatcher.

I look back at Mark and his sincere eyes fill my soul with comfort. "My mother and I haven't been getting along lately. I hope I haven't pushed her to the point of doing something crazy."

"Just relax. I'm sending a unit your way right now. Someone should be there shortly. Wait outside in case there is a perpetrator, he might still be in the house," says the dispatcher.

"Okay, thanks." I hang up the line.

Mark and I walk outside. Five minutes later, we hear a police siren and see flashing lights as we sit on the steps of the front porch. Then, a short Hispanic officer of medium build exits his car. I glance at him. He has long hair like Mark. The officer walks up to us, running his fingers through his slick black hair while saying, "I'm Jose Hernandez." The officer shakes both of our hands. "What's going on? Have you heard from your mom yet?" He asks.

I sigh. "No, this is unlike her." I point behind me. "It looks suspicious inside too." I point to the house again as I place my face atop my thighs. I lower my head in between my legs, tearing up while Mark rubs the back of my neck. "She never leaves the lights on. She's always concerned about saving electricity. She is very frugal. I feel bad, because we haven't been getting along either.

Jose glances at Mark. "And who is this fellow here?"

I respond before Mark says anything. "Oh, this is my boyfriend."

"What's your name, son? And can I see some identification?" Jose places his right foot atop the steps close to Mark. With his right leg bent and his left leg extended on the pavement, he looks over his shoulder to observe the outer surroundings. After his observation, Jose refocuses his attention on Mark.

"My name is Mark Clay, and yes, sure—" He pulls out his wallet and hands Jose his license. "Here you go."

As Jose looks at Mark's license, he glances at me and asks, "What's your name sweetheart?"

"My name is Isabella Smith."

Jose hands Mark his license, then he takes his right foot off the step, positioning himself directly in front of me. "Isabella, I'm going to ask you a straightforward question and I want you to give me a straightforward answer, okay." Jose points at us, waving his fingers side-to-side. "Have the two of you done anything harmful to your mom?" Jose looks forward inside the house, the door is ajar. "It's just protocol, because this whole set up looks suspicious."

I scoff and stand up. "Absolutely not! I would never harm my mom. Why would you even ask me such a thing?"

Jose exhales. "I just told you not to take it personally. It's a part of our standard protocol. We have to ask. Besides, the way you two are reacting just seems suspicious to me. Especially after you said you and your mom haven't been getting along."

I push my hands against the afternoon breeze, disgusted. "Officer, you don't know me or my mother," I say.

Jose nods his head. "I apologize but I am just trying to do my job."

Mark frowns and says, "Well, go do your job and stop accusing an innocent person of something she didn't do."

Jose stares at Mark. "Young man, I strongly suggest that you lower your tone!"

Mark doesn't reply, he looks at me, drowning in concern.

Jose refocuses his attention on me. "Okay, we will do a thorough search of the city. Meanwhile, can you write down your mom's relatives and friends, the places she hangs out, and where she works?" Jose hands her a pad with a pen.

"My mom doesn't have any surviving relatives or friends, and she doesn't go anywhere. I want to file a missing person report," I say.

Jose raises his eyebrows. "Okay, we will try and track her phone calls by pulling up her phone record, which will take a while. We are going to search her house thoroughly and collect any evidence we find. If I need to ask you more questions, I'll reach out to you. As a standard protocol, we search nearby waters and dumpsters whenever we file a report for a missing person."

I start to sob. "Oh no, not my mom."

Mark screams, "Officer, why did you just tell her that? Now she's crying!" Mark consoles me. "It's going to be okay, Izzy. Maybe she's finally changing up a lot of things, maybe she decided to get out of the house or something."

Jose frowns, pointing his fingers as he scoffs. "Listen to your two-strike little boyfriend here. I think he has a good perspective on a lot of things based on this conversation. I apologize if I scared you, Isabella."

Less than a minute later, Jose walks inside and searches my mom's house. While Jose searches throughout the house, I ask Mark to get me out of here.

"Hey, take me away from here. I need to clear my head." We step inside Mark's Corvette and drive away.

***

Reunion at The Blues Café

Also Thursday Afternoon
Sophia

I thought, *a few more seconds and I'll be at the café.* I couldn't wait to speak with Travis.

I pulled up outside the café, then stepped out of the car with a white jogging suit on. I walked up to the entrance door. "Hey, I am here to see Travis."

318

The guard invited me in, escorting me to the bar. The bartender offered me a drink, but I declined his overture. "No thank you. I'll just sit here until Travis comes out," I said. I looked to my left and the wooden round tables reminded me of the many drinks I've had at the club after my performances. I looked around, bracing my arms atop the bar. *I've had a lot of good memories and just one bad one at this café.* I looked to my right, observing the double doors swing open.

That's Travis walking toward the front now. He always dresses so nicely in his suits. Captivated by his appealing look, I entertained my thoughts. *I like the navy-blue suit he has on today—it blends in well with the dim and dark atmosphere inside his club. He's not handsome like Sammie. If his nose wasn't so long, and if his blue eyes weren't pushed back into his head, then he might be good looking. I hate bald guys too. He could use some hair. But at least he's the average height for a guy, and he has a muscular build. His skin is beyond white, though.*

Travis walked toward me and sat next to me atop a bar stool. I smiled and waved. "Hey, Travis."

Travis smiled. "Sophia, sorry that I had to get off the phone yesterday. I had an important call to take."

I turned to my right to face Travis while my left arm rested atop the countertop. "What's the scoop on Sammie?"

Travis leaned forward, placing his right arm on the bar while signaling for the bartender to serve him a drink.

"Sammie is doing out of country tours right now. I called his dad earlier, but Sammie doesn't talk to his dad. However, he does talk to my daughter, Molly. She knows a lot about him, she keeps me in the loop." The bartender handed Travis a glass of red wine.

319

I glanced at the wine while grimacing. "Wait, Molly is the girl that my brother was dating when he was killed. Sammie never mentioned that she was his cousin. I wonder why he conveniently left that part out?" I was confused.

Travis tossed his hands into the air. "I don't know anything about that Sophia. Maybe your brother's Molly isn't my Molly." He shrugged his shoulders. "I think I would have known about him if he was dating my daughter. Anyway, Molly told me that Sammie is touring in other countries. She mentioned that he can't stand the thought of not being able to see someone who he is in love with. She didn't mention any names because he didn't want to talk about the person. She mentioned that he said it brings him too much pain." Travis sipped his wine then cleared his throat. "Which is why, he prefers not to mention her name."

My face lit up with hope like a lamp inside a dark room. I just know in my heart, I'm the one he's talking about.

"I tried to find Sammie's address for you, but Molly said she didn't know his address."

"Huh?" I asked, perplexed.

"Yeah, I know, me too." He sighed. "For some reason Sammie refuses to give Molly his address, he's afraid she'll give it to me."

"Why?" I asked.

"He thinks I will give my brother his address if I found out where he's located. My brother misses him, but Sammie doesn't want to have anything to do with his dad."

That's my Sammie. I know why he doesn't have dealings with his dad. I crossed my legs and smiled.

Travis faced the bar. "I don't have an exact address for Sammie, but I do know that he lives in Arizona when he's not touring. I have been trying to get in touch with him myself to see if he will come and perform at my club again. I have Molly's number, but she's been out of the country. Next time I talk to her, I will try to get Sammie's number, and I'll call him myself." He glanced at me. "If I'm able to get in touch with him, I will call you personally."

I placed my hands over my heart. "This information is really making my heart rejoice. I've been searching for Sammie for most of my life." I withheld my tears as my voice trembled. "Excuse me." I took a deep breath.

"It's okay." Travis patted me on my left thigh.

I wiped tears from my eyes. "It's just that—now, I feel like I'm finally about to find him."

He smiled. "Up until recently, I know you've refused to accept the money that was due to you. You've performed for me for the past five years, and a lot of those performances were for free. I appreciate you helping me out." He reached into his left coat pocket, extracting an envelope. "Here's the twenty thousand dollars that's due to you. I know in my heart that this money will allow you to go find Sammie."

Perfect timing. "Thank you so much, Travis. I plan to heavily pursue my singing career for my daughter. She really needs me. I didn't think that my child would end up being my main source of inspiration."

He sipped his drink again and asked, "What's her name?"

I smiled and nudged his arm. "Isabella Smith, but I call her Izzy."

Travis' eyes expanded like an owl. He faced me and said, "Hmm. That's interesting!"

He looked so surprised. I lowered my tone, playfully dragging his name as I said, "Travis." I smiled. "Travis, do you know something that I don't know?"

He poked his lips out while shaking his head as a tinge of sweat erupted on his forehead. He gestured with his hands, emphasizing that he doesn't know anything. "No! No—no, I don't know her."

"Oh, ok. When I return from looking for Sammie, I'm going to develop the best relationship with my daughter."

"Sophia, I see a certain look in your eyes. You aren't coming back to the Marin County until you find Sammie," Travis said.

I laughed. "If I haven't found Sammie in five months, I will come back to do my audition. I still don't know who the organizer of the audition is, because the segment I heard on the radio didn't mention any names, and honestly, I don't want to know. Not knowing, at least for me, helps me not think of my failed attempt from my past with Duke."

"Duke Proctor?" Travis asked. "I know you don't want to know this, but Duke is going to be one of the judges for the audition that will be at my bar in five months."

My face lit up. "That's crazy, Travis. I auditioned for him about twenty-years-ago. He invited me to audition for his final competition round, but things just didn't pan out."

"Everything happens for a reason." He smirked. "I have some good news to tell you; you're the main reason why he's coming here looking for talent. He heard about your shows on Fridays, way out in Los Angeles. He called me and said he wanted to hold an audition here, and that he remembered you. He didn't ask for your number because I told him you didn't want to pursue music seriously. Today is your first time sharing with me that you would like to go all out with your music career and take everything to the next level. I definitely think you should, because you are an insane talent!"

I can't be mad with Tavis for just now telling me this. Technically, he's right. "This is some incredible news."

He lifted his left hand. "The audition is on June 1st. Don't miss your opportunity to be great again, Sophia. Not everyone gets a second chance to experience this type of opportunity twice in their life. You have to realize that God is giving you another opportunity to use the gift he put inside your heart." He stared at me with endearment. "Sophia, your gift is very powerful. You are just as good as Nancy. Actually, I think you're better."

"Nancy was at my audition twenty years ago when I first auditioned. The only reason she won was because I was pregnant with Izzy at the time." I stood up and stepped away from the bar. "I'll see you in five months. June 1st will be here before you know it."

"Sure. You're right." He smiled.

"Travis, thanks for everything. This is the best news I've heard in twenty years."

We said our goodbyes then I departed.

I got in my car and drove to my house with a big smile on my face. I need to pick up a few of my songs. I hope that Isabella is there too. But if she isn't, I'll just leave her the letter that I didn't write the other day before I fly off to London tomorrow.

A few minutes later, I arrived at my house.

I pulled up and observed several police units at my house. I parked on the street, then jumped out. I hope Izzy is okay. I sprinted to my front door before I was confronted by one of the officers'. "Ma'am, stop right there, who are you?" One of the officers' asked.

While breathing heavily, I replied, "This is my house, and I'm the owner. Why are you all at my house?" I looked around and observed three officers searching my house.

"What are you all doing here? Is everything okay? Is my daughter, okay?" I asked.

One of the officers' walked up to me and asked, "Are you Sophia Smith?"

I held my hand over my chest. "Yes I am. Why? Is my daughter, okay?" I yelled, "Izzy, honey, are you home?"

The officer I was speaking with had a calm tone like rain drops from a drizzle. "I'm Officer Jose. Everything is okay. Your daughter, Isabella, she called us because she thought something terrible had happened to you. She left a number for you to call her on the table in the kitchen. I will personally contact her myself to let her know that you're okay. Do you have the address where she lives?" Jose asked.

"Yes, of course. And thank you for doing your job. Be sure to inform my daughter that I am okay." I can't call her now; it'll just make me want to stay with her. I know I am being selfish, but I don't see any other way. I guess I could just call her, but I just can't right now.

"Of course, I will call her in a second," said Jose.

"Thank you again," I said.

Two minutes later, Jose gathered his squad. The officers started to exit my house, and then Jose mentioned this before he left, "I called her two minutes ago, and she knows that you're fine. She mentioned that she is headed your way soon."

I smiled. "Thank you." *I need to get a move on then.*

The officers' left, then I looked around at the unkempt nature of my home. I see why she panicked. I heard my phone ringing. "I bet you that's Isabella." I stared at the telephone near the coffee table that was inside the living room. I closely watched the phone until the line ceased ringing. *I just can't answer that right now. I need to hurry and write my letter. I'll leave and get a hotel for tonight, like I thought about doing yesterday.*

I picked up a nearby pen and a sheet of paper from the table in my living room, then I wrote a letter to Izzy.

***

The Letter of Departure

I placed the pen and paper down as I teared up while squeezing my eyes with my fingers. I just finished writing my letter to my baby girl. I hope she understands why I had to leave in the manner that I am after she reads my letter. I'll be gone no longer than four or five months. I might even be back sooner. Maybe I'll see and talk to Sammie next week at his concert. I know that he does a thing called the One Lucky Fan Program, which gives you an opportunity to go backstage with him. I need to write several letters to his fan mail address in Arizona. He probably doesn't read his fan letters personally, but I'll take my chances. I exhaled. "I hope my letters stand out."

I stood up from the kitchen table. "Well, here goes nothing." I placed my letter on the kitchen counter for Isabella to see. Then, I gathered a few last minute items before calling a taxi. Ten minutes later, a taxi pulled up outside my home. I knew it wouldn't take the driver long, since Yellow Driver's Taxi Company is only three minutes from my house. I locked up my house, then jumped inside the taxi.

A few minutes later, I arrived downtown at The Grand Lux hotel. I checked in, then I finished preparing for my journey.

***

Meanwhile

Isabella

Mom, here we come.

Mark's hot ride speeds down a street in my neighborhood. He leaves tire marks in the road as we approach my house. We pull up into the driveway, then I scream, pointing my fingers.

"Look! Mark, look, my mom's car is here." I look at him, excited, then he kills the engine. "I'm going in first," I say. I open the passenger door, placing my right foot onto the pavement. I pause and look over my left shoulder at Mark and say, "Uh, wait in the car, since my mom hasn't met you yet. I want to talk to her before the two of you meet."

"Okay, that sounds like a plan," says Mark.

I lean in to kiss Mark.

He places his right index finger atop my lips. "No kisses, remember? I don't want to take advantage of you because you're vulnerable right now. I want you to feel happy and safe with me." He smirks and points toward his right cheek. "However, I'll take a kiss on the cheek, though."

I love him. I smile and oblige his request. "You're so sweet and funny. Thank you, baby."

While walking up the steps, I fumble through my purse, searching for my keys. I slowly open the door as it creaks from opening in slow motion, echoing throughout the house. I scratch my head. The house seems vacant. I walk inside and call out for my mom. "Mom, are you home?" Um, that's odd. The house sounds empty, but her car is still outside. And it wasn't here earlier. I know she was here because she cleaned up a little, but it still looks messy in here. Over the next few minutes, I look in all of the rooms, but I don't locate my mom. I panic and rush downstairs. I pause at the end of the stairway and think to myself. She has to be okay, because Officer Jose just called me less than an hour ago. "I just need to relax." Maybe she has a man in her life now who came to pick her up. I enter the kitchen to get a glass of water. I'm so thirsty from running around looking for my mom.

While swallowing my water, I lean against the refrigerator, and notice a piece of paper on the kitchen counter. Hmm, what's that? I pick up a sheet of paper and glance over it. I sigh and say, "This is definitely a letter from my mom, I can tell by her handwriting." Interesting? She dated the letter for today. She must have just written this. I start reading the letter.

Dear Isabella,

I miss you a lot. I am sorry we haven't talked in weeks. I take full responsibility for this because I am your mom. However, lately, I haven't been a great mom to you. I haven't been a great mom to you at all, but all of that will change starting in June. I am leaving the country to search for Sammie. I will be out of the country looking for him.

I know this might seem odd to you, for me to risk everything like this. But I just have to do this. I'm asking for your support on this. The reason I left without saying goodbye is because I knew if I saw you, I wouldn't be able to leave your beautiful eyes behind.

I sit down, holding my left hand over my mouth as I mourn and moan like an injured lion.

You know you have my eyes, baby girl. When I see you, it's like I am looking at my twin. It's odd but this is the only way I could find the strength to leave you and be true to my soul. Please don't be mad with me, I promise, you're the most important thing to me. I might be back sooner than June because there's a big contest in June, and I'm going to be in it. This contest can change our lives forever. I will tell you everything when I get back home. Meanwhile, use this time to draw closer to God. And remember what I said about saving yourself for marriage.

I love you,

Mom

I dry my tears as I overhear loud knocks on my mom's door. That must be Mark. I stand up and sigh. Mom, I support you. Now, let me open the door for this fool before he breaks the darn door down.

Knock-knock. I open the door.

Mark rushes inside and looks around, then he gently grabs me and says, "Hey Isabella, what's going on? Why are you crying and where is your mom?"

I sob like a newborn. "Mark—" I pause to catch my breath as tears hydrate the inside of my mouth. "Mark, she isn't here." I stutter as my body shakes. "She—she, she's going out of the country to find the love of her life." The paper is soaked with my tears. "Here is her letter, read it yourself."

Mark looks at the letter, blowing on it to dry my tears. He begins reading it as his feet shuffle. "Wow, this is an interesting story, and quite beautiful if you ask me. I wonder what contest she is referring to?"

I fall into Mark's arms, placing my head on his chest. While still slowly regaining my composure I say, "It's probably a writing contest or something." I look up at him. "Mark, can we stay here tonight? I just want to be in my mom's space, you know?"

Mark looks down at me and says, "Yeah, that's fine. I just need to run by my place and grab some clothes. I'll pick up something for us to eat on the way too. What do you want?"

I'll take a burger and some fries, with a milk shake," I reply, still hugging him.

"Okay. And, put yourself in your mom's shoes, try to see things from her perspective too," Mark says.

He's so insightful and smart. "Thanks for being here for me. I love you," I say.

He blushes. "I love you too. I want to ask you something when I get back, and it's important too."

I hate when he does that. "Ahh … ask me now, you know I hate when you do that."

He grins. "It's nothing major, Izzy. We will talk about it when I get back, okay."

I toss my head back like a giraffe. Then I sigh. "If you say so."

He walks backwards toward the front door and says, "Don't be like that, beautiful." He points his fingers at me. "I'll see you in a little."

Chapter 19:
Join the Fan Club:
The Search to Reunite with Sammie Begins

Sophia

I woke up to get dressed and I put on a pink warm-up suit. After getting dressed, I exited my hotel room to walk toward the elevator.

I can't believe that I am about to embark upon this journey to find the man who means so much to me. I've been waiting for this moment for twenty years, and now it's finally going to happen. I glanced at my wristwatch. *Plenty of time. My flight leaves in four hours. I just want to get there super early in case something goes wrong.* I exited the elevator onto the first floor before entering the lobby.

I used the telephone in the lobby of the hotel to call a taxi.

"Good morning, I need a taxi to take me to the airport. I'm staying at The Grand Lux on Blueborn Avenue," I said.

"Okay, Ma'am. Someone will be there to pick you up in about twenty minutes," said the clerk over the phone.

"Thanks," I replied, hanging up.

I looked around before walking near the glass exit doors. I sat down adjacent to the entrance, so that I could look through the window. While sitting, I picked up a recipe magazine to skim over it. A few seconds later, I placed it down. I'm leaving today, but I won't arrive in London until 11 p.m. tonight. I'll purchase my tickets for his concert after I arrive in London, and I mailed him a couple of fan mail letters to his address in Arizona. I wish he had a fan address in London too. I plan to write Sammie a letter every week until he responds. I wish that his letters weren't vetted by his staff. They're probably going to think I'm just some crazy fan who is obsessed with Sammie. I know if Sammie gets his hands on one of my letters, he will reach out to me for sure.

Fifteen minutes later, I looked back, observing a taxi outside the hotel. Finally. I exited the hotel with my luggage bags. I smiled while knocking on the passenger window of the taxi. *Hmm, an Asian male.*

He rolled the window down and asked, "Where to?"

"To the airport," I said.

I stepped into the car, then we drove to the airport.

I didn't know Sammie would go on to become a famous singer without me in his corner. I always envisioned us becoming superstars together. I wonder what Sammie has been doing with his life over the past twenty years, besides singing? We have so much to catch up on.

Twenty minutes later, I arrived at the airport. "Ma'am, we are here. But please, remain in the car for now. I will get your things out for you so that you can relax before your flight," said the driver.

I smiled while reaching into my purse. "Thank you so much. You deserve a nice tip, here you go. I'll take my bags from here. Take care." I exited the taxi, then walked inside the airport. I stopped to observe the scenery. Look at the size of this place, there're so many different little outlets too.

I resumed walking. I needed to check my bag in. While navigating through the airport, I noticed a few people sprinting with their luggage. They're in a rush. I exhaled. *I could really use a cup of coffee. I'll get some before I go to my terminal.* I walked through security, then I got coffee. Afterwards, I walked for three minutes until I found my gate. Once at my gate, I took a seat. *I think I will read a couple of chapters of the Bible while I wait since I have almost two hours before my flight starts boarding.*

Two hours later, I heard an announcement that my flight would begin boarding in five minutes. I stood up, gathering my luggage. A few minutes later, I stepped on the plane and noticed a lot of people. *Seems like a lot of them are from London. Oh yeah, that's right, we just had an international religious conference downtown.* I looked at my boarding pass. *Great, my seat is way in the back. At least I'm close to the restroom.* I placed my carry-on bag in the overhead compartment, then I sat down. A few seconds later, I fastened my seatbelt. I said a silent prayer to God. Ten minutes later, the plane sped against the tarmac, gliding into the sky like an eagle.

Once the plane was above the clouds, I experienced an epiphany. *The reason I love Sammie so much is because he takes my heart so high into love's sky.* I smiled, lifting my eyebrows. *That's a great song title, love's sky. I need to start working on this one right away.*

I pulled out a pen and a note pad, then I started writing "Love's Sky."

***

Love's Sky

Love is like heaven soaring through your heart. Love is change and sometimes love is strange. I chose to love you from my heart, that's why my life will never be the same. Love doesn't have a name; it chooses whomever it wants. My heart chose you, so please don't front.

It's never good to refrain from accepting love's dos and don'ts. Love's sky always takes you higher than what you want. I just pray you fall for me exactly the way I want.

True love comes with abundance; there's never a drought. I look forward to the days when our love sprouts. One thing that's for sure, your love, I never doubt. You inspired me to speak from my mouth, the seasons of love that navigate constantly while still respecting love's north and hate's south.

There will always be two forces in the world, and may you, my girl, always be the good source. I can feel our love in your voice. Your presence is like gold, you are perfect, although you're stuck with me like a mold. A mold can sometimes annoy its host just like a worker does with their boss. Either way it goes, we all must still soar high and pay love's cost.

Love's sky is a mindset only true lovers live by. Love is high and hate is low. Baby, please don't go. Please love me forever, no matter where I go.

I looked around at the other passengers, then I reread my song. *Wow, another great song. Whenever I'm thinking about Sammie, I have the best love concepts flowing throughout my mind.*

I wonder how Isabella is doing. I miss my baby. I hope she read my letter with tears of joy. I smirked. *I can't believe that little sucker moved out on me. She had the courage to stand up for what she believes in. Courage is something Izzy must've received from her father. Kyle was a courageous man, and a good person overall.*

I wonder how Sammie is going to react when he lays his blue eyes on me. I think Sammie will be pleased to see his chocolate cupcake. That's one of the pet names he used to call me. I don't know why he called me that lame pet name, but I think it's cute.

I blushed while laying my head back. A few minutes later, I fell asleep, with love's sky on my mind.

***

The Life of a Superstar:
Sammie, Sammie, Sammie

Sophia

I woke from a little turbulence on the plane. As my eyes slowly began to open, I became oriented to my surroundings. I looked to my left and right. How much longer do I have before I arrive in London? I yawned, placing my hands over my mouth and listening to the captain's announcement through the intercom. "We have fifteen-minutes before we arrive in London. Get ready to experience the time of your lives, especially if this is your first time in the UK."

I can't wait to get myself together for Sammie's concert tomorrow. I really hope and pray that I am fortunate enough to win one of his backstage visits.

A few minutes later, the airplane landed on the tarmac. I tightly grabbed onto the seat-handles, bracing myself as the plane sped down the runway. Thank God, we made it safely. I'm ready to get off this plane. I observed the unfasten seatbelt light come on. I'll be happy when this line starts moving. While walking in line like a prisoner, I realized I didn't have my luggage. Dang. I immediately turned around, maneuvering through oncoming traffic. A few seconds later, I collected my carry-on, then exited the plane. After gathering my bags from baggage claim, I searched for a taxi to my hotel. I hope that Hotel Supreme is extremely nice. I've heard a lot about it through different articles.

I entered a taxi as the driver stepped out to place my bags inside the truck.

The driver entered the car, starting the meter. A thin, elderly European White male glanced at me in the rearview mirror. "Ma'am, where would you like to go?"

Through the backseat I observed the amazing architecture of the buildings in London. *I wish the United States had the characteristics of these buildings. I love the retro and distinctive appeal that the city's uniqueness portrays. London reminds me of The Golden Gate Bridge but with structures like the bridge inundated throughout the city.*

The driver cleared his throat, asking again, "Destination, please?"

I exhaled then said, "Forgive me. Hotel Supreme."

He smiled as the sun shined on his gray hair. "Excellent choice. Where are you from?"

"I'm from California," I said.

He looked to his left then entered onto the street. "Oh, you're from the United States. That's bloody great. There's a place near your hotel that serves the best donuts, you should try them. Blue Heaven Donuts."

The driver must've read my mind. I leaned forward, poking my head out while observing London's roads. *It's so cool to see people driving on the left side of the road. Their way just seems backwards to me. Their buildings look like castles too. It's like they're made for queens and princes.* I laughed out loud. *I forgot, queens and princes live here.* I shook my head.

The driver made a sharp left turn, then he asked, "Verdict?"

"Maybe some other time," I replied. I need to cut back on my calories anyway.

"Of course, and no extra charge for our slight detour. What brings you to London?"

His accent is to die for. Their accents are so bloody cool. "I am here to see Sammie Walker live in concert."

He smiled while stopping at a red light. "Wow, he is a great talent, isn't he? I like his songs, especially The Midnight Forest."

I leaned forward and asked, "Wait, Sammie has a song called The Midnight Forest?"

"Yes, I love that song. It's one of those songs they haven't played on the radio yet." He glanced at me through the rearview mirror with a look of surprise. "You don't know about The Midnight Forest?"

"I actually haven't purchased any of his albums. I haven't been able to listen to his music. It hurts me too much. We used to date, back in the day. I've been trying to find Sammie for years now. We came up with The Midnight Forest together. Well, actually, he named the woods."

The driver pulled up at the donut shop, looking back at me. "Go ahead and take a stab at it," said the driver.

I told him never mind, laughing before glancing at the pristine appeal of the donut shop. "Thank you for showing me where it's located, but again, I'll pass."

He shrugged his shoulders. "Okay!"

"Back to the song though," I said.

"I'm listening," said the driver.

"The song is about a girl who he saved from suicide through his unspoken love for her at the time. His love gave her a reason to live again. He calls it The Midnight Forest because he met the girl in the woods at night. At some point during their numerous encounters, he realizes that he has fallen in love with her at midnight every night, since they enter the woods every night at the same time. At first, the girl doesn't know she's being watched, and the guy isn't aware that what's really attracting him to the girl isn't her beauty, but her gift of music. The irony is, he has the same powerful gift that the girl has too. The Midnight Forest represents hope that they will meet again to rekindle what they cherished in the forest. And, at some point during his life, The Midnight Forest is abandoned by the love of his life. The love of his life interrupts their romance because she's forced to move a long distance away from his heart. The song is about the guy searching for his love after she moves away."

"Wow, that's pretty good since you haven't heard the song," said the driver.

"I am the song!" *It's about me.*

We arrived at Hotel Supreme, and the driver placed my things outside the hotel. I waited in the car until he finished unloading my belongings. The driver reentered the taxi and I paid him. While exiting the taxi, Sammie's song broadcasted on the radio.

"Hey folks, I hope you all are feeling bloody great today. My name is Peter and I have a song for your souls. It's by Sammie Walker. Here's The Midnight Forest," said the radio personality.

My face lit up and I dropped my luggage, racing to the taxi. I reopened the door and said, "Oh my God!" The driver smiled. I jumped inside the taxi, waiting for the song to come on. The driver looked through his rearview, observing me staring at him. I waved and smiled, and he did too. The driver didn't say anything. My heartbeats spoke for me.

Sammie started to sing. "If love is real, it will find you still. No matter where you go my love for you will grow. I didn't know the night we met that love's greatest story was on set. My feelings for you have grown over the years, as I search to find your heart with my tears. I miss you so much. I pray you hear these words: My greatest fear is dying without you near," sang Sammie on the radio.

Abruptly, I jumped out of the taxi. My heart was throbbing. I ran inside the hotel, entering the lobby restroom. I locked myself in a stall, crying uncontrollably. I banged my fists against the door. I just couldn't finish listening to his song. That song was handcrafted for my soul. I know now that Sammie's heart is crying out for me.

A few minutes later, I checked in and purchased a ticket to Sammie's concert through the hotel. What a coincidence, they had five floor seats remaining for their guests. Since the coliseum is supposedly only one or two miles away, Sammie's marketing team probably partnered up with Hotel Supreme to accommodate his fans. I smiled while walking to my room. Once inside, I observed the palace-like features of the room. *Wow, this golden looking brick floor and antique furniture is very nice.* A few seconds later, I started to unpack.

I unpacked, laying my outfits across the bed. *Which one will get Sammie's attention?*

The red dress is the one that will make Sammie turn his head to see who I am. This dress kind of reminds me of the time when I met up with Kyle twenty years ago after my mom's funeral. I think red helps me to relax. I glanced at the clock in my room. The concert started in four hours. "I need to get started on my hair and makeup."

While freshening up in the shower, I visualized a moment that Sammie and I shared in the midnight forest. *I was so used to performing at night. I did that because no one could really see me, at least that's what I thought until Sammie discovered me. Once he realized I was scared to perform during daytime hours, I guess he made it his mission to help me break free of my fears. I'll never forget our early Saturday afternoon together. It was the first time I'd sung during the day.*

The day was bright like a camera flash, shooting directly into our eyes. The trees were our protection from the sun on that day. As we held hands, Sammie pushed me in my shoulder. I could hear the birds chirping. "Hey Sophie, why are you hesitating? Are you a chicken or something?"

I pulled my hand away from his, facing his beauty like a brave woman. "My name is Sophia. Be patient with me, I've never done this before. I'm scared, if I'm being honest with you."

He attempted to run but his leg gave out on him. He fell and I ran toward him, helping him up. He stood up. "Learn something from what I just did. I have cerebral palsy, so I can't sprint, but I went for it anyway." He brushed leaves off his jeans and said, "Sophia you have to release your gift and just be free." These words sealed my heart forever with him.

I placed my hands over my face, turning my back to him out of shame. "I'm trying, Sammie, but it's daytime. Normally, we come to the midnight forest during nighttime, and we stay here until the next morning. I don't want my parents to see me or find me singing in the woods." I turned around to embrace his touch atop my right shoulder. "I'm only comfortable showing you my gift," I said.

That was my only time seeing him shed tears. As his slow-paced tears crawled down his cheeks, he looked at me like I was the most important person alive. "Sophia, I get what you're saying, but you have a dream to become a world class singer. How are you going to perform in front of thousands of people if you can't become one with nature?"

"Nature?" I asked.

He sighed like a disappointed father. "Nature doesn't judge people, it's only people that judge you. I like to sing amid the natural elements. I like the serenity I feel whenever I am singing out here." He looked around. "The breeze carries my voice and my song echoes against the trees. I don't know where these woods carry my voice to, however, what I do know is that the feeling I receive from being free out here gives me confidence. One day, when I'm performing for millions across the world, I'll be reminded of the beauty I feel whenever I sing with nature. My memories here will calm me down and help me to be poised as I tap into my gift. Sophia, you know what the real source of my comfort is, right?" He pulled me into his arms like a grown man.

"No! Sammie, I'm not a mind reader."

He laughed like a little chipmunk. "I thought that's something guys normally say to girls?" Sammie said.

"It is, but you know I'm a tomboy, and—" He interrupted my thoughts.

"The true source of my comfort, Sophia, lies with you. That's why I love to come out here with you. I used to sing just for me and to connect with nature, but now I sing for you too. Listen closely to a new song that I wrote. It's called My Favorite Color is You."

I didn't know twenty years ago that Sammie would turn this into a hit song in London. I stepped out of the shower to put my makeup on. I got dressed and prepared for Sammie's concert. I glanced at myself in the mirror before exiting the room. How can you not see me in this red dress? I caught a taxi to the concert. Once there, I walked in and heard thousands of fans screaming at the top of their lungs. I was cleared by security, then guided to the first floor after showing the attendant my ticket.

I maneuvered through the crowd to locate my seat near the stage. I'm sitting in the front row, about twenty rows from the stage. It's the best that I could do since the other seats were already sold out. I listened to Sammie's opening act say, "Let's get this party started!"

I glanced at the bright lights flashing around the room. The darkness reminded me of the midnight forest. The loudness of the music jolted my heart, sending shockwaves of emotions through my veins. *I'm about to have a great time.* I looked around at the audience, observing thousands of people chanting, "We want Sammie!" I joined in, "I love you, Sammie!" I can't wait to see him step on the stage.

A hush went over the crowd, everything turned pitch black, then everyone went crazy as they heard the raspy voice of the world's leading singer. "London, are you ready to party?" *Oh, my God, that's Sammie voice. He sounds so masculine, and older.* I stood on the tip of my toes in anticipation. I shrugged my shoulders. *Well, duh! That's because he's older.* I blushed. *I can't wait for them to turn the lights back on.* The lights illuminated the arena again, as the sounds of a drumroll intensified. The crowd stared at the stage. The stage moved and opened like a volcano. Sammie came from underneath the stage, jumping out of a golden box. He stood motionless for ten seconds—the audience went wild.

I stared at Sammie like I would never see him again. Tearing up, I placed my hands over my mouth. *His outfit looks amazing. I love his white suit with the gold trim along the sleeves.* I smiled. *He even has a little chest hair showing for us. His hair is very long now. He must've dyed his hair brown too.* Sammie tossed his sunglasses into the audience; his directed aim was a distance away from me. Sammie said, "London, how are you feeling tonight?" He held the microphone toward the crowd. The crowd erupted with a collision of sounds.

I screamed. "I love you, Sammie!"

"Let's get this show going. My first song tonight is, My Favorite Color is You," said Sammie.

I snapped my fingers while moving slowly to the melody of his song. *Oh my God, Sammie sung this song to me, twenty years ago. Is this really happening? It's like I just noticed I'm twenty years into our future. I am at his concert in London and he's singing the song, the same way he sung it twenty years ago, during the daytime in the midnight forest. The only differences are that we are in London, he doesn't know I am here, and he's singing his heart out to me in front of thirty thousand people.*

I started to cry while listening to the second verse.

Sammie was on his knees, tilting to his right because of his bad leg. He rocked his pelvis back and forth while moving to the rhythm of his soul. He sung his heart out as chills captured his number one fan, forcing goosebumps to sprout up like plants on top of my arms.

As my fantasies ran wild with my racing heart, I continued to listen to Sammie sing.

"I knew your love would find me amid the trees. Your kisses freed my need to be free from my loveless spree. You taught me, it's a necessity to be true to you. All that I do is for you. If someone's heart could stand alone forever on its own, then mankind would perish with no moments to cherish. Without great memories, there's no heart to love. All things changed when I met a special girl. I never had a chance to love you, at least not the way I wanted to."

"I'm leaving our future with you but only the nature of true love can draw us together like glue. I miss you girl; your presence is my world. If somehow you could see how my life is torn in two without you; to nature I would confess, I'll never lose you again to life's contest."

"Without you, I'm just a friend to nature but with, I'm befriended by the world. Finding you is what made me great, oh how I plead with nature for just one more date. You're my favorite color, you're special like no other. I love you like no other!"

"My favorite color is you. My favorite thing about you is living my moments with you. You bring out the best in me. I see you and me together as one. I'm only interested in what we will become. Let's be together forever, you're my favorite person now and forever."

Sammie temporarily struggled to stand. Once fully erect, he dropped back down to his knees, then a hush went over the crowd. I can feel his emotions pass through the crowd like a breeze. *I finally understand now what Sammie meant by releasing your gift into nature. Nature doesn't adapt to its environment—nature is the environment. It permits outside elements to use its resources in whatever ways it chooses.* I looked around. Sammie is literally controlling the entire stadium. We all were forced to tap into his heart's frequency. He made all of us feel his pain.

With teary eyes, I spoke out loud, the crowd still going wild. "I can't take seeing my man miss me anymore." Sweat built up around my chin, then its droplets fell into my hands. With courage foisted upon me, I ignited my inner drive while charging toward the stage. I ran with the force of a racehorse. I only have ten rows to pass before I'm reunited with my love. Oh no, he just turned his back. While swinging my arms to increase my speed, a bodyguard built like a linebacker stepped in front of me, picking me up. "No, Ma'am! You can't charge to the stage. You can't jump on the stage and possibly ruin Sammie's concert," said the security guard.

I looked away from the guard and noticed that Sammie's back was turned to the crowd. I screamed for Sammie. He couldn't hear me, because everyone else was screaming his name too. The bodyguard politely took me back to my seat. Less than thirty seconds later, I attempted to charge toward the stage again, only to be cut off again—then escorted out of the venue. "Ma'am, I already warned you not to do that again. I was trying to work with you because I know you paid good money to be here. I don't want you to lose your money, but I'm going to need you to calm down. If you charge toward the stage again, I'm going to have to ask you to leave," said the security guard.

I nodded my head, turning away from him like a spoiled brat. The guard guided me back to my seat once more, as I overheard Sammie performing like the Godfather of Pop music. While attempting to walk back to my seat, I thought, I have to act while Sammie is still thinking about me. He just performed a whole song for me. I know he will see me if I'm able to get close enough to the stage. I have a plan, but I must act right now. I paused before the guard opened the door to let me back inside the auditorium. I faced the security attendant and said, "I am so sorry for my behavior. I'm just a big fan and I love Sammie Walker." I pointed my fingers behind the vanguard, screaming with a dire tone of urgency, "Hey, look at that girl!"

The guard turned his head and asked, "Where?"

This is my moment. I opened the door and went for it. While sprinting, I felt my speed picking up. I know I'm going to make it to the stage. As I got close to the third row from the stage, I heard Sammie finishing another song. Sammie turned around to walk backstage, then I was stopped by security. Three large White men picked me up and carried me outside the stadium as I screamed Sammie's name. While the men held me in their arms like a deranged psychopath, I wrestled to break away.

"Ma'am, we are going to have to ask you to leave," said the guard from earlier. "I told you not to charge toward the stage again. You lied about that fake girl so you could make a run for it. I know you're a fan of Mr. Sammie, but he has a show to put on, and you aren't a part of his act."

I am his main act, you idiot. The men placed me down as I gestured that I would behave myself. I faced the guard that I was most acquainted with and said, "The song he just sung, My Favorite Color is You, was a song he wrote for me."

"Ma'am, I'm sure that the other thousands of women who are at this concert feel the same way that you do. The only difference is they're sane. They aren't delusional and charging toward the stage. Please leave now before I call the cops," said the guard.

I observed four men staring at me like I'm crazy. "Please go grab Sammie's manager and tell Sammie or his manager that Sophia Smith is here," I said.

The same guard replied, "Ma'am, you're crazy. I won't ask you to leave again. I'm just going to call the police, and have you arrested."

I can't get arrested in a foreign country. I don't want to ruin my chances of reuniting with Sammie at one of his other concerts. "Alright!" The guard walked me out of the building.

Then, I caught a taxi back to Hotel Supreme. I rode in the backseat with my arms crossed while lying on my back, stretched out. I cried profusely as the driver repeatedly asked, "Ma'am, are you okay?"

With tears choking my voice, I sounded like a muffled engine, screaming, "Just drive and leave me alone!"

Three minutes later, I arrived at the hotel. I quickly gave the driver his money, then exited the car. Upon exiting, I sprinted toward the door, glancing at onlookers staring at me as they pointed. Why are they pointing at me? Once inside the hotel, I rushed to my room and laid on the floor until I cried myself to sleep.

Chapter 20:
Wondering and Pondering:
Do Dreams Come True?

Sophia

I woke up a few hours later, still on the floor. I stood up and got into the bed, pondering, *those guards thought I was crazy. I was only trying to see Sammie. I probably did look like an obsessed groupie, though.*

"I wonder if Sammie saw me?" I started to sob. Maybe he just didn't care to stop the guards from carrying me out? The hotel has a brochure of his tour dates. I think I picked one up. I stood up and looked on the table by the television for a brochure to analyze it. *He has another show in two weeks in Berlin. I can't wait. What am I going to do for two weeks in anticipation for Sammie's next show? I'll just go out and spend some time in London. There's a lot of stuff to do here. I need to be mindful of how much money I'm spending though. I only had about 22 thousand dollars remaining. I need to make these last few dollars last.*

I went to use the bathroom, then I decided to go look for a religious service to attend. Since I'm going to be in London for a while, I might as well make the most of it. I washed my face. While looking in the mirror I thought out loud, "My mom was raised as a Jehovah's Witness, but my dad was Catholic. My mom and dad respected one another's views, but I could tell that they both wanted each other to join their religious sect." I wiped my face with a towel. "I had the privilege to attend both services, and I think that my heart gravitates more toward my mom's beliefs. I'll find a local Kingdom Hall near here, and that'll be a good way for me to find some people to talk too."

I exited the bathroom in deep thought. What I remember about Jehovah's Witnesses is that they're nice people and God fearing. My mom was studying the Bible with a lady named Sister Grisby. She stopped her study because she became angry about racism and blamed God. I learned about a scripture, Acts 10:35, that helped me to appreciate that God is not a partial God. I learned that during one of the services. I'll find a local service and inform one of the elders that I would like to ask one of the sisters; a few Bible-based questions over lunch or something. I know I shouldn't use the congregation for my association needs alone, but I need people to mingle with right now more so than ever.

Several minutes later, I prepared for bed. I woke up the following morning in emotional pain. After lying in the bed for a few minutes, I rose. I went to the gym and exercised, then I ate breakfast. After showering, I walked downstairs to speak with someone at the front desk. I don't know where to start my search for a local Kingdom Hall, so I'll just ask the receptionist. I walked up to a middle-aged, dark-skinned, Black lady. "Hey, do you know where the nearest Kingdom Hall is located?"

"Kingdom hall?" The lady asked.

She scratched her head. "Oh yeah, the worship center where Jehovah Witnesses' attend."

I raised my eyebrows. I think I looked at the dates for Sammie's schedule backwards or something. I don't know for sure, but something seems off. I looked at the receptionist and said, "Actually, don't worry about it." I walked away.

I rushed back to my room to check the brochure again. I entered my room and picked up the brochure while saying, "That's right!" I smiled. "Sammie will be in Berlin this weekend." I immediately booked a new flight, along with a hotel.

***

Four Months Later

May 30ᵗʰ
1986
Berlin, Germany
Sophia

While having breakfast at Berlin's Coffee Shop, I thought to myself. Over the past four months, I missed Sammie's presence face-to-face at each concert. My concert seats seemed to get further and further away from the stage. And unfortunately, Sammie was getting further and further away from my heart. I looked out of the window into the rusty beauty of Berlin's age-old creativity and culture as I reminisced over my journey. I sipped my coffee while pondering my life's most recent footsteps. I scoffed, twisting my right foot and placing my coffee down on the table. It was impossible to get close to him during his concerts in Germany. I'm so disappointed with my adventure.

I reached into my purse, discreetly counting my remaining funds. "Gosh." My inner thoughts entered my mind. I'm down to two thousand dollars. I'm running out of funds. Good thing I only have one more night to stay in Berlin. I really miss Isabella, but I still haven't reached out to her because I need every penny I have. I know this is the end of my rodeo. I still have two grand remaining for a reason, though. I have to talk to Sammie again, somehow, some way. I glanced at my watch before leaving cash on the table to cover my bill.

I headed back to The Hotel of Berlin, practicing the rest of the day for the audition at The Blues Café. While practicing, I said, "The audition is right around the corner!" Tomorrow morning, I'm headed back to the U.S.

A few hours later after I finished singing, I packed my luggage then prepared for bed. The abundance of new clothes that I've purchased over the four months will have to be shipped separately, I thought to myself, lying in bed during my final night in Berlin. Good thing I shipped my four other suitcases off already. It was smart for me to go ahead and ship those suitcases to my house. I should receive them within a month or so.

Within minutes I fell asleep.

The following day, I boarded my plane. My flight was from Berlin to Atlanta—then Atlanta to San Francisco.

I boarded my last flight from Atlanta to San Francisco.

When I arrive back home, I'll have ten hours before my audition. I hope Isabella is home when I arrive. I've been practicing the song that I'm going to use for my audition. I looked out my window into the darkness of the sky. *I feel slightly like a failure. I didn't unite with Sammie. Maybe he received my letters? I wonder if Travis was able to get in touch with Sammie.* An hour later, I fell asleep.

Several hours later, I arrived in San Francisco. I woke up to sounds of a plane landing on the tarmac, then I stretched, twisting my neck to ease its stiffness from a day and a half of plane flights. *I think my trip to Berlin was healthy for me. I feel extremely confident about my life now. Getting back into the best shape of my life has helped a lot with my confidence too. Just having the courage to finally follow my heart really boosted my confidence. Now the rest is in nature's hands, but most importantly, God's hands.*

I exited the plane and caught a cab into the city. *Maybe I can get a nap in before the audition tonight.* I looked down at my wristwatch. *Good—the audition is ten hours from now.*

Chapter 21:
The Music Within Your Heart:
It's Showtime at The Blues Café

Travis

I sit back in my chair, looking around at my office. *I'm so happy to be who I am. The best talent comes through my café.* I smile. *I'm so proud of my nephew Sammie.* I hear a knock on my door. One of my workers knocks on my door again, then opens it ajar. The worker enters and stands back near the door at a distance. Standing six feet tall, with a bald head as smooth as the floor, the worker's smooth dark skin blends well with the approaching darkness of the night. The worker says, "Hey Travis, there's a guy name Sammie who's on the phone for you. He mentioned that you've been trying to contact him."

I smile and gesture for him to approach me. My loud red suit blends in with my glass desk. I raise my eyebrows. "Is his name Sammie Walker?" I signal for the worker to close the door.

The worker closes the door, standing ready to take charge in a black suit. "I don't know, I didn't inquire about his last name. I'm sorry," says the worker.

I wave my hand and say, "It's okay, Ace! Thanks for picking up the phone. I didn't hear it—I was in the back speaking with Duke regarding the audition tonight," I say.

Ace contorts his lips, positioning his hands in front of him while saying, "No problem, Travis." Ace exits the office.

I really hope this is my nephew. I kiss the glass table while looking up at the ceiling to call upon God. I pick up the phone, taking the caller off hold. "This is Travis."

Sammie sighs. "I know who this is. How are you, Uncle?"

Thank God. I complete a circle in my rolling chair, excited. I make a fist, shaking it back and forth while smiling. "I'm fine. I'm just preparing for the audition I'm overseeing in a few hours. How were your tours in Europe?" I ask.

"They were a blast. I made a lot of money. I had so much fun," says Sammie.

I smile. "Did you run into Sophia out there?" I ask.

Sammie pauses for several seconds then takes a deep breath before saying, "Whoa, whoa, Sophia who?"

That boy is in shock. "Sophia Smith! She told me about her history with you. You know, she's been looking for you for over twenty years now." That's crazy.

Sammie's modulation increases. "How do you know Sophia? Wait, how do you know all of this?"

I twirl the phone cord around my thumb. "She has been performing at my club for five years now. She actually came here to notify me of something before she left for Europe to search for you."

Sammie's voice crescendos like a musical play. "Wait, Sophia came to Europe looking for me?"

"Yes, she showed up here about four months ago. She mentioned she was moving on to bigger things." I lean back in my chair, caressing my chest with pompous strokes. "It seems like my club just continues to push raw talent to the next level. The Blues Café produces superstars. Don't forget, you got your start here as well, remember?"

Sammie sighs. "Yes, I remember Uncle. That was one of the last times I saw her. She came looking for me during my last show at your place." He exhales. "After you fired me, I landed a major deal with J & B Records. I didn't realize how big I was going to become at the time."

"Yep, you're doing well for yourself." Your dad is proud of you too.

"Sophia left me a note indicating how much she missed me. She mentioned in her note that her mom was sick, and that her dad was killed in the Vietnam War. The night Sophia came to find me, Sabrina, that stupid girl, kissed me while I was distracted with Sophia's presence. I can't believe we just kept missing one another for over twenty years," says Sammie.

"Yeah, I could tell she really misses you. I also gave her twenty thousand dollars to help sponsor her four-month journey to find you," I say.

Sammie's voice trembles. "Sophia searched for me for four months in Europe?"

"Yep," I say.

Sammie sighs with a cadence of intense frustration. "Ugh!"

"Nephew, you're a big star now, so it's not like she just has special access to you. I tried to get in touch with you, to notify you while she was in London, but I couldn't reach you. She mentioned she would send fan mail letters to your address in Arizona. Have you received any of her letters?"

Sammie takes a deep breath. "I'll have my assistant go through all of my fan mail letters right now. I only read the mail that they vet. I leave that responsibility up to him; he determines what I read.

However, I told him never to throw away any of my fan mail letters after they're vetted. My fans take the time to write me letters, so even if I never read them, I at least want to honor their letters by keeping them. I'll instruct my assistant to search through my fan mail to locate Sophia's letters. He keeps my fan mail organized in alphabetical order, so it shouldn't be hard for him to find them." Sammie takes a deep breath. "This is exciting news, Uncle Travis. I'm glad you're sharing this with me."

I rub my lips while extracting photos from inside my desk. While looking at photos of myself, Sammie, and my brother I ask, "Do you still love Sophia?"

There's a long pause for nearly forty-seconds. Sammie scoffs and says, "You are asking me about feelings I had over twenty years ago, Uncle Travis."

"She definitely still loves you," I say.

"I don't know about that. When I used to tell her I loved her, she never said anything back. I know Sophia used to like me when she was thirteen, but she's like thirty-six or thirty-seven now. A lot has changed. Besides, that was a very long time ago when we dated. I would like to see her again, but I don't know if we have a romantic future together."

"I want to inform you that she'll be here later tonight at the café for the audition that Duke is sponsoring," I say.

Sammie's voice echoes a happy tone like someone that hears good news. "Wait, Duke is coming to look for talent in Marin County? Wow, that's going to be a big show. Sophia is going to win too. There's one thing I know for sure, she has a very powerful gift. How is she looking nowadays anyway?"

"She's beautiful! Where are you right now?" I ask.

Sammie is silent for several seconds. "Uh, I'm in Arizona right now, but I have to head out tomorrow for a meeting in Brazil. I'm getting ready to do a tour there as well," says Sammie.

I stand up and pour a glass of wine. Shaking the wine glass in my hand, I say, "I think you might want to find a way to get to this audition, Sammie. You seem like you're slightly disinterested, but I know you, I'm your uncle." I sip the wine. "I think you're hesitant because you're scared of being hurt. Sammie, if you see her tonight and the spark is gone, that's okay. Nephew, it's okay if you don't feel the same, but you have to at least chance the opportunity to get some closure with this woman. I feel like both of you need this. You know, there's a saying, 'You only live once'. It's time for you to live and be fearless. Unless you're with someone else?"

"Well, I was dating someone, but we are on a break right now. I love Ashley, so I really don't know if I'm interested in seeing Sophia again."

Not good. I quickly finish the rest of my drink. I clear my throat. Sophia won't like that. "Sammie, get on your private jet and fly to my café. Come surprise my guests with your presence. My guests will go crazy if you come, and it'll be good publicity for my club too."

Sammie chuckles. "Uncle, you have enough exposure. I don't know about making a trip there like this, at the very last minute. I would have to call my pilot to see if he's available."

"Just pay him handsomely, stop overthinking things. Remember this: There are certain moments in life you'll never get back." I lower my tone. "Don't let this be one of those moments. Oh, by the way, Sophia left her address and telephone number with me for you. Sammie, make the right decision, and at least come revisit a love that was lost. Maybe it needs to be found." I hear a knock on my door. "Look, I have to go now. But I love you and I hope I'll see you soon. Take care," I say.

"I love you too, Uncle. Bye, take care." Sammie hangs up.

***

Sammie

I can't believe Sophia came to London looking for me. While walking to my office, I reflect on my feelings for Sophia. My white robe looks like fur off a cow. As my slippers drag against the ground, I filter through my thoughts. I can't believe we successfully missed each other for over twenty years. I always told Sophia I loved her, but she never said it back. I'll get my assistant to go find her letters. Matter of fact, I will go find them myself because if he organized my letters properly, then they'll be easy to find.

I walk downstairs to my fan mail room. I look around at the fancy nature of my home. I can't believe I've had this mansion for three years now. Sophia would love my house. I am gifted in music, but Sophia's gift is in a class of its own. I enter the fan mail room to search for Sophia's file. "There they are, I found her letters." I smile. "Wow, this girl wrote me thirty-two letters. I'll just read a random one." I flip through her letters like an amateur shuffling a deck of cards. "Looks like she wrote this one a week ago." I walk to my desk, pulling a chair out, then I take a seat.

Dear Sammie,

I really miss you. I'm going on tour to find you. I love you. I hope your heart is still complete toward me. I know this is crazy, for a woman to think that a man would still be in love with her after twenty-years. We both were kids when we dated, but I believe in my heart you feel the same way I feel about you.

Herewith this letter are my address and telephone number. Please come find me! Let's have a drink and catch up.

58390 Wholly Ave. Marin County, CA 79606. My telephone number is 555-555-5555.

Sincerely yours,

Sophia Smith

I stand up, fumbling through a few more of Sophia's letters. *I don't know how to respond to these.* I lay her letters out on the table, then walk in a circle around them repeatedly for several minutes. I toss my hands into the air, grunting as I drop to my knees in despair. I stand up, adjusting my robe. I stare at her letters again, as I place my right thumb and index finger underneath my chin. I aggressively rub my chin like a deep-tissue massage. I erupt into a clamor. "Enough!" *I've moved on with my life, so I shouldn't even entertain this.* While staring at the letters like a lion hunting its prey, I decide to read Sophia's remaining thirty-one letters.

I sit down and start reading several letters. While reading, I start to cry. *I'm angry we kept missing one another for all these years.* I immediately stand up after I hear a slow creak as the door opens. I quickly try to compile the letters to return them to their safe haven. With several letters in my hands, I wrap my arms around the letters like they're a cuddly stuffed animal. My eyes are opened wide, like I've been caught committing a felony. Before the intruder reveals their identity, I ponder: Who is this coming in here unannounced? I'm not expecting anyone.

"Hey, baby," says Ashley.

I drop the letters, expelling a sigh of relief. I didn't know who that was, I was a little nervous. "What are you doing here, Ashley?" I ask.

Ashley walks toward me twisting her slim and narrow hips. Her breasts are the most noticeable feature on her body. With perfect perkiness, they call out for my attention. Her long legs propel her to only being one inch shy of my height. With amazing green eyes, like a jungle, she inches closer to me while rubbing her hands through her flawless blonde hair. Her thin eyebrows rise as she observes papers scattered about. With long eyelashes like a deer, she throws herself into my arms, and her full lips embrace my right cheek. She carefully places my hands on her buttocks, and her lavender scent opens my nostrils to new levels of sensations. Her seduction is almost complete until I glance to my left at Sophia's name on one of my letters.

I quickly step back, listening to Ashley say, "I see you're not in the mood to play. But to answer your question, I let myself in. You know I have a key, right?"

She shouldn't be here. I look confused while picking up Sophia's letters. "Yes, of course," I reply.

"Why do you have tears in your eyes?" Ashley points at the floor. "And why are all these papers on the floor?" She bends down, glancing over the papers. She picks one of the letters up and sighs. "You never read your fan mail. Who is Sophia?"

"Hey, don't toss her letters around like that! Besides, I thought we were on a break." I ask.

"Yes, we were, but I changed my mind. I'm not mad with you anymore. I found out you planned to propose to me. I messed up the proposal by being anxious. I flipped out and became angry with you after Tim and Kim got engaged. I mean, they had been together for only six months. And, we have been together for six years, and you still hadn't proposed to me; and I felt like you weren't going to, either—so I broke up with you. I know you tried to call, and you even showed up at my house, but I didn't want to talk to you." Ashley blushes. "I know you didn't mention you were going to propose because you wanted it to be a surprise. My mom told me because she didn't want me to ruin my chances with you forever. She reminded me that you are a high commodity, and she's right." She smiles. "I can't leave you on the market for too long with things being unsettled between us," says Ashley.

She follows me around the table as I slyly avoid her. High commodity, huh?

She rubs her fingers across the table, smiling while slowly circling me. "My mom told me you'd plan on proposing to me tonight. If that's the case, then why are you reading these love letters from Sophia? I can tell that the two of you had a history together because of how you're acting. How long ago did you all date? When is the last time you saw her?" Ashley asks.

"We dated when I was a teenager." I scoffed. "I haven't seen her in twenty-one years." I pause on the opposite end of the table, after observing Ashley come to a halt.

"Wow, she must be crazy to still be chasing you. She just doesn't know that your heart is already taken. She must've decided to track you down once she realized how famous you are. She's probably a gold digger or something," says Ashley.

No way. "Sophia isn't like that," I say.

Ashley charges at me but I circle the table with a faster pace. She screams, "You're standing up for a woman you haven't seen in twenty years! How stupid is that, Sammie? I'm the one that's with you right now." She pats herself on the chest. "I'm the one that's going to marry you and have your kids. You do realize that you're getting older, and I am only twenty-six." She picks up one of the letters from the table, tossing it. "I know you like pretty young things like me, so stop thinking about an older lady that's writing you these pathetic letters."

She's lost her mind." Ashley, I really need the rest of the night to myself." I open the office door, tilting my head to signal her to leave. "Can you please just either leave or go to one of the other rooms while I sort through my thoughts? I need a few days, so just give me that, please. I promise, I'll call you in a few days. I just need to clear my head because I don't know what I want to do with my life right now. I love you but I just need a little longer to get over your immaturity right now. You've shown me a different side of yourself by acting foolishly, simply because I didn't propose to you when you wanted me to. Love is not a sprint, it's a marathon." I exhale while looking into her eyes. "If we are going to be together forever, then we need to run love's race with endurance."

She frowns, placing her right hand atop her right hip. "Endurance? Sammie, you do realize we've never been intimate together. You're the only man that's a thirty-eight-year-old virgin. Your relationship with God, doesn't have to be flawless, so your resolve doesn't make much sense to me. I am starting to think that maybe you don't really like women."

I gently place Sophia's letters on the table then I walk up to Ashley, grabbing the back of her arm while escorting her out of my office. She pulls away as I yell, "Leave, Ashley! Because now you're insulting me. I told you from the beginning that I was saving myself for marriage. My motive for getting married isn't driven by my desire to have sex—because that can wait. I need to find a true companion, so that I can be successful in life. I need some time to think about what I want to do with my life. Besides, the way you're talking, I don't know if you're the woman who God has for me."

Ashley does a gesture with her hands like she's praying to God as the sounds of her heels echo off the floor. "Sammie, I am so sorry. I just want to be with you and start a family."

"Do you want to have children with me, or do you just want my money? Because that's all it seems to be about, lately!"

She frowns then grabs a few of the letters from the table. "You know, I don't need an attitude from you," says Ashley.

"You, better not. Put those down," I say.

Ashley charges toward a shredder and passes Sophia's letters through the machine like an assembly line of destruction. I run up to her, snatching the rest of the letters from her hands. "I can't believe you just put Sophia's letters in the shredder. Leave my house, now," I say.

"Fine, I hope you find your little skank too," says Ashley. She storms out of my office and leaves my house.

I locate the most recent letter that Sophia wrote to me, then I exit my office, walking to my room. I change my clothes and place the letter inside my jacket. I sit on the edge of my bed and ponder. I didn't know Ashley was going to do what she did. If I'd known, I would've protected Sophia's letters with my life. I sigh. I don't know if I should call Charlie and have him get the jet ready, or if I should just let Sophia be. My heart feels like we need to talk and meet again, even if it's our last time. I walk back into the fan mail office, dressed in blue jeans and a red short-sleeve collar shirt.

I go through Sophia's file again and I notice something new. "Wait, hmm … I didn't see this letter, it arrived two-weeks-ago." I read the letter. So, Sophia wants me to meet her in the spot where our love was first formed, tonight—after her audition.

She also invited me to her audition in the letter. It will only take three hours to get to Marin County on my plane. I don't know if I have enough time to make it to her audition, though. I glance over the letter again while rubbing my chin. "I don't know what I'm going to do, but I need to make a decision—really soon."

***

Love's Final Showdown

June 1st
1986
Izzy

I wonder when my mom is returning. I look into the mirror to observe my audition outfit. I am dressed like a superstar. My white sleeveless dress resembles an angel with boldness. The split on the left side of my dress teasingly exposes the beauty of my legs. My hair is styled in a simple ponytail. My gold necklace makes my chest shine as I step forward with blue high heels on. With a natural look of beauty that's devoid of makeup, I stand in my room outside my bathroom, knocking on the door. "Mark, are you ready?" I look at my gold wristwatch. "My audition starts in two hours," I say.

Mark walks out of the bathroom dressed like a million bucks. His elegant velvet blazer fits his body like a glove. As his musculature shines brightly beneath his white slacks, his white dress shoes captivate one's eyes like a fancy car; but a prestigious vehicle model that's rarely seen. I bite my lips. Wow, Mark looks delicious.

Mark smiles. "I'm ready, let's go honey. Your mom should be back in town by now. Do you want to stop by her house before we head to your audition?" He glances at me. "And wow, you look fantastic baby."

I shake my head. It took you long enough to notice. "Thanks! And, uh, no. I'll just stop by tomorrow. I don't want to be late for my audition."

"Okay, sounds good to me." Mark pulls me in close and holds my hands. "I know you're going to do an awesome job tonight. So don't be nervous," says Mark.

I really needed that. I blush while squeezing his right cheek. "Thanks, baby."

We walk downstairs like the queen and king of England, then we hop into Mark's Corvette, racing to The Blues Café.

***

Sophia, You Can Do It!

Sophia

I'm here. I can't wait to see Izzy later. I arrived at the café dressed in a gold dress like a goddess of wealth. I entered the building with my hair curls dangling across my shoulders. With pink lipstick atop my lips, I grabbed my silver necklace, squeezing it for good fortunate. While walking to the singer's lounge, Travis spotted me. "Sophia, is that you? He smiled. "Girl, come over here and show me some love."

I laughed and gave him a hug. "Hi, Travis, how are you?"

Travis waved his hands as he grimaced. "No—no, the better question is, how are you? And how was London, and your four-month adventure?"

I sighed. "Uh, it was okay, I didn't get what I wanted." I frowned, pushing my hands against the air. "Actually, I really don't want to talk about it."

Travis nodded his head. "Okay, no problem." He glanced at his wristwatch. "You're here kind of early, huh? The audition doesn't start until another two hours. I have some possible good news for you." He gestured for me to follow him to his office. I obliged, stepping inside his office then he closed the door.

Please tell me it's something about Sammie. I pulled a chair out then sat down. "So, what's up?" I asked.

He stood in front of me as I sat directly across from him. The only thing dividing our bodies was Travis' desk. "I talked to Sammie several hours ago," said Travis.

I leaned forward and gulped. "Oh my God, what happened, what did he say?"

"Calm down, that's what I'm trying to tell you," Travis said.

"Okay, I'm sorry! Please, tell me. I need to know," I said.

"He's aware that you were in Europe looking for him; he knows you still love him. I gave Sammie your address and telephone number. He's leaving Arizona tomorrow to fly to Brazil. So, I doubt he makes the audition tonight." He glanced at my attractiveness. "And by the way, you look great. You must've lost fifteen pounds while you were in Europe. You look so young and beautiful. You don't look a day past twenty."

"Thank you!" I stood up. "Travis, that was great news. I am so excited. I hope Sammie shows up tonight."

"Yeah, if he manages to make it to your audition, that would be great." We talked for another hour or so, then we exited his office. We continued talking as we strolled along the hallway.

While walking, I glanced to my left. Oh my God, is that who I think it is? He must be the surprise guest. I lifted my hands, signaling for Travis to pause his thoughts. "Hold that thought Travis." I stepped in front of Duke, grabbing his attention. "Mr. Proctor, do you remember me?" I hope he does.

Duke smiled while stepping back in his beige suit. "Yes, you're Sophia, the girl who bailed on my audition like twenty years ago or something like that." He laughed. "How could I ever forget you? You were pregnant during that time as well, right?"

I sighed. "About that! Look, I apologize for my immature actions. My daughter is eighteen now and her name is Izzy." I shook my head. "Well, it's Isabella. Uh, I want to explain what happened that day."

Duke does a gesture to signal that it was okay. "No need to explain. You're looking better than ever. Look, if you sound anything like you did twenty years ago, then I might be signing you to a deal tonight. Smile and get ready, because you have a lot of competition tonight. I'm here to see a young girl who has the same name as your daughter. I've heard a lot about her through lounges and various bars in town." He pointed at Travis. "I think Travis is familiar with her too."

I wonder who she is? Especially since she has the same name as my Izzy. "I can't wait to meet this local phenomenon."

Duke winked his right eye. "Me too. The show starts in 22 minutes, so get ready."

I smiled. "Oh, I am," I replied.

***

Mark and Izzy Arrive at the Café

Izzy

I'm glad we're here on time because Mark was moving slow. I jump out of the car. "Travis told me that I'm the like the second or third performer tonight. Come on Mark, we are late, we have to get in there right now." He just had to stop to get a quick bite to eat. That's how we got stuck in traffic.

Mark sighs as I step out of the car. "We aren't late, Isabella. The audition doesn't start for another fifteen minutes." We walk up toward the entrance, then he points while saying, "We just need to skip these people in front of us. I don't think they're contestants." He looks at me and says, "Just go tell the guard you're one of the performers. I'm sure your name is on a list or something."

I race to the front of the line, only to be stopped by an outstretched arm. The guard says, "What are you doing? You can't just skip the other people in line."

"I know but I'm one of the contestants auditioning tonight. I really need to get inside," I say.

"Name?" The guard asks.

"Isabella Smith."

"Okay, I see your name on the list. Go ahead and get in there before you miss your spot."

"Yes sir!" I look back at Mark. "Come on Mark." I grab his hand. "He's with me."

I walk inside and notice one of the most shocking things I've ever seen in my life. I squeeze Mark's hands as tears explode from my eyes like a tsunami. *That can't be my mom. She's supposed to be at home right now.* I walk forward, maneuvering through the crowd to take a closer look. My mouth opens like the trunk of a car. "Jesus Christ, that is her!" I point toward the stage while jumping for joy, as I jerk Mark's left arm, saying, "My mom is on stage! Look, they just introduced the song she's about to sing. 'The Music Within Your Heart.'"

My mom is singing, and I'm blown away.

"Izzy, your mom is better than you," says Mark.

She most certainly is. I wipe my tears. "Yes, she is."

I look at Mark, standing to my right. "Mark, listen to how good she sounds!"

My mom prances across the stage, nailing high note after high note. The strength of her voice freezes the audience in motion. She moves the mic around while snapping her fingers to the tune of her own beat. Her golden dress shines brightly with the spotlight on her.

"My heart is never alone when I'm next to you. If I could be near you all day and every day I would. After you left my heart, my love went blind. I have no desire to be with or see another man. You are my rhythm and my heartbeat. I want to hold you and imprint your face inside my mind. You make my memories shine. I will love you always and forever."

"The way my heart beats to feel for you is beyond real. With you, I'm more than one I'm two. You make me happy. I love you like an adventure I've never experienced before. You are my heart's core. You're my only spark. Sammie, I failed to tell you before but not anymore, you're the music within my heart."

My mom steps back and bows, as the crowd screams for more. "We want more! We want more!" chants the crowd.

***

Sophia

I can't believe the crowd received me so well. I must've done well in my performance. I walked off stage to enter the singer's lounge. While standing, my adrenaline continued to rush. *I can't believe I received such an astounding standing ovation. I hope that was enough to beat the incredible talent that Duke came here to see.* I kept the door open as I listened to my competition. *Wow, that guy who just finished performing sounded good.* Several minutes passed, then I overheard the MC saying, "The last performer for tonight is up next."

So far, I'm feeling pretty good about winning this competition after hearing everyone perform. Let's see what the last performer is capable of. I heard someone who had Isabella's name being called on stage. That's the girl who Duke came to see. I walked into the wave frequencies of a beautiful voice. I continued to stroll along in the hallway as I walked toward the auditorium. Wow, she is good. I can't wait to see her face.

Ten seconds later, I embraced a prodigy. As I looked out into the mountaintop of melodious perfection, I felt my heart racing. I started to perspire heavily like I was jogging. Placing my hands over my mouth, I bulldozed my way through the crowd to get a close-up on the wonderful sight I saw.

Oh my God, I think I'm going to faint. That's my baby up there singing her heart out. I knew she had my gift of music running through her veins. My baby just received a standing ovation. Oh my God, I'm crying uncontrollably. I have to run up to my baby and give her a hug. Izzy was the final performer for tonight. In my opinion, she was the best. I am so proud of my baby girl. I just know that she won.

Before I could make my way to the stage to hug Isabella, Duke walked onto the stage, immediately after Izzy finished her song. Duke delivered a special announcement that was hard for me to believe. He held his hands up, signaling for the audience to be silent. Then he said, "Everyone did an amazing job tonight. I will take a few minutes to pick the winner. Meanwhile, I just want to say thank you to all of the contestants." He held his index finger up, waving it from east to west. "But there can only be one winner." He remained on stage while staring into the crowd. While in deep thought, he paced back and forth across the stage, then one minute later, he said, "Sophia Smith, you are the top contestant for tonight's audition. I'm signing you to a record deal tonight, if you're interested in making hits with my label!"

Oh no. I wanted it to be Izzy. But I am ready to pursue my own career, too.

Duke called me on stage so that I could express my thoughts. I hugged Duke then took the mic as he handed it to me. I stared into the crowd and said, "First and foremost, I want to congratulate my beautiful daughter, Izzy! In my opinion, she's the real winner tonight. I can't see you, baby, but I know you're here. I love you, sweetheart! I didn't know you had my gift running through your soul." The crowd cheered. "But you know, tonight has taught me a valuable lesson. The lesson is that you should never give up on your goals and dreams!" I exhaled then paused while tearing up. "Sometimes, our dreams take longer to fulfill than we might have anticipated. I couldn't have imagined that it would take me over twenty years to get a record deal." I paced myself as my emotions continued to surge. "Life takes you in a different direction sometimes, but if you stay true to the music that's within your heart, you'll be able to accomplish anything. Life is so interesting. Life is an adventure! I am probably talking too much, but I have something to say, and I think it's something everyone needs to hear, especially, my daughter Isabella. Where are you, honey?" I looked around for Izzy. "Come get on this stage with your mom!"

***

Izzy

I'm coming, Mom.

I make my way toward the stage. *My mom must 've read my mind. I want to be on stage with my mom to help her celebrate this moment. I walk toward the stage of victory to embrace the greatness that's being manifested. My mom is one of the best singers I've ever heard in my life. I can't believe I've lived with her for all these years, and I didn't know she was this talented. She is living proof that all true dreamers can achieve their life's goals.* I walk on stage with her. We hug and share a few words together, then she hands me the microphone. "I'm the happiest daughter in the world." I give the mic back to her. "Mom, I'm so proud of you. Why didn't you tell me that you could sing like this? You did an amazing job. I am so happy for you."

The crowd continued to cheer.

"I've kept this side of myself hidden from you and a lot of people that I love. I'm not doing that anymore. I realize now that I've robbed the world of the magnificence God placed inside my heart. And honey, you were so good up there tonight," says Sophia.

I point at my mom. What my mom is saying right now, in this moment, freezes my heart. I gulp and cry tears of joy. Her words are so inspiring. I could listen to her forever. I am amazed by the things she's saying.

I point to the crowd. "Mom, do you hear that? The crowd is chanting your name!"

"Sophia….Sophia….Sophia….Sophia! Finish your speech, we want to hear the rest of what you have to say," chants the crowd.

I smile, opening my hands while tilting my head, gesturing for my mom to honor the crowd's request. "Mom, don't keep your fans waiting!"

My mom faces the crowd and says, "I really appreciate all of you coming out here tonight, to support all of the contestants. What we do isn't possible without you, the fans. Years ago, I didn't have the courage to pursue my singing career. Fulfilling my dreams used to be solely about me. For a while, my dreams weren't about other people— and that was wrong of me. However, I now know the true beauty of dancing to the music that's within your heart. The truth is, sometimes doing things solely for yourself isn't strong enough to push you into action. Whenever things don't go your way, you have to know that God is still on your side. I've learned that whenever adversities come into your life, Jehovah God is simply getting you ready to embrace a bigger calling. When Jehovah calls you to do something, you'll know. Because he's going to sponsor your dreams." My mom places her hand over her heart. "I encourage everyone out there to believe in yourself and expose your true gift of value. Your gift of value is the thing that comes the easiest to you. It's that something that you love and you're naturally great at it. Your gift is the music you feel within your heart!" My mom bows. "Thank you all again for supporting me."

Duke walks back on the stage, grabbing my mom's hand while holding it up in the air. As my mom stands tall as the winner, Duke says, "I think our first single is going to be: 'The Music Within Your Heart'. That was a beautiful song. I look forward to working with you soon."

My mom says to Duke, "Same here, Mr. Proctor. And thanks so much for giving me another chance." She exits the stage.

A few seconds later, my mom turns around tapping me on the shoulder while she stands in the hallway, leading to the singer's lounge. My mom shakes Duke's hands once more then walks away. "Mom, did you find Sammie?" I ask.

My mom smiles and faces me. "No, I didn't, honey. I didn't see him here tonight either. I need to get out of here because I have somewhere to go. I'll meet you back at the house. We can catch up then, okay, sweetheart?"

I quickly grab Mark's hand, pulling him from behind a table. "Mark, stop hiding." Mark steps forward, waving like a shy three-year-old girl. "Mom, before you leave, I want you to meet my boyfriend, Mark," I say.

"Mark this is my mom, Sophia. Mom this is Mark."

My mom and Mark hug one another.

"Nice to meet you. You were so great tonight! You did a fantastic job," says Mark.

***

Sophia

I see my daughter takes after her mother. She likes a little Caucasian persuasion too. He's a cutie too. "Thanks, Mark! And you're very handsome. I see why my daughter likes you. You have a great smile as well. I look forward to getting to know you and talking to you later. Meanwhile, I have to get out of here," I said.

He blushed. "I understand. Thank you."

I hugged my daughter then exited the café. While driving, I thought to myself. Seeing Mark reminds me of Sammie. I wish I could've seen Sammie tonight. I wonder why he didn't come. But I did tell him to meet me in our spot tonight if he missed my audition. I looked at my watch. "It's almost midnight, and I need to get to our spot before midnight hits." I hope Sammie meets me in the spot, tonight, where our love was brought together.

Fifteen minutes later, I drove into my old Novato neighborhood, then parked at my parent's old house. Surprisingly, the house was still vacant. I parked in the driveway, then jumped out of the car, running into the woods. I glanced at my wristwatch. I have to make my appointment with true love. It's 11:55p.m. I have five minutes before midnight falls. I made it to my destination at 11:58p.m. I looked around, searching for signs of Sammie while rubbing my arms to keep my body warm. It's a little chilly tonight.

Thirty-minutes go by, and I panic. "He's not coming!" I walked near the Tree of Destiny. I see they cut our old tree down. I placed my back against a nearby tree, sliding to the ground as the leaves broke apart beneath my butt. "Why didn't he show up tonight?" I stood up and screamed, "I hate this feeling of not knowing." My voice echoed through the woods like thunder. I cried for a few minutes, then prayed to God. God, please let us be together. I made my way toward my car, strolling through the forest. Abruptly, I turned around to walk back into the forest. *It's 1 a.m. now, I guess Sammie isn't going to show up. I've been here for a little over an hour now. I can't keep standing in the woods alone. I am getting cold, and I don't know if I can stay out here much longer.*

I paused in our spot for five more minutes. "Okay, Sammie, you obviously aren't coming." I tossed my hands into the darkness of the morning sky. I'm leaving. While walking through the woods, suddenly, I heard a magical voice brush against the trees. My heart recognized the voice—then I jumped for joy. I turned around to hear Sammie Walker singing as he ran to my heart.

Sammie was singing his hit song, The Midnight Forest. I was about fifty yards away from Sammie when we spotted each other from afar, staring at one another for a few seconds. What are you waiting for, Sammie? Come here. I could see him standing in the dark like a lamp to my heart. He had on an all-white suit. Maybe he planned on making my audition? "Screw it!" I started to sprint then Sammie joined in. We raced toward one another then Sammie stumbled because of his leg, falling due to his bad leg. I'm coming, baby. Before he hit the ground, I caught him with my arms, pulling him up to his feet.

I am so happy. I hugged Sammie and held him tight as I said, "Sammie, I can't believe that it's you." He hugged me back—but not as tight. He seems reserved.

Sammie smiled. "Sorry, I missed your special night. How did you do at your audition?" He smiled, shining brightly while caressing my face.

I want to kiss him so bad. While still in his arms I said, "I won, Sammie, I won. Duke Proctor signed me to a two-year-deal. My first single is going to be 'The Music Within Your Heart.'" I held Sammie's hands as they rested atop my face. Sammie looks like something is bothering him.

"That's awesome. I'm happy for you. Sophia, I have something to say to you, and I don't know how you're going to handle it." He removed his hands from my face and sighed.

"Sammie, I've waited for twenty-one-years to see you. I could die right now. So, before I die, I must tell you that I love you! I have loved you all my life." I turned away from Sammie then turned back around to face him. "I need to know if you still love me too." I asked.

Sammie turned his back to me, weeping like a man that lost everything. *What's wrong with my Sammie?* I approached him, grabbing his hands as the intensity of his tears increased. Sammie slowly pulled me down to the ground with him, where we sat on our butts. He stared at the sky while I stared at him. *Does he still love me or not?* I sat up on my knees, staring at him while waiting for his reply. I was anxious, desperately holding my hands in front of my face like I was praying to God. *Come on, say something, Sammie.*

Sammie tapped the grass, gesturing for me to come sit next to him. I extended my legs and scooted next to him. He grabbed my hands, staring into my eyes while pushing his hands through my hair. He hesitated then he said, "Sophia, I plan to propose to someone tomorrow, her name is Ashley. We had a huge spat earlier but to be honest with you, I really love her. I just wanted to come and tell you that I read all thirty-two of your letters, that's how I found out about meeting you here tonight in the midnight forest."

I cried silently as tears rolled onto my face. Sammie dried my tears with his thumb while saying, "My Uncle Travis also told me you were trying to find me, and that you flew all the way to London looking for me?" Sammie placed his hands over his heart as tears fell from his face. He dropped his head between his legs and said, "Sophia, that really touched my heart. I know you were in a relationship with a guy named Kyle. Do you remember the day when you were at Marin County University?"

If it touched your heart, then why are you about to marry Ashley? And why is he talking about Marin University? "Wait, what? Huh?" I asked.

"I ran behind your car, but you drove away and left me," said Sammie.

Jesus, that was Sammie. I looked shocked as I sat down on my butt. "That was you? I thought that was a racist boy named Jimmy." I'm so stupid.

Sammie lifted his eyebrows. "I even left you a letter at your mom's hospital."

I grabbed his hand, rubbing it as I said, "Sammie, I didn't know that was you running behind my car. I thought you were Jimmy—I was scared of him. And I did love Kyle, but I only moved forward with him because I thought you had moved on from my heart. And I never received your letter. The staff at my mom's hospital were racist people." He has some explaining to do too. "And who was that girl you kissed twenty-years-ago at The Blues Café?"

Sammie grinned. "That was Sabrina." He chuckled. "Sabrina meant nothing to me, she was just an obsessed woman who tried to stop us from getting back together."

I sighed. *I think she succeeded.*

Sammie continued, "I went out with her one time. I showed her a picture of you and me, when we were younger. I guess she recognized you, whenever you busted into the club. I'm assuming she wanted to send you the wrong message—so you would think I was taken."

I shook my head while smacking my lips. "I should've stayed around that night—and talked to you." I wonder how he's going to react to my next bit of information. "Look, I want to tell you something else too." I scratched my head. "Uh, I have a child now," I said.

He leaned back with a look of shock exuding from his face. "What?" Sammie asked.

I took a deep breath. "I had sex with Kyle twice before he was killed in a terrible car accident."

Sammie frowned. "So, the two of you got married on me?"

"No, we never got married." *He sounds kind of jealous.*" My daughter's name is Isabella Smith, and she can sing too." I grabbed his hands, but he pulled away. *Okay, I knew he would do that. It's my fault, I didn't keep my vow to God.* "Isabella has our gift, Sammie."

Sammie looked at me with disdain. He placed his hands over his chest then increased the bass in his voice as he said, "I managed to maintain my virginity, and I'm thirty-eight-years-old. That was very hard for me to do, but I guess you just couldn't do the same! I've been with Ashley for several years now, and she tries her best to pressure me into being intimate with her, but all I think about is displeasing God. I hate that our story has to end with me moving on, my friend." He shook his head then quickly regained his composure. "However, I'm glad you're doing well and that we finally got a chance to talk. Since you're back into your singing career now, I was thinking that maybe we could do a tour together. Duke is known for dropping his new artist albums fast. I'm sure you will have an album out in a few months. I have a tour I'm going to do in the United States, starting in November. It's called The Holiday Tour with Sammie Walker."

Why is he talking like we will never be? I stared at the sky. *After all my years of waiting for this moment, I don't want to spend it angry.* I'm upset, but I don't want to waste this precious time with him. "I'm happy for you Sammie. I would love to do a tour with you. And stop being so judgmental about me having a child out of wedlock. I made a mistake—and I'm sorry for it."

He grimaced. "That's good to know, but I'm going to propose to Ashley tomorrow morning. I just wanted to honor your request, by showing up to the spot where our love started. I wanted to tell you face to face that I'm taken. I tried to make your audition, but it was impossible for me to make it on time. I figured I would show up to the midnight forest, since you invited me here in your last fan mail letter. I didn't know if you would still be here or if you would come here at all. However, I decided to risk showing up here because a part of me knew you would still be here," said Sammie.

I can't lose him again. "Sammie, please don't marry Ashley. She doesn't love you like I do." I scoffed as I stood up. While standing in front of him, I said, "Why show up here tonight if you don't want to be with me? I gave you my number and my address, you could've just called me another day or wrote me a letter. Why waste your time by showing up here tonight?" *I know he still loves me.*

Sammie stood up. "Sophia, you do realize that the love we shared was when we were kids? If we were meant to be, then reuniting wouldn't have been so hard for us, wouldn't you agree?"

"No, because I know you are the one for me. Sammie, I tried my best to run to you at one of your concerts, but your bodyguards stopped me, kicking me out of the arena."

He laughed while rubbing his bottom lip. "Yeah, they told me about that. I didn't know they were talking about you, though."

I looked serious. "Sammie, answer this for me at least—" I sighed. "I know you said you love Ashley, but are you in love with her?"

He shook his head, tossing his hands into the air like he was frustrated. "Sophia, none of that matters now!" He pointed to me. "I told you, we can only be friends and nothing more."

I walk up to Sammie, circling him while trying to face him. He continued to avoid looking me in my eyes, as he turned in the opposition direction of my footsteps. He's running away from our love. "Sammie, do you still love me? Sammie Walker, are you in love with me?" I managed to corner him in the openness of the dark, grabbing his right hand while firmly holding it, as he tried to hide his face. I yelled, "Sammie, look at me! I know your heart." I exhaled. "Why are you crying if you're not in love with me?"

Sammie faced me with watery eyes. He stepped forward, gently pushing me in my chest with his fingers while saying, "Sophia, I searched for you! I watched your heart mull over another guy as I tried my best to make my way back to your heart." He stepped away from me to his right, kicking the grass. Then, he kneeled, pulling grass out of the ground, tossing it out of frustration. With his back turned to me, he sighed and said, "Why didn't you just love me back, the way I loved you when we first met?"

I tapped him on the back while trying to pull him my way, but he pulled away from me. "I have to go! Look, uh, I'll reach out to you if I want you to tour with me," said Sammie.

No, no, no. "Sammie, please don't go!"

Sammie walked away then he started to run as fast as he could while limping across the forest. He struggled to maintain his balance, but he figured it out. His sobs were so loud that a lion's roar couldn't compete.

After Sammie's body fully left my sight, I fell to the ground, planting my tears into the soil of the midnight forest. If a tree of tears could grow, then I've given it the fertilization it needs in order to sprout. "I didn't think that my journey would end like this." I guess, I'll head back to the house, and let Izzy know what happened. I left the midnight forest with a broken heart and a wounded spirit. I stepped inside my car and drove home. While driving, I listened to Sammie's song on the radio. "'The Midnight Forest' how ironic!"

Twenty-minutes later, I pulled up to my house. I hear the laughter of two people who are in love. I walked inside to a house full of excitement.

"Mom! What's wrong?" Isabella asked.

Mark had his left arm around Isabella as they cuddled on the couch.

At least she's happy. While looking dejected I said, "Sammie doesn't love me anymore. He's going to propose to a woman named Ashley. I just finished talking to him."

Isabella stood up and walked over to hug me. "Aww, Mom, it's going to be okay, it's his loss anyway."

I hugged my child. "It's 2:30 in the morning, I'm beat. Why didn't you tell me you could sing like that?" I smiled.

"Mom, remember, I tried to sing for you a long time ago, but you told me never to sing again. You said pursuing a singer career is wicked, and that I should be a doctor, lawyer, or a nurse," said Isabella.

I tilted my head to the right. "I remember! If I'd known you were in the competition, I wouldn't have competed. You would have definitely received a record deal if I wasn't in your way."

"Mom, I wanted to tell you that Duke offered me a record deal as well. After you left, he said that my skills were too good to pass up. Everything worked out, so you didn't rob me of anything."

That's amazing. "I am so happy to hear that. This gives me a little reprieve from my broken heart. Honey, I need to get some sleep now, though." I pointed at Mark. "And I expect the two of you to behave yourselves."

"Okay, Mom, we understand. Let's finish our discussion in the morning," said Isabella.

While walking up the stairs, I stopped midway then I turned around and said, "It's already morning time honey."

"Well, you know what I mean, Mom."

The sounds of an engine roared then it suddenly stopped.

"What is that noise I hear? Sounds like someone is outside. Do you all hear that?" I asked.

"Yeah, it sounds like someone just pulled up," said Mark.

I observed Isabella looking through the window. "Mom, a White man just got out of his car!" I made my way back down the stairs.

"What?" Why is a man coming to my house at 2:25 a.m., and unannounced? "Don't open the door, Izzy, I'll handle this." I walked to the door with my heart beating fast. I opened the door to see a beautiful scene. A famous superstar bowed, then bent down on one knee. I held my hands over my mouth. "Sammie, what are you doing here? And, why you are kneeling?"

Sammie reached out, grabbing my left hand, pulling me onto the porch. While holding my hand he said, "Sophia, on my way back to my taxi, I decided to pay the driver to drive me around town for a while. I had him take me back to my uncle's club. As I passed by The Blues Café, it reminded me of a feeling I've never been able to achieve with Ashley."

Thank you, Jesus. I blushed. "What feeling is that?" I asked.

Sammie pulled me in close as I stumbled toward him. "Sophia, I ran behind you that night because the thought of you running away from me was too much to bear. But today, I was the one who ran away from you! During my ride in the taxi, I asked myself: If I keep on running away from you, would I be happy knowing that I left you emotionally exposed in The Midnight Forest, as you so graciously confessed your true feelings for me? That's when my heart provided me with the answer I was forced to embrace. You see, I can't marry

Ashley, because it's my destiny to marry you!" He pulled a large, princess-cut diamond ring with gold trimming out of his pocket. "Sophia Smith, I thought I bought this ring for Ashley, but to be honest, when I bought it—I always had you in my heart. That's why I waited so long to propose to Ashley. Sophia Isabella Smith, will you marry me?"

I cried tears of joy while looking back at Isabella. With a huge smile, Izzy signaled for me to go get my man. "Mom, what are you waiting for?" Isabella asked.

I faced Sammie with my hands on both sides of my cheeks. "Yes, of course I will. I've waited twenty-four years to hear those words!"

Sammie and I hugged, kissing each other like two kids that fell in love again, just like we did inside the midnight forest.

***

Epilogue

Always Listen to Your Heart:
How You Finish is What Really Counts

Present Day
Los Angeles, California
2011

While lying in bed, Sammie and I talk about important details involving John Proctor.

"By the way, you never mentioned if you found out what happened to your mom, and if you were able to get John Proctor and Billy Joe indicted." Sammie asks.

"It's been over thirty long years, but I was finally able to discover the truth. Having money really does a lot. Since I was able to pay the right people, I was able to finally get the facts I needed to bring my family justice. I found out the drunk driver who killed Kyle was also a member of the KKK. I think it's possible that John Proctor drove to Marin County after he set my house on fire. The private detective I hired found evidence that John came looking for me and Kyle," I say.

"How did he know to go to Marin County to look for you?" Sammie asks.

"Well for one, he knew I used to live in Marin County, and during one of our conversations, he asked me who I was going to see there. I told him I was going to see Kyle and that I loved Frank's Donuts. John cheered me up, but I knew something was wrong. I couldn't put my finger on what at the time, though. I discovered the drunk driver that killed Kyle wasn't prosecuted. Also, the investigator provided me with evidence proving that my mom was coerced into taking her life. Billy Joe was killed by John because he thought that Billy Joe was a liability. John thought that maybe, I could bring his whole organization down since I knew so much about Billy Joe. That's why John was investigating me. He was trying to determine whether he should kill me. After he determined he needed to kill me, I think he decided to kidnap me instead, or turn me into one of his slave servants. Remember, a lot of people did that back in certain parts of California, especially in the fifties and sixties. I am so thankful that Kyle saved my life. I am alive today because of his intuition."

Sammie smiles. "Sophia, I am so happy that Kyle acted on his intuition because I couldn't handle losing you. What happened to John, though?"

"The private detective told me that he was usurped by some of his members, after they discovered that he killed Billy Joe. One of his own members, Billy Joe's dad, Aaron Saurage, assassinated him to avenge Billy's Joe's death.

"Wow," says Sammie. "I guess justice was served."

We hold hands as Sammie continues talking about John Proctor. While he's speaking, my mind drifts into nostalgia, due to peace and unmatched happiness. I blush while thinking to myself.

I remember the night he proposed like it was yesterday. Sammie and I kissed all night, and we finally got married six months later in Mexico. We had a destination wedding. Only Isabella and Mark were there. They were newly engaged as well. I smile while looking up into the heavens.

I just knew with all my heart that Sammie and I would go on to produce several number one hits together. We have delivered the gift that brought us together to the world for twenty-five years now. Our marriage is still going strong.

The two of us are in our early fifties. My daughter Isabella has produced two grandkids for us, Isaac, five, and Sarah, seven. Sammie and I are inseparable.

The Music Within Your Heart went on to become my favorite song, and it topped the charts as my best-selling number one hit. The Music Within Your Heart encompasses my whole life's search for my true love. It took me over twenty years, but I finally reunited with the rhythm of my heart.

Sammie and I will continue to dance together on beat inside love's heat. We will dance together forever, until the music within our hearts ceases to play its heartbeat inside our souls.

Sammie Walker, I plan to die while still passionately loving you forever. I am happy my dream of being with you manifested its truth. I always wanted to become Sophia Isabella Walker.

Sammie, you changed my world and brought meaning back into my life when my whole world was dark. I take a deep breath and smile with passion. I am a true believer that everyone should always listen to the music within your heart.

The End!

Acknowledgements

I personally want to extend a special thanks to my beautiful and lovely wife, Erika Miller for being a pivotal source of inspiration for my creative love stories. I also want to warmly acknowledge my closest friend, Marques R. Harris for his invaluable feedback. Most importantly, I would be amiss not to commend the following parties: King LeMar Elegba, Lonnie Coleman Sr. (father-in-law), Lonnie Coleman Jr. (brother-in-law), Sherman Dunn (close friend), Montrell Coleman (mother-in-law), Beaux Coleman (nephew), Sarai Coleman (sister-in-law), Jerry Jones (close friend), Brittnie McKenzie (good friend), Deandre Lash (my good friend), Tim Hartland (my good friend), Danielle Hartland, Erin Narcisse, Mark Wilson, Jessica Wilson, Julie Piehiedrahita (my good friend), Monique Jones (my good friend), Herman Thibodeaux (close friend), Michael Francois (close friend), Jerry Jones (close friend), Angie Bringaze (good friend), Lisa Perez (good friend), Erin Narcisse, Jason Gill, Candace Adams (my good friend), Brittany Coles (sister), Anthony Rollo (good friend), Julie Rollo (good friend), Latasha Miller (cousin), Elena Harris (my little sister), Jamal Cordera Boatner (friend), Muriel Duggins (good friend), Catherine Saurage, Zelma Petty, and Tyras J. Walker for offering me valuable feedback regarding their thoughts of *The Music Within Your Heart*.

Printed in the USA
CPSIA information can be obtained
at www.ICGtesting.com
LVHW040718230923
759120LV00031B/179